GRUMPY WOLVES

THE FATE OF THE WOLF GUARD COMPLETE SERIES

AIDY AWARD

INTRODUCTION

Dear Reader,

This book is the Fate of the Wolf Guard complete series, so if you've already read that, you've read this!

But as I was writing Filthy Wolf (the next book in the Alpha Wolves Want Curves series) I realized, Taryn is not only an important secondary character in books 1-4, but that she's important to both the wolves world... and the dragons. I didn't want readers of the series to wonder how in the world Taryn comes to play the very special part she has going forward, without knowing what exactly happened to her if they hadn't read her spin off series.

Unclaimed starts right after the end of Kinky Wolf, but Taryn makes a very mysterious appearance in Hungry Wolf too.

That is why I've decided to include Taryn's story as book 5 in the Alpha Wolves Want Curves series.

Most of my books are simply one shifter, one curvy girl as the main characters, but Taryn is so very special, that she gets a few more wolves in her life. This is a Why Choose romance, meaning there is more than one hero, and she doesn't have to choose between them, she gets them all!

If you haven't read a Why Choose romance before, I think you'll find this is very similar to my standard story, with a bit of a twist. She's still a badass with curves who has to grow into her true authentic self, and the heroes are still sexy alphas who love our heroine and her curves!

But if Why Choose truly isn't your thing, skip ahead to Undefeated, Chapter 10-12 and you'll get all the spoilers of who Taryn truly is and why she's important to the wolves and the dragons.

I'm assuming you've read books 1-4 if you've picked up this one, but if you haven't... I'm about to drop you straight into a void called the Nothing, and then into a secluded paranormal prison island.

I'm not giving you much background or world-building here and *I've done that on purpose*. I want you get to experience this story just as Taryn, our heroine, will. She's got total amnesia and knows nothing of the supernatural.

Getting plunked into a story is half the fun for me as a reader. I love escaping into another world and getting to BE the heroine of the story.

I hope you enjoy the ride!

:)

—Aidy

UNCLAIMED

FATE OF THE WOLF GUARD - BOOK 1

For all the wolves in my life

"The moon does not fight. It attacks no one. It does not worry. It does not try to crush others.

It keeps to its course, but by its very nature, it gently influences. What other body could pull an entire ocean from shore to shore?

The moon is faithful to its nature and its power is never diminished."

— DENG MING-DAO

TARYN

I don't know how long I've been in the darkness. Infinity plus a million feels about right.

I don't know much of anything, really. I must have had a life before the monsters came and shoved me into the Nothing, because the one thing I do remember is that I have a name. Yeah, shocker. I was surprised myself when I realized that little fact.

Except, I can't quite grasp what it is. Sometimes, I'm Anastasia, occasionally Sophia, more often Ekataryn. That name feels the closest to the real me. Taryn for short. I can almost hear a voice calling me that in some distant past.

A beast growls nearby. It's injured and desperate. I know the feeling. This might be more tricks my captors are submitting me to. I reach out anyway, wanting desperately to connect with any other living being.

"I'm here," I whisper.

"No, you're not." The voice resonates through my whole body like tiny spikes. Another painful ruse.

I retreat into myself, trying to protect what smidgen of sanity I have left. On days when they use their magic to make me see and hear others who aren't really there, I have my own tricks to push the darkness away. Saying my name keeps me from falling apart.

"Taryn, Taryn, Taryn." I repeat it over and over to myself, nothing more than a murmur, because I don't want to lose the one and only thing I know is mine.

Even after they've left me alone in the silence again, their shadowy illusions crawl up and down my body, a thousand pinches trying to pull at my skin and find a way in. The only course of action I've devised to fight against power I can't touch, is to imagine a light inside of me burning their black magic.

If that's even what it is. Do I really live in a world where real magic exists? Have I always? If I do, I would happily forsake fabulous powers if I could see some light again. Basking in the sun's rays… No wait, moonlight sounds better.

I don't know when, but I used to enjoy looking up at the moon and breathing in its light, like air. I remember the soft glow on my face. If I have no other shred of my memory, I want to forever hold on to the beauty and power of the moon.

What a weird ass idea. It is just a hunk of rock in the sky. It doesn't have some mystical energy. Not like it turns people into werewolves or something.

Huh. There's a new thought I didn't notice hiding in my mind. Great. I was obsessed with either astronomy or horror movies, or both, in the life I had before. I simply can't remember.

And I'm not sure I ever will.

Trying to figure it out is exhausting. I just want to sleep. No more thinking, worrying, wondering.

I close my eyes, but that's short-lived. In as long as I can think of, I hear something real.

People. Not voices in my head, not scared and hurt animals.

The air around me changes and is so completely different

that I stand up and turn toward the sound, even though I can't see anything. I fucking hear men talking and they're getting closer.

"Hello? Is someone there? I need help." My voice cracks and the words don't echo off any surfaces in this weird void. I have zero sense of whether the sound reaches the men. "Can anybody hear me?"

The blackness around me swirls and nausea roils in my gut. I'm on the brink of losing my balance. What in the world is happening? I throw my arms out to steady myself, but it doesn't help. Through the dysphoria, shapes form, trees, dirt below my feet, and yes, two men. Real, live humans.

"Help." I force my legs to take steps toward them. The sharp, jagged ground pokes me in the bottom of my bare feet and I stumble forward, landing on my knees before what could be my jailers or my saviors.

Except they aren't men at all.

Death, in tattered robes, looms up before me. I don't think those hoods hide faces at all. There's only more of the Nothing where their eyes should be.

"Who you, where do, why you, what help?" The stream of questions stumble out of my mouth, awkward and misshapen. I've not only forgotten who I am, but this disorientation of being in the real world has made me lose my ability to talk right. The ground under me continues to wobble, and I can't stay upright.

The creatures reach for me, and an ominous evil pours out of them. I try to scramble away but instead I throw up. I didn't know there was anything in my stomach to retch, but yellowish green chunks hit the arms of their robes. Gross, but I feel marginally better. The spins are less hurricane-ish and my muscles are shouting at me to get up and run.

Puke does not appear to be a death deterrent. The robed things grab me, one by each arm, and drag me, uncaring of my cries, across the dirt. Maybe I'm already dead because it's fricking cold out here and I am not dressed for Hell frozen over. I don't recognize the thin white t-shirt and frayed, ripped jeans on my body.

In fact, my own limbs aren't familiar to me. My arms are bigger and softer than the thin ones holding me. Gasp. Holding me with hands of flesh and bone. These are people, men, humans, not something ghostly at all.

And I'm twice as big around as either of them. Which means I can use my chunky butt to kick their asses.

I yank my arm and force my feet upright on the ground, but these two douchepotatoes aren't even phased. Maybe I was wrong about them not being supernatural creatures. I know I heard voices earlier, but these two haven't said a thing and they are way strong.

I've got just enough leverage to kick one of them behind the knee. Oh, yeah. That does it. He falters and yells at me. "You stupid, fat bitch."

Aha. Misogyny and fatphobia. More proof they're plain old human men.

The other one sighs. "Shut the fuck up and let's get this over with."

"No, don't." I double my struggles, a fresh surge of energy pulsing through me.

"Tell me who you are. Please, help me. I have a family." Do I? Not a single face or name comes to mind. The longer I'm out here, this cold air helps my brain clear, so it doesn't feel so empty. I know there is something I need to find. Someone?

Whatever or whoever it is, it's important to me and I am to them. I have to get back. "Let me go. I won't tell."

I don't remember anyone, or where I am, or how I'd get to my old life. But it's a bad idea to let them take me anywhere. Especially since that involves me being dragged away by these two minions of evil. The one I didn't kick wrenches my arm and jerks me forward. The other joins us and digs his finger-nails into my shoulder. Try as I might, besides that one knee kick, I cannot escape these guys.

There is little else I can do, so I let out a really nice, gut-wrenching scream. And I scream, and I scream some more. I scream so much, I'm basically howling at the moon at this point. Doesn't matter that the sky is so gray and overcast that I can't tell if it's day or night? There is no sun or moon.

I'm making the biggest racket I can in hopes that there are any other human beings in a ten-mile radius who can hear me. Even if there are other dudes in death drag, at least they'll be a distraction and maybe I could slip away.

But no one comes.

I'm on the verge of going hoarse and my lungs are ready to give out. I can't quit, but so far my instincts on how to fight for myself have sucked a big fat rat. Which is why I'm surprised as shit when they drop me like I'm hot. I am not. This forest is fricking freezing and shivers rush through me deep down to my soul.

Where the hell are we? Siberia?

One guy raises his arm, all spooky-like, and points toward a weird dark fog bank before us. "Go."

"Uh, no." And by no, I mean fuck you.

The other grabs me by the elbow and holds me out, pushing me forward. I simply don't have the coordination to pivot and run away. The shadowed fog looms up and swirls around my legs. That same dizzy disorientation seeps into my head and belly again, and I'm this close to hurling more chunks.

"You're sure this is what he wants?" Death dude number two actually sounds worried for a minute. Perhaps I misjudged him.

"Yes, how else are we supposed to get rid of her? Now do it." Death dude number one, the bigger of the two assholes, gives me a shove, and I go headlong into the nauseating mist. Two or three stumbling steps later and poof, the fog recedes behind me and I'm standing on a rocky beach with a very different tree line in front of me.

I turn around very slowly and blink about a hundred times. The water is frozen solid but so crystal clear I could almost touch the rocks below the surface. My feet are frigid, but there is no way I walked across that stretch of ice. It goes on forever and I don't see land in any other direction.

Where are the death dudes? The forest I was in a second ago? And where in the hell did that weird black fog bank go?

It's as if I've gone through a portal to another dimension.

If this is my normal life, I don't want any of it. Mystery-fog, nope. Guys who act like demonic ghosts, nuh-uh. Freezing weather, yeah, that can eat a bag of dicks.

At least this place isn't the Nothing. I said I wanted to see light. This is a poor excuse for it, but it's better than that never ending darkness.

I don't have a clue what to do next. I can try to go back across the lake, find the portal. At least there are people there, even if they are the bad kind. It wouldn't take long for my feet to turn into cement ice blocks, though. Not that the rocks on the frosty shore are a whole lot better.

Those woods aren't friendly looking either. I don't have any survival skills. Or maybe I do. I haven't died yet. First thing I need is some kind of shelter for safety. Out on that ice, I could run into those minions. So into the woods, it's time to go, where I might come across something even worse. Fan-fucking-tastic.

Anything is better than standing around on the cold rocks. I have no idea if I'm choosing wisely. My feet end up deciding for me because they are done with turning into fleshy icicles. I wonder if I can make some ad hoc shoes out of pine branches.

What I really need is a fire. A roaring one. That should stave off any wild animals and frostbite.

"*You're safe, printsessa.*"

Whoa. What the hell was that? It's as if a sexy voice-over started up in my head. If I'm going crazy now after all that time keeping myself sane in the Nothing, I'm gonna be pissed.

I whip around, searching for where the voice could have come from. About halfway up the beach, I see eyes, two blue moons, glowing from within the obscurity of the trees. Animal eyes, wild ones. My heart goes haywire and does a weird flip-flop in my chest.

Uh, maybe I'll just go a little further down the beach to find a place to take cover and make a fire. I glance down the thin strip of land between frozen water and the tree line to see if there's even the semblance of a shelter, or hidey hole, a fallen tree, anything.

Nothing.

A quick peek over my shoulder to make sure the animal isn't coming any closer, and it's disappeared. Phew. Maybe it was just as scared of me as I was of it.

I start up the shore and dammit, I should have gone looking for that hiding spot sooner. Four more pairs of eyes pop up, these yellow, not like the blue ones I saw before. From among the eyes, a thin man steps forward. His delicate features, have me thinking he is a teenager, until I look closer.

The muscles of my stomach clench. Not that same sick feeling from the Nothing or the portal. My own system is working hard to warn me of danger. The look of this guy is worse than the spooky dudes. Which is ridiculous. He doesn't have a weapon or creepy black robes. He's a real-life human and I should ask for help.

It is that or freeze to death.

I'm not that cold. Blue feet and frostbit fingers are fine.

He narrows his eyes and points a long graceful finger at me. "*Que fais-tu ici, Ekataryn?*"

Say what? I take some real slow steps back. Part of me is saying to get away from this dude fast while the other part

13

chastises me for being a fool because I'm half naked, alone, and cold. Even a creepo is better than freezing to death.

He glances around as if making sure he isn't in danger. From me? Slowly, he comes a little farther out of from the forested area. Two gigantic wolves follow slightly behind him.

Oh shit.

"Chto ty zdes' delayesh?"

That didn't sound like the same foreign language as before. Maybe since he's trying this hard to communicate with me, it's okay? Then again, maybe he's just looking for puppy food for his snarling wolf friends. When I don't reply, he tries again, albeit with some irritation in his voice. *"Was machst du hier, Ekataryn?"*

I do not want to talk to this guy. Everything in me says he's bad news. "Go away."

"English? Strange. Mine is, uh, *nicht* so *gut*. Come with me, now. No one else can find you." He waves me over and two more of his wolves stalk from the dark shadows of the forest.

I hear a growl from behind me. Crap. They were surrounding me all this time, and I didn't freaking notice. Not like I can do anything to defend against a feral animal attacking me, but I whip around anyway and discover those glowing blue eyes staring back. They aren't focused on me though, they're lasered in on creepo.

The wolf is growling hard, and his hackles are raised. He does that angry wild animal thing where he snaps his jaws and making mad barking sounds. Ah, man. I'm about to be a dinner fight.

"Good wolfie, wolfie. You don't want to eat me. I'm sure I don't taste yummy at all." Total lie. I've got way more fat on just my thighs than skinny creepy guy has on his whole body. I'll be frickin' delicious while he's a crunchy, salty snack that makes your face pucker.

"Hurry, come away from that beast." The guy waves me to him again. "I will protect you."

Yeah, you and what army? Creepo might have four wolves, but combined, they aren't as enormous as the blue-eyed one. They're scrawny mutts compared to this huge, angry ball of fur.

This time, creepy guy doesn't address me, he talks straight to the wolf. "I've already claimed her. She's mine."

Hold up. What? Nope. Don't like that. And also, why is he talking to the wolf? "No, I'm not. Officially unclaimed here. No one gets to say I belong to them."

Another man steps out of the trees looking like he belongs in the frozen landscape. His face is covered with a rough beard and he's wearing about four-hundred more pounds of clothes than me. "Smart girl. Nobody else wants to be claimed by Peter, Peter pussy-eater either."

"*Scheiße.*" Creepy Peter throws his head back and stares up at the sky. "This is not your place, August."

The burlier man walks toward me and I already feel safer. Which is probably dumb. The blue-eyed wolf joins him, and I have this unnatural need to reach out and touch his fur. Mr. Burly gives me a quick once over and put himself between me and Peter. "I think you'll find it most definitely is. Unless you're challenging me?"

Peter doesn't reply to that. Not verbally, anyway. He is pissed as hell, but he keeps his mouth shut. A challenge must mean serious business around here. He backs away and so do his wolves. Before he skulks into the trees, he points at me, then his eyes, and back at me.

Okay. I think I just made an enemy. Great. It's only day one of my new life in this winter wonderland. I only hope I've also made a friend and not become beholden to someone worse. If creepy Peter feared Mr. Burly and his giant wolf, I probably should, too.

The wolf saunters over to me and sticks his nose right in my crotch.

"Hey, now, inappropriate. We just met." I try pushing him, but there is no moving this wall of fur and muscles. "Get out of there, you weird pervy dog. I do not need you up in my lady business. Get, shoo. Go on."

I give Mr. Burly a glare that is meant to convey that he should get his pet under control. He merely lifts an eyebrow and watches.

I don't have any luck escaping Snooty Mcgrooty until he gives a final snuff and then sits down on his haunches and lets his tongue hang out, proud of himself. If he wasn't so huge and scary looking, I'd smack his nose and tell him he was a bad dog. But I also would like to avoid getting eaten.

"Right." Mr. Burly says, and I have no idea who he's talking to. He takes one long stride closer to me, and I notice he's got beads of sweat along the coarse hairs covering his upper lip and near his temples.

I thought his face was pink from the cold, but maybe he was running. He didn't seem out of breath when he arrived on the beach. He picks me up and tosses my torso and belly over his shoulder and smacks my butt. "We'd better get you somewhere protected. I certainly don't have shoes for you, but I'm sure Vasily will lick them and let you stick your toes under his belly to warm them up."

My heart does that flip-flop thing again and I still can't I tell if that means something bad. I should know my own body's reactions. I should. But I got nothing. Besides, being carried off like the spoils of a hunt doesn't sit right. Not to mention, I'm pretty sure even someone as strapping and strong as this guy wouldn't be able to carry my ass very far.

"Hey, put me down. Where are you taking me?" I slap my hands across his back, but whatever this coat is made of, it's a fluffy layer of protection, and I doubt he felt a thing. I did though. With each smack, zips of pain rush from my fist up my arm. I think that means frostbite is getting to me.

"You're fine, love." He pats my butt again. "You're safe with me. I'll explain more once we get you inside, warm, and put something in your belly."

That did sound great. My stomach rumbled to agree. I didn't even know I was hungry. I literally couldn't remember the last time I was. My hunger could wait if I had to. "You mean, feed me, not put a baby in me, right?"

He doesn't reply and my heart goes ballistic.

AUGUST

*E*kataryn is here, on the fucking Island of the Damned. More than here, she's in my arms again. Sort of. Thrown over my shoulder. Same thing.

"Put me down, you big burly asshat. I can walk on my own." She pounds on my back and kicks her feet. Good to see there is some spark in her. More than I had the day I was tossed on that same beach.

"Not a chance. I don't want to be the one to have to cut off your frost-bitten toes." I can only pray she still has enough power to heal herself. The warmth of my cabin will help. The warmth of my bed will be even better.

Which is not something I should have thought. I'm going to have to keep my outdoor protective furs on if I don't want her to see how my cock is pressing against my leggings. She's not ready for what I want to do to her.

"Cut off?" she squeaks and her struggles lessen.

I would never hurt her, but she doesn't need to know that right now. I need her to be compliant just long enough to get her to safety. "Yes, with my hunting knife."

I never thought we'd ever see her again, not after two-hundred years of living in this nightmare wondering if she was alive or dead. Joaquim knew though. That son of a bitch. There she was, right on the beach where he said she would be. It took everything I had not to run to her and crush her against me.

There wasn't even a fucking glint of recognition in her eyes when she saw me. Whatever those Volkov bastards have done to her, it's bad. I want to rip the head off every single one of them. Not likely I'll get a chance.

I have to tell her.

I can't.

Fuck.

I hate secrets, and lying, and subterfuge. That's Grigory's department, and now apparently Joachim's. He warned me that she would know nothing of our world, and even less of who we are to her. Here I am god damned scaring her.

Fine. I'd keep my mouth shut, for now. At least I'm the first to touch her, hold her. I can practically taste her. The scent is so rich and my wolf is begging me to drop her right here in the snow and claim her for my own.

Why can't I? It's not like we have an alpha to command us. He gave up a long time ago and his bitterness and anger make this island prison even worse. Pin pricks of guilt poke along the back of my neck. He would know if I claimed her.

Vasily whines and I glance down at him. He knows what I'm thinking, and don't I feel like a selfish ass? I give him a curt nod and he and I go back to our understanding.

My cabin is at the edge of the *derevnya*, on a rocky bank where I can have my peace, but also be near enough to keep trouble at bay. That is when I'm not off rescuing fair maidens from the shadow.

Vasily runs ahead, making it his business to ensure no one lies in wait for us. The flicker from the fireplace still lights the small windows and I don't scent anyone else nearby. None that shouldn't be. The streets of the *derevnya* carry the stench of danger. Damn.

Grigory's been here.

The people of the *derevnya* rely on me to keep them safe. We're the only bastion of decent people on an island of criminals, murderers, and psychopaths. Most of us are some kind of political prisoners and except for Vasily, Joachim, Will, and me, they wouldn't know how to fight if it meant the difference between life and death.

The instinct to go to them is already rising up, calling the wolf forth to do my job and eliminate the threat. I want to check that everyone is okay, but I'll have to see to that later. Ekataryn is my only priority. I focus on her scent, the sound of her heart beating, and the way her ass squirms under my hands, to focus on keeping myself in human form.

The villagers can take care of themselves for one damn minute. I do enough for them. If they can't keep themselves safe with the tools Will and I have given them, then maybe they need a hard lesson.

That's never been my way, which is how I ended up half dead, lying on that very same beach, two-hundred years ago. Hmph. You'd think I'd learn.

I get the yip from Vasily giving me the all clear and he butts his head against the door to open it. I join him quickly, not wanting her scent in the air any longer than necessary. A rush of warm air hits me in the face and Ekataryn's half bare legs shiver.

"Are we there?" She lifts her head and moves like she's going to crawl down my chest.

While I'd enjoy that very much, those toes of hers are not touching cold ground ever again if I have anything to do with it. "We are and if you don't stop wiggling, I'm going to drop you in the snowbank outside the door instead of the bed."

"Bed?" That same squeak is back in her voice and I'm such

an asshole for loving it. So innocent, so sweet, and I couldn't wait to turn those squeaks into moans.

"It's either that or the table. This isn't the Winter Palace, tzaritsa." I drop her onto the bed, even though I want to throw her down on the pillows and follow her into the warm furs and blankets. My naked body against hers would warm her up a whole hell of a lot faster than the fire.

I grit my teeth to hold in a snarl. The fire is what she'll get because I can't trust myself not to do much more than she is ready for. I turn my back on her and grabbed all three logs that would normally last through the night and settle them onto the coals. A few blows and the dry wood takes, crackling to life. In a few minutes it will be roaring.

That done, I have to get a hot drink in her and make sure those soft, delicate feet aren't causing her pain. But I discover someone else is already taking care of warming up her feet.

"Vasily." I can't keep the growl out of my voice. He's curled right up on her lap, his tail wagging, flipping itself back and forth over the round of her ass. Dickhead knows exactly what he's doing. He's missed her as much as I have. Maybe more.

I can see the weariness of being cold and thrown into the prison taking their toll on her. She shoves at Vas to get off her, but he's as big as she is and twice as heavy. She's not going anywhere no matter how hard she fights.

I send a silent prayer up to the goddesses that she trusts me enough to control whatever fears she has left and stay put in my bed. She isn't afraid of Vasily at all. When he doesn't give way, she gives up her fight and pets his head. He closes his eyes and leans into her. Asshole.

"That's his name, your wolf? Vasily? It suits him." Her voice has that note of exhaustion, but it's also timid. I don't like that at all. It's not what I've come to expect from her. Sweet and innocent when she needs to be, fine, but not timid. Never.

21

I send the traitorous wolf guard a death glare that doesn't faze him one bit. "He's clearly yours, not mine."

I have to keep reminding myself she's not the same girl I knew, and my ability to be there for her in this lifetime was non-existent. Perhaps she wasn't allowed to develop her own inner self-assurance. I wouldn't doubt it.

She gives us both a half grin and I'd just about die to see the other half. "I'm Taryn. What's your name?

It hurts more than I expect that she doesn't know our names. I do like the version of her name she's chosen. Will telling her my full name, the one I had the last time we were together, spur any memories in her? Would my house name? I shouldn't try, but I can't help it. I want her to remember me. "I am Stanisław August Poniatowski of the House of the Rising Moon."

Her eyes go wide and she sticks out her chin as if trying to catch all those syllables in her ears and mouth. Guess my name didn't make a difference. "But you can call me August."

"August. I can at least pronounce that."

We've struck a small truce between us and that's garnered me the trust I need from her. Vas gives her a little whine and she runs her fingers through his coat and scratches him behind the ears. I almost shift right then and there just to get the same treatment.

"He's sweet." She yawns and leans into him. Lucky fucking bastard.

"He's something alright. You keep your eye on him. His bite is much worse than his bark."

Ekataryn gives him a good couple of scritches under the chin. "You wouldn't bite me, now would you?"

"He'd love to eat you right here and right now, but he won't." Vas gives me a growl for saying that.

Am I acting ridiculous for being jealous of him getting to curl up on the bed with her? Yes. Is that stopping my own wolf from wanting to burst right out of my skin and fight for that right? No.

It's her shivering that keeps me under control. "I'm going out to get some more wood from the pile for the fire."

I shove my feet back into my boots and throw my coat back on, not bothering to button it up. I'll get some wood, sure. But first, I'm shifting and going for a long ass run to burn off the energy inside of me, burning to ignore everything I know is right and mark her, claim her, and make her my true mate.

"You're leaving me alone?" She scrambles to get up but Vas doesn't move, so she's stuck. Good.

"Don't go outside, don't try to leave. You're safe here." I don't give her more explanation than that.

Being her mate meant protecting her and that's what I was going to do. Having Pyotr find her before I did put a kink in our plans. Him, I could handle. It was his sycophants that would cause problems. How the fuck had he known Ekataryn would be exiled to the Island of the Damned at that moment?

Joaquim would die before he'd tell that puny rat anything. Even if he was Pyotr's confessor. The good father is everyone's confessor. Everyone who still thinks they can be saved, anyway. He knows more about the goings on in the lives of the Island than anyone else, but he keeps his mouth shut. Keeps a lot just between him and his God.

I'm not a hundred meters from the cabin and haven't even shifted yet when Joachim's white wolf darted from behind a copse of trees. He sniffs me and I roll my eyes at him. Her scent is all over my clothes and it's probably driving him as mad as it does me.

"She's safe, in my cabin with Vasily. But Pyotr Feodorovich and his gang of sycophants found her before I got there. He's going to be trouble. As always."

Joachim snorts and puffs of cold air drift up from his snout.

He doesn't shift and uses our pack connection to reply. *"You'll take care of him, just as you always do. Protector of all but yourself."*

"Don't get all fucking up in my head. I know exactly who and what I am." But Ekataryn did not.

"Grigory has been on the rampage again." Joachim's constant composure about matters big and small is his trademark. A God-given talent I do not possess. I knew I scented Grigory in the air and in the destruction in the *derevnya*. That's my village, dammit. He can't go around, killing whoever he wants, whenever he pleases.

Rage filters through me, scorching my senses. My wolf's claws shoot out of my hands and my fangs extend. I look forward to the pain of the shift and rip my jacket open ready to let my beast out. Fuck Grigory.

Calm yourself, August. He's gone back to his lair. She is safe. Besides, it will take you a week to repair your clothes and if you go back to the cabin with them in shreds, Soph-- Ekataryn will want to know what happened.

It takes me more than a few huffed deep breaths to push the wolf back inside. Joachim is right. He's always fucking right. "You keep him away from her and the *derevnya*."

Joachim sits and stares up at the overcast moonless sky. *"He is not mine to command."*

Like I don't fucking know that. "I need to get back. Vas is alone with her and I don't entirely trust him. He could go berserk now that she's here."

"That would be a welcome change."

"You're an asshole." None of us has been able to get through to Vas in over a hundred years. Maybe Ekataryn will.

Joachim stands and shakes the snow off his fur. He takes a few steps back toward the village and his church. *"You have no idea what I am."*

"Don't you want to see her?" I don't understand why he sent me to protect her when he was the one who knew she was coming. His wolf is just as powerful as mine and he probably could have charmed her into coming with him instead of strong-arming her compliance.

He's got some other master plan he isn't letting the rest of us in on. Fine. But I know what's in his heart. How could I not?

Joaquim doesn't bother to answer and his wolf disappears in the falling snow and frozen mist. Fuck him, fuck the island, and its eternal winter.

The conversation has cooled my ire and I head back to the cabin and grab an armful of wood from the pile at the side. I should not have been gone so long. I may hate how Vas has earned her trust and her touch so easily, but I know full well that he would always protect Ekataryn.

He'd been vicious enough in his time here that no one would bother him. Not even Grigory.

I push my way back inside, half expecting her to be curled up with Vas as her big teddy bear and asleep. What I find is a short, puffy *leshiy*, minus of course the snowman and abominable part. Ekataryn has dressed herself in my furs using sinew, from some snowshoes I'm repairing for Maggie, to tie them onto her body like an awkward dress.

While I should be angry that she's trying to escape, a stupid grin creeps up on my face at the blankets falling off on one side and squishing her arm and shoulder on the other. "Oh no, a wood goblin found its way inside. It's not a very big one. Shall we eat it for dinner, Vasily?"

Ekataryn jumped a good half a meter into the air and one of the furs slipped, exposing her lush bare thigh. "Oh, you scared the crap out of me."

Vas didn't think I was half as funny as I did. He stays curled up on the bed watching Ekataryn struggle with the furs. I can't take my eyes off her. God, how I want her. I want to feel every square inch of her body pressed against mine. I need to know she's real, that she's here, and that she's alive. Being inside of her and hearing her moan my name is the best damn way I can think of to prove she's in our lives once again.

"I'm glad you're back. I'm all warmed up. Can we go now?"

"Where do you think we'd go, tzaritsa? Night has fallen and there is nowhere else on this god-forsaken island that is safer than right here." I don't care that there hasn't been a moon in the sky in the two-hundred plus years I've been here. It didn't matter then. I can never allow her to be outside at night.

"Island?" She says the word as if it's foreign to her. "No, no, no. We're completely surrounded by that ice? Can I cross it? Will you show me, take me? I have to get back to... well, I have to get back to my life before."

Icy cold dread runs along the back of my neck. Joachim said she would know nothing of our world, but I thought she would at least understand where she was, could maybe even tell us what happened to get her imprisoned. Vas's eyes narrow and his eyes darken, matching my sentiments exactly.

I may not be able to tell her who or what I am to her, but she needs to know where she is. I can't swallow past the awful knowledge that I'm about to crush her hopes. I don't answer right away. Instead, I busy myself laying another log on the fire and filling the pot to boil some water. She's hungry, thirsty, and tired, but her mind is still in survival mode and hasn't acknowledged it yet.

"Sit, let me feed you." That will give me the excuse to delay destroying her hopes for a few minutes longer.

"I'm not hungry." She looks around the cabin, likely wondering what I'm even offering. Everything in here is sparse, but I've never needed more. That will have to change.

"You are, and you will let me take care of you. We aren't going anywhere until you've rested, actually warmed up, and you'll need energy to survive this harsh land. So, sit." I'd forgotten how stubborn she could be.

Vas jumps off the bed and shoves her toward the table with a butt of his head. She makes a face at him. "You are the bossiest wolf-dog I've ever met."

I cough to cover my snort. "He also wants to take care of your needs."

Vas wags his tail and let's his tongue hang out. Dirty minded asshole. He pushes her again and she's forced to stumble forward and into one of the three chairs. The fourth was broken years ago.

"Why? I don't even know you." She twists on the chair to look at the two of us. "Why are you being so nice to me? It's not like I can do anything to repay you. I don't plan on being here long."

"Forever." The truth pops out of my mouth. It will crush her, but it feels good to say it. Not because I want to hurt her, but for the first time, I'm glad for the curses of this island. She can be mine, ours, forever now. "You're here forever. This place is a prison for enemies of the Volkovs, and there is no escape from the Island of the Damned."

TARYN

*P*rison.
    No escape.
Damned.

That absolutely could not be true. I not only can't believe it, I've just decided I will also refuse to believe it. I haven't done anything to deserve being incarcerated. I may not have much in the way of memories of my life before the Nothing and today's adventures in crazytown, but I know I'm not a bad person.

People go to prison for murder, thievery and corruption. I can't even imagine taking a life. Thinking that I'm now trapped with people like that has my heart speeding up and skipping beats. "There has to be a mistake. Who do I see about appealing? There wasn't a trial, no one read me my rights."

I may not remember squat about squat, but I know there is such a thing as a justice system. This isn't it.

What if I've been framed? Maybe my life before was so messed up that I got involved with criminals. Or maybe my family... a strange flash of a fist squeezes an empty hollow right below my throat. It's not like a vision, just an extremely uncomfortable feeling.

A family. They must be why I feel the need so deeply to get back. I have to take care of... someone. Gather my loved ones together and... I can't quite grasp what or why or who these thoughts are even about.

"The Volkovs don't care about any law but their own." August's eyes go dark and storm-filled. "If they thought you were a danger to them and their power, your punishment is to be banished here, never to be heard from or interfere again."

That doesn't sit right either. "I'm not dangerous to anyone."

But this man who has taken me in is. He was ready to fight that creepy Peter, and it doesn't take much imagination to come up with a whole litany of crimes that guy probably committed aside from the peculiar way he talked to me. I want to ask August what he's done to land in prison, but that feels like opening up a can of venomous worms.

Except from the second I saw him, I curiously felt safe. Which is probably really dumb. Is my own instinct so untrustworthy that I can't tell a murderer from a hero?

That's a big ole yes. For all I know, this guy and his wolf are serial killers and I'm being set up as their latest victim. Vasily whines and sets his head on my lap. He's both fierce and adorable at the same time. I can't help it, I grab his face and give him a snuggle. "You're not a serial killer, are you, poochie-poo?"

Is August the same as his wolf-dog, tough and gentle? Sweet and savage? I just don't know. Which puts me back to square one - do I stay with him where I've so far been safe, or run away from his particular brand of danger because he might be planning to harm me? Both choices give me the heebie-jeebies. Where would I even go?

He's been willing to give me some bits of information, in his gruff way. Even though I only understand some of what he means, without any cultural or societal memories to draw on, I need to find out more to make this decision. I'm certainly not going to straight out ask him what his crimes were in case I really, really don't want to know.

I start with an easy one. "How many people are in this prison island place?"

"Too many."

That's not helpful, but I'll pretend it was a real answer. "And no one has ever escaped? There must be someone, an urban legend of digging a hole and climbing through sewers or something."

"There is no escape."

This isn't working. "What about when the guards come with food?"

August laughs, but not in the fun way. "We provide for ourselves. Don't worry, I'll never let you go hungry."

"Who is this we?" I hope he means there are other non-killery people and not just him and Vasily.

He scratches his beard and his eyes flick between mine. He's trying to decide if he should tell me and I blink my lashes as sweetly and innocently as I can. Come on, you can tell little old me.

"Tomorrow I will take you to the *derevnya*. There are some others you should meet."

Phew. I think I won that round. "What's a *derevnya*? Is it far, can we go now?"

He makes that thinking face again and purses his lips. There can't be that much harm in telling me about a place he's going to take me. Vasily makes a little whine-growl and August rolls his eyes. The two of them have a language all to themselves. "A village where others who have banded together to defend against the monsters and men who seek to destroy us."

Gulp. Monsters. He means bad people, doesn't he? Except what he said there was monsters and men. I think I'm done asking questions now. Those were definitely answers I didn't want to hear. But a village of people who work together must have other good people in it. I'll find out there whether I've gotten in with the wrong man and wolf. "Okay, tomorrow, then."

August pours hot water into a mug from a pot that's been warming by the fire. "Drink. The tea will help revitalize you, but also allow you to sleep."

All my time in the Nothing feels as though I've been asleep and while my body is exhausted, I don't think I could sleep a wink. Not after all I've learned and need to mull over. Besides, there is only one bed, which I accidentally glance toward.

Change of plans. "Wouldn't it be safer if we went to the village now?"

August has been more of the stoic grump up until I asked that question. Sure, he'd thrown me over his shoulder, but he hadn't hurt me and I wasn't scared of him. But the anger that morphs his face now has me thinking he is more of a wild beast than Vasily. I freeze with the mug halfway between my mouth and the table. This is the part where he murders me.

"No."

Uh. Okay. A gruff answer is better than ripping my heart out of my chest with his bare hands, which is strangely what I'm imagining.

He takes several deep breaths, closes his eyes, and when he opens them again he's much more calm. "Just, no."

I can't quite put my finger on what it is that has gone away in his face, but I can quite literally feel the fine hairs that were standing up on my arms and the back of my neck, lay down, one by one. Very weird sensation. I set the mug back on the table and pull the fur I took from the bed tighter around me.

I don't have anything to say. I'm not going to simply agree to his refusal, but he doesn't need to know that. Especially if he's gonna go all beastly on me.

AIDY AWARD

"Go to bed now. You need rest." He snags the mug and splashes the remaining swallow of tea onto the edge of the fire.

I may be imprisoned, alone, and without proper clothing or resources, but I don't like being bossed around. This time I can't keep myself from saying something. "I'm not a child. You don't have to take care of me."

He growls. Growls. At me. "I will always take care of you. You will be safe this time."

Prickly pins tingle across my shoulders and zip down my spine.

Vasily barks at August. He's reacting to the tension between us. He may be only an animal, but he can see what's going on. The conflict creates a rock in my chest. I don't even know this guy and his wolf and I just want to hug them close to me and say that everything is okay and that I'll take care of them.

Dumb. I can't even take care of myself.

I reach for Vasily's back, wanting to calm both him and the situation. I pull the wolf closer and talk to him because it's silly and maybe that will defuse the explosion of emotions we're all sharing right now. "I think August is the one who is tired, don't you Vasily? He's a mister cranky pants. He's the one who needs to go to bed."

Vasily wags his tail and lets his tongue hang out. Yep. He likes the idea. I glance up at August who still has a mad on, but there's the tiniest twitch at the side of his mouth. Ha. I got him. He wants to smile. "I'm not going to sleep until you do. So if you really want me to go to bed, you'll have to entice me by crawling in first."

His mouth isn't the only thing twitching now. His eyebrow is flirting with me. Once again, I should be freaked out. Yep, there's only one bed. Nope, I'm not letting him get in there with me.

He could if he wanted to. He does want to. I weirdly even

32

kind of want him to. I would feel safe and protected wrapped in his arms. But I am not the girl who is too dumb to live. He's also not the guy who would kill me. I know that from someplace very deep inside. I don't trust my instincts, but this is something more than a gut feeling.

"Where will you sleep?"

I watch his face carefully and I see the flash where he glances to the bed and back to me. It's so fast, and there is a longing there that I don't understand. Although, duh. He's probably been in prison for a long time and hasn't had a woman for longer. He could so easily continue to poke at me over this, but he doesn't. "I'll sleep on the floor in front of the fire."

I get up and pull the biggest blanket and the pillow off the wooden frame and sparse mattress. The room is warm and the furs will keep me from getting cold. "Here. I don't want you to be uncomfortable."

He waves me off, but I lay the blanket carefully on the hardened dirt floor, not too near the coals. I need him to be warm and snug. Because the second he falls asleep, I'm taking Vasily and finding that town.

August may not want to harm me, he even wants to keep me safe, but that is not going to get me home. He may think there is no way off this island, but I don't believe it. I don't even think he meant to tell me about the village, and I doubt he'll take me in the morning either. If there really are monsters and other bad men on this island, he'll lock me up in this cabin and I'll never see the light of day. A prison within a prison.

That's hardly better than living in the Nothing.

August sits on the blanket, arms wrapped around his knees and waits for me to get into bed. I'm not taking my clothes off in front of him, but I do drop the furs I'd been trying to wrap around me on the bed.

His big furry coat is hanging on the chair and it's long

enough to be full-length on me. Lucky for me he's a big bulky guy and I'm pretty sure it will close around my butt and boobs. If I'd been stuck with that Peter guy I would have needed two or three of his coats and all they would have covered are my thighs.

I crawl under the furs and Vasily jumps on the bed with me again. I sure hope he's down for my escape plan later, because if he isn't I'm stuck here until he needs to go out to pee. There's no way I'd be able to move him off me.

The heat from the wolf and the furs lolls me into drifting toward sleep. I may as well rest for a little while so I'm ready when I do escape, once I'm sure August is unconscious. I don't know how long I've been out, but a snore from August wakes me. Good. He's deep in sleep and I don't think too much time has passed.

Vasily is asleep too, and definitely having wolfy dreams if his little whimpers and snuffles are anything to go by. He's sprawled across my legs, but I'm able to slip my feet free from underneath the furs. He wakes up anyway and looks at me with those adorable, sleepy, moonlit eyes. I wonder if the color and light in them is a product of this strange island, because the other wolves' eyes glowed too, although not with Vasily's pretty light blue.

I stroke the strip of soft fur between his eyes and hold a finger up to my mouth hoping he understands to keep quiet. I move to crawl off the bed and the wooden bed frame creaks under me. August snorts and rolls over and I freeze.

Vasily jumps to the floor and wags his tail, but doesn't bark. If there is such a thing as wolf treats in the village I'm definitely getting some for him. I gingerly get off the bed and am grateful the floor is dirt and not planks because I'm sure the boards would squeak if they were.

I grab the coat and it's way heavier than I expected. It also smells like August. Woodsy, smoky, man and wolf. I only feel bad for about a half a second for stealing it. Even if he catches me, I might never give it back. I slip my arms in and have to shove the sleeves up. I'm going to be a walking marshmallow in this thing, so I'd better put the boots on and get them laced up before I button the coat shut.

I have to give a couple of big tugs to get the boots over my calves and they go up over my knees. There's more material, but they aren't going any higher up my thighs. They're tight enough, I don't need the laces to hold them on, but I tie them tight around my ankles because there's a whole lot of room in the shoe part.

August's feet are at least twice as long as mine. I think that means something because a giggle bubbles up when I think about it. But whatever it is gets lost in my Swiss cheese brain.

Mmm. Cheese.

God, my memory is weird.

The door doesn't appear to have any kind of lock, which is weird to me since we're supposedly on an island of criminals. But one glance at Vasily and I see why they don't need a lock. It isn't like there's a lot to steal. August lives pretty sparsely, although I liked it. Warm, comforting, safe.

Unlike what I'm about to do. I open the door millimeter by millimeter, trying not to make a sound or let a gust of cold air in. The bulk of the coat, not to mention my rear-end, I mean, I can't exactly slip through a crack. Before I'm able to slip out, Vasily skims right past me and sniffs the ground and the air.

The night has gone as still as the frozen water. There aren't any snowflakes falling, wind blowing through the branches of the trees, or animals doing nighttime activities. I sure hope that's a good thing. I get out the door through the smallest opening I can manage and am very careful to shut the door quietly behind me.

Vasily looks up at me and he doesn't seem antsy or on edge. He'd growl if there were monsters or men. Right? I bend into a weird sort of squat next to him. The coat won't allow for much more. I whisper close to his ear and he holds so still I'm not even sure he's breathing. "That's a good boy. Can you take me to the village?"

I haul myself back up, wait a second to see if he understands me and when he doesn't move, I take a few steps away from the cabin. Vasily sits down.

Great. It's not like I saw a leash or something. Either he comes with me voluntarily or I'm screwed. The cold air is already turning my breath and my lungs to ice. We have to get moving. I pat my leg and loud-whisper, "Come on, Vasily. I'm going with or without you."

That's a lie, but it's not like he speaks English anyway. I take a few more steps and he still doesn't move. He's freaking calling my bluff. Fine. I turn my back on him and walk away at a brisk pace. I figure as long as I can still see the cabin, I'm close enough that I could sprint back in case of monsters.

A good ten feet away, Vasily bounds up in front of me and butts his head against my right thigh, pushing me in a new direction. I have the distinct feeling I'm being herded, but if that gets me to the village, fine.

We go a bit further and he does it again. I change direction heading a little more to the left again. I'm doing my best to pay attention to the formation of the trees and the plants so I can find my way back if I absolutely have to. I can just say I had to go out to pee.

Crud. Now I have to pee.

We keep walking and every so often Vasily moves me in the right direction. The village isn't as close as I'd hoped. I haven't seen a sign of it at all yet. More walking, more herding and I see light up ahead. Finally.

I hurry a bit and then stop in my tracks. Dammit. It's the cabin. Vasily has taken me in a big circle. "You're a butthead."

He wags his tail and is definitely proud of himself. Fine, I'll show him. He followed me last time, so I expect he will again. I turn a hundred and eighty degrees and walk in the exact opposite direction he wants me to. I'm right and he joins me, hitting me with his head to go back toward the cabin.

"I see what you're doing and I'm not playing your game this time. We're going to that village whether you help me or not." I look up at the sky and wish it wasn't so overcast. A little direction from the moon and the stars would be a welcome sight.

Vasily keeps trying to herd me, but even though he stands almost as tall as me, I move only slightly and then correct my course in whichever way he doesn't want me to go. I keep moving fast because I'm definitely feeling the cold now and I need to keep warm until I find a new shelter.

Again I see light up ahead, and this time I'm sure it isn't the cabin because there is an outcropping of rocks I'll need to climb over. This has to be the village. I walk even faster even though I can feel a stitch in my side coming on. I haven't seen any monsters, not that I know what they look like, and if I hurry now, I can avoid them all together.

The light flickers like a fire and the shadows of the trees grow longer and darker. That's just a trick of the light. Except one shadow jumps from one tree to another and a chill unlike the cold night air fills my mouth and throat. The fine hairs in my nose turn to icicles and I can't breath, I can't even cough.

Vasily turns from the affable companion to a menacing guard wolf. He growls low and it turns into a snarl. He's got a whole mouthful of fangs, and while they aren't pointed at me, I'm so scared I take a step away.

He snaps and barks at the shadows that are definitely moving of their own freewill now. Vasily moves right in front of me like he's going to defend me from shadows. We are so screwed. I reach out to touch his back, not knowing if it's to comfort me or him.

One shadow gets enormous, crawling up the side of a tree and I even think I see a face in the darkness. I know as deeply as I know my own name, this is pure evil. Vasily glances back at me and in my head I hear just one word in that same voice from the beach. *"Run."*

AUGUST

J haven't slept so peacefully in two-hundred years. Ekataryn's presence back in my life is all it takes to fill in the holes in my soul. I didn't even realize how bone-achingly exhausted this banishment without her had made me. Never knowing who was caring for her and protecting her, especially after Vasily and Grigory appeared, broken and even more destroyed, on the shore a hundred or so years after I did.

No wolf guard was ever rewarded for sleeping. I should have remembered that.

"August. She needs you. Now."

I go from fast asleep to awake and shifted, bursting out the door in my wolf form in less than a breath. I can't believe I didn't know she was gone. And why the fuck didn't Vas wake me? Until now, he hasn't said a word in my head in a hundred years, but he could have stomped on my balls or something to let me know Taryn was gone.

Her scent is unmistakable to my wolf's nose, but she's wearing my clothes and damn if my smell mixed with hers doesn't turn me the fuck on. If she and I live through this battle, I may be breaking my promise to Joachim not to touch her yet.

And there will be a battle. Vas is a hardened warrior. Survived the Volkovs even longer than I did. If he's calling for help, some bad shit is about to go down.

I follow Ekataryn's scent in a god-damned circle around the cabin before it heads off in the opposite direction as the *derevnya*. She never did have a good sense of direction and could get lost in her own closet. Granted her closets at the Grand Palace were larger than the entire village.

The shadows on the trees are long and dark, and I pray that tonight, the demons aren't out to play. They were only one of the reasons I didn't fucking want her out at night. Not that they would touch her. With her here now, everything about this world could change.

A quick glance up at the sky and it's still overcast. No stars, and definitely no moon. Good. One less thing to worry about. We'll be lucky if Grigory doesn't come just looking for a fight.

I see the light from a campfire that's much larger than it needs to be and I know why Vas called. He's tough as claws, but seven against one is bad odds. Especially with soft, fragile Taryn so vulnerable. If the Naryshkins found out who she is, they'd destroy her, or worse.

When I find them, Taryn has her back up against a tree and is throwing rocks at the other wolves. It doesn't appear she's hit one yet, or if she has, they aren't deterred. Vas has one wolf pinned to the ground, his jaw around his opponent's throat. More are approaching, and he's snarling at them while the captured wolf struggles, but the warning isn't slowing them down.

I have to make a split second decision. Grab Taryn and get her to safety or jump into the fray to better the odds of keeping all three of us from getting killed or enslaved to this brutal pack. My instincts scream to go to Taryn. It is my one duty to protect her.

She hasn't yet seen me as a wolf in this life and won't know if I'm friend or foe. If I drag her away and leave Vas to fend for himself, there's no guarantee some of the pack won't come after us and if he gets hurt, she'll never forgive me.

Fuck. She'll also never forgive either of us if we get killed and she gets claimed by the asshole, power-hungry Naryshkin pack. Okay then, no one is dying on team Taryn.

I pounce from my spot in the trees and in front of her. Both Taryn and the Naryshkin wolves jump back, surprised by my entrance. Her instincts are crap and I understand, but the wolves should have known better. Although, I above all understand being distracted by her presence.

"Get away, you dirty wolf."

A rock hits me directly on the hind quarters. Welp, at least her aim is okay, she just needs to put a little strength behind it. We'll work on that later, after Vas and I take out these dickwads. Two against seven still isn't great odds, but I've tangled with each and every one of them before. I know their strengths, which are in their numbers, and their weaknesses, which is in their greed.

Lev Naryshkin is probably still smarting from the last time I beat his ass for trying to intimidate the people of my village. He's skulking behind some trees and scowls at me when he notices that I've spotted him. He shifts and I am cursing his name hoping Taryn didn't see that.

I can't afford to take my eyes off him to check on her but she's not fleeing in horror, so either she's starting to remember who she is, or she didn't notice Lev.

He throws on some robes and strolls up behind the rest of his pack. If he's got garments here, then this is more than a fire to keep warm. What in the hell are they doing making a camp so close to my cabin and the *derevnya*?

"Peter said there was a new woman here. I didn't believe it

and wanted to see it with my own eyes." Lev keeps his distance, putting his pack between him and us. Of course Peter went running to tell everyone Ekataryn is here. Shit. Half the island will know by morning and we'll have a siege on our hands.

I should have taken her to Maggie and Will right away instead of my cabin. At least all the other scents of the village would have masked hers.

A rock flies over my back and hits Lev square in the chest. "Any friend of Peter's is no friend of mine. Call off your wolves and mine won't hurt you."

Whoa. A spike of pure need and energy burst through me like rays of the moon at her claim on me and Vas. Now, that's my girl. Has she remembered who she is?

Lev smirks and takes a few steps closer. Dumbass. "Your wolves, are they? Do they know that? I think if given the chance, they'd eat you up themselves. Have you been claimed by one of them? Because that's the law of this land and I am prepared to fight to have you."

"What is it with you weirdos and claiming me? This is the twenty-first century, nobody owns women anymore." Ekataryn's words have plenty of bravado, but the scent of her fear is curling up in my nose. I glance over at Vas who still hasn't let the other wolf out of his death lock.

"Vas, we need a plan to get out of this besides standing here growling while Lev gets a hard on."

His only response is to bite down harder making the wolf he's trapped yelp. I guess one sentence in a hundred years is all I'm going to get out of him. It looks like his strategy is simply to go down fighting. That's not acceptable.

"Fine, don't talk to me. But fucking listen." I'm about to come up with a plan out of my ass.

"You have no mark?" Lev's eyes light up and I'd better come up with something fast or Ekataryn is going to see the true nature of us all before she's ready for such truths. Because I will slaughter every man here before I allow him to even touch her. "Then I claim you for the Naryshkin pack. Having you in our beds will bring a prestige no others on this island have seen in hundreds of years. You'll be our queen, as long as you remember who rules over you."

Ah, fuck. Okay, the plan is now just one step. Murder Lev. *"Get ready, I'll take Lev, you cover Ekataryn."*

Vas snorts and that's either his agreement or his acknowledgement that my plan is stupid. What choice do we have? We are not letting her die again. Not this fucking time.

"God dammit. What the hell is wrong with you people? I said I'm not being claimed by anyone and I'm certainly not going to be a brood mare to you." Another rock flies through the air and this one bounces right off Lev's forehead. "Queen, my chubby ass. You mean whore and that means you can go fuck yourself."

If I were in human form, I'd be laughing my ass off right now. I'm also falling in love with her dirty mouth.

Shit. Shit. Shit. I am fucking falling in love with her. That can't happen. I know better. Protect her. Worship her. Don't fall in love with her. She's been back in my life for a few hours and my feelings are already going to get either her, Vas or me killed.

Lev's face turns dark and the other Naryshkin wolves go from alert and ready for battle to menacing and on the verge of attack in a second. He's their alpha and they can't disobey whatever command he's spoken into their minds even if they wanted to. They didn't all used to have darkness in their hearts and minds. I blame the Volkovs for that more than Lev himself.

They've pitted us against each other for the basic right to survive. There is nothing we can do about that now. Ekataryn will survive regardless of the cost.

I growl low and stalk closer to the closest wolf in the semi-circle. They may have no choice but to obey Lev, but they should know they are in for a beating.

"Get that female." Lev points toward Taryn and the wolf in front of me attacks.

I'm ready for him. Just as Vas did, I go for the other wolf's throat. He sees my attack coming and tries to feint to the left. Such a beginner move, I almost hate taking him down. I slash out with my claws, striking him across the belly before he can get away. His intestines spill out and blood spurts across my fur.

Beside me, I hear Vas crunch down on the captured wolf's neck and end that poor sap's life as well. Five against two is already much better odds, especially when the two are elite trained wolf guards.

Rocks go flying over my head and two against five becomes two and a good distraction. That I can work with.

"Call off your attack. Stop this madness, stop it now." Ekataryn yells at Lev and that gives me the perfect opportunity to attack while he's paying attention to her.

I jump over the flayed wolf and sail toward Lev. If he's smart, he'll shift to defend himself. I hope to get there before that happens. Midway to Lev another wolf slams into me, knocking me to the ground. I can't fucking breathe and I'm pretty sure some ribs are broken. My wolf's healing abilities will take care of my injuries but I don't have time to sit around and lick my wounds.

Two wolves attack me, one from each side. I'm able to kick one of them off, but the other claws my shoulder, splitting my skin and fur. I spin to counter the attack and catch a glimpse of Vas in a spitting, snarling furball of terror with the other three wolves.

That means a path to Ekataryn is open for Lev to grab her. Not on my watch. I pivot, nearly losing my footing under the torn muscles. Instead of going for my attacker, I race to get back to her. I don't get very far before my enemy sinks his teeth into my backside. I refuse to go down even if I have to drag him along like a parasite.

Ekataryn sees us coming, but it appears she's out of rocks. She's searching the ground around her, but she's used up her supply. Lev is only a few feet away and I'm not going to make it before he does. Vas yelps in pain and he never does that. If he's hurt that bad, he won't be able to protect her either. We used to work so well as a team and now we are shitty defenders. It would sure as shit help if we had the rest of the wolf guard.

I try to pull from my innermost beast and put on a burst of speed. My injuries are taking too much of a toll. I change directions once more, this time straight at Lev. I may not reach Ekataryn in time, but I'll kill him the second he touches her.

I'm desperate now and that will have to serve me. I break Joaquim's rule and speak directly to her with the mindspeak connection we have, that we've always had. *"Run, Ekataryn. Go toward the sunrise, you'll find help in the village that way."*

She jumps about three feet which ends up saving her. Lev slams into the tree and just barely misses her. She scoots around the back to begin a game of cat and mouse. I'm so close I can taste Lev's salty skin, but he moves too quickly and gets a mouthful of tree bark.

"Come here, woman. I'm claiming you whether you like it or not." Lev reaches for her and gets a hold of the furry collar of the coat.

"Fuck off, tiny dickwad. Help! Can anyone who isn't an evil werewolf hear me? Help us!" Ekataryn's voice rings through the forest with a supernatural power, rattling the branches and rustling the drifts of snow all around us.

A call returns in the form of a lion's roar. Fuck, yeah. Reinforcements.

That gives me a burst of energy I didn't know I had any left. I kick my attacker off and bite at Lev's side. I get nothing but a tearing of robes, as the slippery little sucker darts away from me. He's still got Ekataryn by the coat and she is doing her best to get out of his grasp.

"Help," she shouts again and her call is answered. Will, in his great lion form bounds up on top of the closest pile of boulders and roars so loud it rocks the forest.

Two of the wolves attacking Vas bolt immediately and the third tucks his tail and whimpers, staring up at the great beast. Vas lay on the ground next to him, bleeding, but breathing. The wolf I finally kicked away, limps off into the trees and that leaves just Lev.

Ekataryn's gaze flicks between me, Vas, Lev, and the lion. Joaquim may have told us not to show her our beast forms, but he either didn't say anything to Will or he knows better than to try to order a former king around. Anyway, the chance that she won't find out about shifters now is a mute point.

"This is not your business, Will," Lev shouts but we all hear the feigned bravado.

Speaking of the angel, Joachim walks up beside Will as if he's just taking a stroll in the park. "But it is mine, Lev Naryshkin."

Lev scowls and he's pissed, but doesn't say anything more. Even he is a superstitious fool and won't go against the only priest this island has.

"No, it's mine." Ekataryn says and does something that will make me smile the rest of my life with her. She knees Lev right in the balls.

He groans and drops to the ground, cupping his crotch, rolling back and forth. She got him good.

Ekataryn steps right over him and walks over to Joachim. I'm already having a hard time breathing, but I hold it in waiting to see what happens. This is either going to go great or disastrously.

"Thank you for your help, you and your lion. But if you say

you want to claim me too, I'm going to kick you in the balls harder than that douchecanoe over there."

Will makes a funny lion chuckle sound and sits down, waiting for the show. He's easily entertained these days.

Joachim bows at Ekataryn. If I wasn't so badly injured I'd bite him. "My lady."

"Do I know you?" She looks at him like she's trying to figure out a puzzle.

That's it. That's all I can take for one night. I keel over where I'm standing and until my wolf does some serious healing, I'm not getting back up.

"Oh no. Please, can you help them? These two were defending me. They aren't part of that dickwad's pack or whatever. We can't let them die."

The world around me goes fuzzy and dark. I feel the second she puts her hands on me and pets the soft spot behind my ears. It's probably the only bit of fur that isn't spattered in blood. The only other time I let her care for me instead of the other way around was so long ago, I can hardly remember.

"Shh, that's a good boy. We've got you." Her words barely filter in as I'm losing consciousness. Does she have me. I want her to. She owns my soul, she owns my heart, I want her to own every part of me.

I have the strangest sensation of being lifted and laid across something curved, like the back of a horse. But there are no horses on the island. Another wolf is set beside me and I'm glad to hear Vas's breathing.

We both could have died today. This can't happen again. Yes, we'll heal, but Lev and the Naryshkins won't be the last pack wanting to come and claim the newest woman on the island.

Without telling her who and what we are to her, how can we protect her as she needs and deserves? Fuck Joachim and his premonitions or whatever other spiritual shit he used to find out she was coming. When I heal, I'm not keeping any more secrets from her.

The rest of them can do what the fuck they want. Just like we all have since we were separated by time and past lives, since we were imprisoned, since we failed her all those moons ago.

I will never let her be in danger again, even if it means betraying the rest of the wolf guard to keep her safe.

TARYN

I have never seen so much blood before in my life. Or, well, maybe I have. What do I know? But this is still a lot of blood. Sure, a pet might defend an owner, but when Vas went all growly and snarling at those seven other freaking huge wolves, I thought for sure we were both dead.

Why would he fight such insane odds for me? I don't feed him, he's not mine. I guess August has trained him well.

Oh god. August. He's going to want to kill me when he finds out what happened to his wolf pet. Maybe even double kill me, because there's this other wolf who jumped into the fray and he seems so familiar, that he must also be a part of August's life.

I eye Father Joachim as he lifts these huge ass wolves from the ground and gently lays them across the back of his lion. First of all, what kind of muscles is the way-too-sexy-to-be-a-priest hiding under his robes, and second, who keeps a giant lion for a pet?

I guess if I'm going to be on this stupid prison island for very long, I need to get myself a big, mean-looking, but loyal animal companion. So far I've seen three men with wolves and now the good father with a lion. What's next, a dude with a dragon? Oh, oh. I know. A little girl with a unicorn.

Okay, now I'm being ridiculous, but I'm just having a hard time believing what I'm seeing and experiencing since I was dragged out of the Nothing and shoved into a supernaturally weird prison camp. I have got to get home. But first I need to take care of those that tried to take care of me. "Where are you taking them? Is there a vet in your village?"

Father Joachim doesn't reply right away and I hate that. I need answers and so far I've gotten less than none. Just a crap ton more questions. "Hey, talk to me here. Would it be better if we took them back to August's cabin? I don't think it's very far away."

"There is a healer in the *derevnya.* She will be able to help them. But all they really need is some time to rest and heal." He touched each of their heads and while his lips didn't move and he didn't say anything, I think he said a blessing for them or something.

She? Finally another woman. I was starting to worry I'd been thrown into the men's prison.

I was a bit wary about trusting another man, even if he is a priest, because of all the claiming stuff, but knowing that he's taking me to a woman helps a ton. It's not like I have a whole lot of other choices or know anything about how to fix a wolf's wounds.

"I think they need more than rest, so let's take them there as quick as we can." I give each of the unconscious wolves a quick touch, needing to know for myself that they are still alive. "I hope it's not far. Your lion will be okay carrying them?"

Joachim exchanges a look with the lion which is strange. "William belongs to no man but himself. But yes, he is strong enough and the *derevnya* isn't far." He extends his hand pointing out for me where to go. Of course it's the exact opposite direction I'd been going last night.

At least the sun is coming up and maybe I'll be able to tell my left from my right. Not being able to see the moon and stars really threw me off. One glance up at the sky and I'm equally as screwed. Worst weather ever.

I never did like winter. Spring is more my style. Huh. Something new about myself I've remembered. That's encouraging and I'm crossing my fingers that more comes back with each passing minute.

We walked through the trees and the snow forever. "Hold up. I need a minute. When you said this place was close, I thought you meant less than a thousand miles. God, how is it this cold and I'm sweating so bad?" I cover my mouth and make oops-sorry eyes at the father.

He and the lion stop and they aren't freaking winded at all. "Don't censor yourself for me, *boginya*. Something I learned long ago is that the gods don't care about our small transgressions. It's the big ones we need saving from."

Father Joachim is a puzzle to me. He's like one of those Russian nesting dolls, I think. If I popped open his top layer, this sad, but strong, and entirely too sexy outer coating it's so obvious to me he's wrapped around himself, there will be more mystery underneath.

It's so weird, because I really do feel like I already know him. A little bit like how I knew I could trust August not to hurt me.

I hope my leaving hasn't hurt him. I'm not looking forward to a confrontation with him about why I didn't stay put in his bed like he told me too. Oh to have a bed right now.

I'd happily cuddle up with him on one side, sexy father Joachim on the other and a wolf or two at my feet. I squeeze my eyes shut and have to put a hand out to find a tree to support myself on. Not because I'm that tired. I am exhausted. But because of that thought.

What the hell is wrong with me? My face is tingling and not from the cold. An absolute emptiness opens in my chest and stomach and I long for something so much, I can't even see straight. Thank goodness for this tree holding me up.

The tree says, "Steady, breathe, *boginya,* breathe."

One breath in, one breath out, one breath in. Nope, it's stuck. I've forgotten how to make my lungs work. I lean harder into the tree who is apparently a man, who is both soft and hard and smells delicious. "I'm okay, father. I just--

Oops, there go my knees. I flop down into the snow and it's a good thing Father Joachim said the gods don't care about swearing, because he just let out a stream of them. "Fucking hell, I shouldn't have tried to keep my distance."

He lifts me up under my knees and behind my back and starts walking away, carrying me like I'm not as puffy as a marshmallow and heavy as a rock. At least he didn't throw me over his shoulder like August did. What is it with the men here carrying me around?

A girl could get used to this.

No. I'm not weak, I'm not needy. Or maybe I am. Fine. Just this one more time. I tuck my head against his neck and find myself wanting to bite at his stubbled chin. Jeez. I'm definitely going to hell for the impure thoughts I'm having about this man of the cloth.

"You can put me down now. I'm okay. I can breathe again. I don't know what came over me." I'm not telling him I'm having a panic attack over being insanely attracted to him and wanting him and another man to take me to bed. Seriously. What. The. Shit?

"I will carry you." There is no negotiation in that tone of his. And I also find that sexy as all get out.

Okay, okay. Fine. I'm attracted to a priest. He's still a man. I'm a woman. We're in a Siberian prison gulag together. Nothing weird about any of that.

Siberia? Why do I know, like for absolutely sure, one hundred percent positive that we're in Siberia? At least that gives me something else to think about besides a sinfully satisfying menage à trois with two men, while a wolf watches.

This must be why I'm in prison. No. That's crap and I don't like that thought one bit. It doesn't feel wrong even a little bit that I'm attracted to both of them, that I want them both so bad it hurts. This means something important. There is a key to this in my past. I don't know how or why, but I am going to find out. Because if these two men can help me figure that out, we can escape and save whoever I'm meant to protect.

"August." Now that I don't have to walk anymore, I am feeling the exhaustion for real now and it took half the strength I have left in me to just say his name.

"What about him?" Father Joachim on the other hand isn't even breaking a sweat. He just keeps on clomping through the snow as if this is a walk through a garden. He's not even wearing super heavy garments or anything. I can feel his heat seeping into me even through the thick furry coat.

"His cabin is nearby."

"Yes, it is."

If I could get more than half a sentence out at time, I could friggin get him to understand. "He's probably looking for me. I didn't stay in bed."

Joachim trips a little and jostles me and then gives me a look I can't quite read. Is he judging me for being in a man's bed? Probably. He is a priest after all, even if he is a hot one. I want to explain, but it's just not going to happen.

"August will be glad to know that you're safe and will be protected at Will and Maggie's. Don't worry about him just now."

"But--" I don't know why I'm protesting. If ever there was anyone I should be able to trust, it's a priest. Right?

"He's fine, Soph... my lady. I promise you'll see him again soon. Now rest. We're almost there." We go down a small slope and his steps hasten. The lion is still ahead of us and it too hurries.

In another few feet I see the clearing in the trees and there is a circle of about ten buildings, not much bigger than August's cabin. This is the village?

The lion heads for one of the slightly larger buildings and this one has a barn on the side. He goes into the barn, pushing the door open with his head, and disappears inside. Joachim stops in front of the cabin and sets me on my feet.

"I thought you'd like to meet Maggie standing on your own two feet." Before I can even say thank you, that's exactly what I wanted, he knocks, and the prettiest blonde woman, who is a bit older than me, and just as full-figured as me, whips open the door and yanks both of us inside.

"Don't be letting all my warm air out. I'm not heating this whole island, you know? Now who is this you've brought me, wrapped up in more fur and skins than a selkie wanting to return home?" Her lilting accent is almost magical and I burst into tears at the sound of it.

"Now, now, darlin'. If you are a selkie, you've got your skin and can return to the sea even if it is a bit cold. My William will cut out a block of ice for ya."

I sniffle and do my best to get myself under control. "Your William? He belongs to you?"

I shoot a glance at Joachim. He shrugs. "I said he belongs to no man but himself. I didn't say anything about belonging to a woman."

"That he is." She looks over our shoulders and toward the door that I don't even think the big lion would fit through. "Where is he now?"

Joachim nods toward the barn. "He's taken Vasily... and another wolf to the barn. They've been injured and I think they could use a bit of help to get their healing underway."

"I'll go help them out in a few minutes. Let's take care of

your selkie, here." She wraps one arm around my shoulder and leads me closer to the fire. "Come on, love. If you give me your furs I promise to let no man even near them. You don't have to cry for one more minute."

The tears haven't quite stopped flowing and I don't even understand why. "What's a selkie?"

She leads me to a padded bench and I realize this cabin is actually decorated and filled with life, unlike August's sparse furnishings. Just how long has she been imprisoned?

The fire is burning hot and I don't want to be wearing this coat another second longer. I squirm around trying to unbutton the thing, but my arms hardly reach the fastenings.

"So not a selkie, then. What are ya, love?" The woman bats my hands away and makes quick work of getting me free. I finally slip out of the coat and she gasps.

I must have blood on me or something. I swipe at my face and throat, but there's nothing on my hands. "What's wrong?"

"Why, if you aren't *Tuatha Dé Danann* here in the flesh." Her face flushes and she gets this far off look and smiles for just a minute. "Joachim? Who have you brought me and why on earth is she here in this god-forsaken land?"

Father Joachim hurries over and kneels in front of me and puts his hands on my knees looking up at me worried like whatever Maggie just called me was a bad name or something. Oh god, I mean, oh man, oh crap. I am not thinking dirty thoughts about a priest, I am not, I am not, I am.

"Maggie, she's already had a long night, having just arrived on our shores. Let's not push her yet."

"Oh, go on with ya now, father." Maggie gives him a little shove and he stands, backing off just a bit. "You're looking to coddle the girl and she needs none of that, now do you?"

"Uh, maybe a little coddling?" I hiccup and sniffle a little, doing my best to look a bit more dejected than I am. The warmth of the cabin and Maggie's bright and cheery welcome have restored me more than I would have expected. Ten minutes ago, I was ready to sleep for a week. Here in her presence I'm, well not great, but slightly re-energized.

I can see why she's their healer.

She laughs at my comment and shoots a side-eye at Joachim. Please don't let her be thinking that I have a crush on the hot priest. How embarrassing. "A little coddle it is then. I'm Margaret de Hythus, but you can call me Maggie."

"I'm Taryn." Thank goodness I know my name. It feels so good to say it out loud, like I'm claiming it for myself for the first time.

"Are ya now? Isn't that a pretty name?"

"It is," Joachim says and also smiles at me.

Ah crap on a cracker. He was good looking when he was all serious and broody. He's fricking magical when he smiles. Stop it, stop it. Stop making goo-goo eyes at the man.

"Here comes my William." Maggie stands and the door pushes open. The big lion, who does barely fit through the door pads in and pushes it shut with his back paw.

"Don't you be getting muddy paw prints all over my clean floor." Maggie wags her finger at the lion and I can see how much she loves this creature and he loves her right back.

He plops his rear end down, not taking another step and I wonder what she expects him to do. Give himself a kitty bath right then and there.

That is not what happens.

He stretches his neck back, rolls his shoulders, swishes his tail and with a couple of snaps, crackles, and pops, an enormous naked-ass man with golden hair and beard as bushy as the lion's mane is standing in its place.

What the shit? I know my jaw is hanging open but I can't seem to close it. I rub my eyes and look again. Maybe I did fall asleep in Father Joachim's arms and I'm dreaming? Yes, that makes much more sense than a lion turning into a man and then walking across the floor and giving Maggie a kiss.

"Hello, my love. The lads are cozied up in the barn and they're pretty torn up. They're healing already, but I'm sure they'd appreciate a little of your secret salve to speed up the process a bit."

I look over at Father Joachim to see if he's as shocked as I am. He is not. In fact, he looks a little bit mad. He's got a hand on his jaw and mouth as if he's trying not to say something harsh. He sees me gawking and that hand goes from his jaw to his forehead.

"Will, I thought I asked you not to do that." I want to rub across the spot his fingers are stroking and ease his worry. Later, when I wake up.

"Sorry Father. It's just too cold to shift outside. I'd freeze my balls off."

"William. We have company for goodness sake. Watch your language." Maggie chastises the man-version of Will just the same as she did the lion. She turns to me and rolls her eyes. "Sorry about my husband, Taryn. We haven't been around the likes of you for a very long time and I believe he's forgotten his manners."

Will trots over to me and Father Joachim puts himself between the two of us. "Ahem, you might want to put on your robes. It's still quite chilly."

Will snorts and side-steps the father. "Taryn is it? So you're what all the fuss is about. I like you, girl. You're going to be loads of fun. We haven't had anything worth fighting for around here in a long time."

Will takes my hand and gives it a kiss. Joachim growls at him. Exactly in the same way that August growled at Vasily when he curled up on the bed with me.

The sound goes straight down to my belly and swirls

around somewhere lower. Okay then, this is a sex dream. Sweet. I'm in.

"Taryn, sweetheart. You doing all right, there?" Maggie set hand on my shoulder. I jumped about a foot and smacked my knee right on Will's junk.

"Whoa there, chickadee. I've seen what you can do to a man's privates. Keep those knees to yourself."

Uh-oh. I don't think this is a dream. Did Maggie slip me something? If she didn't, could she? I need some serious drugs if I have to deal with people who shift into animals.

JOACHIM

*J*esus, Mary, and Joseph, and all the saints. I can never touch her again. My soul is on fire and my skin is scorched from the smallest brush of her body.

Is this how August felt carrying her from the frozen sea to his cabin? No wonder he's already had her in his bed. I can't even blame him because if I had her alone, I wouldn't be able to resist her either.

Carrying her through the forest, I could do, because of that single-minded need to get her to safety. I almost lost my balance and dropped her when she tucked her face into my throat and her hot breath blew across my beating pulse. That forced need has turned to something much more sinful now and I don't know how long I can resist her siren's call on my heart.

No. I cannot think that way. I can make the easy choice and make all of our lives hard. Or I can make the hard choice and make her life easier. Like right now when she's being initiated into our world by rapid fire and egotistical lion kings.

"Taryn." Her new chosen name tastes like home on my tongue. "Please allow me to help you understand."

I shoot Will a reproachful lift of my eyebrow. The twinkle in his eye says he knows exactly what he was doing shifting in front of her even though I specifically asked him not to.

I squat down in front of her again, knowing it will help settle her for me to be at eye-level instead of towering over her. This time, I'm smart enough to put space between us.

"Understand what? That I've been drugged? Or that I was thrown through a wardrobe into magical fog and ended up in Hellarnia with the lion. Oh, does that make Maggie the witch? What am I even talking about?"

She must have a love of books and stories in this life, just as she did when we were young. It will be hard for me to give up thinking of her as my Sophia. I suspect it will be easiest for August since she was his Ekataryn Velikaya and the one life she's lived where she almost beat the bastards who steal her life and memories at each new rebirth.

"I understand how your brain feels as if it's betraying you. We all experienced something similar when we arrived. I swear to you that in this place and with these people, you are safe." These are words I wish someone had said to me when I arrived.

"What people? That guy over there is apparently a lion." She's a little hysterical and I can empathize. I may have pitched my own fit after being thrown in here. It took all my faith to get myself under control.

The stories August tells on the coldest of winter nights here in our personal hell, are the ones that have helped me survive the last few hundred years. A pang of regret hits me square in the chest that I missed her reign as Catherine the Great. I would have so loved to see her rule over both man and wolf once again.

Grigory never speaks of that time, nor of her next life that I also missed, as a Romanov princess, and the final betrayal by Rasputin. The bitter blackness in my alpha's soul is both my bane and my penance. I will do better by her than I have for him.

"Yes, he is. Magic exists. William's gods gave him the gift of two forms and the ability to shift between them. When you know nothing of the supernatural that can seem strange and scary, but I promise it is a part of everyday life all around us."

I see something spark in her eyes, a flash of memory perhaps. If we're lucky, someday she'll remember everything about who and what she is. I can only pray.

No, that's a lie. Yes, I can hold tight to my faith, but I can and will do much more than that. I have been working toward bringing her back for even longer than I can remember. This time, it must work. It will. Because for the first time, the Volkovs have made the mistake instead of me.

"Is everyone here a, uh, scary-ass shifter?" She pulls her arms away from me and I hadn't even realized I'd moved closer to her. She is the moon and I am the waves trying to reach her with every beat of my soul.

That is not a question I'm ready to answer. It is hard to lie to her. I am prepared to sacrifice everything for her, but she is the one who bestowed my vows upon me in the first place. Lie and save her more fear and anxiety or break the most sacred of covenants.

I want her trust more than I want my next heartbeat, but do I deserve it? That is a resounding no.

I'm a coward. "Maggie is also a shifter, and you're not scared of her, are you?"

Maggie smirks at me. Yeah I just threw her under the horse-cart to save my own skin and she knows it. She turns her frown into a soft smile for Taryn. "That I am, love."

"What are you?" Taryn looks Maggie up and down and takes a deep breath. Some of her anxiety goes out with that exhale. "Oh, let me guess, a giant pink polka-dotted bunny rabbit?"

"Now doesn't that sound fun, but no. And I won't be revealing my other form to ya. That's only for my William." Will kisses Maggie's cheek and Taryn leans in closer to me.

She whispers and I have to clench my jaw tight not to allow my inner beast to take over. It almost works. The wolf remains within, but my cock on the other hand stands up to take notice. Good thing I'm fucking wearing robes.

"She's something naughty like a sexy mermaid with tentacles or something, isn't she?"

I swallow my tongue and have to cough to recover and hide my burst of laughter. Taryn winks at me. Okay, she is taking this much better than I expected her to. This is the side of my Sophia I fell in love with so long ago, before I took on my calling and pushed her away, to protect her.

"What is a mermaid octopus even called? A merpuss? No, I think that's a mermaid cat. Merctopus? No wait, mer is the ocean dweller part. Octomaid? That's a horrid word. But, come on. What other magical creature could charm a freaking lion like she has. He's besotted."

I'm doing my best to keep a straight face. "Indeed. Stories have been written about their love, wars fought over it."

"Is that how they ended up on prison island?" Her question is so innocent that it sobers me from the intoxication of her. There are not enough Hail Marys or Our Fathers for the impure thoughts I'm having of her.

Maggie clapped her hands together in an attempt to let us know she could hear every word we were saying and that was quite enough. "That is a story for another time. Now, sweetness, if you're done having your whoopsy-sad, come to the larder with me and first we'll feed you, and then see if we can find something for you to wear besides a smelly coat and your tattered underthings."

Pretty sure I've just been dismissed from my duties of explaining our world to Taryn. Maggie and Will only know part of the wolf guard's story just as we only know part of theirs, so there is no harm in letting her talk with Taryn without me.

I swallow hard. So many things could go wrong, but I'm going to have faith in that very special creature that is Margaret de Hythus and trust that she will keep my Soph... Taryn, safe within her purview.

Shit. No. I can't do it. I have to be there. I don't know what Maggie is going to tell her. Not about this island, not about me, and fuck what if she tells her about mating. I take one and a half whole steps before Will grabs me by the shoulder and forces me to sit down on the bench.

"Hold up there, father. Maggie will take care of your girl just fine. Leave them be."

I sigh and put my head in my hands. "I do wish you would put some clothes on, Will."

"My house, my rules." He crosses to a wooden cabinet and pulls out a bottle and two mugs. "You need a drink. I shall imbibe with you."

"It's barely daybreak." Not like I can refuse an offer from Will. He hasn't been the King of Scotland since the year of our Lord, 1214. But no one has told him that.

Will pours the homemade liquor into the mugs, hands me one, and slaps me on the shoulder. "Start the day with a good stiff drink, or a good stiff cock, I say. You interrupted me enjoying the latter, making me rush off into the freezing cold weather to roar at some glaikit bawbags, so we'll partake in the other."

He clinks his mug against mine. "Slàinte mhath."

"Slàinte." I down the drink in one swallow and let it burn away the need I have inside for Taryn. It's going to take a lot more than one drink to do that, but it does clear my head and give me the resolve to remember who I am, and my duties to her and my God.

I need to think about anything else but her.

"I see our friend, the Dark Prince, was about yesterday. August is upset that he missed all the fun." I had more pressing tasks for August yesterday than playing streltsy to the *derevnya*. I already knew the death and destruction wrought here, but I need to focus on something instead of Taryn.

"Yup, he killed that poor bugger who came to the island a few months back. I never did like that fella. He wasn't our people, but these villagers want to believe the best in everyone. Good riddance to him, I say." Will has seen more death than the rest of us combined so very little bothers him. Except maybe danger aimed at his mate.

I'm not surprised or shocked that Grigory has murdered another inmate. Again. He continues to spread his black mood around so that all may fear him. I'll have to take the trek out to his lair. I can't absolve him of his sins, as he will not promise to stop committing them.

He's not ready to hear that Taryn is here. Even less so than she is ready to know that he has been waiting for her. I will have to tread very carefully with the two of them or the devastation will be worse than any of us can handle.

"Did he damage anything else?" Besides his own soul.

"Nothing that can't be fixed. A few frayed nerves when he prowled into town with murder on his mind." Will refills his cup and offers more to me, but I refuse it. "You know even I can't reason with him or scare him off when he gets that way. It terrorizes the others when he does that. They're all worried they'll be his next victim."

They won't be. Not that they will ever believe it. "I have full faith that you will continue to protect them. Although, it wouldn't hurt for some of them to hone their weapons skills a bit more."

I glance toward the larder and realize I'm waiting to hear exclamations of distress. All is quiet. Too quiet. What are the women talking about in there for so long?

"Nah." Will doesn't miss my overt glances and refills my mug despite my protests. "These people are just trying to rebuild their lives here the best way they know how. They don't need combat skills. The marauder packs can play at war all they want. They deserve that harsh life, we do not."

He isn't preaching anything I don't espouse myself. Sometimes I wonder if he's got a better relationship with his God than I do mine. His faith certainly gives him more patience than mine.

Finally the women come out and if I thought I needed to chastise myself for lusty thoughts before, I'm a dead man now. Maggie's put Taryn in a simple full length dress, lined in fur around the collar, sleeves, waist and hem. It's tight across her chest and ass and I want to rip it off of her, mark her covered throat, and claim her for my own here and now.

Hail Mary, full of grace. Blessed art thou amongst women and blessed is the fruit of thy womb.

Fuck, I can't even recite the simplest of prayers correctly. I look away from her and take another swig from my mug. I'm going to have to find a way to excuse myself. I'll make an excuse to check on August and Vas. I'll tend to the households who are distraught over the death in the village. I'll gather firewood, break ice for water, kneel at the makeshift altar in the church we've forged in the frigid wilderness of this harsh land.

And at the end of my work, I'll lay in my bed, cold and alone, and take myself in hand, thinking of her in this very moment staring at me like she wants to mark and claim me for her own.

I stand up, knocking the bench over, and pull my robes tighter around me. "You appear to be well taken care of here. Please excuse me, I have many duties to tend to today."

I can't stay here with her a second longer. I just need one

day and one night. Then I'll get myself under control and I can continue to do what I must. Just one day, Lord, give me that so that I do not fail you or her again. I cross the room in just a few long strides.

"Hey. You can't just leave her here, father."

Damn. My fingers are already wrapped around the handle of the door. I'm so close. "I will send August for her. She can stay with him. It will be good for them both."

I yank the door open, and August is standing there, wind whipping through his hair, snow blowing around his bare legs. Well, shit. At least he didn't shift in front of her too. He basically falls into the room and I can see from the angry red marks on his skin that he's not entirely healed yet.

He's awoken too soon just to see that Taryn is all right. He can be here with her while I cannot. He's a better man than I ever was.

"August?" Taryn calls his name and I hate that I wish it was my name she was saying with such care and worry in her voice. "Why are you naked?"

August stumbles across the room and pulls her into his arms. "Thank God, you're okay."

I can't look away, I can't help but watch them together.

"Oh gosh. Eek. Yeah." She pats him gingerly on the back, but I see the way she melts into his embrace at the same time. "Sorry I up and left. Vasily and I ran into a bit of trouble. But I'm okay. Vasily got hurt though. I'm really sorry."

"Vas can take care of himself. You're the one I was worried about. I told you not to ever go out at night." His words chastise, but his tone belies his worry.

"I know, I know. Wait." She pushes him away, holding him at arms length and examines him. "Oh my god, sorry father, what happened to your shoulder, and your leg, and your side?"

Shit. I see the exact moment when it clicks together in her mind. She's always been so smart and I love that about her. I should have known I couldn't keep secrets from her for very long. Still there is much I cannot reveal.

"It's nothing, tzaritsa. Pay that no mind." He glances over at me, like I can do anything now. Then he sees Will lounging around naked and shrugs his shoulders.

"No mind, my ass." She runs her fingers along the nearly healed slashes along August's shoulder. He sucks in a breath and someone needs to get that man a robe because he's about to have a big problem on his hands.

I shut the door, resigned to the fact I'm not getting away. Lord give me strength. There's a scratch at the wood and I open it again. Vas limps in and over to Taryn and August.

She looks down at Vasily, touches the spot between his nose and eyes, then back up at August. She glances back and forth between them trying to decide if she's really seeing what she's just discovered. "You're the other wolf, aren't you?"

August stares into her eyes for a long time. He blinks, blinks again and while I know him as well as I know myself, I do not know what is going through his head right now. If it was me, I'd be wondering how long before I could haul her back to the cabin and claim her.

Finally he clears his throat and speaks. "I am, my lady. I swear as neither guard nor beast will I ever cause you harm. Can you accept me as both wolf and man?"

Christ in heaven. Every single one of us are frozen waiting for her answer. This is the first hurdle and the one I feared the most. Once she knocks it down, there is no going back. Her world and ours will be forever changed.

TARYN

*F*or some reason the phrase - not my circus, not my monkeys - pops into my head. Except more appropriately, it's not my prison island, not my wolves.

Except this is my temporary home for the time being, so it is kind of my island, and it's weird and crazy, but I do feel a connection to August.

Not as crazy as turning into a wolf, but still weird.

I see Will watching me and taking a drink from a mug. If that's alcohol, I want some. Because this is one wackadoodle-ass life I've walked into and I'm gonna need a minute and a tiny bit of loosened inhibitions to get through the first day. Hell, the first morning.

I side-step naked August and his question, cross over to naked Will and extend my hand. Thankfully, he doesn't pretend to not know what I want and hands his mug to me. I empty it in one long gulp. It burns going down, but it's not unfamiliar and I think I've had a drink like this before.

I hold out the mug and he instantly refills it. I swallow that too and then set it down on the table.

"Okay, raise your hand if you also turn into a wolf." I slow blink and pull my eyes over to Father Joachim.

He scrubs his hand over his face and then slowly raises his hand. Maggie twists up her mouth trying not to I-told-you-so smile. She doesn't raise her hand, but I didn't think so. Sure, these guys are all predators, but I don't think she is. I'm still going with bunny.

I flick my gaze over to Vas curled up in front of the fire. His wounds are healed far beyond what I would have imagined was possible, but I must remember this place is filled with magic. The fur around the red marks hasn't grown back though. Poor puppy.

No way he's a man too, is he? Nah. Maybe? I'm keeping my eye on him.

While she was finding her daughter's dress for me, she told me I needed to keep an open mind about this place, the people here, and who I might be to them. I don't understand what she means, but fine, mind open. Clearly having a closed mind would have one going insane inside a day.

"I can't believe I'm saying this, but yes, I accept you all as man and beast."

August's shoulders release and he takes a deep breath. That was at least partly the answer he wanted to hear. Funny how he was holding on to so much tension over my answer. I know I've got this intense attraction to him, but why does he care about what I think about him?

"Since you've got these supernatural powers, can you please help me get off this island? I don't belong here." I don't mention the part about having someone to go back to. Partly since I have no idea who the someone might be, and it gives me a weird pang in the very center of my chest.

What if I want the someone to be August or Joachim, or both?

Open mind, open mind.

"Love," Maggie starts and I can already hear the denial in her tone. "Our powers can't help you."

The way she says that makes me think there is someone else with the ability to get me out of here. August and Joachim stay entirely too quiet. "Is there someone's powers who can?"

Joachim lifts his chin and looks upward as if talking to God. "There is no way off the island for a mortal. Only the power of the gods or goddesses can break the dark spells that keep us here, frozen in time."

Open mind. "I thought priests were all monotheistic."

August snorts and Joachim gives me a look like he very much wonders what is going through my head. Hell if I know.

"Most priests don't know what I do."

He means about the supernatural, people who shift into animals, and magic and stuff, right?

"How do we find a god or goddess to help us then?" At least this time no one outright said there is no way off the island. That's progress. "Are there any imprisoned on the island with us? No, wait, they could just escape. Is there a prayer or an incantation?"

Will quirks his head like he's thought of an idea. Then he grabs Maggie's arm, pulling her into his lap. "I'm pretty sure I saw God the first time I made my lovely mate call out my name in pleasure with my cock inside of her."

Maggie smacked him on the arm. "You're a dirty, dirty man, and don't think I missed the reason you've pulled me onto your lap. I can feel what you're trying to hide, poking me in the tush right now."

"Blame Father Joachim. He's the one who interrupted our, hmm, morning attempt to spot God."

"Uh, should we, umm, go?" Awkward. That's what you get when you let guys run around naked.

And no, I haven't been sneaking peeks at the very naked August at all. Not even... crap. I just looked. I really had done a good job of keeping my eyes above the waist until now. Holy tree trunk. How does that thing even fit in his pants? Or inside anyone.

I'm not thinking about him inside of me. Yes, I am. No, I'm not. I totally am. God. Ack. I stare at a point on the wall near the ceiling and blink about four-hundred and twenty-seven times until I'm sure I can control my wandering eyes.

When I'm sure I can keep my gaze at eye-level I bring my head back down and find August, with a twinkle in his eye.

Busted.

He leans back on the bench and spreads his legs as if daring me to look again. Father Joachim elbows him in the ribs. "Ouch. I'm still healing."

In a calm, measured tone very opposite to the irritation on his face, the Father says, "Your wounds are on the other side."

"What the girl needs before going on an adventure to find a goddess, is protection." Will hasn't let Maggie up yet. I'm a bit grateful I don't have to look at his manly bits any longer.

Funny how I can't stop thinking about August's, or what Father Joachim is hiding under his robes, but I couldn't care less about William's.

"I will keep her safe." August's sexy relaxed slouch from before is gone in an instant as he straightens up. For the first time since he came in, Vas raises his head and stares at us, sleepy, but interested.

He gets up from his warm spot and comes over, plops down right on my bare feet, and curls up, asleep again in no time.

Will nods a bit too solemnly. "I know you've already sworn to protect her, but as proven today, one may not be enough against the packs who will continue to come to claim her."

Two thoughts hit me on either side of my brain. First, what the hell is up with all this claiming stuff? Ugh. Second, if one isn't enough, I could think of a second wolf-shifter I'd have on my protection detail. Because if they end up naked every time they shift back into human form like Will and August did, I wouldn't feel even the slightest bit bad about accidentally seeing hot priest's bod.

I keep that second thought to myself. For now. "Why does every man, woman, and wolf want to claim me? I get it. Everyone's been in prison for a while. They want to get some lookie and nookie, but that's not what anyone has said to me. Not that they want to have sex with me, but that they want to claim me. That Peter guy, the guy in the woods. What does claiming mean?"

Suddenly the guys are all tongue-tied. Maggie rolls her eyes as if to silently say to me, "Men, am I right?" "Claiming is part of the mating ritual of all shifters. To be claimed means to become that shifter's mate and he become yours."

"They want to marry me?" That was not what I was expecting.

Father Joachim finds his voice. "The mating ritual is much more than the human marriage convention. To be marked, claimed, and mated is a joining of souls."

Marked.

Claimed.

Mated.

His words send a shiver through me that bounces up and down my spine. I'm about to reveal a vulnerability to these people that I was holding close. If this mating thing is so important, maybe they will understand. "I think maybe I am already mated. I have someone I need to get back to in my real life. That's why I have to get off this island."

August growls, Vas whimpers in his sleep, and Father Joachim's eyes go from his brilliant bright blue to a dark and stormy winter squall.

Maggie holds up her hands and August stops growling, but the mood in the room is as frigid as it is outside. "There's an easy way to tell. You'll bear a mark on your skin, given to you by your mate. I didn't see any such thing when I helped you don Yvaine's dress, but I wasn't looking for it either."

My hand automatically reaches for my neck of its own accord. That's where a mark would be. I know it. I rush over to the one glass window and pull back the furry collar of the shirt. Even though the reflection is faint, I can see perfectly fine.

Nothing. No mark.

I was wrong. I don't have a mate.

That doesn't feel right though. I do, I do have someone. But if I did, why would I be thinking such sinful thoughts about August and Joachim? Is this why I've been imprisoned? For cheating on someone I was supposed to be mated to?

Also no. In fact, the thought of that gives me the heebie jeebies. I may not remember diddly squat, but I don't believe my core values could have changed. I'm not a bad person. I know the difference between right and wrong, and I wouldn't do that to someone I had formed such an important bond with. Hmm.

I gasp but try to hide it. What if I'm here because my mate cheated on me, got caught, and got rid of me? "Is there any way to get rid of a mark?"

I swipe my hand across my neck and examine it again. I can almost feel where a mark should be, as though I remember one being there. If my guess is correct, that would mean my overwhelming need to get back would be for revenge. But I'm sure it's to protect someone, to take care of them.

I'm so confused.

Father Joachim comes up behind me and looks into the window at my reflection too. "There is not. A true mate's mark is for life. It does not appear that you have been mated in this lifetime, Taryn."

"What if someone's mate dies? Can't they find love again?" It breaks my heart even thinking about that. I can even feel tears pushing at my lower lashes.

The father places a hand on my shoulder and looks into my eyes in the reflection. He's saddened by this question too. "That is a complicated answer. The short version is, it depends. If the pair weren't true mates, then yes, and her new mate can add his mark to the old one forming something new. If they were fated mates, then --"

He can't finish his sentence and I think I'm going to cry.

August joins us at the window. "If fate takes a mate away, only the goddess can decide if that wolf is worthy of finding his true mate once again."

Finding her again? That's not what I was asking, but his answer appeases my heart more than the one I was looking for.

I swallow down the tears and slip away from the men and the window. I need a minute to think, to clear my head. I pace back and forth from the door to where Vas is still laying, and back again. "So Peter and his wolves, and the other pack think I'm their true mate? Isn't there a way to know besides marking and claiming me? And how does one mark a mate?"

I think I can figure out the claiming part.

"Not all wolves care about having a true mate. Some believe that any mate will do."

Well, I don't like that. I'm not sure when I bought into the woo-woo of fate and true love, but choosing to be with someone who isn't meant for you. Gross. Dumb. Bad. Yuck. But it gives me an idea.

"You're telling me that to get the other packs to stop trying to claim me, some other wolf needs to."

"Yes," August says it with such force.

Joachim gives me that same what-are-you-thinking look and I'm starting to get uncomfortable about how he's all up in my head. "Where are you going with this?"

I don't want to be claimed, I might be lusting after these guys, but I think that has something to do with the island too, it doesn't mean I'm ready to be mated for life to one... or two of them. I also don't want to spend anymore time than I have to looking over my shoulder and worrying that some misogynistic alphaholes are coming to kidnap me because they need status and a baby maker.

Except there is no way August is going to go for this. If he doesn't, maybe Father Joachim knows of some other unmated guy in their little village of decent people who will.

I take a deep breath, turn to August, nope, I can already see the no way on his face before I've even asked the question. I'm going to have to ambush him. Instead I look at Father Joachim. Crap, again, nope. He'll see right through me.

"Maggie, can you help me with something in the larder again. My, umm, furry undies need adjusting." I spin and head back into the little pantry storage room before anyone else can say anything, hoping that Maggie doesn't call me out on the fact that I'm not wearing any kind of undergarments.

She comes in, closes the door behind her and crosses her arms. Even she can tell I'm up to something. "What is it, love?"

"If wolfman claims me here and now, on this cursed island, he doesn't have to be my true mate, right? Then, I'll still be able to find my true mate someday, if I am claimed while I'm here on this island, right?" A plan as strange as this land is forming in my mind and I only pray that I can convince my only allies to play along.

"Technically that's accurate."

"I need August to--" the words won't come out of my throat past the lump of anxiety blocking it up. I clear my throat and try again. "I need him to claim me."

"Love, I want to say that's wonderful news, we should all be so lucky as to have a mate like August. But you're not talking about mating, are ya?" She blows away a bit of curl that's fallen into her eyes.

"Kind of. I need a fake mate. Just to give me some breathing room, long enough to figure out how to get off this island and

75

back to my real life." I'm praying that Maggie doesn't choose their side and go tattle on me.

"August isn't going to go for that." She shakes her head. "He almost gave up his life for you. That boy was already half in love with you the moment you set foot on our shores, selkie or not. Haven't you seen how he looks at you?"

I don't think anyone in my life outside of here has ever sacrificed a thing for me. It's like I already know him and he knows me. I'm half in love with him too. But come on, that has to be the lusty hormones this island is making me produce talking. No one falls in love overnight.

"Which is why he's the right choice to be my mate while I'm here."

Maggie makes a tsk-ing sound at me and if someone can fold their arms harder, she does. "Child, I am telling you now that if you and August mate, he is never letting you go, and that is not a bad thing. But don't you go trying to break his heart. That is something I can't heal, and I'm fucking magical."

Eek. I've gotten Maggie all riled up. "I swear to you I don't want him hurt. What if I make it all about sex? No emotions, just tab A into slot B."

Maggie closes her eyes and laughs at me while shaking her head. "You're going to do what you think you need to do and I can see there's no talking you out of it. Just be careful. August's heart may not be the only one getting torn apart."

"I'll be fine." Probably. Girl's gotta do what a girl's gotta do to survive. I won't apologize for that.

We go back out into the room and the guys are deep in some kind of discussion. Even Vas is up and watching the men talk. August and Will have finally put on clothes which actually makes this easier. I walk over to August, take his hands in mine and, I don't know why, but I get down on one knee.

August looks at me like I really am on drugs this time and tries to pull me back up. I don't move and I don't let him get away. I can't believe I'm doing this. Please let him say yes and please don't let him figure out my plan, oh, and please don't let me break his heart when I finally escape this island. God, this is a horrible idea. "August, I mean... Stanisław August Poniatowski of the House of the Rising Moon, will you marry, uh mate with me? Please?"

I can't remember my own last name, but I remember his mouthful of a moniker. Eyeroll to myself. My heart is pounding a million beats a second and I'm definitely going to pass out soon if he doesn't answer.

August drops to his knees, getting down on my level and squeezes my hands tight. His eyes flick back and forth looking between mine and I know he's trying to figure out what this means. Then his gaze drifts down to my lips and back up making the beats of my heart drop down to the very bottom of my belly and between my legs.

He leans in so slowly, I think maybe time itself has taken a little break from it's busy day just to stop and watch us in this moment. He brings his lips so close to mine I can feel his warm exhale. I close my eyes and lean in that last ten percent of the way searching for the kiss that is so close I can taste it. His mouth brushes against mine, not in a kiss but in a word.

"No."

AUGUST

I stand up, pulling my hands from Ekataryn. I can't look at her or I'll cave. Fucking hell, I want her so badly and that tiniest taste of her lips against mine almost broke me.

I cannot be with her in half measures and I am done with lies. I won't.

How could she even think I didn't see exactly what she was doing?

My throat has gone as dry as the coals in the fire and the arid air trying to get in is making it hard to breathe. I am the fool, not her.

I want to shift and run into the woods, howl at the moonless sky, look for another fight. Anything but be here looking at her shock and disappointment. It takes me only two long strides to cross to the door, yank it open, and walk out into a howling wind that whips cold air and snow all around as if it's been made especially for my mood. I don't bother to shut the door behind me and let myself disappear into this cold squall.

"August, wait." It's Joachim's voice calling to me and not Ekataryn.

She is still and silent and I do not stop. If he wants to find me, he can.

I'm only wearing the light robe borrowed from Will and my human form gets cold faster than my wolf. Yet even though I had every intention of shifting, my wolf won't rise up. It too thinks I'm the dumbest fucker ever for saying no to her. I head back to the barn because at least the wind won't whip through my bones and I can figure out what the hell to do next.

Joachim has followed me out and I don't want to hear anything he has to say. Whether he's going to tell me all will be well or that I've fucked up, I don't care either way. He knows so much more than he's telling the rest of us and that makes me want to hit him in his beatific face.

He's followed me to the barn and I might actually do it. "Go away, Joachim. I don't need your counsel."

If I could just be open and honest and straight with Ekataryn, tell her who and what I am to her, and what she means to me and the rest of the wolves stuck here in this shit-hole, everything would be so much easier.

But easy choices make for a hard life.

Never once in all the lives I have lived with her has she ever gone quietly into that dark night. She fights for every scrap of her existence over and over. I don't know what made me think she wouldn't do the same in this one. That she'd sweetly acquiesce to letting me claim her, mate her, make her mine once again.

She's likely been doing everything she could somewhere out there in the god-damn twenty-first century all alone, just to survive. None of us were there for her, to guard her, to steal her away from the Volkovs plots and ploys. None to help her ascend.

The Volkovs once again took everything away from her, thinking they could get away with it this time, crush her, eliminate the threat she poses to their control over all of wolfkind. She will never break.

But I might.

If I don't calm down, I'm going to break something all right, and then Maggie will kill me. I flop my ass down onto the nearest bale of bark strips and fist the sharp, dry bits of wood.

Joachim sits next to me and rolls his prayer beads through his fingers. "You have to mate with her, August."

"No. She wants a fake mating. I cannot do that, and will not force her into a real one without her consent." For the mating to even appear real to the other wolves who will continue to hunt her, I would have to mark her. That can't be faked even if I wanted to. A claim could be made and not meant, but every shifter who isn't dead would know if I didn't fuck her.

"Her plan wouldn't work anyway." I'm sure she imagines a mating ceremony to be like a human wedding. It's so much more. "She doesn't understand how the mating ritual works."

Mark.

Claim.

Mate.

Give over your soul into the safe keeping of your mate.

Joachim knows exactly what I must do to mate her, even if he decided to forgo the mating in his last life with her. "The joining doesn't have to be witnessed by the whole *derevnya*. It's an old tradition that I'm sure I could persuade the others to forgo."

I want to take her, push my cock into her, let her body take me in, mark her with my seed in front of witnesses. I need everyone to know that she is mine and I'm hers. That's what a true mating ritual is and I'll have nothing less.

Except for the part about mating under the full moon. She's the one who wanted true mates to meet and join together under the shining rays of the goddess. "I wouldn't think you would be willing to compromise."

"I'm not." There's a new vehemence to his voice.

Here is the Joachim I knew. Always planning, always scheming, eternally ten steps ahead trying to make things right. I think it's time he let me in on his goddess-forsaken plans.

"Her wolf guard will witness the mating. We will be there. We have to be." He rolls those damn beads in his fingers again as if they hold the answers to the universe in them. Maybe they do. "This is our chance. We haven't all been together in the same life with her in over two thousand years."

My skin tingles with a push from my wolf. Is he ready to break his vows? Even if he is, the rest of the guard are not prepared to work again as one team.

"You won't get them to do it. Vas is too broken and--" We may all be imprisoned on this island at the same time, but we are by no means together. Our alpha has abandoned us all.

The beads, click, click, clack as he twists them through his hands rhythmically. "He'll come. He's angry and even he thinks he's given up, but he hasn't."

We're all fucking angry. But knowing a fellow guard has your back has made the difference between wallowing in that darkness and deciding to go on random killing sprees to appease the demons that haunt us. "You talk to him?"

"No." His hand stills and the beads drop, dangling by the cord between his legs. "But everyone needs a confessor. Especially those who are sure their soul is damned."

"He has a lot of sins to confess." Murder isn't the only one.

"Don't we all?" He slips the rosary back into a pocket in his robe and folds his hands. He pauses for a moment and I'm sure he's asking whichever higher power he prays to these days for help convincing me to do his bidding. "Which is why you have to agree to mate Taryn. We can end this all and begin everything anew, together."

His prayers are going to have to be unanswered today. "I won't trick her into it. I'm done lying."

Joaquim stands up and snarls at me. His wolf flashes in his eyes and mine rises up to meet the challenge. "Dammit, August. Get off your fucking moral high horse. We're trying to save her. If I have to break every single one of God's commandments, you'd better believe I will murder, steal, covet, and bear false witness to do that. She is the alpha, she is the omega, and we are but her servants. Her will is your command, and you would do well to remember that."

Jesus. In the two hundred years I've been imprisoned with Joachim there to greet me on day one, I've never seen him lose his temper. I bet if I think back to the lives he and I have lived together, I wouldn't come up with a single instance where he spoke a word in frustration or anger.

He stomps off and I notice the claws of his wolf extended from his hands still. He never loses control.

Dammit, I am not in the wrong. He wants me to sacrifice who I am for the folly she has planned, not yet understanding who and what she is.

I sit in the cold barn alone letting the chill seep into me. It's good for clearing my head.

The barn door opens again and I see the squall has receded to just a light snowfall. Will leans against the open door and Vas is seated next to him. He yips at me.

"Not you too. Why don't you do this fake mating thing with her?" I toss a piece of wood his way.

He whines and turns his back on me. Asshole.

"So, you're getting mated, are ya?" If I didn't know Will was an ordinary shifter, imprisoned here like all the rest of us, I'd swear he was a god. He's clairvoyant as hell.

Fuck. I guess I am. Because Joachim is right, I am hers to command. If this is what she needs from me, I am not the one to deny her. I simply have to figure out how the hell to make this mating real to her. It's the only way I know how to be.

"Yep. It seems so. You'll witness?" I may be the protector of the good people, but Will is the rock that holds the *derevnya* together. He and Maggie have been here longer than the rest of us, and welcome those that are undeserving of this banishment into their community. They gave me something to fight for when I was sure there was nothing left even worth living for. His stamp of approval over this mating will send a message to the outlaw packs not to even think about trying to come for Ekataryn.

He has been the alpha I needed in my life when I had none.

Will smiles and shakes his head. "Not just me. They're planning a whole damn celebration for you. Every man, woman, and wolf will be coming to town for this party. Have fun with that."

Ah, fuck me. I'd better get back in there and see what kind of bullshit Joachim is cooking up now. While I do want a proper mating, I don't need everyone to witness. Especially not Peter, Peter pussy eater. He had his chance with her and screwed the... well, he didn't screw anything, the impotent bastard.

I never did trust him. Who the fuck can't get it up for a woman like Ekataryn. Someone with an agenda of their own, that's who.

Vas curls up in the pine bough bedding we woke up in. He needs more time to heal and I'll ask Maggie to come out and give him some of her special salve for his cuts. I trot back to the cabin with Will to talk them out of this party idea. Assuming she agrees to my terms, there is no reason why I can't mark her, claim her, and mate her right here and now. I don't know what Joachim's plans to get Vas and shithead to mate with her too, or him for that matter, but those are details for later.

I want to complete this mating, then take her back to my cabin and give her so many fucking orgasms she won't be able to see straight. Or walk. Or remember why she ever wanted this to be a fake mating. My wolf is aching to rise up and sink a bite into her soft, sweet flesh to give her a mark.

My mouth waters and my cock grows hard.

Will opens the door and waves me in. I hold up my hand. "I need a minute."

Will laughs. "Get it in the snow, not on my house. I don't want my cabin smelling like your seed, you degenerate." He shuts the door and I turn my back to the door, reach inside my robe and grab my stiff cock. I could very easily jack-off right here, right now. I haven't been with a woman in two-hundred years. I've never been with anyone but her.

Even thinking that she could be ready and waiting for me to take her just on the other side of this door has a bead of pre-cum seeping from my tip. I'm intent on giving the bulge at the bottom a hard squeeze, forcing my cock to go down. Instead, I indulge in a brief moment and give my length one fast stroke from base up, and swirl that drop around my thick head.

The wolf's knot is already beating at the root, ready to plunge into her and lock us together. Fuck, why am I doing this to myself? She knows what I am, but she's not prepared for how my beast will take over, make her body submit to mine, and drive me to fuck her hard.

I should jerk myself until I come so the need building inside of me isn't so intense. I slide my hand up and down and lay my head back against the door, closing my eyes. Her lush body glows for me in my mind. She's on her hands and knees, her ass in the air, her cunt dripping and exposed for me.

I fist my hand tighter around my cock and pump faster, harder. I want to take her in every way. In her hot cunt, in her lush mouth, in her tight ass. I grit my teeth and groan, but the orgasm won't come. I need the real her, not my dry hand and a fantasy.

This moment of hedonism has made things worse and now I'm more than ready to make this mating happen. I can only pray she'll understand. I sigh, let my cock go, and wipe my hands in the snow.

When I open the door, Ekataryn rushes over, squealing, and wraps her arms around my neck. She peppers my face with tiny kisses on my cheeks and I forget that I'm angry. "Will told me. Thank you, thank you for helping to keep me safe."

"I will always keep you safe, tzaritsa." I brush my lips across hers and want to deepen the kiss, to taste her for real, but that will come soon enough. What I need to do is give her my terms. She can have her fake mating, but to me it will be real. I will mean every word and action we're about to take.

"I know this isn't what you want and I swear I'll do everything I can to get you out of this prison too so that you can get back to the real world and find your true mate too."

"You are my--"

Joachim is growling in my head and glaring at me. But I will not lie, not even if he thinks I should.

"Oh, come and see what Maggie has planned for the ceremony. I know it's fake, but won't it be nice to have a celebration with everyone. It's got to be the worst, living in this eternal winter. This town needs a party."

"That isn't a good idea. We're inviting trouble to come to town. We should do this here and now and as quickly as possible. The sooner you're marked, claimed, and mated, the sooner you're safe." At least from other packs. I can't guarantee she'll be safe from the Dark Prince of Wolves.

Because as our alpha, Grigory will know the moment I take her, and he will come to destroy what peace we've found.

Joachim quits growling at me and gives Ekataryn an easy smile. "Your soon to be mate is overly cautious, and I can't blame him. But if we want you to be truly safe from other packs coming to claim you, we have to get the word out. The best way to spread this announcement far and wide across the island is to invite the alphas of each of the packs.

"Not every alpha. I do not want Peter or Lev anywhere near her." Or Grigory. "In fact, none of them. You can send out your invitations, but it should be to a party to celebrate the fact that we're already mated. You said yourself that everyone doesn't need to watch me take her. We have enough here to witness."

Ekataryn tips her head to the side and lifts up one finger. "What exactly do you mean by 'take her'? Take me where?"

This is what I was afraid of. I send a quick glare Joachim's way. "The ritual. I can mark you now, but until we have sex, you are unclaimed."

Her eyes go as wide as the moon and she looks around at the others. "Excuse me?"

"That is our wolf mating ritual." I pull her back into my arms and dip my head so my lips are against her ear and my words only for her. "First, I will find just the right spot on your neck to mark you, by kissing and teasing you soft skin with my tongue and scrapes of my teeth. When your body responds with a shiver of need, I'll know that's where my mark belongs on you."

"Oh." She's barely whispering and I love the breathy sound of her arousal rising up.

"I can mark you then, or wait until I'm buried deep inside of you. Either way, your body will succumb to a pleasure like you've never known and will push you to come with my teeth in your skin."

"I don't think I'm into biting." That's a lie. The scent of her arousal is already filling my nose. She's definitely turned on by the idea.

I move my mouth to her other ear. "Then I will declare my claim on you for all to hear, and that's when the fun begins."

"Fun?" Along with her arousal, she's got the tangy scent of nervousness. With her lack of memories, she may not remember exactly how good sex with the right partner can be.

"Yes."

"What kind of fun?" The best kind.

Mmm..., she knows, she just doesn't want to acknowledge how badly she wants and needs the scene I'm laying out for her. "The kind where I fuck you so hard you beg me to let you come."

"Why do I have to beg you? I'm pretty sure..." She swallows and bites her lip trying so hard to hide her lust for me

But I know, and now I've got her.

"Because until you come with my seed deep inside of your cunt, and we're locked together in a true wolf's mating, everyone will know this is fake. There is no way my wolf will lock us together with the knot making my claim on you and our mating official, until you agree you are my one true mate."

TARYN

*A*ugust wants me to fuck him... and he means fuck, not make love, not have sex, fuck him in front of a whole bunch of other people while he does whatever this knotting thing is and he expects me to come. Yeah. No.

Well, maybe. I don't think I have ever been this turned on in my life. Like, I would remember my body doing this sometime in the past wouldn't I? The intensity of his words and the way he says them burns through me like the liquor Will gave me. Except that only pooled in my stomach. August's words have me clenching my thighs together because this heat is melting between my legs.

That has to mean I don't have some mysterious lover back in the real world. I wouldn't want and need August to do everything he's saying if I had someone else. Or even if I was meant for another.

Once these guys told me about fate mates, I was in. Seems weird that I could go from zero to one true love in nothing flat, but I think that means that I believed in this stuff on the outside. The more I learn about shifter culture, the more it feels comfortable.

Gasp. Maybe I'm the bunny.

Because right now, I'd sure like August to eat me up.

I shouldn't, but I blink slowly and open my eyes focused on Father Joachim. He's watching us and there is a deep blue glow in his eyes. His cheeks are pink just across the top of his cheekbones and I think mine match. I have a terrible urge to tell August yes to everything he's whispered in my ears, if Father Joachim is there too, doing the same things to me, at the same time as he is.

Even I know that being a priest means women are off limits. No matter how badly the woman wants him.

Vows are important and I pray to whatever God Father Joachim believes in that I'll be forgiven for breaking any vows, even ones that remain unsaid. Because I'm going to say yes to August. I'm going to let him make me his true mate.

It doesn't mean I'm going to stay and live some kind of happy ever after on the Island of the Damned. It may not be a mate I need to get back to, but I still know in my heart of hearts, there is someone I need to protect and take care of and that the only way to do it, is to escape this place and it's eternal winter.

I can't let anything, not even a true mate get in the way of getting back to my life before the Nothing.

My arms are still wrapped around his neck, and his lips are pressed to my ear. I want to hold onto this brief, perfect moment for a little bit longer, burn it into my memory so if and when things go wrong later, I can pull it out and remember exactly how I felt when I said yes. No one is taking this memory from me. They can throw me back in the nothing and slice up my mind again. I would still know my name and have this memory. It's mine now. Forever.

"Yes, August. Make me yours." I feel lighter and brighter the instant the words are out of my mouth.

Father Joachim closes his eyes and lifts his face upward as if sending up a prayer of thanks.

August growls and lowers his lips from my ear to my neck. He growls, but this time it's a sexy sound that makes my insides all jelly and my knees just as weak. He scrapes his teeth across my skin and holy canines, sparkles of freaking magic jolt through me. I think he found that spot he was talking about.

"Hold up there, big guy. I'm down for being your mate, as crazy as that sounds when I say it out loud, but I need a little time to come to grips with the whole having sex in front of other people." Except maybe Father Joachim. God what is wrong with me? Oops, sorry God, didn't mean to bring you into this. Pretend you didn't hear that. I am not thinking naughty thoughts about one of your guys.

Oh, but I am.

"Are you sure about that? The scent of your arousal is strong enough to--"

Ack, what? "Shush your face. Do not tell everyone here that you can smell me."

Will chokes on his drink. "Don't worry your head about that. It's not like the rest of us didn't notice."

Oh my God. Dammit. I need to find another name to take in vain. "You can all smell me?"

Maggie raises her hand. "I can't, but I'm a vegetarian. It's not like we can't all see what's going on between the two of you though."

I take a nice big step back from August and I purposefully look at the wall instead of Joachim. "I think I need shifter-world lessons. There isn't like a book or something I can read about how to date and mate a shifter, is there?"

No one else seems to think I'm funny. I'm adding that book to my to-do list for after prison. "I'll take that as a no."

August closes the space between us again and I'm going to

have to give him a lesson in personal space. "You don't need a guide. I will teach you everything you need to know."

That look in his eyes says all of those things he wants to teach me are dirty. Very, very dirty. "I'm sure you will, after the party. I still want to have it. If I'm getting true fated mated, I want it to be special."

Something goes through August's mind when I say that. I see his brain click on and get busy thinking about something besides sex. Phew. "I will make our mating as special as you desire, sweet one, and give you your party, but I still don't want all the other alphas there. I don't trust any of them not to try and steal you away before you are marked and claimed."

"You should mark her now." Father Joachim's voice is raspy and insistent.

Eek. Now that I know everyone except Maggie can literally smell when I'm turned on, I really need to start thinking about anything but how his words make me feel all squirmy and needy. Think of snow, think of ice, think of sultry summer nights, think of volcanoes exploding and... crap that didn't work and I think even I can smell myself.

Hopefully everyone thinks I've got a biting kink.

"Yes, I should." I know August is a wolf-shifter and all, but does he have to stalk me? I am definitely the bunny, and he's the big bad wolf.

I take a few steps back and run into the table. Ouch. That's going to leave a bruise on my butt. "Wait, didn't you say that bite is going to, uh, make me come. I'm not ready to go all porn star in front of everyone."

Will leans over to Father Joachim and loudly whispers, "What's a porn star? Is it a star that makes one's mate orgasm? I would like to get one of those for my Maggie." He winks at her and adorably, she blushes.

I slip around the edge of the table and put a chair between me and my wolf. This is futile, I know. He can catch me anytime he wants, or anytime I want. Dammit, I want. But seriously, not in front of everyone.

"Look, I get that I have to follow your ritual, but can I have something private and romantic? Can we do the marking without the whole world watching?"

August stops and exchanges a meaningful look with Father Joachim. I don't know the meaning, but they just had a whole conversation with their eyes and the wiggles of their beards when they clench their jaws. I need to learn this language. The only part I do understand is when Joachim narrows his eyes and August gives a quick jerk of his head. They come to some kind of decision between the two of them.

"My tzaritsa, I will try my best to do as you ask, but I cannot be sure that I can stop at just one taste of you. Marking you will affect me too."

Of course it will. "What if..." I can't believe I'm going to say this out loud. "What if Father Joachim, umm, watch... I mean, chaperones?"

August doesn't say no. His chest rises and falls faster than before and he licks his lips.

Those red slashes across the father's cheekbones flare back up. "If that is what you wish, I am but your humble servant."

I am so going to hell.

Maggie clears her throat and breaks all the delicious tension in the room. "Is the party on then? We sure could use something to celebrate around here."

August is shaking his head no, Joachim is nodding yes.

Vas comes trotting in the door unaware of anything but his wagging tail, and he's got a mouthful of some kind of vine with white flower buds running all up and down it. He comes right on over and drops them at my feet. "Ah, what a nice pup to bring me flowers."

The rest of the room has gone so silent I can hear myself breathe. When I look to see what's the matter, everyone is staring at the flowers. "What? Are they poisonous? Do we need to get Vas to a vet? Do you have a vet?"

Maggie is the first to move and she comes over, pats Vas on the head, picks up the vines, and hands them to me. One by one the flowers slowly open and their fragrance tickles something in my memory. I've seen these flowers before. I think maybe they're my favorite and perhaps someone has given them to me on special occasions. Or maybe I've given them to someone else. The someone I have to get back to.

Tears glisten in Maggie's eyes as we watch each bud spread its petals. "No, love. This is the first flower any of us have seen on this island. Ever."

Right. Eternal winter, no spring, no flowers. Father Joachim looks at me, and it's not like I know, so I shrug. "So where did these come from?"

A knock sounds on the door and two men and one woman stand outside. They've got vines of buds in their hands too, and the flowers are opening one by one. Out the window and the wide open door, a half dozen more people are making their way toward Maggie and Will's cabin.

Joachim pushes through the people and out the door. "Come out, look. They're everywhere."

We all rush out and while, I wouldn't say everywhere, vines with the white buds and a few opening flowers on them are poking up from the ground near the cabin, over by the barn, and I even see a few blooms along the trees where we came into the village.

"Father, what does this mean?" someone from the gathered crowd asks. I'd like to know too.

"That it is time to rejoice." He holds out his hand to me, and I give him the vines. He holds them high over his head and then lays them gently around my neck as if they are a blessing. For a brief moment it's just him and me and this isn't a blessing, it's a

93

gift. He cups my cheek and the blue of his eyes dances and flickers like a fire within.

He's going to kiss me. My heart skips a beat and then another when August steps up behind me and wraps one arm around my waist. I stand between these two men, never wanting to move. Joachim says in a quieter volume than his big announcement. "Tomorrow, we will celebrate with a true mating."

Then he casts his gaze around the circle of gathered people and steps back, withdrawing his hand. "Moon flowers have returned to the island, and we will give thanks and praise that something special has come into our lives in our darkest hour. You are all invited to the mating ritual for our newest arrival where we can one and all celebrate love and life."

Murmurs turn to happy exclamations, pats on the back, and congratulations to August and me from all around. I smile at each well-wisher and introduce myself to them, trying hard to remember the litany of names. I won't remember a single one. I'm too distracted by the ping-ponging of thoughts in my brain.

Ping. This moon flower thing means something. I am so damn tired of not being able to access my own memories. It's as if they are right there in front of me, but there's a wall between me and what I want to know.

Pong. Was Father Joachim going to kiss me? I was sure he would. I even think August grabbed me not to pull me away, but to hold me in place for the kiss.

Ping. These flowers don't grow in the forest, and they certainly don't bloom in winter with snow and ice all around. These vines are supposed to surround... gah. I can almost see it in my mind.

Pong. Will August hold me like that when he marks me? My back to his front, supporting me with his body, protecting me in his arms, Father Joachim in front of us, watching, with that same need burning in his eyes?

Ping-pong. The flowers belong around a church or a temple or whatever kind of building or structure people worship in. That's where August should mark me. That's where Father Joachim belongs. We should all be in the temple surrounded by the flowers.

I can see every single building in the tiny village from where I'm standing and Maggie and Will's barn is the biggest one. We need a better gathering place than either that or the street and I really like the idea of a flower covered temple. I'm shaking some guy's hand and he seems as good as anyone to ask. "Hey, is there a temple or a church where we could have this celebration?"

The guy stops pumping my hand and he looks like I slapped him across the face. He stiffens up and looks to Father Joachim as if he needs permission to tell me. He opens his mouth two or three times, like a caught fish gasping for water, then pulls his hands from mine and takes several steps backward until he's back in the crowd of people.

"Uh, did I say something wrong? I just thought it would be nice to have a space where everyone can get out of the cold for our party." I'm a liar. I don't care if everyone else comes to the temple or not. That's not entirely true. They are all good people, like Will and Maggie and August and Father Joachim. It means something that they can maintain their integrity after being banished or imprisoned with horrible creepy men like Peter and Lev.

I just know that I want to have this mating ceremony in a place that has meaning. I don't know why that's important, but I'm sure if we do, I will remember.

Father Joachim lifts his arms in the air and uses his announcement voice again, "Thank you everyone, now head back to your homes and do what you can to help prepare for the celebration tomorrow."

A woman steps forward out of the gathered group. Her chin

is set and the others are looking to her. She's been tasked to say or do something by the rest of them. I like her already. "Father, what about the Dark Prince? What if he finds out? He killed again last night and if we're all in one place together he could take us all out in one sweep of his razor claws."

Ping, ping, pong. Dark Prince, killed again, razor claws? Just how many bad guys are on this island. It is a prison, I get that, but a shiver goes through me at the mention of this guy.

August and Vasily both growl at the mention of this Dark Prince. They do not like him. Yikes. I slide my hand into August's and my other into the tuft of fur at the top of Vasily's head to give myself some comfort. Having them to protect me from another new threat is keeping me from getting mad about this whole prison island situation.

Someone should be able to save these good people from this horrible fate.

"Alida." Joachim says her name and I'm suddenly irritated as hell at her. Uh oh. Jealous much? But also... back off of my priest lady... who I also admire and want to be friends with. "We all know the Prince is unpredictable, but look at who will be at this celebration."

Vasily yips and stands up, wagging his tail and letting his tongue hang out in that adorable way he has. August seems to puff up and stand taller, Will gives the woman a salute, and even Father Joachim looks less like a priest and more like a warrior right now.

The woman nods as if talking herself into the fact that these shifters can protect her. "The Streltsy will all be there, you'll keep him away and us safe?"

I like this word, Streltsy. It means guards. I shouldn't know that when I can't even remember my own last name, but I do. It suits the wolves I've gathered around me and I have full faith that they can ward off this Dark Prince and keep everyone from harm.

"I trust them," I blurt out. It's not really my place because she doesn't know me from a tree, but I can't help it. It's my mating they're all coming to celebrate, they might as well know I'm not afraid.

Alida comes over to me and takes my hands in hers. "We all want to trust them too, but you haven't met the Dark Prince of Wolves yet. He just doesn't kill, he steals your soul."

JOACHIM

*D*ear sweet Goddess of the Moon, what are you doing to me?

"Father?" Taryn looks to me like I have all the answers to life, the universe, and everything.

"The Dark Prince is no demon." Although, he thinks he is. "He is simply a wolf shifter like me. His claws are no sharper than mine, and I promise, he cannot steal anyone's soul."

Alida harumphs. "Maybe, but he did burn down the church and you couldn't get me to go anywhere near that place. We'd be better to host the party in our make-shift church in the woods." She knows the others look to her for guidance. With so few females, they quickly become fast friends when a new woman arrives, and I can see she wants to find a bond with Taryn. Who doesn't?

"Burned down a church?" She always did like a little religion in her life. I'm not surprised she's angry over the desecration of holy ground. "He is so not invited to this party. What kind of an asshole is this guy?"

The kind that needs saving from himself, more than we need to be saved from him.

I avoid answering her question because now is not the time to explain. "Alida, I think the church in the woods will be perfect. We will create a new sacred circle. While the moon cannot yet shine down on us, we can hang the moonflowers from the branches and feel as though the goddess watches over us all."

Taryn makes a cute little moue at me with her lush lips. How I'd like to see them wrapped around my cock. "What exactly is the religion you are a holy man for?"

I choke on the air I breathe and August laughs, patting me on the back to help me recover.

In one day, Taryn has come closer to understanding who and what she is than she often times does in entire lifetimes. I have to believe it's because we're all here on this damned island together. For the first time since I fucked us all over, we're together, and I can atone for my mistakes.

No, it wasn't a mistake. I thought I knew better, that I was stronger, smarter, and could keep her safer. Hubris was my sin and I fear I'm on the same path again. They're all so angry now, and finding out the damage I've done will only sink them deeper into darkness. Maybe so far that even her light can't save them.

This is a trial I must pass alone if I am ever to reunite the wolf guard. I must stay firm to my vows and stop imagining the sins I want to commit with her.

August takes Taryn's hand and nods to me. "Let's show her your church, Father. A marking is a fitting way to christen a new sacred circle, don't you think?"

Taryn grips his hand tight enough that if I couldn't scent her nervousness rise up, I'd be able to see it in the tremor of her muscles. She doesn't let anyone else see. Her head is held high and she takes the first step toward the woods. Not two feet away, she looks back at me and her eyes say, "you're coming, aren't you?"

Maybe I'm not entirely alone. She wants me there. It's going to kill me but I will be what she needs for her marking and her mating with August. He's the wolf she deserves. He'll take care of her when the rest of us can't.

I want to give her more time, ease her into remembering, let her take the power she wants and not force it on her. There are no easy choices this time around. We know better than to take them.

But I will make sure the rest of the guard gets their fucking heads out of their asses and is at this mating too. Once they see August taking her, they won't be able to resist her pull. They'll join and finally, finally, we will be whole once again. Only then can I relent. It's been so long.

I'm ready to follow them into the forest, but pause to find Vasily. His paw prints in the snow lead in the opposite direction. He should be there for the marking, but I will settle for only the mating. The only way to heal his broken heart is to open it up to her again. He knows that, he's just afraid. I can empathize.

I will join him later tonight in the woods. He's more comfortable when we're all in wolf form. I will do what I can to help him see his path to salvation. Then I'll go to find Grigory in his burned out lair.

I catch up to August and Taryn and we leave the safety of the *derevnya* for the dense trees that cover most of this land. The outlaw packs roam the woods looking for prey, but August does a good job keeping them away from here. To have both Peter and Lev's packs so close makes me wary and on high alert.

There's a place not too far into the forest where Will and Maggie cleared out saplings and debris below a row of tall leaning pines who've grown into a natural arched roof. Maggie said she felt the magic of Tír na nÓg there when she was first exiled, and she and Will have searched many times for a way out of this eternal prison in this hidden chapel of nature. In eight-hundred years, they haven't found anything.

I choose to believe that this place is more holy than magical and August and Taryn are about to prove it.

While I watch.

My wolf howls at me inside. I learned long ago to suppress those base instincts. I thought I had my beast under control. I haven't been face to face with my one true mate in so long and her presence is bringing out both the best and the worst in me. I have a very tenuous hold on the thin thread of my restraint.

One wrong move and it will snap. I can't let that happen.

As we approach the entrance to the make-shift church Taryn's nervousness turns to awe. She hurries into the shelter of the trees and smiles and spins, laughing with the joy of the place. Nature's handiwork is a sight to behold, but it's nothing compared to Taryn's excitement and pure beauty.

August and I stand together, both taken by her and not wanting to break into her moment. He speaks softly and with reverence. "I never could resist her."

"Nor I." But I must. At least for now. Only when we are all together as one once again can I finally be hers once again. If she'll even still want me.

"You have to help me, Joachim." The scent of August's own trepidation is a new smell to me.

I've never once known him to be nervous about anything. He dives in head first to every struggle, every challenge, any battle that needs fighting, especially for right, especially for her. "I want her too badly. I won't be able to stop myself and that's not what she wants."

"August--"

"No, really, Joachim. My wolf is tearing at me to get out and my cock is throbbing. I tried to tell you this was a bad idea, and now I'm enlisting you to make sure I don't hurt her."

He would die before he caused her harm, but his emotions

are running too high to hear that. I'm certainly not going to admit my own wolf is pushing at me so hard to mark her that my fangs have already dropped and my own cock is hard and aching. "I'm here and I'm not going anywhere."

August gives one curt nod and strides into the center of the chapel to join her. She pauses in her twirling and looks up at him with the glow of the moon in her eyes and the flush of excitement and arousal in the pink of her cheeks. August's fists open and close rhythmically as he stares down at her.

I can do this. For him, for her. For us all.

Taryn looks from August to me and back again. "Will it hurt? The marking? You said you're going to bite me."

He can't answer her so I do it for him. "Yes. In the pain, there will be pleasure. This is part of what it means to be a wolf. When we shift, our bones break and reform, our skin splits to make way for our fur, but for that pain we get heightened senses, supernatural healing, and some even develop psychic abilities."

Remember.

Remember who and what you are.

"The bite used to mark a mate is the same. For the pain, you get a connection with your mate that will allow you to communicate with mind-speak, and a sexual pleasure that will leave you satisfied longer than any ordinary orgasm."

I long to see her come, to stroke her hair and take care of her in the aftermath as she comes down from the high of her body's bliss. It will be pure torture because this one is not for me.

August takes a step closer so they're almost touching. "And a mark that represents our bond so that all might see that you belong to me."

And him to her.

She touches her neck and licks her lips. "Will you shift into the wolf to do it?"

"I am always the wolf." He puts his hands around her waist and turns her so that she is facing me instead of him. They're both pleading with me through their eyes for my strength, though neither realizes they don't need it. August's wolf ripples across his skin and stretches, sniffing the air around them, taking in the scent of her. "One does not exist without the other."

August holds her tight against him and lowers his face to her throat. He puts his other hand on her thigh, pushing her legs open. Though she's covered in thick woven fabric, he's inches from her pussy and he bunches up the skirt in his fist. His wolf's claws have extended from the end of his fingers and if he's not careful he'll scratch her delicate skin.

Her eyes go dark with arousal as he scrapes his teeth across her throat, but they're also wide with fear. This is why she needs me, why he asked me to help.

All I want is to push her head back against his shoulder and find my own spot to sink my fangs in and mark her too. I must be stronger, I must be better. For her. For her, for us all.

I push the wolf down, although my cock will not obey. I'm throbbing and my balls are already drawn up tight. She may not be the only one who will come when August marks her.

She bites her lip and her eyes are blinking a million times a second. She's trying so hard to be brave, but her muscles are tense and she's on the verge of bolting.

I know her better than she knows herself in this moment, and what she doesn't need is for me to be the gentle priest. I step up to her in this all too familiar position and grab her chin, tipping her head to the side and giving August more room to find just the right spot to bite her. "Listen to your body, Taryn, not your mind. Your body knows this is your mate and it wants the mark, it is waiting to revel in that sting of pain."

She tries to shake her head, and squirms to get away. August growls and nips at her shoulder. His beast is rising up to claim his mate. I hold her face tight and press myself against her to pin her in place. August pulls her skirt up higher and I push his hand away, replacing it with my own.

"He won't do it, *boginya*, if you fight him. He wants your consent. He needs you to need him as much as he does you."

She whimpers and I have to give her more if she's going to submit. August is breathing hard and the rise and fall of her chest matches his. It's not her that's fighting against August but the walls in her mind blocking her memories. I will tumble them if it's the last thing I do.

God, forgive me. I yank up the front of her skirt to her waist and slide my hand down, pushing her soft thighs apart. What I wouldn't give to feel those thighs pillowing me as I push inside of her, or cupping my head while I lick the sweet essence from her dripping cunt.

She's already wet enough that I can slip two fingers between her plush pussy lips and I press hard against her clit, feeling it throb and grow hard beneath my fingers. "Do you feel how wet you are? That's for him. Your body calls to him, it wants him. But you have to say it. Tell him you want him to mark you."

Her eyelids flutter shut and she instinctively grinds against my fingers. "Look at me, Taryn. Look at me, and tell him you want this. End this sweet torture."

Mine, hers, and August's.

If she doesn't give in soon, both August and I will be fucking her right here in this sacred circle and she won't know what's happened. She'll only know the pleasure of being our mate once again.

Not. Fucking. Yet.

August gives her small bites all up and down her throat, nipping at her, marring her skin in warning. He's rubbing himself against her plump ass, anxious to claim her. I move my fingers back and forth over her tight clit in time to his futile thrusts. He's on the verge of frenzy, but I push at his mind and lend him some of my own control. He lifts his mouth from her throat and licks the shell of her ear. "Say it, tzaritsa. Tell me you want to be mine."

Her throat bobs up and down and she sucks in a shuddered breath. "I..."

Her need and arousal permeates every bit of the air in the chapel of trees and the longer we let this go on, we're putting her in danger. Any wolf worth his salt will be able to smell her a mile away and will come running. I need to end this now.

"Taryn, let go." I let my wolf rise up and I pour all my lust and need for her into the words. "Dammit, mate, look at me and say it."

Her eyes fly open and she wraps one arm around me and the other around August's head, pulling him back down to the crook of her neck. "I want you, mark me, please, mark me."

I don't know if she's saying the words to August or me or both of us. August doesn't care. That's all he needed. He sinks his teeth into her flesh and I can feel him pouring all that he is into the mark.

She grabs onto my arm and holds my hand between her legs and she gasps as the orgasm hits her hard and fast. The pent up tension is so intense that I can literally feel the pulses of her clit beating against my fingers. My own cock responds to her pleasure and my seed shoots from me landing mutely on the inside of my robes.

How I wish it was my cock sliding between her legs instead of my fingers. It is not to be. By denying myself, I've given her and August what they needed.

Taryn moans and pleads for more and August groans out his own pleasure. He too has come from this first bonding between them. I can smell our combined scents in the air and it's so heady that I get no relief from coming. I'm still hard and my cock is going to stay that way, tormenting me.

Slowly her arms drop and August lifts his head, licking her

wound to soothe the sting and help her heal. Already the bite marks are moving and shifting into the form of his white wolf. When it also forms the rising moon, the symbol of his station, her first mark will be complete.

August stares at the beginnings of the mark and his wolf rises up again. He tears himself away from her and she falls into me, weary, depleted, and satisfied. I let her skirts fall and hold her to me, tucking her head against my chest. He lifts his head as if to howl, but takes a long deep breath and stares at us embraced. He mouths two simple words to me. "Thank you."

They are the last thing I want to hear. "She is marked as yours now, guard her well."

He nods, pushes his own beast back down, and comes to take her from my arms. It's not the first time, but I hope it will be the last.

August croons to her with nonsense words of love in our native tongue and strokes her hair. I should clean up and let them have their bonding in peace. I find that I cannot. I don't want the scent and taste of her erased from my fingers.

A few moments later, not nearly long enough for me to indulge in the continued need for her, she rouses herself and gives August a long, lingering kiss. He should take her back to the cabin and to his bed. There's a new resolve in his eyes and he'll be able to control himself until the claiming tomorrow. She'll be well pleasured through the night by his tongue, teeth, and fingers. Not mine. He'll help her be comfortable giving him her body and be fully prepared for their claiming and mating tomorrow.

Taryn turns to me, and there's a new glow to her skin, eyes, and being. Has she remembered more of who and what she is with this first step in the mating?

"Father Joachim?" My name on her lips pushes at the control over my wolf in my mind, like she's in my head.

I take a step away, needing to separate myself from the two of them. "Yes, my lady?"

She takes August's hand in hers and holds it against her chest, his palm to her heart. She looks deep into his eyes and I watch him melt for her. Then she brings her gaze back to me. "I want to say that I'm sorry if I've made you cross a line or break some kind of vow to your God."

I should tell her none of it matters if it's what makes her happy and whole. "There is no need. I have done what was asked of me in service... to my higher power."

She pushes August's hand tighter to her chest, showing me the intimacy of her new bond with him. "You didn't let me finish. I want to say I'm sorry. But I'm not."

A soft ringing shimmers through my mind, like bells on a church exalting in praise and joy. She stares at me and it's almost like I can see some of the fog clearing from her mind, filling in a few of the holes in her memory.

Her voice bursts out beautiful and clear, not just in my mind but August's too. *"Because I need you both."*

I stumble back and throw up every block and defense I know to keep her from the darkest places in my memories. "*Boginya,* I can't."

She reaches for me and thank God, August can feel my sheer panic and wraps her in his arms so she can't come any closer.

I turn my back, drop my robes and prayer beads, and let my wolf out. My bones break and transition from man to beast, my skin bursts with the force of the fur pushing out, and I've never felt the agony of the shift so fiercely. I welcome the pain and this time, for me, there must be no pleasure.

I howl to the open air rafters of this church in the trees and the chapel resounds with my prayer. I pray to God, pray to the Goddess, to give me the strength, the will power, the control to make this sacrifice. I must deny her need and both of our souls crying out to join, so that I can keep my vows and save us all.

Even my howls cannot drown out her voice in my head. *"Forgive me, Father, for I have sinned. But I will not confess, I will not give up my need for you."*

They are the same words she said to me over three hundred years ago in the last life we lived together, when I became her priest instead of her mate, giving her into the care of the Volkovs.

TARYN

*T*hey are mine and I am theirs.

I know these two men. Not like I met them yesterday and now I can call them by name and recognize them as friendly faces. I know who August is as if we've been together for hundreds of years. He is my protector, my lover, my ally. I know Joachim deep in my soul. There was a time when he and I were friends, then we fell in love.

I still don't have a good sense of who I am or where I lived before the Nothing, and I'm grasping at ghosts of memories that are right there in front of me, yet I still can't hold them in my mind for more than the tiniest of moments. Never long enough to examine them until I understand what I'm feeling and seeing.

He is hurting now and I don't know why. His howls are a wounded prayer and I want to answer them for him. I want to wrap him in my loving arms and tell him he doesn't have to suffer. I will take care of him.

I keep August's hand to my chest, needing his touch like I need to breathe. "We have to help him. Please, August. Tell me what to do."

I feel as though I should know, but I don't. Have I hurt him so much by telling him how deeply I need him and his love? I swear I will give back to him tenfold what he gives to me.

Another wolf howls nearby, repeating Joachim's soulful cry and I'm worried one of the other packs have heard and will come to start trouble. I don't want to see this perfect, peaceful chapel in the woods disturbed by fighting. Especially not over me.

I squeeze August's hand. I feel so much better knowing I have him to support and uplift me. I want to make sure that I don't take advantage of that from him because I can see how he could so easily give too much of himself in any relationship. "Are we in danger? Are the outlaw wolf packs coming?"

"No danger." He squeezes my hand back and I think he likes that I'm already relying on him. Although, I'd rather just be lying on him, in bed, after a long naughty night.

Oh geez. We were all up in each other's heads a minute ago. I hope he can't hear all my thoughts. I bring up an extremely graphic image of something I hope he does to me later and he doesn't even flinch. Okay, phew.

"It's Vasily," he says and then looks toward the entrance to this peaceful sanctuary.

Vasily comes rushing into the sacred enclosure and straight over to Joachim. He butts his head against Joachim's dark furry shoulder and I'm more convinced now than before that Vasily is more than a wolf. He hasn't shifted like August and Joachim have, but there is definitely more to him than meets the eye.

I want to ask August. I decide instead to let Vasily show me himself who and what he truly is.

He comes over and is headed straight for my crotch to sniff me like he did before. I'm a little uncomfortable that he'll know exactly how my body reacted to August's marking and Joachim's, uh, help. If he is nothing more than an animal, he won't understand or care about the significance of the marking.

Vasily doesn't get all up in my business this time. He goes straight for August.

August swats him away. "Back off, Vas."

Vasily snorts, gives my hand a quick lick and then trots back over to Joachim. He grabs up the discarded robes and pushes them toward the other wolf. Joachim turns his back on the offer.

"Vas won't take no for an answer, my love. This is how you can help them both." August lifts my hands where I'd been holding him to me and gives my wrist a quick kiss. *"Go to them."*

It is going to take some getting used to having someone else in my head. But August's words feel so much more intimate when he speaks into my mind and it makes me go all squishy inside. My heart is all gooey for him and I am so looking forward to the mating.

He gives me a little shove forward and I hurry over to Vasily and Joachim. I try to take the robes from Vasily because I want to drape them over Joachim and encourage him to shift back so we can talk. Vasily won't give them to me. He's tugging back like we're playing a game.

"Hey, let go. I'm only trying to help." I give the robes a yank and now I am thinking Vasily is a pet, because why would a man play tug with someone's clothes like this?

He finally lets go and I stumble back. I kinda want to smack him on the nose. Sigh. He's such a sweet defender. I can't forget how he was ready to sacrifice his life for mine hours after we met. If anyone is going to be my rock on this island, it's this pup. And by pup I mean big ass scary looking wolf who's eyeing me like his next meal.

If he does turn out to be a shifter, that's when I'll smack him on the nose for keeping himself hidden from me.

I let go of my irritation and I wrap my hands around the scruff of his neck and press my forehead to his. He too was just trying to help and I love him for it.

He gives a little whine and drops the robes. He squirms out of my hold, gives me a big wet lick from my neck to my cheek and then as fast as he came in, he's gone. All that's left is his pawprints.

Weirdo. Adorable freaking weirdo.

I like him so much and I hope someday if he is a shifter, he'll trust me enough to let me see him as a man. Mostly because I want to give him an enormous hug. And smack his nose. Maybe his ass.

I pick up the robes and lay them across Joachim's back. I'm not sure he'll let me, so I very carefully hold my hand out over his ears in case he doesn't want me to touch. He leans into me and I stroke the softest fur just behind his left ear.

"I won't push you, Joachim. I don't know how any of this works. I only know I want you in my life. Today, I'll take that however you can give."

He doesn't reply with words, but with shifting back into his human form. My chest caves in a bit with the harsh reality he tried to tell me about the pain of the shift. I can literally see his muscles and bones going all wacky cracky under his fur and then his skin.

I'm pretty glad I'm not the shifter in this relationship at the moment. I'd much rather endure orgasmic bites than that.

Joachim slips his arms back into the robes and when he stands up straight, fully clothed again, the man once again becomes the priest. "I apologize for losing my control. It won't happen again."

Ooh. Is it bad that I want to push his control? I don't want to see him break down, but I do want to see him break apart and let me in.

To his pants.

Crap. Priest. Vows. Sorry, God.

He takes a step away from me and I don't like it so I move closer. Father Joachim holds up a hand and looks over to August, and I can see the request for help in his eyes. August comes over but gives Joachim a huff. The look on his face says he thinks Joachim is being a dumbass.

He squats down and retrieves the string of beads from the ground and hands them to Father Joachim.

Joachim rolls them between his fingers and even I can see how they bring him back to his focused self. "I can't take you as a mate, *boginya*. You need me more as your priest than you do as a lover. I promise."

Uh, that's a lie, straight from the pits of hell. But I promised I would take whatever he could give today. If that's being my priest, that's what I get. For now.

"So, what happens now?" I vote that we all go get warmed up back at Maggie's with a cup of Will's moonshine mixed into a hot beverage and sit around telling each other our life stories. Mine will be short. I was born, then there was the Nothing, now I'm here and wanting to get in each of your respective pants. The end.

Maybe they can fill in some of the holes in my memory. The sense that I've known them each for a long time isn't going away and if I can blink away the mind fog, I'd be able to look back at when we were last together.

"August takes you back to his cabin and tomorrow you come back here to be mated." Joachim puts the beads back in his pocket and backs even farther away from the two of us. He's inching his way to the nearest exit.

"Couldn't we just do the claiming and mating now. I'm ready." More than.

"Yes," August says and grabs me around the waist in a way I'm coming to get excited about.

"No," Father Joachim says, slashing his hand through the air.

"We must have witnesses. You've been marked, but it isn't enough."

He continues and he thinks it's just in August's head, but I hear him too "*You will make her safe this time, August. We can't afford to make any mistakes.*"

I expect some ruffled feathers or tuft of fur as the case may be from the demand. But my August, he's a smarty pants and he clearly cares for Joachim in a way I don't yet understand. "*She is safe with me, Joachim. Go. Seek your solace.*"

I keep quiet. I wasn't meant to hear this exchange anyway. I've poked and prodded at Father Joachim too much and I have to believe that he'll come to me when he is ready.

They are mine and I am theirs, and not having him here with me now isn't going to change that.

Joachim bows his head to me. "Until tomorrow night, my lady."

I watch him retreat for the area that should be his domain not mine and worry that I've broken something between us before it's even started. I touch the mark on my neck, wanting that connection and it shoots a warmth through me like electricity. I feel both loved and a heated passion.

August lowers his head and pushes my hand away with his lips. He kisses the mark and that simple touch sends a zing all the way south to between my legs. "Why do I have a feeling you're thinking dirty thoughts about me right now, my sweet tzaritsa? Like lay me flat on my back with your lush ass in my hands while you sit on my beard?"

Oh my God. Sorry, Father. That is exactly the image I sent him earlier when I was testing to see if he could read my mind. "Can you see everything I'm thinking?"

He laughs and I forget my embarrassment. "No. But you were projecting that thought loud and clear."

"I was? How about this one?" I think of another thing I'd like to do with August and I wonder, for just a moment, where I'm getting all these ideas. I think I might have been kinda slutty in my life on the outside. Thank goodness, because having August in my bed is going to be a lot of fun.

August fake gasps and swats me on the rear. "You are a dirty woman, mate. But you'll have to wait until tomorrow night. You're not getting any of this until then."

He grabs his cock through his robes and my hands go straight there too. He snags both of my hands into one of his and holds them up over his head, then backs me up to the nearest tree. I get a flash of an image where he and I have done this dance before.

I wrap one ankle around the back of his calf and pull him in closer. He attacks my mouth with his and in moments our tongues are dueling. He's fierce and passionate and I want him now even more than I did before. With each passing second my arousal for him grows.

I was just the tiniest bit worried that without Father Joachim here pushing me to accept August that my body would cool off. Yeah, that's not happening. "Please, August. Claim me, mate me now. I need you."

For a hot minute he grinds himself against me and I think he's going to do it. Then he nips my lip with his teeth and breaks the kiss. "You always were a greedy thing for my cock. I promise you when we mate tomorrow night, I will leave you satisfied."

Always. I'm disappointed that he's pulled away but he's opened a door that I'm not passing by. "Tell me about our life together before? How is it that I feel like I know you so well, now that you've marked me?"

A dark shadow crosses his eyes, but if I hadn't been staring right into them, I might have missed it. He uses his free hand to stroke across my mark. "It's the connection. Some of my own memories are flowing into you."

I don't think that's right. The feelings I have for him now

aren't filtered through his perspective. But what do I know? Hardly anything.

He brushes his lips across mine and while I want so much more, he releases me from this lovely vulnerable position he has me in and waves me to the exit. I don't want to leave, but I realize it's probably not all that safe to be out on our own. Especially if we run into a big pack again like last night.

He guides me back toward the *derevnya* and we see people hurrying to and from Maggie's house. Alida and another woman have gathered armloads of the vines with dozens of white buds on them. They're headed toward the trail we just came from accompanied by four big fierce looking men.

"They aren't in danger going out there are they? I don't want anyone to get hurt because of me." I feel a need to protect these people.

"They'll be fine. With both Will and I here and Vasily out patrolling, the outlaw packs will keep their distance."

"Until the mating ceremony." When the whole island is going to watch me have sex. An hour ago that freaked me the hell out. Now I'm looking forward to it. Not the everybody watching part, but the mating with August so that everyone knows we belong to each other.

August growls. "Yes. Until then."

"And what about that Dark Prince guy?" I don't like the fear I saw in Alida's eyes when she spoke about him. Nobody messes with my people.

Whoa. Okay, calm down there, me. I've been here barely a day. Nobody needs me claiming them. I'm the one who needs to be claimed.

"Father Joachim seems to think he can control the whims of murderous assholes." August's anger at either the Dark Prince or Joachim or both rolls off him so strong I think I can smell it. Bitter, burned sugar.

"What? No, no, no. August, go get him. Don't let him put

himself in danger like that." I mentally call out to Joachim, but there's no sense of him in my head.

We've made it back to Maggie and Will's cabin and we pause in front of their front door. August chucks me under the chin in a way I think he's done a hundred times before. "Don't worry, my love. I have no intention of letting the good Father anywhere near the Dark Prince of Wolves tonight. Now, in you go. Maggie will let you bed down in their care tonight."

"Wait, you're not staying with me?"

August smiles and his wolf's fangs drop giving him a demonic look that makes my stomach go loopy-loop. "I don't think Will would take kindly to me bending you over their kitchen table in the middle of the night to fuck you until you're screaming my name as you come."

Oh.

"And that's exactly what will happen if I stay with you tonight. I've wanted you from the second I saw you on that beach cold and lost. It has taken all that I have not to claim you already. But both you and Joachim insist you'll be safer if we do the mating ritual the way it was ordained in the beginning of all wolf kind. So, yes, I must leave you tonight." He presses me up against the door with his big body and grabs my butt, one cheek in each of his massive hands, holding me still while he pushes our hips together.

He wasn't kidding about the wanting me part. Either that's an entire tree trunk in his pants or he's happy to see me. And boy, oh, boy are my girl parts going to be happy to see him tomorrow night.

I'm not letting him off so easily though. I wrap my arms around his neck and lift one leg and then the other until I've wrapped my ankles around his waist. I kiss him, sucking his lower lip between my teeth and then run my tongue along one of those big, sharp fangs and then the other.

He groans and kneads the curves of my ass, hiking my skirt up further and further.

A voice calls from the other side of the door. "Don't get your wolf seed on my door, you horny toad. We talked about this."

Out of anyone I've met so far, Will is the last person I'd have dubbed a cock blocker. August sighs and slowly steps back helping me lower my legs of jelly to the ground. "You are a thief of self-control, tzaritsa. Dream of me tonight, but do not dare touch yourself. I'll know and your orgasms are mine now."

He throws off his robe and indeed his cock is hard and ready for me. He strokes it once while I watch, swiping a tiny drop of come from the tip onto his thumb. He raises his hand to my mouth and pushes that small taste of him into my mouth and swirls his thumb back and forth across my tongue.

If I thought I was turned on a minute ago, I was wrong. My heart is beating between my legs and if he thinks I'm not touching myself tonight, he's wrong.

"You're projecting again, my love. If you make yourself come without me, you'll regret it when I withhold your orgasms later as punishment."

Oops. Too late.

He shifts into his big white wolf and runs off into the woods, while I melt against the door.

I sit there on the cold ground for a long time, needing to cool off. Dusk is darkening the sky, but because the clouds cover every inch of the sky, there is no sunset. I stare up into the bloom of night and for just a moment, a tiny sliver of the sky is visible, and I can't be sure, but I think I see a glimpse of a crescent moon.

A dozen wolves or more howl somewhere far away and I want to join my voice with theirs. I open my mouth for a silly little howl, but before I can even squeak a new voice pops into my head. It's not August, it's not Joachim, but I know I've heard it before.

"I'm coming for you, princess."

I shiver at the darkness that rolls across me with his promise, and jump up, pound on the door until Will lets me in and fall gasping for air into Maggie's waiting arms.

AUGUST

*J*t's a damn good thing Joachim and Vas had a plan for keeping me busy all night because with nothing to do, I would have either fucked my own hand raw, or Ekataryn. She and I have mated in every single one of our shared lives and I have never felt a need for her this intense before.

Joachim is right. This time is different with all four of us here and alive at the same time. The Volkovs have won too many rounds in our war for her soul. It's about fucking time we win a round. More than that, we need to take the fight to them and end their tyranny over wolfkind. With her, we can.

If Grigory will get his head out of his ass. Which, right now, seems unlikely. Not that I ever thought he would. Especially now that I'm standing in his lair.

I fucking hate this place.

Vas is sniffing around the entrance to the ruins of what used to be a beautiful onion-domed church that brought us all back to our lives in Kievan Rus. The first thing Grigory did upon being thrown into our eternal prison a hundred years ago was burn this church to the ground.

That was just the beginning of his descent.

He turned his back on us and I'm having a real hard time seeing why we're here in his lair seeking him out. He doesn't deserve her anymore.

Joachim is inside the main sanctuary like a dumbass. If Grigory was in there, he'd already have Joachim pinned to the ground by the throat.

I call to them both. *"He isn't here and there isn't even a scent of him."*

If we didn't know this was where he spent his time between his vigilante murder sprees, I'd think this part of the island was completely abandoned. It smells like shadow and nothing.

Joachim lies down at the front of the church and I get the feeling he's not going anywhere. *"He'll be here. You two go on and get to the alphas you want to come to the mating ritual. I will take care of Grigory."*

Vas doesn't need to be told twice. He may not have said anything, but it's not hard to tell how much disdain he has for the lair and its master. More even than me. He takes off toward the coast and I follow. It's not like he's going to invite anyone to this shindig. I have to do all the talking.

There are a few packs that aren't outlaw, but aren't political prisoners either so don't live in the *derevnya*. We talked about inviting them into the fold, and even brought one small group as a trial. Each and everyone of them were dead by the next day. The Dark Prince of Wolves decided for us that no other packs could live in the little community of good people.

Not that it's any safer on the coast or in the forest. He kills indiscriminately when the fancy strikes.

It's why I built my cabin just outside the *derevnya's* boundaries. It's why Joachim roams the forest and has no home. And why Vas splits his time between the two of us.

I don't like it, but we pick three packs with alphas who aren't complete shitheads to come and witness the mating. They'll spread the word among the other packs by telling the tale from wolf to wolf. It takes us well past dawn to find each pack and its leader, then to convince them this isn't a trap and that yes, I've found my true mate. Clueless bastards.

When we get back to the *derevnya* I expect to see people going to and fro, making preparations for tonight. Every home is shut up tight and quiet. Then I see it. The well in the center of the circle of cabins has been burned and the carefully placed stone wall torn to shreds.

Vas and I go on high alert and sniff the air and ground looking for the scents of our foe or foes. The snow around the well is trampled with a half dozen paw prints including one lion. Thank goodness Will was here. But if he's gone off chasing the miscreants who've attacked while Vas and I were on invite duty, then who is protecting Ekataryn?

The hair on the back of my neck and tail stand up, alert and reaching out to sense the danger among us.

I bolt for Maggie's cabin and find the door broken off its hinges. Dear Goddess, no. My feet are made of lead, stalking into the room and looking at the signs of struggle and clues to where the bastards have taken my mate. The door to the larder is covered in scratch marks, but it stands.

I paw it open, it's not even locked. My heart pounds in my chest so hard it physically hurts. The room is empty. But there is no other exit. They've been taken. I will kill every wolf on this island and burn it to the ground if one hair on her head is harmed

Vas starts tracking the scents from the larder door, nose to the floor and walks straight into the little room. He sniffs up the walls and then scratches at the shelves. He's the best tracker and my nose can't smell anything but my own damn anxiety. I wish he would fucking talk to me.

He turns and yips at me. *"She's safe."*

For one brief moment, I bow my head and thank whatever God Joachim prays to these days. *"Take me to her."*

We run back out the front door and straight to the barn. Maggie and Ekataryn are huddled together, holding on to each other. I don't smell blood and don't see any bruising or any other injuries. The pain in my heart releases and I can breathe again.

I shift and go over, dropping to my knees and wrap them both in my arms. Maggie takes a deep breath, but Ekataryn is trembling. "Was it the Prince?"

I don't smell him, but I couldn't earlier either.

"No." Maggie responds with a firm irritation. She gives Taryn a squeeze and they release each other, safe now. "It was the Naryshkins and some other wolves I didn't recognize. Will went after them. Is he back yet?"

Fucking Lev. I have no problem hunting him down and tearing his throat out for this. In fact, where did Vas go? "He isn't back. I'm sure he's fine, just chasing them off. How did you escape? We followed your scent to the larder, but then Vas found you here."

Maggie stands up and brushes the dirt off and pats me on the shoulder, then touches Ekataryn's hair. "That's between me and Taryn." She leaves the two of us to comfort the residual fear out of each other

I shouldn't have gone off and left her alone when I knew damn well that she was still vulnerable. "Come here, my love."

She hasn't said a word, but she isn't trembling anymore. She crawls into my lap and wraps her arms around my neck. Before I can ask her anything more, she kisses me and pushes her hands into my hair. This is no soft welcome home, she's dueling with my tongue and biting at my lips like I did to her yesterday.

"Claim me now, August. I don't care about the ritual." She reaches for her skirt and pulls the hem up to her waist. She's naked underneath and I can smell her arousal. But the scent of her fear and frustration are also in my nose, pushing into the places of my mind that wants to do as she asks.

"Ekataryn, stop." She doesn't listen and slides one hand down my side, tracing over the scars from yesterday's battle then across my thighs and between my legs. My cock is already hard for her and I can't resist letting her touch me.

She wraps her hand around my cock and I cover hers with my fist, letting her lead, but showing her how much pressure I want her to use. Together we stroke up and down and I love the sound of her breath hitching as she watches my cock grow bigger and harder for her.

"Are you ready? Because I am." She puts her hands on my shoulders and straddles me, ready to sink down onto my cock and ride me.

God, I want that, want to feel her cunt squeezing me in her tight heat as she bounces up and down on me, using me for her pleasure. But not until after I properly claim her and we mate in the way that will satisfy my wolf. It needs her submission, to dominate her and her pleasure.

My mouth waters and the wolf pushes at me to flip her over and take her hard and fast, right now. Then she will be mine and she will be safe.

But no one else will know and she and I both need that. We can draw this community together and make it a safer, stronger place by doing the mating ritual in the traditional way. I know that I pushed against it, but Joachim was right all along.

"Ekataryn, no. I'm not ready. This is not the way."

"I'm pretty sure this is exactly how it works. You're a man, wolf, man-wolf, and I'm a woman. Your cock is hard, my pussy is wet, and we both want it. This is the way." She sinks lower and I can literally feel the heat between her legs.

Fucking hell, what is wrong with me?

I want this to be right for her, that's what. It is what she would want if she truly knew who she was. Since I can't tell her, I will be stronger than my fucking libido and do the right thing. I grab her waist and hold her still, barely poised over my weeping cock. Damn, it would be so easy to thrust up into her and... no. "We will wait until the mating ceremony."

She wiggles her ass and fuck, I almost cave. "You know you want this, August. There is no need to wait."

"You're a temptress. Which I love, by the way, but we will wait." But not if she wiggles that ass again. I stand up, hauling her up and over my shoulder. I leave her skirt pushed up and her ass bare under my hand. It is in for a spanking later that we'll both enjoy.

She kicks her feet, but that does nothing but make me dig my fingers into her soft flesh. "August, please. I'm scared. Those wolves today wanted to take me."

Her words are less filled with fear and more frustration. Good, I'd rather have her irritated with me than frightened. "I know, and I will fucking kill them. After they get to see me claim you."

"I don't want to wait until tonight." She sighs and hangs like a limp bag of potatoes. "I didn't even want to wait until this morning."

I don't like waiting either, but there is something more going on than just her fear of Lev. Will and Maggie took care of her and she is safe now. Besides, the attack on the *derevnya* just happened. What had her nervous through the night?

I carry her back to Maggie's and a few of the others from next door are already helping to repair her door. That gives us a minute to talk alone inside. I slip past Maggie and she nods, understanding that we need a minute.

She slides off my shoulder and sits on the bench in front of the fire, staring into it and not at me. I squat beside her. "What aren't you telling me?"

Her eyes flick down, then back to the fire. She's about to lie to me.

"There's nothing else. I just want us to be mated." She wraps an arm across her body. "That will make me feel safe."

And there it is, the lie. Not the part about nothing else. That's just her trying to protect me. She doesn't think she'll be safe once we're mated.

Is it because she needs Joachim to mate with her too? She hasn't even formed a bond with Vas yet. I don't believe she'll ever be able to reach Grigory.

Grigory.

That fucker.

He's figured out she's here. I don't know how, but he has and he got to her.

I will not allow his mission of vengeance to hurt her. She's going to think I'm insane for doing a one-eighty from a moment ago, but everything just changed. "Come on. We're going to get mated, in the sacred circle. Right now."

I grab her hand and haul her up. Where the hell are Vas and Joachim? They're the only witnesses I care about. Shit, and Will, who isn't back from chasing Lev and his cronies off. I stick my head back out the open door. "Maggie, you have a way to communicate with Will? I need him to meet us at the sacred circle, I mean the chapel in the woods, as soon as possible."

She looks at me like I'm a recalcitrant child and stares at where I'm holding Ekataryn's hand. "Hold your horses, boy. He and I have mindspeak the same as you, but what's the rush?"

"Change of plans. Mating ceremony is right now." I take a half a step before Maggie waves one single finger at me in the no-no-no motion.

"Nope. You've got these people here all worked up. They fought off Lev and Peter and some other yahoos today when you weren't available because they want this mating ritual to happen. Bridget and Killisi want to renew their bonds with their mates seeing as they never got a proper ceremony. You're both running scared but you will calm your tits and bide your time to do what is right for your people, dammit."

Our people. Ekataryn's. She's been here a day and they've taken to her as the wolves under her care always do.

Ekataryn squeezes my hand. "Sorry Maggie. You're right. We can wait. I want to give everyone a reason to celebrate. I just got scared is all and I put that on August. I'll be okay now that he's here with me."

She's being brave and I love her for it. But she needs more than just me. *"Vasily, Joachim. We need you back here. Come as soon as you can."*

I don't get an answer from either of them and that worries me. I can't do the ritual without them anyway.

I take over fixing Maggie's door and the women invite the other she-wolfs over to do whatever it is they do to prepare for a mating ritual. I may have claimed Ekataryn for my mate more times than I can count over the years, but I have never known what they do before a ritual. They always smell so nice though, so I assume it has something to do with flowers.

One by one, the alphas of the three packs we've invited roll into town. None cause even a bit of trouble and indeed help with the preparations. This is too easy and it's making me nervous as shit.

As the sun sets, Vas and Joachim still aren't back from wherever the hell they are, and it's making my skin itch. Will returned as if he'd only been out on an afternoon stroll, but I did see Maggie treating a wound on his forearm with some of her silver magic healing balm. Something went down out there and he's brushing it off like it's no big deal.

"Where the fuck are you two?" I call to the other wolf guard again and this time Joachim at least replies.

"I'm on my way to the sacred circle. Vasily isn't coming."

Dammit. She would want him there. I get that he's still hurting from when he lost her in their last life, but I thought he'd come around. The two of us will have to be enough.

There's no way I'm letting Joachim get out of this mating

tonight. He can keep whatever secrets he wants, but he will be there for her as she wishes, just as he reminded me that I needed to be.

I glance up at the sky and know that if we could see through this damn ever-thick cloud cover blocking out the moon, it would be shining bright in the sky. I have to set aside my fears and put my faith in the good people I've protected these past few hundred years that they will now protect me and my mate.

I haven't seen Ekataryn since she sequestered herself in with the women, so I reach out to her mind. *"Ready now, my tzaritsa?"*

Her words come back to me with a laugh and I'm grateful that she's feeling better about whatever had her so worried earlier. *"I was born ready."*

Ah, if she only knew how true that was. *"I will meet you in the sacred circle. Don't be long. I'm anxious to make you my true mate tonight."*

She gives me a mental shove and that's all I need to ensure that she's ready and just waiting on me to get this ceremony started.

I run through the forest in my wolf form, wanting to check the surrounds out and make sure there are no unwelcome guests hiding about. Every few minutes I run into another of the male wolves from the *derevnya* standing guard along the path to the chapel of trees.

We are blessed to have these people here with us, though I don't wish this fate on any of them. I give each of them a mental nod and my thanks knowing that they have my back and will keep Ekataryn, Joachim and me safe.

When I get to the chapel in the woods, our newly designated sacred circle, I'm flabbergasted by it's new appearance. We all know that the true mate bond must be fulfilled under a full moon and that there is no way for us to have that with the constant cloud cover.

The chapel entrance has been covered with the moon flower

vines, and when I go into the sanctuary, a sort of chandelier has been raised in the center and is also covered in the white flowers. It's as if the moon is glowing down on us. It's absolutely perfect.

A few more male wolves join me and I'm glad to have them as witnesses. A few are mated and I swell with pride that they will be renewing their bonds with their mates along with us. This is what it means to be part of a community, part of a pack.

I shift and they follow suit. I wish Joachim and Vas were here with us too. While everything about this mating ceremony will be ideal for Ekataryn, it's missing that something special without the rest of the guard here with me.

As if I've conjured him with my thoughts, Joachim finally walks into the chapel. Where the rest of us are naked, he is wearing his robes and looking very official. There are lines of exhaustion across his face and the set of his shoulders too. It's more than lack of sleep.

I won't press him on where he's been or what he's been doing because I know wherever and whatever, it's all for her. He joins me at the front of the circle and claps me on the arm. Despite his trying night, he's here when I need him the most.

"Vas?"

Joachim shakes his head.

"He'll come around." He's broken and angry with something to prove. I get it, I was in his same mind for a long time too.

The forest around us goes quiet and Will, in his enormous lion form strides into the sanctuary. He truly is the king of all beasts and they still in his presence. I'm grateful he's here.

Behind him a row of women in wispy white robes and moon flowers in their hair walk in single file. Maggie leads them and Jeanette, Bridget, and Killisi follow behind. They each pair off with their mates who stare at them moonstruck. Poor saps.

Then I see her.

Ekataryn floats in like something out of a dream. She's draped in flowering vines to make up her mating robes and they perfectly outline her lush curves, those gorgeous hips I want to grab onto and never let go, her full breasts that I want to get lost in, and that ass and those thighs that I will spend hours worshipping with my mouth, tongue, and cock.

I feel as though she has both taken my breath away and breathed new life into me. She makes me whole and I hope I can do even a part of the same for her.

Joachim leans over and whispers to me. "She's glowing for you."

It shouldn't be possible, since there is no full moon and that's when true mates glow for each other. But she is glowing for me, and I am for her. She is my moon.

TARYN

*M*aggie and the other women in the *derevnya* made the chapel more gorgeous than I ever could have imagined. I don't know what a mating ritual is supposed to be like, but if this isn't it, it should be. The moon flowers decorate the walls and are hung from the branches of the trees in beautiful designs. In the center, all the biggest blooms are grouped together in an enormous ball that I swear is filling the whole place with a romantic light just as if the moon was shining down on us.

At the very front of the sanctuary is the best part.

Both August and Joachim are waiting for me. I want to run to them but control myself because this feels like a more solemn occasion and less like the orgy sex party I thought we were having.

I don't know if it's the light from the moon flowers or if I'm imagining things, but I swear the two of them have a shimmering glow to them. None of the other people gathered have the same radiant light and I decide it must be my feelings for them manifesting like an enchantment. Strange and special magic happens on this island, even if it's supposed to be for the damned. I'm going to take advantage of every moment I have here.

And I know one thing for sure. When the opportunity comes to escape and get back to the real world, I'm taking my wolves with me. Whoever is waiting for me on the other side will understand. I have to believe that.

August takes my hand and for the longest time we just stare into each other's eyes. I'm not sure when it happened, but I've fallen in love with him. It's not only the intensity of the marking, or the way he lives to protect me and keep me safe.

He sees me. Even when I don't know who I am, August does. Not the me from long ago, but the woman I am here and now. I didn't know how much I wanted that in my life. I think I didn't have that in the world on the other side of the fog and the Nothing.

I want to reach out for Joachim too, but he's keeping himself guarded. He isn't ready and I worry that it will be hard for him to see August claim and mate me when he won't allow himself to do the same. But at least he is here and I'll have him any way he wants to be tonight. When he's ready, I'll find out what is keeping him from opening his heart to me.

For now, I give him a smile but keep my hands to myself. He's done so much to make sure I have what I need, am happy, and comfortable. I will do the same for him.

Relief passes across his face and he nods to me, then to August. "Are you ready, *boginya*?"

"Yes. Very." My nerves are gone. I want this joining. I want more, but it all starts with August and that feels right in my soul.

"Ready, Guard of the house of the Rising Moon?"

I've never heard Joachim call August anything so formal. I know he told me part of what he was called had this title in it, but there's something extra special in the ceremonial ritual sound of it. August nods and replies, "I am."

Father Joachim holds up his hands and spreads them wide over his head. "We gather together in this, our sacred circle to honor the Goddess of the Moon who bestowed upon us the very nature of our wolves and gave us the light by which to find our way to our true fated mates."

Ooh. The Goddess of the Moon. Fancy. I knew Father Joachim's belief wasn't simply in any ordinary religion.

"If your fated mate be here, declare your claim on them and let your pack know that they are yours and that you belong to them."

August takes my hand and holds it over his heart just as I did after he marked me. "I claim you, Ekataryn--"

He's so serious and it's abso-freaking-adorable. I don't want to break the moment, but I have to make sure one thing is clear before we get to the good stuff. "Taryn."

He frowns and gets this cute wrinkle between his eyebrows. "What?"

"I know I am Ekataryn to you and I want to remember when you called me that, but right now I don't and I want you to claim me here and now as I am." I hope this mating ritual pushes my mind like the claiming did, but even if it doesn't, I want to belong to him and him to me as we are in this time, in this life.

"Taryn," he nods and I see the satisfaction in his face at saying my name, "I claim you as my mate. You are mine and I am yours for all time."

Joachim takes up August's hand and places it over my heart. "You don't also have to declare your claim, but I think you'll get a lot of satisfaction out of doing so."

I place my hand over the two of theirs. Joachim swallows and pulls his away. I get a little ping of sadness and see in the set of his chin and the shadow in his eyes that he doesn't think he's worthy of my love. He is and someday I'll prove it to him. Before we leave this prison.

I let him go, but am pleased that he doesn't step away. Maybe there is hope for him yet. "August, my rising moon, I claim you as my mate. I am yours and you are mine for all time."

A blue light ignites in his eyes and I swear the wolf is looking back at me. He throws his head back and howls, sending a quiver of desire spiraling from the top of my head, down my belly and across my legs. Joachim joins his howl and then another wolf's cry from far away echoes through the night.

The howls resound through the chapel and each and every person lifts their voices up. I am overwhelmed by their chorus and the love and joy in their song fills up all my empty places inside until I feel like I'm overflowing.

August ends his call, smiles down at me, filling me with all the good ooey gooey warm and fuzzies on the inside, and then gives me a fast, deep kiss that is much too quick. "Friends, join us in the sacred circle to witness the claiming and renew your own bonds."

The other men and women move forward and the ones who are paired off begin their own dances of love under the moon of flowers. Dresses drop, they reach for each other and a few even shift together to mate in their wolf forms.

A few of the men gather around us but not too near. I'm slightly nervous about them watching even though I know this is an important part of the ritual to August. He cups my cheek and gives me another kiss, this one slower and more sensual. "This is just you and me and our pleasure. Don't worry about anyone you don't want to."

Okay, that I can do. I bring August's hand up to the edge of the filmy dress that the women gifted to me. He growls in that sexy way and I can't wait to hear him say my name in that same husky bass when he comes for me. I take a quick inhale and reach for Joachim's hand again hoping that he won't pull away. He swallows hard but doesn't retreat.

134

Together they find the loose ties of the flowery vines holding it on and the dress falls to the ground, pooling around my feet. August licks his lips and if I wasn't so excited about what was coming next I'd tease him for being a drooling wolf about to eat me up.

Joachim is breathing hard and I can see he is about to pull away from us. I don't want him to so I'd better do something fast. With a quick glance back at August, I send him a mental image of what I want.

"Fuck, yes." He steps behind me and pushes me to a kneeling position on the ground in front of Father Joachim. I bite my lip, wanting so much to open those priest's robes of his, but knowing that if I don't let him do that himself, it won't mean as much. He has to choose this.

August drops to the ground behind me and pushes my legs open with his. He wraps one arm around my waist and pulls me tight against his body. "Do you feel how hard I am for you, sweet tzaritsa? I'm going to fuck you so deep that you won't know where I end and you begin."

I lay my head back on his shoulder, relishing his touch, but keep my eyes on Father Joachim. August slides his hand lower and cups my pussy, then he drops his face to my throat and scrapes his teeth across my mark from him. I shudder and press my hips forward against his hand.

It's hard not to let my eyes drift shut and revel in the sensations running through my body. I want to be present and deliberate about every moment. I'm already missing so many memories and I never want this one taken away from me. I'm searing everything about tonight into my brain, all of August's body, his love, his claim on me.

I also want Father Joachim to experience them too. I want him to see me becoming August's mate and I want him to join us.

"You're already so wet for me. After I fuck you and mark you with my seed, I'm going to spend a long time licking this delicious cunt." He slides two of his fingers along my pussy lips, teasing me and drawing more juices from me, circling my clit, pushing me too close to coming with just his simplest of touches. When I'm sure I'm about to go insane if he doesn't make me come, he opens my legs wider and pushes his way between my legs, but not into my pussy, taunting me even more.

"August. Please."

"Soon, love. I want your body to be more than ready for my claiming because it will not be soft and gentle." He withdraws his fingers and brings them up to my face, painting my lips with my own juices. Then he turns my head and nips and licks at the side of my mouth.

My heart is beating so fast and I'm dying for him to complete the claiming. But I do want him to tease Joachim. He knows exactly what to do before I even think it. August holds his wet fingers out to Joachim. "Taste her, Joachim, and see what you're missing."

Joachim's adam's apple bobs up and down. "I can't."

"You can," August growls and dips his fingers into me again.

Joachim's eyes are dark and on fire at the same time. "I won't."

"Then you can watch as I take her knowing she wanted you as well." August slides his cock between my legs and I groan as he pushes the tip through my folds. "Watch as I claim her, fuck her, and make her mine, knowing she could also be yours."

He lowers his head to my throat again and sets his teeth at my mark. He pushes his cock inside of my channel in one long, deep thrust, pinches my clit between his fingers, and bites into my skin. It's so much more than I ever imagined and I'm soaring through the sensations. My body clenches around his and the orgasm I've been waiting for slams into me. I shut my eyes, seeing lights and rainbows explode behind my eyelids. August doesn't move, just fills me with his body.

A thousand million trillion years later he licks my mark and his fingers begin a slow swirl around my clit, drawing the orgasm out. "I love to feel your cunt trying to milk my cock."

Having him inside of me is better than I could have imagined. Everything is... more when we're joined like this. The scent of the moon flowers mixed with the tangy pine of the trees is everywhere. The air around us is thick on my skin and the noises of both love making and fucking are like a song I'd forgotten.

When I open my eyes again, I see exactly what I've been craving. Joachim has his robe open and his hand on his cock. August makes his first long withdrawal and thrusts back into me. Joachim's hand slides up and down his cock, matching August's movements.

With each stroke, August whispers in my ear. "I claim you, you're mine, you're safe, I'll protect you, you're mine, you're mine, mine."

I am. I'm totally and utterly August's in this perfect moment, and he is mine.

The same for Joachim. He may not be ready to share his body with me, but in my mind, I have claimed him and I'm not letting go of either of them. Ever.

With every thrust now, August is growling and pushing faster, harder, and deeper. I swear he feels bigger each time he pushes into me and the head of his cock is hitting me in all the right places. And still I want more of him. There is something not yet fulfilled in this mating and not knowing what is consuming me.

I want to be even more connected, bound to August in a very real way, not just with words. He's panting in my ear, groaning, and growling and I want to push him over the edge into his own orgasm. I'm so close, but my body keeps building and building, winding so tight, but won't break and let us both fall into the bliss of coming together.

Joachim stares down at us and bites his lip. He's holding himself back too. That's not what I want at all. His teeth digging into the soft bow of his mouth so hard and it gives me the idea I've been searching for. I grasp August's wrists and pull his hand from between my legs. His fingers glisten with my juices, and I know seeing me taste his fingers will spur them both closer to coming.

I want their seed, it's mine and it's what I'm missing.

With my eyes on Joachim's, I suck August's fingers into my mouth and swirl my tongue around, tasting the tang of my arousal mixed with the salty sweetness of his skin. Joachim's wolf flashes through his eyes and his glow intensifies.

"Taryn, yes." August falters in his rhythm and squeezes my hip even tighter than before, holding me in place, then fucks me even faster. My pussy is fluttering, my clit pounding, along to the beat of my heart.

Joachim's lips move, murmuring an incantation or prayer I can't hear. I release August's finger and lick my lips. I'd love to use my tongue on the drops forming at the tip of his cock. I know he won't let me, yet. I'm not done pushing at either of their restraints.

I open my mouth and bare my teeth. I may not have the fangs of a wolf, but my own little canines will do. I lift August's wrist back to my mouth and scrape my teeth across his skin, in the same way he did to me.

"Fu-uck." August growls and presses his flesh harder against my mouth, wanting me to bite him.

Joachim's thighs tremble and his cock jerks. A bulge near the base swells and grows into a knot of flesh. He snarls and grips the knot with his other hand. His seed spurts from him and baptizes my chest and throat. He slashes his hand over his cock again and again until he's given me every last trace of his essence.

He drops to his knees and hangs his head in front of me. No, no, I don't want him ashamed of what we've done. I grab his chin as he did to me during the marking and make him look at me. When his eyes have come up and he's holding my gaze, I let his face go and swirl a finger into the seed on my breasts.

I bring a large drop up and smear it on August's wrist, then I bite down, combining Joachim's seed with August's blood in my mouth.

August roars and shoves into me deeper than he's ever been. I can feel the same knot that swelled on Father's Joachim's cock push into me and my pussy stretches to take August in all the way. His hips jolt against my butt and he snarls. His front pushes against my back and then he rips his arm from my mouth and digs into my shoulders, pushing my face to the ground. Instead of dirt, my cheek lands on Joachim's thigh and he shoves his hands into my hair, holding me down for August to truly complete the claiming.

My heart is beating so fast and hard that it's going to explode. Instead of it going, my whole body detonates into an agonizing release. August rocks his hips, pushing that knot harder and deeper into me until we can't be separated ever again. Finally his cock convulses inside of me and he empties his seed into my channel, calling my name and claiming me in the way I need.

"Mine, Taryn, mine."

I close my eyes and savor the fullness of August's body locked with mine. Joachim's grip on my scalp releases and he pets my hair, crooning a prayer over me.

Behind my eyes, in the floating bliss of being so well claimed, I find a memory of me and August in an opulent Winter palace that I've built as the gem of the empire. I'm changing life for both peasants and wolves.

August and I are locked together in this same way, becoming mates once again. Two other men are watching us together, witnessing his claim on me. I feel I know them, but can't place either of their faces in my memory, but I know their bodies because they have also claimed me.

Joachim is missing from this scene and I wonder where he is.

My memory flashes again, and I remember being on my knees at the altar of a huge church where Joachim is bestowing the church's blessing on two young men. He's going to declare my brothers tzars of Russia, but everyone knows I'll be the one ruling.

Ruling over men and wolves.

Another figure is there, hiding in the shadows and he scares me. He wants something I don't like giving him.

My mind flashes again and I'm in another palace. I'm a princess and my father is the Tzar of all Russia. The man in the shadows is there again and he's with my mother. But she's not a wolf, so how can she be?

The men from the memory in the palace are there and they're hurrying me from my bedroom. The Volkovs have made trouble for my father and there's a revolution. We have to escape. "Anastasia, hurry, come with me."

The memories are all right there in my head, but I don't understand them. I only know that I've just seen pieces of my missing soul and a shadow that will never let me regain all that has been stolen from me.

AUGUST

I told Taryn that at some point tonight, I will be buried so far inside of her, that she won't know where she ends and I begin. That was close to being accurate.

My cock is held tight in her cunt, my wolf's knot locking us together, my seed filling her, but I'm the one who can't comprehend how we aren't one soul reunited.

I've had a lot of sex with my tzaritsa over her lifetimes, and it's always mind blowing. Those times were tiny blips compared to the ferocity of our mating tonight. I thought I could control her, make her submit to me as is the way in a claiming and mating.

When she bit me and put her moon mark on my skin, I was transported back to the night I was first initiated into the temple at Uruk and became a member of the house of the rising moon. Joachim, Vasily, and Grigory were all there too although we had very different names back then.

Her love for me then was just as strong then as it is tonight and I am humbled. Where did it all go so wrong?

I won't think about that now. I have her in my arms once again, and she is safe now with my wolf's claim on her body to keep any others from trying to use her or take her away. My wolf is not yet satisfied and until I am sure she is no longer vulnerable, we will be locked together by the bulging knot at the base of my cock.

Not that I mind having my dick all up in her delicious heat. It gives me time to trace her gorgeous curves and imagine all the ways I will pleasure her body in the nights to come. I love that she has meat on her bones. It means that she has been at least well cared for and fed in her life outside this prison. I've worried a thousand nights, wondering if the sycophants the Volkovs charged with raising her this time would treat her well or abuse their place of privilege in wolf society.

I send one hand caressing down her side, loving the feel as my fingers dip into that favorite curve where her waist meets her hips and then run my touch over the swell of her rear nestled against me. I love the plump globes of her butt cheeks. They're going to cup my cock and hips fantastically when I get around to fucking her ass.

Which would be even better if Joachim or Vasily would join me, taking her between us, one in her cunt and one in her tight rear. My cock gives a jerk, liking that idea very much, and this is no way to calm my wolf so that the knot releases. At this rate, I'm going to have to make her come again and milk my cock dry before we can go home.

Or even better, if Joachim would quit his quest to destroy his own soul for some damn reason and put his face between her legs to get her off while I'm buried inside of her, she would fucking love that. It's always best when two or more of us take her at the same time. But never as good as when all four come together to worship her as she deserves.

Taryn rouses from the blissful aftermath of her orgasms and moves like she can get away. "Ah, ah, ah, my love. You're not going anywhere. My wolf still wants to know that you are mine for a bit longer."

She reaches between her legs, but I'm filling her so deep she can do nothing but scrape her fingers across my balls. "August, you make me feel so full, so complete. I don't ever want to move. Can we just lie here together forever?"

"Yes," I say and cuddle her in my arms so she doesn't get cold. Except I notice for the first time since I came to the Island of the Damned, the ground isn't frozen. Perhaps we melted all the snow and even the permafrost with the heat of our love making.

I lift my head and look around. There are three other couples resting in the sacred circle with us and a half dozen men and wolves surrounding, keeping guard. None are shivering in the frigid Siberian winter air. There is no snow on the ground in the chapel. But there are more sprouts of moon flowers and incredibly, fresh green tufts of grass.

"Joachim." He's still on his knees near our heads, rolling his prayer beads between his fingers. Atoning for his sins tonight, I'm sure.

He pauses in his prayers. "I know. Look up."

The trees overhead form an arch creating the enclosed space, but the sky is still visible through the pine boughs. The clouds have parted and a crescent moon, a rising moon, hangs in the sky. "Holy shit."

"That isn't what I'd say is holy, but yes." He glances down at Taryn and the look on his face makes me want to tear his heart out for keeping it from her. He gets up, his robes back in place and raises his arms. "Come one and all, rouse from your mating bliss, and join us back in the *derevnya*, to revel in this break in the eternal winter, share a meal, and raise our cups to our friends lucky enough to be mated. Praise be to the Goddess, thanks be to God."

Chittering goes through the people about what could have caused the weather to change for the first time in all of our combined years in this frozen hell hole. Some are worried it portends destruction and others the end of our banishment.

Taryn grabs my arm thrown over her hip and gives the mark of the crescent moon on my wrist a soft kiss. My wolf likes that and the knot in my cock wanes and I reluctantly pull myself from her body. She gives a little groan and then a light laugh. "I hope there's more where that came from later."

"Oh, I promise there is plenty more for you. If all stays calm now that she is claimed, and it should, there is no reason for the other alphas to come trying to steal her away, then we'll have plenty of time to spend hours and hours, days and days in my cabin fucking each other's brains out.

My cabin is absolutely the best place for her to be. Even that sliver of moon could expose her to the Dark Prince and that is a risk I'm not willing to take. I didn't want her going out at night before, when the clouds covered the sky and there was no chance of the moonlight shining down upon her.

Now with the rising moon staring right down at us, she needs to stay hidden away safe from his vengeance.

"Joachim, we need to get her inside as soon as possible." He nods and picks up her discarded mating dress and brings it over. It offers little protection, but it's better than nothing. For the first time in my life, I wish the sun would rise already.

I would worry less about our trek back to the *derevnya*, if Vas was here to help guard her. I try calling out to him with no reply. I heard him raise his voice with ours in our howl during the mating ceremony so I know he's about. I have to trust that he isn't wallowing in misery somewhere, but out patrolling the area around the chapel to keep her safe.

I don't scent any disturbance, battles, or blood in the air so for now, I'll leave him be and see to her safety myself. But some time soon, he and I are going to have a come to Jesus talk. Or maybe that's better left to Joachim.

"Taryn, we need to hurry back to the *derevnya*. I don't want you out in the open at night, but we're not waiting for sunrise. Walk with Father Joachim. I'm going to shift and scout around to make sure there aren't any dangers waiting along the path."

We get up and she gives me a soft, lingering kiss. "Okay, my protector. I'm sure everything will be fine and I'll see you back at Will and Maggie's in no time."

Will left soon after the mating began, taking Maggie with him, I suspect for a little love-making of their own. Lions' mating rituals with whatever Maggie is doesn't involve witnesses, and they prefer to keep their sex life private. I find that thought strange, but to each their own.

The path to the *derevnya* is littered with flowers and not just the moon blossoms. All kinds of plants are pushing up through the ground and if this continues, we'll be having a gorgeous Russian summer before long.

I scent fire somewhere far off, in the direction of the burned church. Either the Dark Prince has been on the hunt or a pack has ventured into his territory. Either way, he will be occupied and not anywhere near our neck of the woods. I'm grateful at least for that.

There are many more delicious smells coming from the circle of cabins and I can hardly wait to see what kind of treats the good people have made for this shared celebration. Maggie and Joachim were right, our people needed something to celebrate. While I'm angry that something happened in Taryn's life to get her thrown in here, I have to believe fate had something to do with bringing her to us, and what better honor is there to celebrate among wolves?

I trot back and forth along the path, relieving the other sentries of their guard duty. Taryn and Joachim come down the path past the boulders on the west side of the *derevnya* and the moon is going down in the sky behind them. The way she glows takes my breath every time I think about the fact that she is mine once again. I'm happy to see he's let her take his arm and they're walking together and not acting awkward. She'll win him over yet.

I run back up to the boulders and nip at her ankles to get her to move faster. She gives a playful swipe at my snout, missing by a long shot, but my task is accomplished. In no time she's at the doors to the barn and being greeted by Maggie.

I shift near the entrance and Will hands me a robe. "Maggie says no naked penises near her food. I'm inclined to agree. Especially those creamy-filled pastries, she's magicked up somehow. Wouldn't want any questions about what's inside."

I shake my head and wrinkle my nose at him. But that's the first table Taryn has gone to and I laugh out loud as she bites into the long, round dessert and white goo squirts out the end. She knows exactly what she's done and waggles her eyebrows at me.

I join her and kiss the cream right off her lips. "I hope there's more where that came from, tzaritsa."

She grins and arousal dances in an adorable blush across her cheeks. "Why do you call me that? I like it, but does it have a special meaning?"

I've seen flashes of recognition in her eyes when I use the pet name, ever since I marked her. "In our last life together, you were the queen of all Russia. Ekataryn Velikaya, Catherine the Great, Empress of both man and wolf. But you were my delectable tzaritsa."

She gasps and clasps me on the arm. "Oh, that's when we lived in the Winter Palace together. I remember, not all of it, just a little, but I have a memory of--

Taryn blushes and I think I know exactly which particular memory she's recovered. "Is it the one where I fucked you in the royal baths then we fed each other and planned out a whole curriculum of courses in how to sexually pleasure your partner for your new university?"

She smacks my arm. "We never did that."

146

Pushing her memories could be fun. "Indeed we did. Perhaps it was the time when everyone mistakenly took me for a horse and accused you of bestiality."

"August," she snort-laughs my name.

"I've heard from newcomers to the island that this particular rumor has lived on well past our lifetimes."

A dark cloud passes through her eyes and she lowers her voice. "And do you know how we died?"

Shit. "I did not die. That is the life in which the Volkovs discovered who I truly am to you and threw me in this banished hell to live an eternal torment without you. But I have it on good authority that you died peacefully as an old woman." I leave out the part about a peaceful death being a rare occurrence for her.

Maybe someday she can get Vas to tell her the story, because he was the lone guard at her side on November seventeenth, seventeen ninety-six.

"Hold on, I don't know much about history," she taps her forehead indicating the lapses in her memory, "but the reign of Catherine the Great was a long time ago. Are you telling me you've been here all that time? How are you not dead?"

Oops. It appears none of us took the initiative to explain how time doesn't move forward on the island of the damned. Save for grievous wounds, we are essentially immortal. "I have been here without you for over two-hundred years."

"What?" She turns to Joachim for confirmation. "And you?"

He nods in confirmation. "More than three-hundred years."

"You guys are making a joke, pulling my leg, this is insanity. Next you'll tell me Will and Maggie have been here for like a thousand years. She looks great for being a millennium old." Taryn rolls her eyes and takes another bite of her treat.

Will comes over and hands out a round of his famous brew. "She's not a day over... wait, what year is it?"

"Uilliam mac Eanric, if you even dare to forget my eight-hundred and fifty-first birthday, you're never getting laid again," Maggie calls from the other side of the barn.

Will leans over to me and loudly whispers. "You have no idea how hard it is to come up with eight-hundred years worth of birthday presents."

Joachim takes a swig of the brew and hands the empty cup back to Will. "I recommend multiple orgasms. Mates always appreciate those."

I nearly spit my drink out my nose. Joachim walks away to greet Jeanette and her mate to the party leaving the three of us to stare at each other open mouthed.

More people and wolves file into the party and behind their heads in the open door, I can see the sun rising high into the sky. Relief washes through me like a cool drink of water. The Dark Prince never attacks during the day. I can let my vigilance over her safety loosen up just enough and let her have fun at her own mating party.

I hug her to me and give her a quick kiss on the head. "Your memories will return in time. Then you can tell me about the lives I've missed since you were Empress."

Taryn's smile lights up her whole face and I look forward to many years getting to bask in her glow. But a moment later that light is darkened by the worst kind of shadow. Fear.

A chorus of unholy howls blasts like an alarm outside. My guard goes right back up and I push Taryn behind me. The Dark Prince may not attack during the day, but the Naryshkins would. If ever Lev needed to get his head ripped off, it's now.

"Stay with Maggie." I point to the other women, Alida, Jeanette, Bridget and Killisi. They've all had to deal with the realities of being unmated on this island and survived, and they are each fierce wolftresses in their own rights. "Keep her surrounded."

Joachim and I drop our robes and shift. This time we have the might of the community, and the other three alphas who have witnessed the miracle that is Taryn. They'll all stand by our side and keep her safe. Together the group of us hurry out into the center of town, prepared for the attack.

Lev, in his big brown wolf form jumps on top of the structure of the rebuilt well. As an alpha he can mindspeak to any and all of us and he uses this as a fear tactic. *"I hope your whore enjoyed your mating, streltsy, because I'm going to rip your dick off and feed it to her."*

"She is claimed and you have no right to her now, Lev Naryshkin. Leave this place and harass my town no more."

Will roars behind me to lend my demand his solidarity. The other wolves with Lev, only some of which are from his own decimated pack, cower at the sound of a lion declaring this his territory. Lev growls and jumps down, stalking toward us.

"You streltsy think you own this island and the rest of us are tired of your tyranny. This is the day you pay for making this prison into your own personal playground."

I'm strict about not letting anyone terrorize the *derevnya*, but that's not what Lev is talking about. He thinks the actions of the Dark Prince of Wolves, with his vigilante killings, is a treachery by all of us imprisoned wolf guards. He couldn't be more wrong.

"Look around you, fool. Does it look like the Dark Prince is here? The derevnya *is full of life, light, and love unlike your pathetic lives, and he has no part of this. Take your vendetta elsewhere and leave my mate out of it."*

Lev yips, irritated with my truth. He turns to his pack and communicates something that only they can hear. When he turns back I see the wrath in the baring of his fangs. *"She may be claimed, but she is yours no more."*

A scream and then the sounds of wolves fighting to the death come from the barn. Fuck, they've ambushed Taryn and the women and distracted the rest of us. I turn tail and sprint into the barn. It takes only minutes for the wolftresses to dispatch their attackers.

But once the dust clears, Taryn is missing. Maggie is slumped against one wall and couldn't have used her magic to whisk Taryn away this time.

My vision goes red, my wolf completely taking over. I hear the yips and yowls of the rest of our pack destroying Lev and his rogues outside and still, I get no satisfaction. All the wolves from his pack who entered this barn are dead. I can tell by the scent trails.

But there is one more scent that doesn't belong, that of Nothing, mixed with the smell of a burned out church.

I have failed my only mission since Ekataryn came to this island and saved me from a life of solitude and anger. I let the Dark Prince find her and take her away to seek his revenge on her.

TARYN

One minute we're being attacked by a bunch of wolves and my new girlfriends are exploding out of their clothes to shift into a badass team of wolf-women, and the next I'm falling through thick black fog ready to puke my guts out.

For a split second that weird feeling of all my hair standing up across every inch of my skin skitters across me as if it's trying to get out and my senses go into hyper-heightened. Crap, this is exactly how I felt when I was first pulled into the Nothing. I remember something dark and evil shoving me into that empty place. Is that what's happening again?

I kick and scream, fighting and clawing to get away. I'm not going back there. For all my flopping around in the darkness and fog, it doesn't seem to do a thing and I land on my hands and knees in the dirt and snow. I've gotten the wind knocked out of me and am trying to suck in a breath while looking around to see where I am.

I'm still on the island. The trees are the same, and the sun is in the sky overhead in about the same place, so I haven't lost any time.

"Hurry, Ekataryn, get up. We have to hide." The creepy guy

who was there on the beach when I got thrown into this prison a few days ago grabs me by the arm and is trying to help me up. Peter, that's his name. August called him Peter, Peter, pussy eater and that niggles something in my memories.

I brush him away, cough to cover my snort-laugh because I just remembered who he is, my impotent husband in the 1700s. Like, literally, he couldn't get it up no matter how hard I tried. I thought it was me, but then I met August and... someone else and my life was filled with plenty of lovers.

I finally get some air into my lungs on a gasp. "Get away from me."

"No, I can't. We aren't safe out in the open." He grabs for me again and yanks my arms so that I have to follow him into a shadowed hidey-hole among a clump of bushes. "Here rub this on your skin and hair so he doesn't catch your scent."

He shoves a chunk of burned charcoal wood at me and I notice the streaks of ash on his face and arms. He's scared of something or someone, all right, and since I haven't got a clue what, I do as he instructs. "Who is this he?"

He eyeballs me like he's wondering if I'm trying to trick him. "Your streltsy have done their jobs well if you haven't crossed paths with the Dark Prince of Wolves yet."

Uh, dumbass says what? "You brought me to the Dark Prince? You are such an douchepotato. God."

Sorry Father.

I stare out of our hiding spot and can see the remains of a burned out building silhouetted by the afternoon sun. Crap, this must be the church Joachim mentioned. We are in deep shit.

"He's not here and we only have to hide until dusk." He points to the horizon. "When the moon rises we can escape."

"Escape what? Being murdered for walking right into some evil wolf's lair? This isn't a game of toy soldiers, Peter. You've put our lives at risk."

"The island." Peter keeps talking, but all I hear is mwah-mwah-mwah-mwah, like an out of tune trombone is talking to me.

Escape the island? For one whole day, I let go of that deep need I have inside to get back to my real life. It comes swooping back like a tornado trying to whip me back to Kansas. It's something I can't contain and it scares me. I need to go, but I won't without August and Joachim. There's no way I'm leaving adorable Vasily behind either.

How can I leave and not take Maggie and Will? What about my wolf shifter girl power squad and their mates? If there is a way to escape, we are all going to use it. But they all said there was no way. Wouldn't they have found this secret in the hundreds of years they've been here?

Or is this why the Dark Prince of assholes burned down this church and instills fear and terror everywhere he goes. Is he actually a prison guard keeping us all under his watchful eye and making sure none of us escape?

I grab Peter's shirt and give him a shake. "Shush your face and tell me how this escape thing works."

He grins in a gotcha way and I hate it. "There is a shadow portal in these ruins. When the moon rises, it will open and we can use it to get back to civilization."

"What the hell is a shadow portal? That is not a real thing. What do you really want?" Yeah, there is a lot of weird stuff that happens in this paranormal prison that I'm not privy to, but Peter always was a manipulative dickwad.

"I know you don't trust me, Ekataryn, but I have no reason to trick you." He holds his hands out, palms up trying to look all innocent. "I cannot make you my mate. I simply want to get out of here. You're the key."

How can I be? I'm not a god or goddess. Father Joachim said only higher power could get us out of here. I sort of thought he meant I should pray more. The way Peter is looking at me, he clearly thinks I have some kind of supernatural powers. He never was very smart.

I scowl at him and scoot away. I'm crawling out of here and getting back to August and Joachim right the hell now.

"You've had a sense since you arrived that you have something you need to get back to, haven't you?"

I fold my arms. Am I shocked he knows this? Yes. Am I willing to let him know that. No fucking way. "I'm sure everyone here has someone or something they want to get back to. This is prison. Duh. Don't try to manipulate me with your wild ass guesses."

"At least I'm not manipulating you with sex." He blinks and glances away like he's the pious one, judging my mates.

"If you had a true mate you'd know it's more than sex." Not like he knows anything about love or sex. He certainly never had either in our life and it's not looking like he's exactly found his one true love in prison either.

"True mates are a myth." He shakes his head like I'm the fool. "Something pussy-whipped wolves say to get their chosen mates into bed."

If there was more space in this hiding spot, I'd slap him. "You don't know anything."

That's it. I'm done with him. I don't know how he got me here, but I'm prepared to walk back to the *derevnya*, Dark Prince or not. Even if there is that curiosity about his escape plan.

"Maybe not, tzarina. But never, not even in our last lives together when you banished me to this goddess forsaken prison, did I ever try to use my love for you to get you to do what I wanted."

I banished him here? Shit. "We were never in love."

"Exactly. We ruled Russia, wolves and humans alike, without that complication. Can you say the same about your lives with your guards?"

Crap. He knows I don't remember much and he's using it against me. "I...don't know."

"They haven't told you, have they?" That smug smile is back and that means he knows something he thinks I should. Dammit, he's right. I'm cursing my own brain right now and whoever did this to me.

"Don't you want to know how you died in your last life, a hundred years ago?"

"No. That's fucking creepy, Peter. What is wrong with you." I'm lying my ass off. Of course I want to know.

"You're not a very good liar. You were much better at it when I was Tzar."

I'm rolling my eyes so hard right now, I'm giving myself a headache. "Fine. Tell me then if it will make you feel better. How did I die?"

There's a glee in his eye that I don't like even a little bit. "First they shot and bayoneted your mother and your father, they murdered your sisters, and then they killed your poor little brother. All while you watched. Then they shot you, mutilated your bodies and buried you in hidden graves."

Holy Mary, Mother of God. "Who? Why?"

I can't imagine August allowing that to happen. Except he wasn't there. He said he was imprisoned over two-hundred years ago.

"Vasily and Grigory, your guards."

He can't mean Vasily, the wolf. I don't even know who this Grigory guy is. I don't know if he's bluffing, but I'm calling it. "I don't even know those names. Your little shock tactic didn't do a thing for me."

Except it did. His little story time has given me an ache in my heart. I know there are two more men who are important to me and that they were with me in several of my past lives. It feels so strange to even think that I've been dying and reborn

155

again and again. Something tells me if I can figure out why that is happening, everything will change.

Peter knows way too much about me and my lives. We only had a relationship in one of them as far as I know. "How do you know all of this about me?"

A weird flash of nervousness shoots across him and he doesn't want to answer my question.

"Peter," I growl at him. Not in the sexy way August growls at me, but more like a mother to a bad child. "What aren't you telling me?"

"There are things on this island that you don't understand. Which is one more reason we should escape the second that sun sets." He points to the horizon and I'm shocked to see that dusk is already getting warmed up. Man, the days here are short.

He wiggles his way out from the brush and stays low to the ground, looking around. Watching him being so cautious, I suddenly realize that he isn't a wolf shifter. That's strange. I get that Will and Maggie aren't either, but they are shifters. I'm almost positive that Peter is simply a human like me.

How the hell were we the rulers of the wolves?

If he isn't a wolf himself, who were those wolves with him at the beach? They were clearly following his commands. Or am I wrong about that, and he was following theirs? "Peter? Where are your wolves, your pack?"

"Shh. Come on, this is our chance." He reaches for me, but I shrink back. I scramble away, but there's a rock behind the bush and it's too thick to go sideways.

"No, I'm not going anywhere with you."

"You're the reason I'm in this prison and you're going to get me out. Right the fuck now." He swipes at me again and I duck, but he grabs me by the hair and wrenches me out of the foliage.

"Ouch, let go of me, you weasel. Let me go and I won't have

my wolves eat your face off." I'm flailing and clawing at him but I can't get away.

He's literally dragging me by my hair into the burned out church like I'm some cave woman. "Shut up. This will all be over soon and you can meet your makers and I can finally be free."

I stumble over the remains of a wall separating the sanctuary from the nave and I realize it was the iconostasis. Only the clergy are allowed behind the religious paintings of the saints and I get an overwhelming sense of wrongness being here.

Oh, or it's the swirling black hole of death opening up in front of us. "No, no, no, no, no. Peter, don't do this. I'm sorry I put you in prison, I promise I'll never do it again."

He doesn't even acknowledge me. "I've brought her, now get me out of this hell hole."

Who is he talking to? I don't get to find out. Peter shoves me straight into the blackness and I'm once again surrounded by the black fog. This time I do puke and it lands all over the cold wet stones of the beach where I first arrived. I do not like black magic holes.

"No, dammit, fuck, shit, no." Peter shakes his fists and yells at the sky. "Let me out of here."

No one replies to him and I want to stick out my tongue and say I told you so. Instead I throw up again. Mid-retch, Peter hauls me to my feet and shoves me toward the sea and the rolling dark fog bank out on the ice.

"We're getting out of here with or without their help. Go." It's only a few steps to the edge of the ice and that's exactly the direction we're going.

There are little pools of water dotting the surface and I can see through parts where it was solid, thick, and pure white before. The nicer weather has melted it so it's no longer safe to walk on. "Peter, we'll fall through."

He sneers at me and looks me up and down. "Fuck you and your fat ass. We just need to make it through the fog. If you fall through after that, you fall through."

Jesus.

Sorry Father.

Peter takes a tentative step onto the ice and it definitely squishes beneath his feet. "It's fine. Come on."

"No way." I'm not dying to escape. I've only just figured out what I have to live for, and it's not on the other side of that fog.

"You don't have a choice." He pulls out a long, deadly-looking knife and presses it to my cheek. "For every second you waste, I will cut a chunk out of you. Maybe I should anyway, so you aren't so fucking heavy."

No wonder we never fell in love. Regardless, no one should treat a person like this. If we do make it out of here, I swear I will find a way to get back. If I have to commit crimes against humanity or wolf-manity to do it, I will. But I also think we are doomed to fail and are both going to die falling into that frigid water.

I take a tentative step out onto the ice, and thankfully, it holds. Although if it's going to break, closer to shore would be better. Peter notices and pokes his knife further into my skin. "Keep going."

I try to go slow, but he's not having any of my delays. The fog roils and bubbles ahead of us, like some kind of living being. It's seriously creepy. A few inches from where it rises up from the ice, I get that same nauseated feeling. Whatever magic Peter used to steal me away from the party is the same as that shadow portal and this fog.

"Yes, into the fog and get me off this island once and for all." He pokes my face with the knife and I swear to all that is holy, I'm going to shove it up his ass the first chance I have. Like in that fog where he can't see me grab for it.

I take another step and crr-ack. The ice under my feet shudders and the sound of it fracturing echoes behind us. The nausea bubbles up my throat and I can taste the bile burning my throat along with the adrenaline of fear. I don't know what's going to happen when we cross into that fog, but it's better than becoming a popsicle of death.

I bolt into the darkness with Peter right behind me and in three more steps, poof, we stumble out the other side of the fog and onto another rocky beach. I get a very eerie sense of déjà vu. Is this the same island? Did we just walk through the fog bank and land right back where we started? It's not like we wandered around in circles. I took two or three steps. The little bit of light from the crescent moon gets dimmer by the second as clouds blow in above our heads and I think it's going to storm.

"God dammit all to hell." Peter throws himself on the ground like a toddler and screams and yells.

I get up off the ground and move as far away from him as fast as I can. But far away is like ten feet, where I freeze like a frightened deer with not enough sense to flee or fight. Coming out of the tree line is the biggest, blackest, meanest looking wolf I have ever seen and it is stalking toward us like it's on the hunt.

"Well, well, well. If it isn't Peter, Peter, pussy eater."

Does everyone call him that?

The voice is definitely coming from this wolf and all of the alarms are going off in my head, plus some in my chest and a few more in my belly. I shrink down into the rocks, because I don't think he's seen me yet. Thank goodness for Peter and his tantrum.

I'm going to army crawl along the shore until I can find a better hiding spot or a place to sprint off into the forest. Then I am fleeing straight into August's arms and I'm never leaving them again.

The wolf lowers his head and sniffs the air. He snarls and

spittle drips from his mouth. I really don't want to watch him eat that man and that's exactly what I think is about to happen.

"You've been in my lair. I smell the shadow on you. For that you'll have to die." He snarls and I'm still so close I can see his muscles bunch to pounce. Peter has curled up into a ball and is whimpering and crying.

Come on, Peter. You're killing me. Literally. Because I can't slink away while the wolf kills him, even if he deserves it. Crap. This is the dumbest thing I have ever done. I grab one of the rocks, pull myself up to a crouch to get a bit more leverage and hurl the rock at the wolf.

It doesn't even land close to him and merely skips across the other wet, slippery stones, clattering to a stop several feet from Peter and the wolf. They both look to see what's caused the commotion and I know I'm screwed. Go big or go home. In a coffin.

I grab up another stone and stand up to give myself full range of motion. The clouds part the tiniest bit allowing me to see even better and the wolf glows in the sliver of moonlight giving me the perfect target. I draw my arm back and catch sight of my own arm and back of my hand. I'm glowing too.

The wolf pivots, turning away from Peter and one-hundred and eleven percent of his attention is now on me. *"Hello, princess."*

I try to swallow past the giant lump in my throat but I can't. He's come for me, and now I'm going to die. But I'm not going down without a fight. I hurtle the rock at him, then spin and sprint down the shore. I can take my chances trying to outrun him, or I can bolt back out into the fog, knowing that I'll either end up under the ice or thrown back onto the shore. At least that would confuse him.

The rocks are too slippery and I'm not moving fast enough. I can hear his snarls and the beat of his feet catching up to me. I give one last ditch effort that I sure as shit wished I'd thought of when Peter had me trapped in the bush. I call out to my mates with the gift of mindspeak. *"Help. Beach. Dark Prince. Running."*

From out of the edge of the trees, another glowing wolf bursts onto the rocky beach and darts straight for me. It's Vasily. *"Go, prinsessa. I won't let him get you. Run."*

He bolts right past me so fast he's like lightning. He and the Dark Prince of Wolves clash together and blood sprays across the ice, the rocks, and my face.

VASILY

*S*he needs me. My Anastasia calls out for my help and I will not fail her this time. I will not let Grigory hurt her. He's angry. Well, guess what fucker, I am too. Alpha or not, he has no right to scare her, and treat her like prey.

I crash into him and go right for his throat. He's the one who trained me to fight, so he's ready for the move. What he isn't prepared for is that I will fucking kill him if he even looks in her direction.

He doesn't deserve her.

But neither do I. The difference between us now is that I'm willing to give my life for her's to make up for my mistakes. He wants vengeance on the whole damn world.

I draw first blood, but he rolls and throws me off of him. Out of the corner of my eye I see Peter run for the woods and I'll kill him too for putting Anastasia in danger and then abandoning her. He'll pay for his treachery, just like he did when they were the rulers of Russia.

Grigory tries to use Peter's escape as a distraction and lunges toward Anastasia. I block him with a swipe of my claws. We've done this dance before and if I don't die tonight, we'll do it again. I've been on his tail all day, doing everything I could to keep him far from the sacred circle and her mating with August.

As soon as I heard the howls and knew August's claim had been made, I went on the hunt. But Grigory is a sneaky fucker and I lost his trail late in the day. At least Peter was good for something. Now I know why the church he haunts smells like nothing and neither does he.

He couldn't resist the shadow, or her.

"She's not worth it, Vas. None of this is. Haven't you figured that out yet?"

I don't bother replying to his venomous thoughts. He's tried for a hundred years to poison me against her. I will never lose faith. Never.

"Vasily, look out," Anastasia screams. I'm ready for Grigory's attack, but she needs to get out of here. She never liked it when we fought. If she tries to interfere, it could be disastrous.

I can't handle seeing her hurt ever again.

Grigory and I tussle, our claws lashing out, and I lose a tooth in his bones. He loses blood. The injuries don't bother either of us. Our wolves heal them almost as fast as they happen. We are too evenly matched.

I don't need to take him down, only keep him distracted and occupied long enough for the other streltsy to get here and get Anastasia to safety. I can trust August and Joachim to rescue her from harm, although I don't know how we'll keep her safe after that.

That's something to think about later. For now, my only goal is to make sure Grigory can't hurt her before she can escape. I'll defend her with my life. Something I did a shitty job at doing in her last life.

I have failed her so many times.

"Streltsy, hear her cry. Hurry." The connection we all share is stronger because she is here.

Joachim's calming presence replies. *"We're almost there, brother. Keep her safe for a few more minutes and we'll be at your side."*

Grigory can hear them too and he gnashes his teeth at our exchange. He's blocked us for too long, but now that he's linked with her, he can't escape the unity of our bonds. He circles, trying to get an advantage to attack, angrier now than before. I'm not stupid. I can see his plan as clear as the bright shining moon. If I let him get between me and Anastasia he'll turn and attack her. My job would be a whole hell of a lot easier if she would back off.

I hate doing this, but I swing my head around for a brief moment to snarl and snap at her. I don't care if it makes her afraid of me, as long as it kicks in her fight or flight response and she flees. Grigory lunges, just as I knew he would, and I kick out at him.

Anastasia throws a god-damned rock at us. It bounces off my back and smacks Grigory in the shoulder. She never was one to shy away from a fight, not even when she's afraid. "You two stop that right now. Bad dogs. Bad, bad, talking dogs."

Grigory growls. Big baby doesn't like her insult. I like her twisted sense of humor. Only she would think to treat two rabid wolves like her pets.

She throws two more rocks and both hit Grigory. They're small, and there's no way they're doing anything more than tickling him. He actually backs away and that gives me the break I need to push him away from her. I attack head on with all my might. We go tumbling onto the ice and toward the shadow fog.

Anastasia yells and runs down the beach toward us. "No, get off the ice, it's thawing and cracking."

We've all been on this ice at least once since getting thrown into this prison. Everyone walks into the dark fog at least once trying to escape. Each time, the portal throws us right back out on the waiting shores of the island. Never have I seen anyone fall through the thick layer of eternal ice. Even attempts to drill through it to fish have failed.

When it cracks beneath us sending the terrifying sound like breaking bones reverberating toward the shore, I can't believe it. For a hundred years I've looked out over this frozen lake, it never changes. But never have the clouds parted and the moon shined it's light down on us either.

"She's making changes to this place with her powers, Grigori. Even you must be able to see that."

We circle each other again, even with the cracks in the ice visible below our feet. *"No, fool. It's merely another trick of the Volkovs. They're torturing us with hope."*

Hope. That's what she's given us all. It's something I've needed badly. *"Why do you fight against her pull?"*

"Why do you continue to fight for her?" He snaps at me and the ice tremors beneath our feet.

I hold very, very still. *"She will save us all."*

"You're stupid to believe that. It's been more than two thousand years and countless lives. She will never save anyone. Grow the fuck up, Vas. Live your own life. I'm finally free."

I live all my lives for her. Grigory used to, until last time. Her death broke us both. *"You're not free. You're trapped in your own rage and you want the rest of us stuck there and miserable with you."*

That rage he has inside is contained no more. It roils out of him like a putrid disease and he's acting like a wounded animal to anyone who wants to help. He'll get us all killed. He lunges for me and we collide, skidding across the ice. I can feel the cracks multiplying under my paws and claws.

"Vasily, no," Anastasia screams and my world is plunged into ice and darkness. The chill of the water is like a thousand knives skinning me alive and I can do nothing to stop it. I scramble to get back to the opening we fell through, but it's already formed another layer of ice over it. We're fucked.

Grigory is clawing to get out and dark amorphous shapes dance on the surface. She's come to try and save us. The freezing water is numbing my brain, but I must warn her off. *"Get off the ice, don't you dare die for me."*

Two more shapes join her and drag her away. *"No, no. We have to save them."*

August and Joachim have arrived to save the day. Grigory scratches at them through the ice, but he too is feeling the effects of the frozen water and his anger can only drive him against this death for so long.

Will we be reborn again in a new life without her?

"Swim down." Joachim's voice filters into my head. I know I've only caught a part of his message and I don't understand. It doesn't matter. Death's cool hand is already reaching for me.

The shapes are back above us. No, wait. This time it's only one. Joachim crashes through the ice and snags Grigory by the scruff of his neck and dragging him down. With our alpha in tow, he swims straight for me. I must be turned around. I can't tell up from down.

Grigory fights against Joachim's hold on him, but the water has made us both too weak. Joachim swims fast and crashes into me, shoving me deeper into the darkness of the lake. I'm swallowed up by the inky waters, and my heart pounds against my chest, my lungs rebel against the lack of oxygen, and my stomach clenches. My back hits the stones at the bottom of the lakebed and I close my eyes for the last time.

Death doesn't feel like I thought it would. I'm still cold, but wind whips through my fur and I can breathe. Anastasia's warm breath blows across my face, her lips so close to mine, and I can't wait for her to kiss me. She laughs and her air swirls into my lungs.

"Wake up, Vasily, wake up for me." Death and rebirth has been

my constant battle for centuries. Am I being rewarded for sacrificing my life for hers and allowed to crossover into the afterlife?

Grigory's voice is the one that replies, and I know that I have not died, but am now back in Hell. *"You should not have saved me, because now I'm going to kill each and every one of you."*

I tear my eyes open and find myself on the same damned beach. Fuck. I thought only the fog surrounding the island was a shadow portal that keeps guard on the inmates of this god-forsaken prison. We can't even escape through a watery grave?

This is some dark damn magic and even Rasputin doesn't have this much power.

Grigory crawls to his feet, fueled by his rage. August and a sopping wet Joachim swoop in, heads lowered and growling. Anastasia gives her two fingers a kiss and then rubs them across my fur in a long caress between my eyes. "You're okay now, Vasily."

I am far from it. Not with those caring eyes glowing down at me. Goddess, she is beautiful.

I tremble, trying to get up to join the other streltsy and protect her. With a pat to my shoulder, she pushes me to stay down. She has a new confidence in her scent and she stands as if she's going to protect me. Anastasia stares through the space between August and Joachim, extends her arm, and points at the black, slathering mess of a wolf that is Grigory.

"You're mine." Her words ring out into the night with a thundering boom. Lightning crashes across the sky as if trying to catch up with the sound of her voice. Rain pelts us in big, fat drops that seem to come from every angle, but it's warm, so unlike the frozen sleet that normally comes with the island's wintery storms.

Those are the words I long to hear from her lips to me. Not this time, not in this life. I must forsake them. In this vow, I find the strength to rise to my feet.

"I am here and will not fall until he does." I join August and Joachim in forming a wall between her and Grigory. I must fight one more time since it's my fault he's found her. We are stronger together.

Grigory steps back as if she smacked him on the nose. His shock is a pungent bitter almond scent that he can't hide. The mask of his anger falls back into place almost as fast as it slipped and he regains his ground. He bares his teeth at us all and in a growled, turbulent voice, he replies, *"Not anymore, princess."*

He lunges, not for us, her guards, but for Anastasia. He's going directly for her throat. I stand my ground in front of her and rear up to block his attack. August launches himself and the black and the white wolves clash in such a frenzy of teeth, claws and fur, that they blur until splashes of red spatter the rocks.

Joachim gives me a quick nod and joins the fray. The priest becomes the warrior he tries so hard to suppress. It is left to me to get Anastasia to safety. I shove at her with my head and nip at her ankles to get her to run. "No, we're not leaving them. We have to stop this fight before someone gets killed."

She always was hard headed. I'm this close to shifting just so that I can pick her up and carry her off this beach. But my wolf howls inside my head. My beast won't allow that. It was my human flesh that couldn't save her before. I must never allow that frailty to come between her and safety no matter what.

I growl at her and push her away. I never should have turned my back on the fight, because it's left an opening for Grigory and he takes advantage of it. I know because I see the fear shoot through Anastasia's face a second before the searing pain of his nails raking across my belly flashes through me.

I want her to run, I want her to hide, I want her to live.

Grigory pushes off me, tears his jaw open wide and wraps his teeth around Anastasia's throat. She screams out words so ancient I can't understand, lifts her face and arms to the sky and pure white light explodes from her eyes and mouth, her fingers, and from between her legs.

The raindrops halt their downward fall, a flash of lightning cracks the sky like a gash in space and time, and the sliver of the moon shining through the clouds is no longer a crescent but whole, unbroken, full once again. Grigory's wolf is frozen in mid-bite and his mouth is full, not of her blood, but of moonlight.

A magic as old as the earth and sea, stars and moon sparkles in the air all around us and we four wolves are snatched up and separated into the four quadrants around her by vines of moon flowers that shoot up from the ground.

None of us even dare to struggle and I can literally feel her energy flowing through me. My bones crack and reshape themselves, my fur splits and the millions of hairs recede as if chased away, the fangs in my mouth and the claws on my paws shrink, my vision goes dark, and my heart is ready to burst from my chest.

The wolf part of me that I've clung to for a hundred years is pushed back inside and my human form ruptures out, too cold, too hot, too sensitive to the sensations of the world. I blink fast, trying to regain my equilibrium. I'm naked and afraid, not for my life, but that she'll see who and what I am and know that I am not worthy of her.

She's remembering who and what she is, and I am not worthy of her.

TARYN

$\mathcal{I}$ don't know how long I've been in the darkness. I don't know much of anything really. I must have had a life before my light was stolen away, but the one thing I do remember now is that I am powerful.

~

~

TARYN and her harem of wolf guards' story continues in the next book in the Fate of the Wolf Guard Saga - Untamed.

CAN'T WAIT to read more of the Wolf Guard's story?

I've got a special bonus chapter for my Curvy Connection email newsletter fans. Get it here--> geni.us/MoreUnclaimed

---

WANT to read my next book as I write it?

Sign up to be one of my Patreon Book Dragons and get the newest book before it's available anywhere else.

UNTAMED

FATE OF THE WOLF GUARD - BOOK 2

For Elli - who makes me think I can

"Love is an untamed force. When we try to control it, it destroys us. When we try to imprison it, it enslaves us. When we try to understand it, it leaves us feeling lost and confused."

— PAULO COELHO

TARYN

I am powerful.

Whoa, holy shiznit, am I ever powerful. Yikes.

Like floating in the sky, magic all around, changing the world powerful. While it is tons of fun to think about casting a love spell, or making cake ingredients dance around the kitchen, ooh, or doing chores with a flick of the wrist, I don't have any idea what I'm doing with this much unexplained mystical energy thrumming me through me.

I'm nothing more than the chubby lost and alone girl with amnesia, or I was when I first landed on this island. Mentally scanning my body, and yeah... no. Nothing has changed and I don't feel like I'm anything special.

Except maybe I am? I'm gonna need some help to figure out what all this means. I've got butterflies or magic or magic butterflies in my stomach swirling around making me feel incredibly squirmy.

Or, more likely, that's my too-sexy-for-their-fur wolf-shifter mates giving me the hot flashes.

Being surrounded by four super-hot naked men is not as

much fun as you'd think. Especially when they're all pissed off. Which, of course, somehow makes them each even hotter.

Lucky me. I've got them all trapped in beams of shiny magic flowing out of me. I don't have a clue how I'm making it happen, how to control it, or if I can make it stop. Might as well take advantage of this moment of peace while they're suspended in mid-air with me and looking high as kites. Pardon me while I drool over each and every one of them as I figure out what in the world is happening to us all.

Okay, let's see. They were all fighting on the beach, I got bit on the throat, more fighting, and then boom. I went all supernova. Nope, still not a clue. Perhaps my mate, August, can clue me in?

August is looking all delicious with his naked mountain man thing he's got going on. All he needs with that beard is a flannel shirt and an axe. No, no. No shirt. It would be a crying shame to cover up those eleventy-hundred pack abs.

Father Joachim could be a fricking movie star. Gasp. Amnesia block busted - I remember movies. This damn prison island could sure use a movie theater, and popcorn, and peanut butter M&Ms. Oh, yeah. And Father Joachim would definitely be the latest heart throb, untouchable and yet so, so touchable. Yum.

While both of them make my insides go all flippy floppy, these other two naked dudes, who I accidentally poofed out of their wolf forms, have all kinds of magic butterflies doing the merengue in my girly parts.

When this magic light poured from my head, shoulders, knees, and toes, knees, and toes, I didn't exactly pay attention to who was where. But I'm pretty damn sure that the hunka-hunka burning love floating dazed to my front and center is none other than cute AF wolf-dog Vasily.

That butthead. He full on let me think he wasn't one of these wolf shifters. I let him curl up and sleep on me for goodness' sake. I gave him scritches behind the ears. Now he's about as big as horse...no a centaur...or, wait are those real? Anyway, he's ginormous and uh... so is his junk. This guy is hu-ung. And hard. His cock is pointed directly at me like a compass.

I'd be his true north. Eyebrow waggle.

Then there's Mr. Grumpy McAssFace. He looks like he'd eat my heart out and give me a squirty orgasm at the same time. I kind of want to let him try too. Those dark eyes are staring into my sloppy little soul and making me all fidgety.

I'm being absolutely ridiculous. This has to be the Dark Prince of Wolves, and he literally just tried to bite my face off. Good thing he missed.

There's heat at the spot on my neck where he bit me and something I can't identify swirls around on my skin. The feeling is remarkably similar to when August marked me. That has to be what set off the surprise magic coming out of me like I'm Emperor Palpatine or Lord Voldemort. I can hear Hagrid now. "Yur a wizard, Taryn."

Am I? Don't wizards need magic wands? It's not like I said a magic spell or anything. I just got so mad that everyone was fighting. Then the Dark Prince attacked me, and the blue light exploded from me, grabbing them all up and turning them into humans like me.

I just wanted them to stop fighting.

Now, I'm not totally convinced I'm simply human. Because, well, duh. Normal women don't go around picking up packs of terrifying wolves with sparkly blue light coming out of... I glance down and yep... yep...I've got magic coming out my vagina.

That is not a sentence I ever thought I'd say in my life.

I'm not the only one staring at my magic vagina either. August, Father Joachim, and Vasily are all blissed out on what-ever this superpower I have is. But that Dark Prince guy? He's focused on me and fighting against my hold on him.

181

"I said I'd come for you, Princess." The same voice I heard in my head, back at the village before I mated with August, rolls into my head like a storm. The kind of whirlwind that could send me spinning off to Kansas or North Korea, but only to end up crash landing directly on him.

I concentrate and try to send another wave of magic over the Dark Prince so he can't look at me like that anymore. I can't even think about what to do next with him staring at me and talking in my head. Why can't he be zoned out like the others? Blue sparkles of power flicker out and I think I'm doing it.

The sparks of magic don't go where I want them to at all. Instead, they slam into Vasily, and he snaps to attention like I just mainlined caffeine into him. Oops. Hope that doesn't have any adverse side effects.

Neither of them can move more than some jerks of muscles and glares, but Vasily's eyes find mine. *"Anastasia, free me so I can destroy him."*

That pisses off the Dark Prince and he growls like thunder. I didn't think he was supposed to be able to hear Vas talk in my head. The form of his big black wolf rippling out from within is like a ghost in the darkness. *"No one can protect you."*

His mouth moves and he whispers some words in a language that's so old I've forgotten it. Whatever it is he says, it makes my magic flow back toward me and the blue light holding him up in the air dims and fades.

Vasily is fighting against me too, but he's drawing more magic to himself, taking what the Dark Prince is rejecting. His wolf also shimmers up, flashing across his face and chest until I can't tell if he's man or beast. His voice, darker and rumblier, grabs my mind. *"Ana, let me free. Now."*

Ooh. Forceful Vasily is schmexy. Wait. What is wrong with me? I'm mid-magical battle with supernatural beings and all I can think about is how I want to rub myself up and down and around Vasily's... gah... stop it weird, horny lizard brain. I need to concentrate, or someone is going to get hurt, or killed, or pregnant.

The light binding me and the Dark Prince together, sloshes like a wave, but as the tide is going out. With each second, I'm losing my hold on him. Not that I know how I've got him in my grasp. If I don't do something, he's definitely going to attack me again.

He's dropping closer to the ground, and I just know the second his enormous feet hit the rocks he's going to shift and charge at me. If I can figure out how to float up higher, I could protect August, Father Joachim, Vasily, and myself from another attack. But I bet this guy can jump pretty fricking high.

The magic is clearly coming from inside of me, which must mean I'm a witch or something. I can control it then. I take a deep breath and close my eyes, trying to feel for where it's coming from. Aside from having blue light bursting out my limbs, I don't actually feel any different.

That's good, I guess? Means that this is part of the real me I just don't remember. I hope it doesn't require me to remember any spells. No, it wouldn't, since I didn't say anything to make it start up. So, it must run on intention.

Fine. I intend to float up to the top of the trees to keep my wolves safe.

Oh, oh, oh. Something is happening. The air is moving around me. I'm too afraid to open my eyes in case it breaks the magic momentum. Perhaps we're floating up too high though, so I take one peek, cracking open my right eyelid.

Shoot, crap, abort, abort the mission. Houston, we have a problem. Instead of floating the four of us up into the sky, I've pulled August, Father Joachim, and Vasily directly in front of me like an impenetrable wall of muscle. August and Father Joachim are to my left and right with their fine, fine butts pretty much smack dab in front of my face.

Vasily is dead ahead, facing toward me. So much of him is... right where I could lick it if I wanted to. And I want to.

Inappropriate. Even if the idea of tasting him, giving him pleasure, has my libido on overdrive.

"*Anastasia, let me defend you against our enemies.*" His words are getting more demanding and gruffier in my head. Why does that turn me on so hard? This is not the time nor the place for sexy fantasies.

I really want to do what he's telling me to do. I close my eyes and will the magic around him to dissipate. When I open them again, I'm not even a little bit surprised that nothing happened. Grr. This power is clearly not something new. I should be able to control it. "I don't know how."

It would probably help if I could look away from the giant peen in my face. Oh wait, something did happen and Vasily's cock blocked it. The Dark Prince is the one who I've floated down to the ground and the magic barely has a hold on him. Great.

He growls at me and Vas snarls back. "*Stay away from her, traitor.*"

Traitor? That's an interesting tidbit I'm filing away for later when I'm not about to be attacked by a naked angry, hot, angry, did I mention hot and angry and naked, man.

Okay. This magic flowing out of me is some bullshit. I flail around in the air trying my best to swim with my arms toward the ground. That actually sort of works. Oops. No, it really works, too well. The wet rocky beach is coming toward my face at an alarming rate.

I wrap my arms around my head to bear the brunt instead of my skull, and a moment later a wall of rock slams into me It isn't the shoreline, but the Dark Prince. I freak out and push against him even as he tries to grab me. My actions send me flying through the air, head over ass until someone grabs me, tucking me against his chest, protecting me from the fall.

Even though I can't see him, I know it's Vasily. He smells of ice and forest and power. Not mine, but something of his own. I want to lick it.

We tumble across the stones and not a one touches my skin. "I've got you, prinsessa."

I'd believe that if I didn't hear the snarl of a giant, cranky wolf nearby. I peek an eye open and yep, the Dark Prince of Wolves has shifted back into his beast form. It's my fault that August, Father Joachim, and Vasily are human right now and I sure as shit hope I haven't broken them. Humans are fragile, especially against snapping wolf jaws.

In the tumble, the other two men have fallen to the ground as well and my magic powers have subsided. The guys don't appear to be conscious, and I don't want Dark Princey Poo to get any ideas about attacking them when they can't fight back.

The three of them have done everything they could to protect me since I landed here in prison-island-palooza, and I've gone and screwed that up. Now we're all gonna die.

I scoot and flop about to get out of Vasily's grasp so I can try to call my magic up again, but before I get anywhere the sound of cracking bones freezes me. Vas's skin splits right in front of me and fur bursts out. Before I can even gasp, I'm underneath his enormous wolf.

I want to reach up and snuggle into his fur. He's sexy as hell in his human form, but ever since I was thrown into this stupid prison, Vasily the wolf has made me feel safe. The least I could do is return the favor.

In one badass ninja move, which probably looked more like a dying fish trying to flop away, I roll out from beneath him. August and Father Joachim are less than a foot away, sitting where they dropped and looking like they've been hit by a steamroller or a Mack truck. Maybe I should beep when I back up.

No time. The Dark Prince of Wolves is charging toward us,

jaw open wide as if he's going to try and eat me up in one bite. Not again.

There is a part of me that wants to try and talk, to ask him why he's so angry and find out who he truly is to me. I can feel our connection, but I can't believe he's a mate to me like August is. The angry wolf running straight for me doesn't appear to be in the mood for a deep talk or even chit chat.

"Ana, no dammit, look out," Vas yells straight into my head. His warning should have me stop-drop-and-rolling, but it gives me the strength instead to stop the attack of the Dark Prince. I'm going to do everything in my power to save these men who have stolen my heart.

I throw my hands out and the blue beams of magic pour from me once again. "Stop. I am not your enemy."

The sound of my voice reverberates like we're in a cave, and the magic hits the Dark Prince head on. He's pushed back for a second and then he lowers his head, and claws his way forward, blue shining eyes lasered in on me. This has just become a power of wills between the two of us and if I'm going to win, I need to throw him off his game.

If only I knew how to do that. My mind is blank, swiss cheese, filled with nothing but fluff. The Dark Prince is getting closer, and my magic is flickering like a bad connection. We are totally going to die if I don't come up with something fast.

But I don't know how to fight. I don't understand where his anger came from, and I certainly don't want to hurt him.

One really dumb idea that probably wouldn't work, pops into my head. It definitely won't be what he expects. "Hey, what do you call a wolf who uses foul language?"

The Dark Prince growls and inches closer.

"A swear-wolf."

For just a moment I see the flicker of something other than pure anger flash through his eyes. That is my chance. I turn all my power on him. Instead of pushing him away it opens one of those freaky portals and he's sucked into it, snarling and growling and howling the whole way.

Then poof. The portal is gone, the Dark Prince is gone, and so is all my magic. I collapse onto the rocks, breathing hard. Magic is some serious cardio. If I didn't lose five pounds today, I'll be surprised.

In less than a second, I'm surrounded by August, Vasily, and Father Joachim. They're pulling me up and patting me down at the same time. "I'm okay, I'm okay. No need to get handsy."

August does in fact get handsy. He grabs me around the waist and pulls me in for a hot and hard kiss. I love melting into his love for me and I kiss him right back. I know he needs to make sure we're both still alive and safe. I won't mind if we reaffirm our lives together in the bedroom later either. Especially if Father Joachim and Vasily are watching... or participating.

But that's wishful thinking.

Or I believed it to be until Vasily grabs me out of August's arms and shoves his fingers into my hair, tugging the strands into his fist. I'm both in awe and a little scared of him at the same time. My fight or flight response is on over drive already and it's telling me Vasily is a predator.

He growls and narrows his eyes like he's angry, but then he lays a toe-tingling kiss on me that has me seeing stars and moons. I'm mid-swoon when he breaks his lips from mine way before I'm ready. He whispers against my mouth, "I'm never losing you again."

Again? When was the last time he lost me?

VASILY

My Anastasia is so much more powerful in this life than in the last, or even the ten lives we lived together before that. She is magnificent and I will murder anyone who tries to dim her light.

It is hard for me to be in this human form again. I've let the beast rule me and all my most base instincts surround my mind like an aura.

I can't help myself. I grab her from August and without her permission, I claim her mouth. Jealousy rears its head and wants that final thrum of her power to sing through my soul once more. In any other life she would slap me for the indiscretion, but I don't give a fuck about impropriety anymore. I need to feel her body pressed to mine, to know that she is unharmed.

Not this time. Not now. I will take what is mine so I can protect her.

She responds to my kiss with a passion of her own, one that I have sorely missed. She gives and takes, her lips and tongue mashing and dueling with mine as if she is the one who can't get enough of me. I may not have sought her consent, but she is giving it to me now with her fervor. She kisses me with as much lust as when she was a beautiful young Romanov princess, and we were sneaking kisses in the golden, bejeweled rooms of the palace.

I push those sweet memories away. They have no place in this time and situation. Fire Island is a cruel prison shithole, and I will not let it or anyone in it take her away from me.

I want her even more than I did a hundred years ago. Her insistent kisses now are nothing like the soft, tentative first brush of my lips over hers that last Russian spring before everything went wrong.

I can't keep a groan in, my human body thrums with lust, and my wolf's need to mark and claim her rule my every move. It's been so hard to keep myself away from her. Even allowing my wolf to curl up on her that first night was almost more than I could take, and I was grateful when she tried to slip away into the night.

Not like I'd let her. She is mine to protect. Forever. I've just done such a shitty job at it in the past. I was too soft, too weak. I can't let anything happen to her this time. That includes not letting Grigori ever touch her again.

"Vasily," she whimpers my name so deliciously between breaths and I want to eat her words. She's so soft and compliant in my arms that I ignore her warning signs. She struggles and pulls away, then slaps me across the cheek. Thwack.

Her hand probably stings more than my skin, but the brunt of her anger bites regardless. "Why did you hide yourself from me?"

I deserved that. I linger over the taste of her lips a brief moment more, grasping for what to say.

There is hurt in her eyes and the rock of guilt I've been carrying around in my gut since I first saw her here on this very beach, aches in a way I didn't expect. My pain doesn't matter, but hers does. The only words I want to say will make her mad or sad. I know because I've said them before.

I don't react to the slap across my face. She only did it to get some of her adrenaline out. Because I haven't been human for so long, I'm not sure how to respond. I risk a quick glance at August and Joachim for help. I find none. Shit, they're angry with me too.

My skin itches to shift. At least in wolf form I know what to do to keep her safe, to keep August company in his rough-hewn cabin, to stand guard over Joachim as he tortures himself with prayer to a long-lost god. My hands and feet and words can't help me anymore than they can my brethren. "I thought I would better serve you as a guardian than a confidant."

Her anger fades, the scent of it moving from burnt leaves to the gentle perfume of the moon flower. She touches my cheek, caressing the same spot she hit me with the lightest of brushes. Even though she doesn't know the extent of my sins, she forgives me. "You were, you are a great defender. I owe you my life several times over. But we both know you are more to me than either of those things."

That dense guilt in my gut pulsates, growing inside, making me wish I could tell her everything and ask for her whole forgiveness. I lean into her touch, trusting August and Joachim enough to close my eyes for a brief moment and revel in my princess.

In the warmth of her love, so easily given, I can be anything she wants me to be, do what she needs done, fight her fights. I would bare my soul for her.

Joachim clears his throat, and damn if that bastard doesn't always know what I'm thinking. I'm not ready to give her the truth I've hidden away in the soul of my beast yet anyway. I place my hand over hers and draw it away. "I don't like us being out here and exposed."

The Dark Prince of Wolves isn't our princess's only enemy.

She gives me a look that promises we aren't done with this conversation, but she is still rattled from the battle. The scent of her worry and fear rising back up permeate my pores and I want only to grab her up and carry her away to safety. I will not. She is stronger than my inner beast gives her credit for.

There are so many thoughts unsaid in her eyes, but she placates me with a nod and turns her attention to the others. "Uh, are you three gonna walk around butt naked?"

Her gaze flashes down to my cock and her pupils dilate, making her eyes go dark with pleasure. My wolf preens inside, loving her lusty looks. The beast wants me to throw her over my shoulder and drag her off to the woods where I can mark her and claim her, and make her mine once again, in private, just her and me.

That is not our way.

August laughs and I wish I had his easy relationship with her. "You've warmed our island quite a bit, love. My cock and balls are enjoying a bit of summer and fresh air."

While this is no summer, the ice surrounding the island has cracked, and glistens with a layer of melted water atop it. The trees have new growth, and then there are the moon flowers.

She tips her head to the side, thinking in that adorable way that she does, her eyes flicking back and forth. "I warmed it up? Is that what my magic does?"

Is she testing us? She's gotten a huge chunk of her powers back, but does she have her memories as well? We've all learned the lesson more than once that if she doesn't discover her powers on her own, the whole incarnation goes to shit. None of us want a repeat of the Kamchatka earthquake and tsunami, or worse, the catastrophic eruption of the legendary mountain volcano *Hara Berezalti*.

My wolf whines inside. Is a natural disaster any worse than the death and destruction I'd wreak on this island and its people if I lose her again?

Perhaps all three of us feel the same. None of us reply to her question. Joachim is the one to break the silence. "We can shift, my lady, if you are uncomfortable."

She smirks at him and gives his erect cock the eyebrow raise of disdain she's so very good at. I'm not coming to his rescue on this one. We all know he's the one who can't handle being naked around her. Dumb fucker.

Not that I am one to talk. I don't trust myself near her either. One whole minute back in human form and I've already stolen a kiss and got a slap for it. And I'd do it again in a heartbeat. Even now I inch closer to her just to feel her warmth.

It isn't enough. I want her under me, crying my name, coming on my cock, ascending to her rightful power and position.

This human form has too many feelings, an overwhelming amount of emotions. I need to shift back to my wolf before I lose my mind.

"This isn't about comfort. Our wolves are the best way to guard you from any further attacks." I wave my arm toward the forest, in the direction we'll travel to take her back to the safety of the political prisoners of the Volkovs. Back to those that already worship her and don't even know why.

My feisty prinsessa isn't having any of our bullshit. "Don't you think we should talk about what happened a minute ago? Or did you all not notice that I have a magic vagina?"

August sidles up to her and presses his lips to his mark on her throat. "I can personally attest to the magic of your lush cunt, tzaritsa."

She rolls her eyes at me and Joachim, but there is a smile too. Once again, I envy the way August can flirt with her and put her at ease even as he moves to protect her. Which is of course what he's done.

More than that I'm envious of his mark she carries on her skin. Mine should be on her throat too.

"Don't tzaritsa me. The three of you know a whole lot more than you're telling me and that ends right now. I'm a fricking witch or something, you all are werewolves, and I just shoved a dude through a black hole. I want to know what's going on here."

Joachim holds up his hand to halt our protests before August and I can even spit them out. "I'll explain everything when we get you back to the *derevnya* and we're sure you're safe."

He will? Joachim's the one who first learned how dire the outcome of our lives were when we revealed her true nature, before she discovered it for herself. He's sworn us all to secrecy in every life we've lived with him.

He shifts and sends a warning through our connection. *Don't say a word.*

I see. He has no intention of telling her anything but is willing to bear the brunt of her anger when she finds that out. He has a skill with her that I do not wish for. Lying.

August hates it as well, but we will do what it takes to make her safe. This time we must succeed where we have failed before. But I don't know how. We have no plan, no alpha to guide our path. Only lies and secrets.

The same as always. That hasn't worked in the past and I'm tired of failing her. I don't shift as Joachim intends. This time I will not retreat to the safety of my beast. Instead, I take her hand in mine and bring her wrist to my lips even though I know it will test my willpower. "Anastasia--"

"Someday I hope you'll tell me all about when I was your Anastasia. In fact, I'm hoping I remember. But I am not her. I am Taryn. I don't have much besides my name, but I'd like you to call me by it." Her words and meaning are firm, but her voice is gentle, and quiet enough that it's meant only for me.

Her tenderness makes me feel fragile and I can't be. The

wolf inside pushes me to be harsh and hard. My words come out in a snarl. "You have more than that, Taryn."

Her name feels awkward on my tongue. I'm always the worst at adjusting to the changes of each new life. I would be perfectly happy going back to calling her my Goddess.

She doesn't flinch away from the angry wolf lingering at my surface. She bites right back. "Like what?"

Me. I want to say it. I won't, not yet. Not until she wants me like I want her. Not just physically, that part is always the easiest. I want her love. Fuck. I want her everything. "Us."

August joins with his easy truths. "The devotion of the people in the *derevnya*, and your newfound powers. That is more than most who are stuck here in this prison."

She glances up at me and pulls her arm as if to take it from my grasp. I don't let her. It's too late for me to let her go. We settle for twined fingers.

"I need more than that."

Joachim growls at the three of us and Taryn growls right back. It surprises her and she covers her mouth and glances back and forth between August and I, all wide-eyed. She doesn't understand what's happening to her, and I can't stand by and watch her struggle alone.

"You have more power in you than any of us even know. I will help you find it, use it, and then you won't need guards any longer. You'll be able to protect yourself, better than any of us ever could." This promise breaks no vows and yet allows me to stop lying to her.

August sighs and Joachim bares his teeth at me. I don't care if I've made him mad. His way wasn't working.

"What kind of powers? Where do they come from?" Her frustration physically hurts me, and I want to make it better for her. I want to destroy those who've hidden and quashed her soul away. I will kill them, so she doesn't have to.

"How do I use them, and can they get us off this god-forsaken island?" She stomps her foot against the unforgiving stones.

Her stream of questions doesn't bother me because I know that means she wants to fight for herself. Fighting is something I'm good at. "Only you can uncover your true power. I will be there as you do."

August slaps me on the shoulder. "If I'd known all it took to get you to be so damn talkative and helpful was to make you shift, I'd have found my own alpha voice and made you shift a long damn time ago."

I shake my head and give my smile to Taryn. "Yours is the only voice I care to hear."

Taryn grins up at me, and I forget for just a moment to be hurt and angry. She's not only bringing sunshine back to the island, but back into my life. I shouldn't have avoided her and her love for so long. August gives me a good-natured punch in the arm, but Joachim is still pouting. This isn't the first promise to him I've broken. He'll forgive me once he has some time to think about it. Nowhere did we say we couldn't help her figure out who and what she is, we simply can't tell her. He'll understand this way is better for us all.

Especially now that the Dark Prince of Wolves knows she's here. My number one priority has to be keeping her safe from him, and the best way to do that is for her to learn how to defend herself. We clearly cannot keep her alive on our own.

"I'm going to get you to tell me what you know, you three. I don't like secrets." She wags her finger at us.

I don't suppose she does. Even if she doesn't know, her whole life is a lie. Every family the Volkovs steal her from, every faux mother and father they give her to, and even we, her guards, lie and keep secrets from her. I hate it and am going to do everything in my power to make sure this time, it ends.

I'm done standing around. "The quicker we get you to safety, the sooner we can start searching for your powers."

TARYN

*I*t seems silly, but I'm hurt that Vasily didn't reveal himself to me like August and Father Joachim did. I'm chastising myself for feeling that way because I also know that he has something broken deep inside of him and that is what kept him from letting me in.

I'm sure it has to do with our last life together. I've got the tiniest snippets of memory. I'm a princess. He's a guard. We're in love even though the idea of us even talking to one another is forbidden.

Sounds like the beginning of a great book. Oooh. I wonder if any of the women on the island have romance novels. I'd kill for a hot cup of tea, a warm and fuzzy blanket... or a wolf, wrapped around me, and a dirty romance to keep me warm.

Vasily is practically vibrating with his need. I'm just not sure if it's to go back to his lone wolf ways, or if that need rolling off him is for me.

Oh, wait. That's me. I think the adrenaline from the battle is taking a nose-dive because I'm suddenly shivering and so is the rest of the world around me.

"Crap, I'm so cold. I wish I could shift into a hairy beast like you guys." It looks way warmer, and I can't blame Father Joachim for staying that way. Except I know he's avoiding letting me see something about himself too.

The three of them share a look between them that either means they're talking in each other's heads or more likely, they've got another secret they're keeping from me.

Secrets. I frigging hate secrets.

I'm going to find a way to make them all tell me everything. I want to know about them, their past lives too, and most importantly who I am and who we are to each other. That includes that damn Dark Prince of Wolves.

"Come here, tzaritsa. I'll carry you to back to my cabin, and then I can warm you right up in the bed we haven't taken advantage of yet." August waggles his eyebrows at me and I'm amazed at how he can go from warrior to lover so fast.

Vas steps in the way of August's attempt to grab me up. "We need to get her back to the *derevnya* so she can start her training."

I have a feeling Vasily is going to be a task master, and that it's going to be super sexy. His promise to help me figure out my powers fills that scared empty place inside of me.

August will help too, because while his mind is in the gutter right now, at his core, he is my fervent protector. The sooner we can get to work the better. I shudder and look down at my toes. I'm surprised they aren't blue. Why is it I never seem to have proper clothes whenever I'm on this beach?

A howl sounds from the tree line and I whip my head around to see some of the other wolves from the village racing toward us. They're led by my new friends and girl gang, Alida, Killisi, Bridget, and Jeanette. They have satchels strapped to their bodies. Leave it to the women to come up with a smart idea like that. If I was in charge, I'd declare that everyone has some kind of emergency shifting kit for when they all burst out of their clothes all the time.

Whose idea was it for them to ruin everything they wear? Why couldn't they just have magic clothes? Not that I mind my guys having to shift back all naked and delicious.

A big roar greets them, and Will comes barreling down the beach, back to us. Funny that my magic didn't grab him up too. Not far behind him is Maggie in human form. I was sort of hoping I'd get to see what she shifts into as well. Nope.

She's carrying an armful of the robes the men like to wear. Probably because they can shed those faster than pants and t-shirts. I'm getting it now. Shifter life is weird. I'll keep my warm wooly dress, thank you very much. I hope Maggie brought it and some shoes. The mostly see-through shift I wore for the mating ritual doesn't do a thing to keep the cold away.

My friends shift and slip on the dresses they've brought in their packs and each of them check in quickly with their mates. I'm glad they got to reaffirm their bonds at my ceremony with August. But something strikes me like a metaphorical snowball to the face giving me an instant shiver and worrisome chill.

Vasily looks from the women and then back at me. He squeezed my hand and frowns. "What's wrong?"

"Nothing, I'm just cold is all." He knows I'm lying. Of course he does. I'm not ready to say anything. I need to figure out what I think first. Because here's my problem.

The women of the derevnya are all mated. To one man. Not three, not four, but one.

There do seem to be a lot more men than women on the island, so why don't they all have multiple mates like I know that I do. I hadn't even questioned it until just now. Are my feelings abnormal? It certainly doesn't feel wrong.

August is mine. If the two of us having sex in front of everyone doesn't establish that, then I don't know what would.

Down to my soul, I know, that as much as he's holding himself back from a relationship with me, Father Joachim is mine too. He belongs to me and I to him. And now that I know

Vasily isn't just a pet, but a hot-blooded, virile man, my heart has a claim on him.

I'm going to have to ask someone about this. I wonder if girls' night out is a thing here.

Maggie comes over to me with my dress and some shoes in her arms, as if my thoughts conjured them. More likely she's done all this battling bad guys business a hundred times before and knew what the rest of us would need. "You're all right now, aren't ya, love? I could feel the power of the *Tuath Dé* coming from ya like a beam from the sun or the moon."

Moonlight. That's exactly what the blue light of my magic reminded me of. Had I called it down? Psh. That's the weirdest thing I've come up with so far. I shake my head at myself as I pull the warm wool dress on over my head. "I'm..., huh, I don't know what I am. I meant to say I was fine, but something has changed, and I don't entirely understand it."

"No, I suppose you don't. But it will come to ya. We all are a bit messy in the head when we get thrown in here through the shadow, but your memories are coming back faster than most. I suspect that has something to do with them." She nods toward August and Vasily who have accepted clothes from my smarty-pants, well-prepared girl gang.

"Oh, is that Vas? He's a fine bit o' man, isn't he?" Maggie fans her face and I think I see Will scowl at her. "You'll have to be careful with that one."

I slip into the boots and sigh in relief. "Maybe we could talk about them, my situation, geez, my whole love life, later when we aren't in after battle crisis mode?"

Maggie tilts her head, and I can practically see the wheels turning in her head. "Now that we've defeated Lev and his pack, we know you're safe, and no one seems to be badly injured, I think we could all use a good gathering around the campfire tonight."

"Another party?" That doesn't sound like a good idea to me.

We should hole up in the village and build a big wall around it. I already feel horrible that it was the shindig they threw to celebrate my mating that opened us up to the attack. "That's what got us into this mess in the first place."

Maggie laughs. "Naw, that'd be you drawing in the trouble. But don't you worry none. We've been waiting on you a long while. We're ready."

Before I can say anything, Maggie's already turned like she didn't just accuse me of being a weapon of mass destruction and is gathering our cavalry to head back. August reaches over and closes my wide-open, gaping mouth with a knuckle. I swallow hard and glance up at him to see if he agrees with her. I don't want to cause these good people to fight horrible criminals like Lev and his pack.

Vasily pushes a stray hair away from my face and tucks it behind my ear. "There's not a one of us who wouldn't die for you."

No. No one is dying for me. I want... I... my chest is thrumming like I've got a ticking time bomb behind my heart. I want them to live for me. "But I don't want anyone to be hurt or worse because of me."

Father Joachim, who has been stand-offish since he shifted, trots over to me. *The distress of your mind is like bitter lemons in my nose,* boginya. *It is my duty to be your advisor in all matters. Let me help.*

Even in wolf form, his calm demeanor permeates my unease and makes me believe everything will turn out okay. And that isn't enough. I need so much more from him. "Is that all you are to me, Father? My advisor?"

Wow. Something else has changed inside of me besides finding out I have magic powers. The world has become clearer. No, not the world, but myself in it. My wants, my needs, and my feelings have become more important. If that makes me selfish, so be it. Because in that selfishness lies the happiness I'm sure is there for us all to have. We just need to take it.

I have to convince Father Joachim to give up his vows.

Shit. What am I saying? I can't believe I even thought that. Yeah, now that is wrong. Doesn't matter that we both want this. There is something bigger and more important out there than wants and needs.

"It's fine, I'm fine. Let's get back to the village. I'm cold." Cold-hearted, that is.

The wolf eyes me, but he doesn't say anything more into my head. I'm grateful he's giving me some space for the moment.

It doesn't take long for everyone to organize into a clumpy line to make the trek back. I'm the weak link and stuck in the middle so everyone else can keep me surrounded and safe. I'm more determined now to learn how to use my power for all these good people.

Vasily and August are never more than a foot or two from me on the walk through the trees, but neither of them push me to say anything. They're probably all up in their heads just as much as I am. Or they're being smart and making sure there aren't any monsters in the trees.

I should know better by now to keep more aware of my surroundings. If I had the senses of my wolfy friends maybe I wouldn't get into so many scrapes. I could have avoided the whole thing with Lev and his pack wanting to claim me, and I certainly would like to have skipped being kidnapped by Peter. That rat.

But once again, a threat appears right in friggin front of me and I'm unprepared.

We walk into the village and a pack of disheveled and shabby looking wolves are waiting for us. My friends surround me in a circle and prepare for another battle. Great. Just great. What did I say? I'm trouble with a capital T.

I grab Vasily's arm, knowing he is ready to shift and protect me. "Wait, please. I don't want more bloodshed."

He nods, but steps in front of me anyway. He snarls in a way that makes me think he knows the intruders. I don't get to August in time. He drops his robes and shifts so fast, I hardly see the transformation take place.

Hackles are raised all around, and I just want it all to stop. No more fighting over, or for, me. No. More. I raise my hands in the air and search for the feeling I had inside of me when I spurted out all that magic at the beach. Power crackles in my palms, and... crap, between my legs too.

If it takes a magic vagina to stop the fighting, fine. I'll use the gifts I have at my disposal. I take a deep breath and open my eyes again to see what kind of havoc I've wreaked. No one is floating, they're not all caught up in my magic moon beams, but they are all staring at me, and with glowing eyes.

Two of the interlopers shift, a man and a woman. They look at me, then to each other, and the woman smacks the guy. "She is Goddess touched. I told you."

She approaches me, but August growls and stands in her way. The woman tilts her head to the side and down, exposing her neck, looking away and at the ground. To my surprise, August quiets and lets her pass.

Vasily is not so lenient. "Showing your throat won't save you if you harm even a hair on her head."

I had no idea the sweet wolf I though was a pet was going to be such a dangerous man. It's a little overwhelming to have him being a protector. I'm not sure what I've done to deserve such fierce loyalty from him, but I'll take it. I'll work on being worthy of it a little later.

To both Vasily's and my surprise, the woman goes down on one knee and bows her head. "We've come to pledge our fealty to your, my lady."

"Me?"

The man approaches and when Vas snarls at him, he too gets down on his knees in front of us. "Clearly the Goddess has sent you to save us from this hell."

He's got one of those pretty, white flowers in his hand and I swear it's glowing the same color as my magic. "I don't even know who your Goddess is."

Maggie comes over and gives the two people a nudge to get up. "That's something we ought to remedy. Don't you think, boys?"

August snorts and tries to cover it with a cough. "Yes, we should."

I give him a what-is-wrong-with-you look. Apparently, this goddess of theirs is just another secret they've been keeping from me. I wonder how much of this I knew about before I got my brain cells zapped in the Nothing. When I find out whoever did this to me, I'm going to give them a concussion and see how they like it. Or, I'll have Vasily do it for me. I think he'd enjoy that.

There's chatter among the villagers and the group of new people.

Will joins us and gives a big old roar, silencing everyone else. Then he shifts and raises his voice so everyone gathered can hear. "I know there's more of ya hiding out there in the forest. Come on out and bring some firewood. My mate insists on a bonfire to celebrate our patch of good weather."

We all wait in silence for at least a count of ten and then a face, and another, and another pops out from various spots nearby. Slowly a dozen more come forward, each with twigs and fallen logs in their arms as commanded. One by one they drop their firewood where Maggie directs them and soon, we've got enough for a fire that will last all night.

No one says much, but they all stare at me, which has Vasily bristling. I get the feeling that hospitality isn't something very common outside the *derevnya*. I like that our community could bring other people together who've been imprisoned here. So far it seems it's about fifty-fifty on whether people are good and decent or bad guys. I'd sure like to know who it is that's thrown us all in here.

"I don't like having all these people around you. I could keep track of them all when they were hiding in the trees like scared animals." Vasily grabs my wrist and pulls me closer to him. August closes in beside me, forming a barricade between me and the lookie-loos.

"You knew they were there?" I didn't see anyone and that gives me the heebie-jeebies.

He rounds on me and there's a wildness in his eyes, that same blue glow as when he's a wolf. "I will teach you to open your senses. You need to be more aware so you can protect yourself."

"I doubt I'll need the skill. I have the feeling you, August, and Father Joachim aren't going to let me out of your sight." I look around for the Father and don't spot him. Not even in wolf form.

August turns toward me too and runs his thumb across the mark he's given me on my neck. It sends a billion tingles across my skin that flow like a wave to my breasts and between my legs. "Your growing powers will attract more attention. That puts you in danger."

Vasily's eyes are glued to where August is touching me, and he clenches his fists. The one holding my wrist squeezes tight around my skin and bones, almost to the point of pain. "We can only guard you against so many."

JOACHIM

*E*verything I know about Taryn is wrong. In my hubris, I assumed I knew how and when she would remember who she is, and her powers would come back to her then.

Clearly, I don't know shit.

I don't even understand how she could pull the light and magic down from the moon and not realize she was doing it. When her powers hit me, shifting me from wolf to man, my blood tingled in all my arteries and veins as if this was my first shift and she herself was blessing me with the sacrament of her very soul. I've never felt such bliss.

Finally, we four were together again, united with her, and all my plans and machinations weren't needed. All was forgiven.

Then I woke the fuck up when she opened that portal.

Good God. I thought the Volkovs and their demons would come rushing out to take her away from me once again. I was even sure I heard Rasputin laughing at us all for thinking we could defeat them and allow our true queen to ascend to her rightful place.

We are safe, no thanks to me, and I watch August and Vas dote on her, keeping her under their watchful protection among the crowd of people coming to see her. How my body and my wolf long to touch her soft skin. I want to run my hands along every one of her lush curves and whisper the truth of my need for her as I take her in our own mating ritual.

I need her so much, it physically hurts. Because of that, I've once again retreated to my wolf form, so I don't have to face her. I need time to reign in that overwhelming hunger for her. I'll be more in control if I meditate on all that's happened. Today's events have forced me to reconsider the plans I had, and everyone's roles they must play.

This all should have been so easy.

She shows up.

We all claim her, helping her remember who she truly is.

She ascends and we are free.

She never finds out how I've betrayed her, my brethren, and all of wolfkind.

But no. None of them can do as they're told.

If Vasily and Grigori would have just fucking showed up to the mating ritual and done as I asked this could all be over. They all know the consequences if we fail her.

I had everyone prepared. Well, almost everyone. I would have convinced Grigori.

My last look through the shadow and into her world did that for us. I didn't tell them that's how I knew the Volkovs had made a mistake and that she was coming. They don't need to know the risks I take to bring us all back together. Now they're slipping through my fingers. Because I'm no alpha. But I'll do what I must since Grigori won't fulfill his duties to us all.

God damn them all to hell.

I flinch at my own thoughts. Hell is exactly where we already are.

Taryn searches the crowd even as they glom to her. She's looking for me. I can feel her pull. But I keep myself at the edge of the circle of buildings that make up the small *derenvya*, away from the others as they prepare for the celebration of surviving for a time longer.

We haven't done enough of that. With no passage of time here, each day is like the last. No one ages, no one changes, except inside where we all die a slow death. With that and the harsh living, there wasn't a reason. The Volkovs knew exactly what they were doing when they requested this demon's prison for unruly foes.

Slow, torturous death, and no hope of hope. Until now. Maggie and Will aren't even wolves, and they can see how her people need to gather around her and rejoice in her return. More will come and she will unite them.

It's not enough.

She never did love the attention. Her people can't help wanting to be near her. Vasily can't keep his eyes off her, and his wolf hovers near the surface. He may be a man again, but in his mind, he's still wild and broken. I know that look, though. He will mark and claim her soon and I envy him. She will heal his broken soul like no one else could.

I tried, and in recent years the violence in him has waned a little. But perhaps that was only his mind losing his humanity. We've all lost a piece of ourselves without her.

With Vas on the path to her, I must turn my attentions to the final phase. We must come together to complete her. And there is only one way I can ensure she gets everything she deserves. I have to sacrifice everything I am, everything I have, for her.

Dusk is upon us, and the first flames of their bonfire are crackling. I stare across the open center square, allowing my wolf's supernatural senses to track Taryn's every movement. August and Vasily are at her side, naturally defending her from anyone getting too close.

I turn my back on the festivities. She is in good hands with August and Vasily. As long as they don't reveal too much. At least we all know she is safe from another attack by the Dark Prince. For the moment.

Above all others, his is the soul I worry the most about. I will save him, and in return Taryn, even if I have to give up my own soul in return. An eternity in hell is not punishment enough for my sins.

The chatter, laughter, and revelry fade as I make my way into the forest toward the old church. I can only pray that's where Taryn's portal sent Grigori. I don't get more than a few minutes away from the derevnya, before I encounter a small and terrified pack.

"Father Joachim? We've been searching for you. What's happening?" An old man who's been in this prison longer than I have calls out to me.

I shift so I can calm his worries. "Do not fear. You are safe in the arms of the Lord and the Goddess tonight, friends."

"We saw the magic in the sky. The moon, Father, we saw the moon."

Old superstitions and fears are hard to combat with prayer alone. Especially when what they've been taught is a myth is real and here in the flesh.

I pat the man on the shoulder and find the eyes of each of his small and tired looking pack. Life here is hard on the strongest of prisoners and this group, both young and old, are not the toughest. They've given up hope more times than there are stars in the sky. "I know. A new hope has come into our lives, and it's hard to trust, but go to the *derevnya* and be with others who believe. You'll find peace there, if only for now."

I wish I could tell them this is the end of our suffering, but even in the best of circumstances, a battle lies ahead of us.

Without Grigori leading the Guard, things aren't even close to good, much less the best. I must continue on my journey and hope I find him at the end.

I can sense more packs moving through the woods in search

of the source of the magic, so I remain in human form. Few will need convincing that change is in the air for us all. Only a fool could ignore the end of our eternal winter, and the moon flowers.

But I know one who will.

After sending a few more peace-seeking packs toward the *derevnya*, I approach the no man's land around the ruins of the church. Even a hundred years later, I can still smell the scorched wood as if it burned only yesterday.

It is the same scent as Grigori's anger.

Today, though, it is more subtle, or rather there is a softer scent intermingled with his. The fragrant soft scent of moon flowers.

Taryn.

The essence of her swirls around me and my blood races. There's nothing I can do to stop my cock from getting hard and aching for her. No amount of prayer, no self-recriminations, nothing can cleanse my soul of my sinful need for her.

I let the lust pour through me and try to use the energy to focus on the push to get done what I must to help her ascend. The first thing I need to do is find Grigori. Even with my senses wide open, I don't feel his presence.

Fuck.

If he isn't here... fuck, fuck, fuck.

Either Taryn's powers have far exceeded what I expected at this point, and she's pushed him out of this prison with that portal, or he's stuck in Hell. Either way, I'm going to have to open a portal myself and that opens us all up to dangers we aren't prepared for.

I've only done it a few times in the four hundred years I've been here and never twice so close together. Before I had to look through the shadow to see her coming to us. This time, I must look for an old friend.

I hurry into the shell of the sanctuary, picking my way

through new piles of rubble. "Grigori, if you're here come out now. Neither of us want to fight off shadow demons if we don't have to."

I'm sure he isn't going to respond, but I have to try. Even with only a small chance of Grigori being stuck in the shadow portal and exposed to the monsters within, there is no choice. As much as I want there to be a better way, I have to open a shadow portal. Neither the guard nor Taryn are ready if the shadow demons decide to come to Fire Island to claim a few new souls for Hell's army.

I set aside the prayer beads I always carry with me, regardless of if I'm in wolf form or human. They are my anchor to this world if I get sucked into Hell.

The dark mark on my soul flexes itself, knowing I'm about to call on it. My wolf snaps and snarls, letting it know that this small amount of freedom does not mean it's in charge.

Sometimes I wonder.

I step into the area where the altar used to stand and feel for the shadow. The black stain of sin inside of me reaches for it and the disoriented feeling of Hell's element washes over me.

Hello, darkness, my old friend.

The portal to the underworld is anything but silent. The cries and moans of the demons are a constant din. I don't know how the beasts under Ereshkigal's control survive such an environment. I certainly don't want to draw the attention of any of the dragon-demon hybrids to take notice of me, so I shift into my wolf form and drop through the shadow into the darkness to look for my alpha.

I am not your alpha anymore, priest. Grigori's denial is tired and defeated. Regardless, I celebrate because he is within a stone's throw of the portal.

After I check the surrounds for demons or worse, I hurry to him and push him to his feet. *I didn't say you were.*

If not for his wolf's healing abilities, he'd likely be dead. His skin and fur are hot to the touch and he's panting, trying desperately to cool down. Brimstone and fire aren't the ideal environment for creatures of the wild like us. Especially not after a century or more of living in a Siberian winter.

He's limping, but we move together toward the portal I left open. If we hurry, perhaps we'll get out without any demons escaping with us. I can hear their screeching not far away. The last thing we need is a haunted fucking dragon to terrorize our people. Grigori terrorizes them enough.

Your thoughts are not as silent as you think, and you smell like them. Haven't I been punished enough? Leave me be.

You know I cannot. No more than I can leave August or Vasily to their own devices either. Without one, we fail. I won't allow that, not when we're so close to succeeding.

Why? Grigori snarls at me. *Because you need to save my soul? Isn't it obvious? I'm beyond being saved.*

Not yours. Hers.

The moment I say it, I can feel a shift in the very fabric of Hell. Above our heads, the light of the moon glows as if the Goddess herself has hung it up to illuminate the underworld. The light does not reach out into the other tunnels and caverns of rock. It glows only for the two of us.

In that light we can see the silhouette of Taryn. She is surrounded by shadows of other people, some whose souls shine and others with swirls of darkness like my own. Two of those tainted souls guard her. August and Vasily.

Grigori growls with such force it rattles the rock walls around us. *Those fuckers. They can't keep her safe.*

He sprints toward the light, and I have to push myself to keep up. Dammit. What the hell is he doing? *Grigori, stop. We can't get to her that way.*

He ignores me completely, which is nothing new. But it's been a very long time since we faced actual danger together, and then he was the one giving the orders.

The time and space in Hell aren't the same as in the mortal realm and we make no progress running toward her light. We do however attract our own admirers in the form of a pack of demon dragon wyrms. Shit.

We have both died and been reincarnated more times than we can count, but I have no idea what will happen if we die on Fire Island or in Hell. Prisoners of the Volkovs don't age, we don't get sick, but we can be killed. Grigori has proven that more times than I'm comfortable with when he goes on his vendetta murdering sprees.

We've got maybe thirty seconds before the demon horde is upon us and no fucking plan for how to fight them off. One or two I could manage on my own, I've done it before protecting Taryn. But not this many and that was literally lifetimes ago. My fighting skill have atrophied. I was always better at subterfuge than killing.

The demon dragons spread their puny wings and climb the walls around us. They're going to surround us and then eat us alive. Yet still we run toward a goal we cannot reach. *Dammit, Grigori. I have no wish to die this day.*

He glances back and snarls. *Then don't. Go back through the portal and leave me be. Save yourself.*

Jesus. Not this again. *I'm tired of your death wish. Get your shit together and do your fucking duty, you asshole.*

For the first time in the hundred years since he was thrown into this prison with me, his step falters. *Careful, Father. Someone might actually mistake you for a warrior instead of a peacemaker.*

Ouch.

Grigori pivots and bounces off the side of the tunnel we're in, landing behind me and face to face with the demons. Finally. I skid to a stop and cover his flank. Some of these wyrms are smarter than we give them credit for.

In the blink of an eye, we're surrounded, but they don't advance on us, nor shoot their spittle of fire. Their red eyes burn and the hunger behind them fuels that fire. Are they taunting us before they eat us?

Grigori lunges at the closest one, but the group of them waver away. *What the fuck are they waiting for?*

Another behind us nips at my heels but doesn't actually strike. When I move away, they push closer, but still don't attack. *They're herding us.*

I'm no fucking sheep. He lunges again and swipes one of them with his claws. It screeches and the black oil that is their lifeblood seeps out. Still the rest do not move to strike back.

"Stop. No harm." A much bigger demon dragon pushes through their ranks and to the front. The others move for him, and I wonder if we're meeting the Black Dragon, father of all demon dragon wyrms. If this is their AllFather, we are definitely fucked.

It reaches its arm out and points at me. "How portal?"

What? Is this creature seriously asking me how I've opened a portal? This is not the Black Dragon. He would have had to shift to be able to speak, just as we do. But whoever this is, he is no ordinary demon.

I'm not sure if it's asking me how I have the power to open a portal, or how to open one itself. Demon dragons use shadow and travel through it, but they don't have the magic required to open a portal themselves. Only gods, goddesses, and some dragons can do that. And me.

It's not as if I can answer his question anyway. I'm not about to shift into my fragile human form. I growl low and shake my head. The demon dragon doesn't like that.

He spreads his wings, and a black smoke pours from his mouth. "How portal or die."

I'm not saying you should tell him, Joachim, but how about you just open one and we hop on out of this hell hole? Grigori backs away and I can see why. The black smoke coming from our new demon dragon friend is turning the craggy stone below our feet to lava.

I can't. I left the one at the church open. I'm tethered to that one.

Then we make a run for it.

At least we have a plan now. A shitty one, but a plan none the less. That's all I ever asked for.

I tense my muscles, preparing to sprint and barrel my way through the demon wyrms but, before I can, the strangest voice rings out through the tunnel. "Jett, no. You quit that right now."

A little girl, no older than six-years old, runs toward us with sparks of fire magic shooting from her hands. She looks directly at Grigori and I and says, "Run, puppies, run home."

This is possibly the strangest thing that has ever happened to me and that is saying a lot. But neither of us hesitate and we both take off. This time I lead, because I can feel exactly where the portal is despite the darkness and winding tunnels we've already run through.

The big demon dragon roars and flaps his wings. I think for a moment he's letting us go because that little girl told him too. But a moment later, he gives chase. He's too late though. I can see the portal and the instant I'm back into the mortal realm it will close behind me.

Grigori, go, quickly. For the first time in his fucking life, he does as he's told and takes an enormous leap up into the portal, slipping through.

The demon dragon swipes his claws at me, and splits open my left flank. I howl with the pain but draw on every ounce of my training as a Wolf Guard to make the jump into the portal. I land on the hard burned ground, feeling the cool earth under my overheated body and thank the Goddess of the Moon for bringing us both back to safety.

The portal zips closed behind me and I can breathe again. No monsters from Hell have escaped, unless you count me and Grigori.

Grigori circles me, a low growl emanating from him that I don't even think he realizes he's making.

Be still. *We are safe, old friend.* On the ground at the site of the portal is a snipped off claw and a few black scales. The wound that same claw inflicted on me is already healing, but I'm going to need a minute to recover from that bullshit journey into Hell. And who in the world was the little girl with fire magic in her soul?

He snaps his jaws and snarls at me. *We may be, but she is not. We are not the only ones who've used the shadow to travel. There is a minion of the Volkovs on Fire Island.*

Grigori's black eyes turn bright blue, reflecting the light of the moon, and he takes off running toward the *derevnya.*

At this point I don't know who he's headed to kill. Because his short stint in Hell has done nothing but darken his soul even further and I'm not sure even the Goddess can save him now.

TARYN

*W*hile I was warm and content sipping on some kind of hot cider and cuddled up in front of the bonfire squashed between August and Vasily, the two of them are on edge. Vasily keeps grabbing my hand, stroking his thumb over my wrist and his wolf lights up his eyes. He takes long, deep breaths like he's doing his best to control the beast, which I don't understand because we're just sitting here listening to stories.

Maggie's just finished one about the fae queen of Christmas whose been a changeling in the mortal world and doesn't know it. I shiver thinking about how everyone in her life had been lying to her until her nutcracker guards show up to take her back to her realms.

"It's just a story, my lady." Killisi notices how uncomfortable the tale made me and brings me a fresh hot mug of the cider.

"Aye. But all stories come from some kind of truth, don't they lassies?" Will winks at the two of us. "Even your own wolf lore had to come from somewhere."

"There's wolf lore?" I want to know more about what makes

my guys who they are. Especially since I can never be like them and shift into a wild animal running free.

"Yes, but our stories aren't just legend. The Goddess is real." Bridget's tone is pretty damn adamant. "Taryn is proof of that."

August and Vasily both go still like ice, but the other people in the circle give a cheer and hold up their mugs in toast. It makes me happy to see the villagers and the newcomers unafraid and enjoying life. So different from the day I walked into the *derevnya* with two injured and dying wolves, when everyone was afraid.

I didn't understand then what living in this prison meant. But now I have friends and my wolves.

Including the Dark Prince of Wolves.

Will he come back to terrorize them or is it only me he's coming for? I'm not even sure I'll ever see him again. I pushed him into that black hole. He could be dead.

No. I can feel him. He's alive. I don't know how I know that, but I do. He both scares and excites me, which means I'm mentally unhinged. I need to think about something else.

August nods toward the girls. "Tell Taryn about the Goddess, then. She doesn't know."

Bridget blinks. "Shouldn't Father Joachim do that?"

The guys both said they weren't freaking out because Father Joachim wasn't at the impromptu party with us. I lean into August. "You're sure he's not in danger? I don't like him being off on his own."

"Yes, love." He strokes my hair, comforting me. "He often needs to spend time alone in the forest. He's fine."

Praying probably. To keep himself from breaking his vows with me. It was really horrible of me for sending up prayers of my own that his would go unanswered. But I absolutely wanted him to be with me, and not whoever or whatever his God had planned for him.

I should feel awful about thinking that, partly because what

I found so attractive about him was his intense spirituality. I like the idea of a higher power who looked after a flock like a shepherd, keeping them safe, cared for, and even loved.

Would this God really want the two of us to be apart when it was so clear we should be together? All I could think about tonight was how I wanted to run my hands over his body, and then August's, and then Vasily's. I wanted to find pleasure with each of them, both with each individually and with all four of us together.

Warmth pools between my legs and I take a quick peak at Vasily and August to see if they noticed. I know they can smell emotions and my arousal. Vasily's nostrils flare and he grabs my wrist again. This time kissing my pulse point. I'm melting and not because of the heat of the fire.

Oh my God - sorry Father - why am I so fricking horny? You'd think with the day of excitement with being kidnapped and becoming all powerful and stuff I'd be tired. Yeah...no. I've got two dudes stuck like glue to me and I'm super hawt for both of them. Like I kinda want to drag them off into the forest and have my way with them. Right now.

So inappropriate. There are so many people here to cele-brate... me. I don't know why, really except for the whole mating thing. Okay, and the magic vagina. But none of these people know about that.

I need to focus. It's nice to have other people around us that aren't weirdo bad guys who are trying to claim me. Maggie said they were taken care of, and I'm pretty sure that means dead. What happens to someone who dies when they're on this island where time doesn't pass? Like, are there a bunch of dead bodies that aren't decomposing laying scattered around somewhere?

Blech.

I haven't seen any. Weird. Oh, maybe that means the people who've imprisoned us come in and clean up. That could be our ticket out of here. Uh, except we'd have to kill someone, and

I've had enough death and destruction to last a lifetime. From here on out, I'm choosing life.

"Yes, please tell me about this Goddess." Perhaps she can come and get us out of the prison with her powers.

Bridget fidgets and looks to the others. Jeanette gives her a nod and the other girls follow suit. "You do it, Alida."

Alida was the first of the wolftresses to decide she wanted to be my friend and she would never truly know how much that meant to me. She stands and moves to the center of the circle near the fire. The crackling fire behind her with the dark backdrop of the night set the stage for a great story.

"Okay then." She lifts her face to the sky and then raises her arms up to the clouds. They aren't as thick tonight, and we can almost see the moon. Not quite, but the sky is illuminated. "We are the people of the moon. In ancient times, when there were many gods and goddesses, we worshipped at the altar of the Goddess of the Moon."

Ooh. Ancient times. Fun. I settled in to enjoy this story.

"Tell her about the persecution," someone shouted from the crowd.

"Shush. I'm getting there." She wags her finger at the man and then continues. "We were blessed by the Goddess, and we prospered under her care. Others who chose to worship lesser gods were not so lucky."

Uh oh. I think I could see where this was going.

"They were jealous of us and called forth demons from the underworld to hunt and kill us so they could take what they wanted."

Nope. Don't like that. What makes some people so selfish? It makes me so mad that anyone would do that to these peaceful people.

"We didn't know how to fight back. We'd never needed to be warriors, as the Goddess took care of all of our needs. These tormentors were slaughtering our people. The Goddess could not abide that, but she couldn't outright kill the followers of another god, or she would incur his wrath."

Wrath schmath. I would have slapped this other god upside the head given the chance. I wonder who he is.

"But she could give us the ability to defend ourselves. By taking some of her own power and pouring it into us, she gave us the ability to free the beasts that inhabit all souls and shift into fierce wolves."

"Ooh. I love that." I clap excitedly, and August chuckles at me.

""Our people defeated the demons and the worshippers of their god, sending them all to hell. But in doing so, the Goddess was weakened by giving so much of herself so that we could save ourselves. She could not shine bright in the sky every night like she had for eons. She needed to rest and recover. As her light faded, she was half of herself, then a quarter, and then her light disappeared altogether."

What? I did not see an origin story of why the moon goes through phases coming. Awesome.

"In our hopes to bring the Goddess back, the strongest warriors among us offered themselves up as her guards, her priests, each one taking on one of her phases to protect. The guards of the rising and setting moons, the guard of the half moon, and the strongest warrior of them all, who must protect her at her weakest, the guard of the new moon."

Guard of the House of the Rising Moon.

That's what Father Joachim called August during our mating ceremony. I turn to him and he's already looking down at me like he's been waiting for me to realize all this time. "You're descended from those warriors, aren't you?"

He swallows and licks his lips like he wants to tell me something and doesn't know if he should. I thought out of all of them, he and I were past keeping secrets. "Something like that."

August glances over my head at Vasily and I gasp. I spin on

my seat to face him. He's looking anywhere but at me. The ground, the fire, Alida, August, but not at me. This is crap.

I grab his chin and turn his face to mine. The wolf is glowing bright in his eyes. "You are too, aren't you? Which house or guard or whatever are you?"

Vasily rips my hands from his face and stands. I think for a second, he's going to walk away without answering me, but then he picks me up and throws me over his shoulder, just as August did. "I can't protect you with all these people around."

The crowd grumbles about the interruption but I lift my head and find Alida. "Don't mind us. Keep telling stories. I'm sure we'll be back in a minute."

Hopefully. I didn't mean to freak him out. I just wanted an answer about who he is. They seem to know everything about me, and I know nothing about them except they're wolf shifters and we've met before in past lives. I'm not wrong about the both of them being from this ancient line of warrior guards.

But what does that mean about me? Why would this Goddess have them guard me? Is she the one who gave me the magic powers? Why? I have so many questions and I'm not getting answers being hauled off like a sack of potatoes.

"Vasily stop. Put me down." I smack him on the back. Ooh, but his cute butt is so close I smack that too just for fun.

He doesn't flinch, just keeps going with those long strides of his toward Will and Maggie's house. "I refuse to lie to you. You've discovered who we are, so I'm breaking none of Joachim's rules."

August isn't far behind, and I give him the what-am-I-supposed-to-do-now look. He's no help because he just shakes his head like he doesn't know either. I suppose if your bestie was a wolf up until this morning, dealing with a grumpy, slightly off his rocker warrior is a bit discombobulated.

Vasily veers from the little wood cabin and heads toward the only barn in town. I don't know why they even have a barn. It's not like I've seen cows or chickens around. Although, I do think I saw deer and small game in the woods around the *derevnya.*

But come to think of it, the barn is where Vasily and August were laid to rest and heal after their first battle against Lev and his pack. So maybe it's more like a temporary bunk house or an inn for newcomers to the island before they get settled or join a pack. Maggie and Will do play the part of hosts pretty well. This community would be lost without them.

I can't see it but hear Vasily kick the door open and once we're inside, he slides me down his body and backs me up to the wall, all up in my personal space. And I love it.

He snarls at August. "Something is coming. Can you feel it?"

August scowls and gives a curt nod and closes the door behind him before joining us, filling any remaining space around me. I don't know what's about to happen but with the way they're both looking at me with brutal desire in their eyes, and their wolves hovering near the surface, I. Am. Here. For. It.

"I will not leave you unprotected." Vasily grabs one arm and pins it over my head, and August takes the other, pushing my shoulder back, and exposing my neck. The place where the Dark Prince bit me is still tender and I wince a little without meaning to. I don't want that to stop what I'm sure is about to happen between the three of us, so I let out the whimper I've been holding in, hoping my lust for them will be distraction enough.

"Fucking hell. He's marked her." August runs his fingers over the spot on my throat and it sends skyrockets in flight right between my legs.

"What?" I squirm in their hold, like I'm going to be able to see how my skin is marred. Marked me? The Dark Prince attacked me, he bit me. When August marked me, it was sensual and loving. I wouldn't call trying to chomp my face off real romantic.

Vasily snarls and narrows his eyes, mad at my very skin.

Then he looks at me and I fall deep into the blue glow of his wolf. He's hypnotizing in his anger and heat, and I'm melting. From the very beginning when I first saw him on the beach, he's guarded and protected me. He almost gave his life for mine and demonstrated his devotion over and over.

I've done nothing to deserve this, and yet I'll take it anyway. I wish so much that he'd let me see this more vulnerable side to him from the first. I barely know the man, but I know his soul. And it belongs to me. Just as much as August's.

"Mine." The word rolls out of Vasily's mouth on a deep, harsh grumble. His eyes flash down to my lips, then to my throat, and back up to my face. He presses his body closer and even through my wool dress and his robes, I can feel the bulge of his cock. He grinds against me and reaches for my skirt, hiking it up to bare my legs.

I'm dying for him to mark me too. I need everyone to know that we belong together.

Honestly, I thought I'd have to woo Vasily, which is very different to how my relationship with August happened, and I don't know what the crap is happening with Father Joachim, not to mention the freaking Dark Prince. All I know, is that it may be their tradition to claim me and have a whole mating ceremony and all that jazz, but in my heart, I've claimed each of them.

"Taryn," Vasily bares his teeth, and I should be afraid, but I'm not. "I am Alexander Vasilchikov, Guard of the House of the Setting Moon, and I claim you for my mate."

Whoa. No ceremony, no ritual? "Vasily, I want Father Joachim to preside over our mating. We need him here."

"No. I'll claim you now and keep you safe." He lowers his lips to my neck and scrapes his teeth across the spot where the Dark Prince bit me. "I will erase this blight with my own mark."

My body is singing under Vasily's attention. Being in his arms, about to be claimed by him feels so right. Yet, I don't want to be only a ward, a weak thing that needs to be protected. I want him to love me.

August pushes a hand into my hair and turns my head so I can see him. "Let him take you, love. His broken soul needs this bond with you. His claim will only make you safer."

"No." This isn't right, it isn't how it's supposed to happen. I want his claim, but I want it to be a celebration of our joining, not done in fear of losing me to some unknown threat. "Please, Vasily, wait."

He stills, with the tip of his teeth already pressing into my skin. I can feel him warring with himself and I don't have a clue if he's going to do as I ask or not.

"You promised to help me find my powers so that I can be strong and defend myself. Don't make me out to be weak. I want your protection, Vasily, but I want your love more."

He stops breathing and I think I've broken him. Then he sucks in a breath, grips the arm over my head tighter, wraps his other hand under my leg, yanking me halfway up the wall and straddling his waist. My heart is beating through my chest. I'm turned on and my adrenaline is pumping through me like I'm about to die.

August grabbed the back of Vasily's neck. "Control your wolf."

Vasily snarls and shakes August off. He pinches my skin between his teeth but doesn't break the skin. Then he brings his mouth up to my ear and whispers, "Remember me, prinsessa."

He doesn't give me a chance to respond, although I think I could only moan out his name at this point. I want him so badly, but not this way. Vasily lowers his mouth to my neck again, avoiding the tingling mark from the Dark Prince, and grinds his pelvis against mine. He says the word again. "Remember."

I am both cursing the world and being grateful for the fact that I haven't had a pair of underpants since mine were destroyed days ago. The rough material of Vasily's robe rubs against my pussy and I'm already seeing stars from the pleasure his movements are creating in my core. I want nothing more than to open those robes, find his cock and guide him into me.

But everything is wrong about mating with Vasily here and now without the others.

"Dammit, Vas." August huffs and then brings his lips to mine, giving me a hard, intense kiss, claiming my mouth with his. When I'm more than breathless, he pulls away and murmurs a demand, "Mark him as you did me. He's fighting every instinct he has not to take you against your will. He won't hurt you, but it will destroy him. Let your magic flow, my tzarina."

Before his words even finish, the room fills with that same blue light of the moon. I'm not even sure I'm controlling it. Vasily's hips jerk and he grunts as he spills his seed. He sinks his teeth into my flesh, and I cry out, not in pain, but with the pleasure of being marked by one who is mine.

A flash of soft winter snow in a long-ago time and place flashes through my mind. I'm still pressed up against a wall, but with Vasily's hands between my thighs and only his kisses on my neck. Then a shot rings out and we're running, running. Running so fast away from the danger.

Vasily is in his beautiful wolf form, his feet pounding through the snow, but I'm keeping pace with him.

Because I too am a wolf.

I gasp and the moonlight recedes, we're back in the barn, and I'm clinging to both Vasily and August. They're both studying me, waiting. I touch Vasily's cheek. "I remember."

He drops his forehead to mine. "Thank the Goddess."

In that past life with Vasily, I too could shift into a wolf, but I turn my thoughts inward and search for an inner beast within me. Is this who I am? I don't see how I wouldn't know that I too was a wolf shifter. Alida said the Goddess gave her people the

225

ability to allow their beasts to run wild and free so they could defend themselves.

This must be what Vasily was trying to get me to remember. But there is no beast in me. I can feel the magic thrumming through me. But no wolf.

I'm about to ask Vasily and August when the barn door slams open and Maggie and Will hurry in. "Sorry to interrupt, lass. But a man has just run to the village from the beach."

"Oh, uh... that's bad? That's nice? I don't know what you want me to say or what it has to do with us."

Will eyeballs the three of us and smirks. "While I hate to break up the fun you're all having, what my mate has neglected to tell you is that he's asking for you by name, Taryn Crescent."

Taryn Crescent. Holy guacamole. That's my name. I hadn't remembered my last name until Will said it just now. "Who is this guy? How does he know me?"

Will raises an eyebrow and folds his arms. "He says he's from your pack and that the Wolf Tzar has murdered your father and taken over as alpha."

What. The. Ever-living. Fuck?

GRIGORI

*B*eing in Hell is fucking exhausting. But so is an eternity in this Siberian prison. I've had a hundred years to sleep and yet I can't. Because every time I close my eyes, I see her, and everything goes red.

I never thought I'd see her again in the flesh.

Death.

Murder.

Betrayal.

And it's starting all over again. I cannot allow that to happen. I will not.

No matter how much Joachim thinks he knows about the future, no matter how badly August wants to protect her, and even if it breaks Vasily even further, the Volkovs can never have the power of the Goddess again.

I can smell the soft wildflower scent of her in my sanctuary and I'm instantly nauseated. Peter will suffer long-term for bringing her here. He doesn't deserve the kindness of death that I mete out to the other traitors sent to Fire Island.

And yet, still another minion of evil and chaos comes and

thinks he can win the princess over, that he can take her power and escape. Not on my watch, not this time.

Hell has sapped my energy, but I draw upon my training as a guard to push my wolf to the absolute limit of my endurance. I can rest when I'm dead. Or when everyone else is. Joachim is right on my tail, as he so often is. He's kept me from the brink of self-destruction, and I hate him for it. *Leave me be, priest. This is not your battle.*

His mental sigh is as loud as the beating of my heart in my chest. He puts on a burst of speed and races ahead of me to block my way. But his footsteps falter and he doesn't get the opportunity to counsel me for the four billionth time, because a new shot of moonlight and magic shoots up from the village.

Fuck. Has the Volkov minion reached her before us? No. This magic is not defensive as it was at the beach when she used it against us. She is remembering.

I swallow the howl my wolf needs to release. I know how to be a silent predator better than most.

Joachim recovers and his voice has that tinge of awe that only a man of true spirituality can. *Vasily has marked her.*

But I know that Joachim has not so the circle of protection around her is not complete. She is vulnerable. That is something I can take advantage of.

The *derevnya* is as far from my lair as it can possibly be, and it takes much longer to get there than I'd like. For a brief moment I see a break in the clouds and the rays of the crescent moon shine down to illuminate my path. Her power has already changed our little slice of hell and she is only just getting warmed up. I've seen what she can do when she is at her most powerful. But that was a long time ago.

The Volkovs have kept her weak without her knowledge, using her magic for their own gain. Joachim is right in one thing. They've made a mistake putting all four of us together with her. This is my chance to make sure their reign comes to an end and her powers can never be used to control wolfkind forevermore.

The stream of light pools in streaks through the trees like a beacon made especially for me to her. One way or another this will end tonight. I race ahead of Joachim so that he has no chance of stopping my attack. He may yet warn August and Vas, but it doesn't matter. I trained them both how to fight, and while Vas is as skilled as I am, he is weak now that he's taken on his human form after all this time.

Weaker still if he's claimed her. I know better now.

Yet even now the lust for my long-ago princess boils through my veins. She has been mine so many times before and I can practically feel her cunt pulsing around my cock, hear her gasps as I make her come for me, taste the love...

I must use those memories to fuel my rage because they were all a fucking lie. Every second of every life I've lived for thousands of years were nothing but a deceit of the fates.

Finally, the *derevnya* comes into view from the top of the hill to the south. Instead of identifying the traitor among the small group of good people who've banded together to survive in this wasteland, I'm shocked to see hundreds. The town square, which only yesterday was nothing more than a barren patch with dilapidated well in the center, is now filled to overflowing with almost every wolf on the island.

This must be the doing of the King of Scots and his willful bride. They throw everything off kilter with their mere presence. How the fuck am I going to find the Volkov minion in this crowd? It's not like I can stroll into town and ask around. The people of this make-shift community are scared to death of me, as they should be. They've all seen me kill before.

Not to mention a lot more alphas who would defend their packs if they felt their people were threatened. I'm not here for any of them, but they won't know that. All they see is the murderer in me.

A long time ago I was good at strategy. I haven't had to, or wanted to, use that part of my brain. God dammit. I don't care what the rest of them think about me, but I won't kill anyone who isn't deserving. If I go running in there now, I'll have to worry about not hurting them to get to the Volkov and the princess.

Joachim trots up next to me, not hurrying since I'm no longer rushing in to attack. *You couldn't expect anything less once they saw her magic. In a way, you brought them to her.*

I want to tell him to fuck off, but he's right. If I hadn't gone to the beach and allowed Vas to pick a fight with me...if I had been able to resist fucking wrapping my jaws around her fragile precious throat - no, it doesn't matter now. I have this situation in front of me to deal with and nothing else. The past is the past and I will not be sucked into the mistake of thinking the answers are there.

Do you see the Volkov minion? If Joachim is going to be by my side, I may as well put him to good use. He may have the spirit of a holy man, but he has the training of a warrior.

No, nor do I see Taryn, August, or Vasily. Perhaps they have already taken her to safety.

Good try. I can smell the sex in the air just as well as he can and they are nearby. Her powers are already erratic. If Vasily has claimed her, she may have already remembered too much. My wolf begs to reach out to her mind. Nothing but the wounds of betrayal lie down that path.

There. A man in clothes tattered enough they speak of a recent shift, stumbles out of the trees and toward the bonfire. Damn. We should have started by going to the beach, but I didn't think the Volkovs were stupid enough send their minion in through the same portal as new prisoners arrive. If I'm lucky he won't have retained his memories coming through the shadow and his life can be spared until he does.

Or perhaps not. I will not allow her any contact with the taint that is the fascism the Volkovs call safety. We almost escaped their rule when she ruled as Catherine the Great. That was the closest we'd ever come to breaking the curse.

I watch the man and the crowd to see how they react to his presence. The fools should destroy him themselves. I can smell his blight from here. I will rip his fucking head off. Right now, or when he's not in a crowd is the question.

There's a commotion and we're far enough away I can't hear what he's saying. *Go, play your role as their spiritual advisor, and see what kind of threat this piece of shit presents.*

My gut tells me he's the worst kind of dangerous. Ignorant and brainwashed.

So that you can murder him with a clear conscience? His tone is both chastising and resigned at the same time.

My conscience is far from clear, Joachim. You know that better than anyone. Now, go. We're wasting time. My eternal soul is already damned. No use worrying about it now.

He doesn't move a fucking inch. *Are you asking? Or are you demanding as my alpha?*

My chest collapses in on itself and I round on him letting my wolf control my emotions like the wounded animal it is. *I am not your alpha.*

Joachim doesn't even flinch. The bastard. Four-hundred years on this island has taught him the patience and peace I can never hope to have. He simply stares at me like he fucking cares and then gets up and trots off as if there wasn't a walking bomb ready to go off.

About halfway to his destination, Will and Maggie move quickly to the barn where I know Vas and August are with the princess. I don't like that one bit. The lion is no danger, but they may be unwitting accomplices. I'm still undecided whether to interfere until Joachim goes from his easy lope to a full-out run.

Fuck. He's learned something and didn't bother to tell me. Fine. That makes my decision easy. Whether those other alphas perceive me as a threat and attack or cower as they so often do is no longer a factor. Especially when I see her walking toward the Volkov minion with open arms.

I take off at a dead run, my sight only on the man, set on his total annihilation as soon as possible. Or that's what I meant to do. I am distracted by the flush on her face, the scent of her arousal, the very beat of her heart pounding in my ears in time with my own.

My mark on her has bonded us once again and I am so fucked.

"Someone get this man a robe. Please, sit. Tell me who you are and how you know me." She sits as if the stumps around the bonfire are her throne, and the people around her are subjects come to beg her favor.

The man is out of breath, which is a ruse if I ever saw one. His wolf is stronger than that. The closer I get, the more I can sense the chaos in him. "Taryn, do you not remember me? We've been searching everywhere for you."

I bet they have.

"I'm sorry, I don't. "The whole being imprisoned in the Nothing and then on this weird prison island has messed with my memory quite a bit. What were you saying about my pack and some Wolf Tzar taking it over?"

The Wolf Tzar? Whoever they've roped into being their puppet these days deserves as much punishment as the Volkovs themselves. Then again so does her so called pack.

"Niko Troika murdered your father right in front of you and you don't remember?"

That conversation comes to an abrupt end as someone finally notices Joachim and I running toward them. Someone screams and another shouts, "Oh, Goddess, no. The Dark Prince is after Father Joachim."

Perfect. This is a distraction I can use. While they're focused on Joachim and saving him, I can rip the head off the false pawn.

"Run, Father, run." The little princess has much less fear than the last time I saw her. I blame that on Vasily. She should be afraid.

August and Vasily shift and move in front of her. Several other alphas and a group of wolftresses shift as well and form a phalanx guiding Joachim to the protected center. But the stupid minion hasn't moved into the safety of the group. He still stands near the stump seats merely watching the scene, not understanding the danger.

Joachim dashes into the crowd and shifts, holding his hands up over his head and shouting. "Do not fear, brethren."

His declaration has everyone's attention and I speed up, and leap over the side of the line. More people scream, more shift into their wolf forms to defend themselves, and this confusion leaves my prey open and exposed.

I dash past the King, and he does nothing to stop me. He knows.

In three more heartbeats I tackle the minion to the ground, dig my claws into his chest deep enough to break his bones and feel the beat of his heart. He screams and I see his wolf fighting to rise up and shift. Too late. In one swift bite I tear his throat out, nearly decapitating him. The blood spurts warm into my mouth and I spit it out onto the snow.

Drops of it hit the petals of a blooming moonflower.

Death.

Murder.

Betrayal.

All I see now is through a red haze. The red of my rage, the red of her blood, spilled on the ground.

I can't breathe, my heart races as if it is the one speared by claws and is fighting to keep me alive. I hear nothing but the buzz of my own blood rushing through my ears. My limbs are dead weights and I'm glued to this spot. I came here to kill the traitor, but I am the one who has betrayed my pack.

Now I must face the consequences.

Because I am the one who murdered the Princess Anastasia.

TARYN

*M*agic is everywhere... and yes, that includes my va-jay-jay. I blame that on Vasily. The second I get August and Joachim in the same room with the two of us, I am riding him like a freaking cowgirl.

Too bad they didn't save that guy who said he knew me. I sure as shit would have liked to know more about this Wolf Tzar and why he killed my father.

August and Vasily are boxing me in with their big old wolf butts so I can't see the Dark Prince of Wolves. He's cornered, or rather circled. Pretty much everyone turned into a wolf when he ambushed us, and we have him surrounded.

I say us, but he didn't touch anyone except for the newcomer. That's when my magic went haywire again, of its own accord. I sure wish there was an instruction manual or an on-off switch. Although, it does seem to turn on every time someone bites me.

Marks me.

I touch my neck, first where Vasily... lost control... marked me... made me remember and feel and wish for... things I will think about tomorrow. When I'm more in control.

Then I move my fingers slightly higher and find the tingling spot where the Dark Prince attacked me. But was it an assault? Clearly, he could have ripped my head off just like he's done to the Headless Horse...err, Wolfman over here. But he didn't. He bit me. Just like August did, the same as Vasily. Well, not exactly the same. Their marks came with, if not love, at least desire. And orgasms.

I'll be asking a lot of questions about that later. One answer I finally have is why I've felt compelled to get off this island so badly, aside from the whole wrongfully imprisoned thing. I have a pack. They're clearly in danger and my need to get back to the real world to help my people is back as my number one priority.

I push forward to see the carnage, but don't get much farther than squashing myself closer to my wolves' heads. At least I can see the Dark Prince now. He's the biggest wolf I've ever seen with fur darker than a moonless night. His mouth is bloody, and his mind is broken. But I feel the light in his soul.

He said he would come for me. I'm starting to wonder if that was the threat I thought it was.

"What does he mean I have a pack?" I shout at him. The Dark Prince only snarls back, and August growls back so much more menacingly than I've ever heard before. I'm glad he's on my side. Father Joachim comes up and stands between the three of us and the Dark Prince. Yay, team Taryn.

The thing is, a pack implies I am a wolf and I've already searched my soul for an inner beast brought forth by the Goddess of the Moon and found nothing. Yes, I've got some kind of magic from this Goddess, but it isn't the ability to shift.

Until I look down at my hands. When did I get the werewolf manicure? These are some badass claws coming out of the end of my fingers. Then something swishes behind me, a little too close to my butt for comfort. I spin and catch a glimpse of a silvery grey tail. I spin again the other way and it disappears in the other direction.

Holy stars in the sky. I am literally chasing my own tail right now. I smash my hands down over my butt trying to get the damn thing to stop wagging. I glance back up and around at my wolves and the crowd around me. So far, I seem to be the only one that's noticed. They're all absolutely focused on the Dark Prince.

All but Vasily. He's staring at me and I'm pretty sure he just raised one wolfy eyebrow at me. Like I've got something on my face. My hair twitches and while I keep one hand on my freaky tail, the other goes up and... wah-ha-ha... I've got fluffy puppy ears.

What the hell? I also still have arms and legs, so it's not like I shifted the same as everyone else. I'm somewhere in between. Like I'm wearing a sexy werewolf Halloween costume.

There you are, prinsessa. A little more and you'll be the wolftress we all remember.

Is this what he wanted me to remember so much back in the barn when his was driving me crazy with desire? I could definitely defend myself better as a snarling, slobbery werewolf. Rawr. But I don't feel like a wolf, or a shifter, or anything but a regular human. My skin didn't split to let the fur out, my bones didn't crack like I've seen everyone else's do. I didn't even burst out of my clothes.

None of which I have time to think about because there's a big snarling Dark Prince to contend with and I can feel the fear, anger, and turmoil in the crowd around us. Ack. No, I don't feel it. I smell it.

Someone way back in the circle hasn't shifted and they shout out. "Attack the murderer. Give him a taste of his own medicine."

A few other voices rise up in agreement and some barks and yips from the shifted crowd too. To be honest, I'm a little surprised Vasily is so focused on me and not the Prince. If anyone was going to bite our attacker's face off, I would have guessed it would be him.

The Dark Prince lowers his head and growls, more blood dripping from his jaw. *Tell your people to back off. I don't want to hurt anyone else.*

"Are you talking to me? What makes you think they're my people or that I control them at all?"

A few more around us shift back into human form. Alida and Bridget among them. Alida looks at me with a certain awe that makes me uncomfortable. "You can communicate with the Dark Prince?"

"Uh, yeah. Can't everyone?"

"No." Bridget shakes her head like I'm insane. "We can only mindspeak with those of our pack and our mates."

Uh-oh. That explains a lot. The crowd, as one giant collective, gasps.

"Alphas can also talk to other alphas. No way he's her mate, August is." Alida waves her hand between me and August. "If what that dead guy said was true, that means Taryn is the alpha of her pack."

Once again, the crowd collectively emotes in a big sigh of relief. Nope, wait, that's the just scent of their relief. Smelling emotions is so fricking weird.

No one mentions that maybe I have more than one mate. And that answers that little question. Shit.

I am no one's alpha.

I'm not repeating what the Dark Prince just said out loud if no one else can hear him. Vasily's ears twitch and he bares his teeth at the Dark Prince. August does too. Only Father Joachim has remained calm through this standoff.

That same shouter from the back of the crowd speaks up again. "We've got him surrounded. Let's kill him and end his reign of terror."

238

I've had enough killing for one day, thank you very much. I'm about to say so, when Father Joachim shifts and holds his hands up, drawing everyone's attention. Wait, what was I saying?

Did I mention how much I enjoy the fact that wolves don't have clothes on when they shift?

"That's enough killing for one day," he says parroting my thoughts.

Wait, can he hear me too? I think something totally inappropriate involving him and me and a vat of melted chocolate, and he doesn't flinch.

Your thoughts are very loud, love. You'll make the good Father blush. When this is over, I will do my best to find something resembling chocolate for you, though. August's stance relaxes and he presses his body closer to mine. Vasily closes in on the other side and I'm once again squished between them.

"Tell that to the murderer, Father." More people are feeling confident, and I sure hope it doesn't have anything to do with them thinking I'm an alpha. I don't know what I am.

"How can you defend him?" Jeanette joins the rest of the girl gang and points at the Dark Prince. "Killing is the worst of the sins."

"I assure you, there are far worse offenses some of us will be judged for someday. We will not be adding to that list today. Allow the Wolf Guard to deal with the Dark Prince."

"How? What will you do to him?" Killisi asks.

Enough. I will not be judged by these weak fools. The Dark Prince lifts his head and howls at the clouds so fiercely and loudly that those of us in human form duck and cover our ears. The wolves among us cower and even lay down.

The five of us are all that remain standing. My Wolf Guard and I, in a face off against the Dark Prince of Wolves, who either wants to eat me... or uh, you know... eat me.

Vasily is practically vibrating with his need to attack, and

August's muscles are bunched and ready to pounce. Joachim looks me dead in the eye and slowly shakes his head.

I don't know what that means. Is he saying no, don't attack, or no don't let the Dark Prince go, or is he just shaking his head in frustration, and he doesn't know what we should do either?

The Dark Prince makes the decision for us. He turns his back on us all and walks through the crowd of cowering people and wolves. The clouds overhead turn gray and dark, socking out any light from the moon, and it starts to snow. Those big old fat flakes that should be pretty but are simply a dreary reminder of the eternal winter.

Even the light from the bonfire flickers and fades and in a moment, the darkness has swallowed the Dark Prince of Wolves up and my fingers ache for wanting to reach out to him.

Ouch. No really, my fingers hurt. So does my head and my butt. No more werewolf claws. The ears are gone, and no more swishes are to be had with my fluffy tail.

I few moments later a sad wroo-wroo ahroo sounds from somewhere far away and I let out a breath. I didn't even realize I'd stopped breathing.

August shifts back to his human form, picks up the robe he dropped and hands it to Father Joachim. "You've got some explaining to do, my friend."

The Father pulls the robe on and slips his prayer beads into the pocket at the front. "Yes. When the time is right."

Vasily stays in his wolf form by my side, and I push my fingers into his fur just the way I used to before I knew he was a shifter. It's just as comforting now as it was then. Although, I hope he doesn't decide he's going to stay like this again. We have unfinished business.

"Were you going to tell me I can shift?" After his declaration to help me find my powers and use them for my own defense, I feel like this was exactly what he was talking about.

No.

"You're a butthead."

You have no idea.

"I have a clue."

Father Joachim gives me a look and Vasily a nod. Yeah, he knew too. Double butthead. He walks around helping people up and encouraging others to shift. The party is clearly over, and it ended once again in bloodshed. What did I say? Trouble.

Maggie comes over and gives my arm a squeeze. "I can offer hospitality to a good couple dozen of our guests overnight in the barn, unless ya've need of it."

"Oh, uh, I don't think I, uh, we, uh, no thanks." Does everyone know what went on behind the closed barn doors? With shifter senses, I think that's probably a resounding yes. Awkward.

There's at least a hundred other people who found their way into the town and there's no way there is enough shelter for them all. "Alida, ladies? Do you think everyone could double and triple up so we could find a warm place for more of our new friends? I don't want anyone to have to stay out in the cold tonight.

More snow is falling, and a blanket of frost has covered the ground. All those beautiful flowers are going to die.

"Yes, of course. we'll make it work." Alida gives me a smile and then spreads the word among the rest of the girl gang and other people of the *derevnya*. There still isn't enough room for everyone, and Will suggests we put together a quick, but sturdy, temporary lean to made of some nearby trees and branches.

August leads the way, and it happens to go right past the place where the dead body of that guy should be. But he's not there. There's not even any blood except for on one spattered moonflower. "Where did they take him?"

Joachim sweeps his hand through the air above the empty spot. "The island has taken him. We are not allowed to bury our dead here. No ashes to ashes, dust to dust. Bodies simply fade away as if they were never here in the first place."

What? "That's creepy, dude."

I'm not in as good of shape as the people who've lived here for years, but I like helping how I can. I sweep the ground under the shelter, so it's free of rocks and debris and spread the unused bits and bobs of branches around to soften the area just a little.

"Don't worry, my lady," one young man says to me. "Most of us don't have anything fancy like these cabins. We're used to sleeping in the cold. I've got a good thick coat of fur for that."

I catch Will's eye and he's heard too. "Tomorrow we'll have a right proper barn raising and get to work on expanding our little village for all your new friends, lass."

When everyone is settled in and the *derevnya* is quiet, August asks, "Shall we head back to my cabin, love? It's cozy and warm and we can rearrange so all four of us fit."

I give him a soft, lingering kiss. "I love that you know exactly what I want. But there's something we need to do before I'm ready to rest."

I understand now what they've been waiting for me to remember. Is this why Vasily has been in his wolf form for so long? I think there's more to it than that. I hope when I can truly call up my inner wolf, I can understand him better.

"I thought you might say that." He glances at Vasily and Joachim in that same old mind meld way they have.

I'm ignoring that from here on out. "Take me to the church in the woods. I want you all to teach me to shift."

VASILY

*E*ven a glimpse at Taryn's silvery wolf has every cell in my body screaming to claim her. I was this close to losing complete control to my wolf a few hours ago and that can't happen again. I haven't had to think about anyone's needs or wants but my own, August's and Joachim's for so long that I've forgotten my place.

At her side.

I'm too wild for her and while I need her to remember who and what she is, I must do the same. I am her guard, her protector, and soon, her lover. I serve at her pleasure, not my own.

My wolf isn't even a little bit sorry that I've marked her. Especially since it's brought her back more of her memories, and possibly even her wolf.

Although, that might have also been fucking Grigori.

He doesn't deserve to even look at her, much less help her ascend. Which is something I'm going to have to deal with. But not yet. Tonight, she's asking for something I am well equipped to help her with.

Finding her inner beast.

It is the rare lifetime where she finds the wolf within her. I wonder now just how much of the stinking Volkov traitor's claims are true. There are always those loyal to the regime placed in positions close to her. He could have been from her pack. But what is going on in wolfkind that the Wolf Tzar has usurped her.

Perhaps she is once again a princess or duchess. Although, the most recent arrivals to the island have updated those of us that have been here a long time that there is very little royalty left in positions of power.

Will found that hilarious. I am unsurprised after seeing the Bolshevik revolution play out before my eyes. I'd like to see this new world where regular people have a say in the way they are ruled. Perhaps even someday wolfkind can follow suit.

My prinsessa would be the one to lead her people to that new way of life. Just as she changed our fates so long ago.

But first we need to get her back to full power and that means helping her control her wolf. I can hardly wait to run free with her through the forest and the snow.

"There is it. Look, the flowers in the chapel are still blooming. The cold hasn't gotten to them yet." Taryn rushes ahead and into the holy spot we've created in a copse of trees that have grown together at the top to form a makeshift vaulted ceiling.

I've spent many a long day and night here watching over Joachim as he beseeches a long dead God. Someone had to make sure he didn't get lost in his prayers.

Taryn spins, her arms spread wide in her joy at simply being here. It's hard to keep a tough shell of anger around her childlike excitement. In some ways she is like a young pup, since she is just rediscovering the magic of the wolf in her soul.

She stops suddenly and points directly at me. "Don't think you're getting out of shifting back into a super-hot guy again after this. But I think you're the one who can best help me learn how to be the wolf."

She thinks I'm super-hot, which I assume means handsome. That stupidly pleases me enough that my tail wags all on its own.

"What would you like me to do?" August smiles at her like this is just a lark and not the most important thing we've done since she arrived.

"I think you're meant to be my tether back to the human part of me. Does that sound ridiculous?"

"Not in the least. We are here to help in whatever way you need."

Joachim clears his throat. I scent the uncomfortability in him. This place of peace means something different to him tonight. Or perhaps it was the night of the mating that changed this chapel for him.

I know that he has not marked or mated with Taryn, yet I've smelled his seed on her. I never understood his decision not to mate with her and remain celibate.

"My lady, if you don't need me, I'll—"

"Don't even think about it, Father." She points at him and the interior of the chapel in the trees shimmers with a faint blue glow. "You know that I need you too."

Joachim visibly gulps and I must admit, I'm enjoying seeing his normally calm façade shaken. She is exactly what he needs to let go of his control and be free again. He didn't always have such a stick up his ass.

Speaking of asses, Taryn's tail has popped out again. *I think you're enjoying chastising the good Father a little too much, prinsessa.*

She looks behind her and swears under her breath. "Is that always going to happen? I don't see you guys going around with your tails out projecting all your emotions for everyone to see."

"No, love. Once you learn to control your shift, your tail will appear only when you want it to. Or perhaps when I ask you to as I take you from behind."

She laughs and the sound fills the chapel like the notes of the most holy of songs. "You're naughty, mate."

"Indeed I am."

"Oh." Her eyes go wide, and she slaps her hand over her mouth. Then she slowly slides her fingers down and whispers. "Do, uh, wolf shifters have sex in their animal form too?"

August is the one that laughs this time. "We can if you want. It's just as natural to us as in human form."

I almost let a whine escape me at the thought of fucking her in our wolf forms.

"I don't think I'm ready for that." She turns to me and lets out a long breath. "Okay, what do I do?"

This isn't the first time I've taught her to shift, but this time feels more important than in any of our previous lives together. Funny, since she's the one who taught us to shift. I circle her, scenting her emotions, her tinge of desire, and her soft magic. One of those holds the key to helping her let go and finding her wolf.

Her magic shifted the four of us when she was in danger, and parts of her wolf manifested when Grigori attacked. I know what to do.

I round on her and leap directly at her, jaw open in a snarl meant to scare her. She squeaks and drops to the ground rolling to avoid my attack. It doesn't take but a small adjustment and I land above her, my front paws on either side of her head.

Vasily! You scared the crap out of me. Her heart is racing, but there's a laugh in her voice too.

It fills my soul to know that I didn't truly frighten her. That means she has at least some level of trust in me. *Yes. I did.*

She blinks her eyes and snorts at me. She hasn't yet realized she shifted. *My lips aren't moving. Why can't I move my mouth?*

I reply by licking her snout.

Whoa. Do that again. No wait, let me do you. Her tongue lolls out the side of her mouth and she makes an adorable little growl. Then she tries again and licks my eyeball. *Oops, I missed. Do over.*

It might be easier if you stand up.

I move and she rolls first onto her side and then onto her belly. *Yay, look. I shifted my face and my arms. Did I get more of my butt than my tail this time?*

August laughs so hard he snorts. "You definitely got more of your butt."

Taryn tries to stand and falls forward doing a full-on somersault. I lope over to her side and give her shoulder a push with my nose to help straighten her out. But she simply falls to the other side.

I think I'm drunk. Was there alcohol in that hot cider? My body isn't working right. Her rear end scrambles until her back end is sticking up in the air, but her face is planted in the dirt. Then her tail goes double-time wagging.

August is cackling so hard now that he's doubled over. She is awfully cute and adorable. Even Joachim has let a small chuckle grace us all.

You're thinking of your arms and legs, feet and hands. Try imagining four legs and paws. I give her another small push and send an image of how I see her into her mind.

Oh. Is that what I look like? I'm so pretty. There's an awe in her voice, as if she thought before that she wasn't so beautiful. She takes my breath away every time I see her.

Joachim is the one who voices what we're all thinking. "You are more than pretty, *boginya*. You are beauty and passion incarnate."

Not exactly how I would have told her how gorgeous we all think she was, but the sentiment is there. At least he's willing to admit it to her. He wasn't always.

Taryn finally gets her front feet under her and takes a few wobbly steps. I press up against her to at least keep her from falling to one side. After a few more tentative paces forward, she finds her stride and walks forward without me supporting her.

She gives a little yip and a jump then, of course she loses her balance and sits down in surprise. Her tail whips back and forth in the grass and dirt. *Okay, so how did you know scaring me would work?*

Shifting is instinct. If you think about it too hard, it won't happen.

She thinks about that for a minute. *You've taught me how to do this before, haven't you?*

Yes. And it never ends well in those lifetimes.

How many times?

Joachim growls and shakes his head. I don't think it matters if she knows this kind of information. She'll remember all of our past lives soon enough. He's too cautious and I've already decided his wary way doesn't work.

More times than I can count. That answer should satisfy them both.

In our last life together? The one I saw when you marked me?

Flashes of her running through fields and woods but as a young princess in a pretty white dress, not the silver of her fur, race through my mind. She ran for her life that day. Perhaps she would have escaped if I had taught her to shift then. *No.*

She doesn't say anything more, but looks back and forth between my eyes, as if studying my soul. I don't flinch under her examination. I would have her know me, the broken parts and all.

Okay. She stands back up and carefully trots back over to August. *How do I shift back?*

August has the lucky job. He strokes along that soft spot between her eyes and then under her chin until she is melting for him. "Imagine I'm kissing you. I'm nibbling my way along the spot where I marked you, working my way up to that sensitive spot behind your ear and…"

In a flash of moonlight and magic, she is human once again,

with a look of longing and desire on her face. She looks down at herself and her disappointment is palpable. "Hey. I've got my clothes on."

August lifts her chin with his knuckles and gives her a soft kiss and a chuckle. "Unfortunately for all of us."

"Your magic allows you to shift in a different way than the rest of us." Joachim tells her.

"Does that mean I'm not a real wolf shifter? Was that guy lying about me having a pack back in the real world?"

I have to grit my teeth not to shout out the truth of who she is. I may skirt the edge of what we can and cannot do to help her learn who and what she is, but I can't risk revealing more than I already have. She's already made such progress today.

"None of us know what is waiting for you off this island. We've all been here a long time, and there is no one here that would have known you there." Joachim leaves off the part about no one alive.

"But have you heard of this Wolf Tzar, guy? Would he do that? Kill my family and take a pack, if I had one?" Taryn gnaws on her bottom lip. She has so much caring in her heart for people she doesn't even know.

I want to take away her worry about some dead father-figure. If the story is even true, this man wouldn't have been her real father, but a pawn of the Volkovs. She would have been given to him in exchange for favor by the regime. Just like the Romanov's, just like every other family she thought she belonged to.

It makes me so angry my teeth ache.

"The Wolf Tzar is often the puppet of the Volkovs, and they will use any means possible to control you and your powers." Joachim's tone is gentle as if he isn't delivering horrible news.

At least he's telling it to her straight. He thinks he knows what's best for her, but I think today he's learned something new about Taryn and how she's built inside. Either that, or he's allowing himself to trust a little bit more than he usually can.

"Well, that stinks and I'm going to...," she looks at each of us, drawing us to her light, "we are going to stop them. So, let's practice that shift some more."

Fuck, yeah. That' s my girl.

We help her shift from one form to another a dozen more times until she doesn't need either August or I to coax her into changing. She spends a bit more time as a wolf experimenting with her body and what it can do. But it isn't long before she's running circles around us all and nipping at our heels.

We ought to be teaching her how to use her teeth and claws to defend herself, but I can't help but be sucked into her charming glee. I haven't felt anything like it since I first shifted myself. *It's playful you want to be, is it, prinsessa?*

Catch me if you can, Vasily. She darts around the back of August.

I decide I can play with her and teach her a lesson in strategics at the same time. I shoot August a look and we've battled side by side so many times, I don't even have to tell him what I'm thinking. He shifts and turns on her, giving her a nip on the hindquarters.

Hey, no fair.

August runs after her, chasing her directly towards me. She's looking back at August and not ahead, so it's easy to tackle her to the ground and we're back where we started, with her trapped under me. *All's fair in love and war.*

August joins us and lays down beside her just outside my paws. *Be careful who you trust.*

In a flash of blue, she's a human again, this time without her usual clothes. She's gorgeously naked, and I can scent a new burst of desire and arousal from her. She reaches out and puts her hands on both of our faces. "I trust both of you with everything I have."

That same blue magic washes over both August and me, and without the usual sharp, quick pain of the shift, we too are back in our human forms.

There is nothing anyone can say or do to stop me from taking her as my mate now.

TARYN

I never knew I could feel this way. The magic August and Vasily have helped me find flows through me, in and around us all and it's like a drug. A love drug.

Vasily and August have spent the whole night with me finding the power within me to free a part of myself I didn't even know was locked away. I still don't entirely sense the wolf within me, but maybe it's just because it's not supposed to feel any different. Like having a certain color of eyes or being female. I just am what I am.

I want them both so much and yet there's something missing. Or rather someone.

Since I captured all four of the wolves in the midst of their fight over me, Joachim has been withdrawn. I've known since the beginning that there would be a battle for his heart, even though we both understood from the second I saw him that it already belonged to me.

But he doesn't want to be mine. Or maybe he does, but there is something holding him back. I want to see him as wild and free and untamed as I feel with August and Vasily. I refuse to believe that any god worthy of true belief in, and worship of, would condemn the feelings I have, the feelings I share with these three men.

Today, I intend on showing Joachim exactly that.

I can still smell the freshly fallen snow, but the sun has risen again and while it does not break through the cloud cover as the moon did for a while last night, the little chapel of trees is illuminated beautifully. The wreath of moon flowers the girls hung to represent the all important moon catches and reflects the light just as the real moon would and Vasily's eyes are wide with awe.

"Prinsessa, you are glowing for me." His voice is filled with wonder, and I can't help but reach out and run my thumb across his lips. His mouth has been a harsh thin line every time I've seen him in human form, but not now.

"You shine for me too." I tilt my head toward August prone beside us. "You do too, just like when we mated."

"Yes, love. You're just as beautiful now for Vasily as you were for me." His eyes have gone dark with desire, and it sends warm tingles racing down my belly and between my legs.

"True mates," Joachim says from much too far away. "The Goddess gave us all the gift of knowing who our true mates were by making them glow for each other in her light."

I can't see Joachim from my position under Vasily, but if I think back to the mating ritual with August, did they both glow? Doesn't matter, we've yet to see the actual full moon. It's only the reflection of the light from the moonflowers giving this glowing effect. Doesn't matter to me, nothing could be more perfect.

Well, except having Joachim... and maybe the Dark Prince of Wolves here too. Oh God - sorry Father - why did I just think that?

The Dark Prince and I obviously mean something to each

other, but he isn't one of my mates. Is he? Deep in my soul, I know he's mine but not like that. It can't be. He tried to kill me, he did kill someone coming to tell me about my life back in the real world, and then he just left like nothing happened. That can't be what comes before falling in love.

I push thoughts of the Dark Prince out of my mind and tell myself I can think about it later. Right now, I want to be in the moment because I do know I have deep and important feeling for Vasily. I look up at him, and then softly brush my lips across his.

He freezes except for a couple of rapid blinks. I'm not sure this man has experienced any kind of gentleness in a very long time. He knows how to be tough, he definitely knows how to be rough, and I look forward to that with him, but right here, right now, I'm going to show him the warmth and tenderness of my love for him.

I skim my fingers across the skin on his neck, in a mirror spot to the mark he's placed on me, with the softest of butterfly touches. He sucks in a breath and the muscles in his chest contract like his lungs are squeezing him from the inside.

The more of his body I caress, the stiller he goes. Until he can't stay frozen any longer and his arms begin to shake as if he's at the end of his strength and can't hold himself up anymore. But I know that isn't the case. It's not his body giving out, but his mind giving in, to me.

"August?" Just looking at him, you'd think he was relaxing, enjoying the show between me and Vasily, but he's on high alert. The wolf in him sparkles out of his eyes, and I can feel the connection between us, just as tight as it ever was.

I love that he's not jealous. I think he's like me in that he knows when we're all connected, everything will feel right. "Yes, love?"

"I know the mating ritual is supposed to be witnessed by--"

He holds up a hand, halting my question. "Stop right there. The mating ritual is whatever you want it to be. Old traditions can be turned into new ones if it's what pleases you."

"I like your traditions. But I do want to the ceremony to feel special for each of us. Will you be the witness for me and Vasily?"

Vasily groans and lowers his forehead to mine. "I am not worthy to be your mate, prinsessa."

Oh boy. "I don't know why you feel that way, but whatever it is, doesn't matter. I choose you, and I think you want to do the same. If I'm wrong and you don't have feelings for me, say so now, or agree to be mine forever more."

I'm pretty damn sure he's punishing himself for whatever happened during our last life. I don't care. It's nothing I remember, and if even I did, that was before, and this is now. But I won't force him, just like he wouldn't do that to me.

"I am not worthy, but I also can't resist you. I will be your mate and you mine." The blue light of his wolf shines as he says the words and it makes my heart sing.

"Good. There's just one more thing." I move to get up, and even as I do, my two mates stand on either side of me and hold out their hands to help me.

We are all three naked in full glory and this time I don't feel even the least bit uncomfortable. There's just one person out of place. "Father?"

I cross to him, hiding in the darkened space behind the light of the moonflowers. He's wrapped tightly in his robes and has even drawn a hood up to cover his face. That won't do. "Father Joachim, will you perform the ritual with us?"

He turns what I can see of his face down and away. His breathing is more rapid than it should be for simply standing here and I can smell both desire and disgust coming from him. But that disgust is not aimed at me, but at himself.

That breaks my heart.

"I can't give you what you want from me, Taryn. There are some vows that cannot be broken." He doesn't look at me when he says these words and I think he's forgotten that I found my wolf and her senses. He's lying about something. But I can't tell if it's a lie to me or to himself.

I hate that he's hurting, but I'm sure that if I don't bust through these barriers he's put up between us, I'll lose him forever. Even if it's painful for us both, I will break him down. But not tonight. I don't want him running scared.

I step a little closer, knowing Vasily and August are at my back and the thick tree trunks that make up the base of this inner sanctuary block any escape from that direction. Carefully, I take his hand and then brush the hood away from his face. "Then for today, give me what you can. Conduct the ritual as you did before. It won't feel right without you. Then stay and witness, celebrate my mating with Vasily."

His hand shakes in mine. I can see the denial on his lips again and I can't let him say no. I should. But I can't. So, I press my free hand to his mouth, and then follow it with my lips. The moment our mouths meet the magic sparks between us, and he lets out a sound that's somewhere between a growl and a sigh.

Joachim pushes his free hand into my hair and the other, that's holding mine, pins my arm to my back. He's kissing me like he can't get enough, and I can't get enough, and it will never, ever be enough. But it has to be, because he breaks the kiss and nips at my bottom lips with his fangs that have extended down from his mouth. He whispers against my mouth, "We gather together in this, our sacred circle, to honor the Goddess of the Moon who bestowed upon us the very nature of our wolves and gave us the light by which to find our way to our true fated mates."

My heart goes pitter-patter then skips a beat and does it again. Could it be that easy? Did I just have to kiss him?

He lifts his head and looks over at Vasily. "Ready, Guard of the House of the Setting Moon?"

In one swift move, Joachim hands me off to Vasily and my head is spinning. Vasily lifts me into his arms, princess carrying style and walks back into the light. "I am."

August and Father Joachim join us, and I want to yell, 'stop, wait'. Joachim's serene look and Vasily's lips pressed to my throat stop me. This is what's right for this moment. I don't want Vasily to think I don't want him, and now at least Father Joachim isn't going to hide or run away. Just having him here feels correct.

Although something is still missing.

You're not safe. I'm coming for you.

I don't know if I remembered, imagined, or actually heard the Dark Prince's words in my head just now, but I'm ignoring them. This moment is about me and Vasily. I snuggle into his arms and look at Father Joachim to continue.

He nods at me and raises his arms as if the chapel is filled with the whole village. "If your fated mate be here, declare your claim on them and let your pack know that they are yours and that you belong to them."

Vasily holds his head high and says, "I claim you, my Anastasia, my Taryn, as my mate. You are mine and I am yours for all time."

A rush of energy flows through me at hearing his claim on me and I can't wait to say the words myself. Father Joachim takes my hand and places it over Vasily's heart, and I know just what to do this time. Before I can say anything, August steps forward and places my other hand over Vasily's heart too, leaving his on top. He doesn't say anything, but I understand.

August is blessing my union with Vasily too, and I feel the tingling of tears tickle my eyes. I slip my hand out from the middle and press it on top of August's so that I am the one holding his hand between mine, all pressed to Vasily's heart. "I claim you, Alexander Vasilchikov, my setting moon, as my mate. You are mine and I am yours for all time."

Vasily drops to his knees, lift his face to the circle of moon-flowers hanging above our heads and howls as if baying to the actual moon. His cry is joined by first August, then Joachim. I even join in because it feels so joyous. We are so loud, the leaves and needles on the trees of the chapel shake, and a few of the flowers dislodge and their petals float down around us.

When Vasily stops, he presses his lips to my ear. "You have claimed my heart, now I will claim your body with mine."

"I'm so very ready for that." I grab his chin and kiss him, showing him with my mouth just how ready I am for him. He kisses me back, our tongues meeting and clashing roughly.

He sets me down on the ground, still kissing me, and then spins my body around so he's behind me and August and Father Joachim and in front of me. Oh God - sorry Father - nope... not sorry this time.

August strokes his cock and he's already thick and hard. Father Joachim had opened his robes and is doing the same. Vasily presses against me from behind and notches what I assume is a damn tree trunk against my ass. "My wolf needs to make my claim on you, and I'm already on the verge of losing all my control."

"I don't want you in control, Vasily."

He growls and he slips his tree trunk between the globes of my ass, sliding up and down. "I'm going to fuck you, prinsessa. I need to mark you in a way no one else has."

Vasily presses his cock against me, but not my pussy, my ass. "Oh. I... ohh."

As with every other aspect of my relationship with Vasily, he's unexpected and pushes me just to the edge of fear, but not over that cliff. It's exciting and I can hardly wait.

August drops to his knees in front of me and cups my pussy, stroking his fingers through my already wet folds. "Don't worry, love. While Vasily stakes his claim on you. I'll be here to make sure you get every bit of pleasure out of this as you did our joining."

I say the words they all need to hear so they know I want this as much as they do. "Take me."

VASILY

*M*y wolf growls at Taryn's demand to be taken. It is exactly the permission I need from her to claim her as I need.

Thank the Goddess that Joachim and August are here because my control is on the very edge. The second she said my name and claimed me as her mate, my wolf rose up with such ferocity I had to fight to keep it contained.

While I'm grateful they're here to help me make sure she's pleasured, a spike is controlled somewhat by jealousy, and even more is the complete need to dominate her in every way. I've shared her with the other Wolf Guards since the beginning and it's never bothered me before.

A hundred years of dreaming about how I didn't claim her when she was my Ana, have turned my fantasies into a harsh demand for her submission.

This time I have to prove both to myself and her, that she is mine, absolutely, and that she can never be taken away from me. The only way that feels right, is to take her in a way no one else in this lifetime has. I'm not sure I could even stop myself from taking her ass, and marking her with my seed there, if she begged.

A hundred years ago, I never would have even considered these kinds of thoughts. Now they are my truth.

I can smell the tinge of fear on her at my declaration. It's the same as in the barn and again, here in the chapel as I taught her to shift. It's a deep instinctual fear and it spikes her adrenaline. Adrenaline feels a hell of a lot like lust and desire.

My cock is wedged between the lush pillows of her ass and fuck, I could come just from rubbing myself along her soft flesh. Someday I will and come all over her backside. Then I'll do the same to her big round tits. I want to see my seed all over her body. My scent will be forever mingled with hers and no one will ever mistake that she is mine.

My wolf howls at me to push her to the ground and shove my way into her body, show her and everyone watching, exactly who her mate is. I will never hurt her. I will take her hard, but I want her to enjoy it.

To do that she must be made ready, and she must be begging for it. She's not the kind to beg, so I must make sure that she gives up any and all control she has. Since I have very little of my own, I will rely on my fellow Guards to do part of the work for me.

I scrape my teeth across the mark on her neck and she groans. I'm literally salivating for her. I lick two of my fingers and slide the wetness across her hot pucker. She gasps and squeezes her muscles. "Vasily, I... don't know if I can do this."

"You can, and you will." This isn't going to happen if she doesn't relax, and I can't exactly demand that of her.

Immediately August gets up close and holds her chin, making her look directly at him. "Shh, look at me. Don't fight against his touch. He doesn't want to hurt you, he won't. Remember, we only want your pleasure."

I move my hand forward, pressing between her legs to both test if she's paying attention to August and to pull some of her wetness back. I'd rather use her natural lubrication than anything else. This time when I circle her anus with my wet fingers she only flinches for a moment and then stretches her arm back to search for my intrusion, instinctually pushing at me.

"Sorry, I didn't mean to do that." She clenches her hand and moves it back again, trying to let me do what I need to prepare her and blows out a breath in an effort to relax.

It's not enough for the urgency of my wolf's need to be inside of her. I need to take away more of her control. "Joachim. Take her wrists."

He hesitates for only a second because it doesn't take him but a thought to see that what I'm asking him to do will put his cock directly in front of her face. He's not the only one who can see what the others need when it comes to claiming Taryn.

August grabs both her arms and lifts them over her head for Joachim to capture. He holds both of her wrists in one of his fists and strokes her hair with the other. For once he has no platitudes or prayers. None that he shares with us, anyway.

She fights him for a brief moment and my wolf loves to see the fight in her. Taryn is no easy prey, no willing submissive. She is not weak and that's exactly the way that I love her. She is brave, unbreakable, and for those close to her, pure magic.

Quickly, August wraps his arms around her waist and stills her, giving her a deep, sensual kiss. He breaks the kiss, leaving her breathless, but he continues his hold on her. She can't move and her muscles tense everywhere. "We know what you need, love. Allow us to give it to you."

He is being to kind to her and it's not what she expects. She snarls and snaps at him, her own wolf coming up to make her displeasure known. My own wolf reacts with just as much force and I drop my mouth to her neck and sink my teeth in. She tenses for a moment and then I feel the moment her wolf lets go and Taryn takes over.

Her muscles release and she moans. "Please. I don't want to fight you, I want this. I need this. But I can't seem to control it."

I bite down harder and reach between her legs. This is mine, she belongs to me and I will claim her. August sends me a warning growl. "I know, it's okay. We've brought your wolf out to play and now she wants to assert herself. She won't accept being claimed by anyone weaker than you."

"Yes, yes. That's it. I need you all to be strong for me."

Those are the words I needed to hear. I release her neck and snarl her name. "Taryn, you are mine. Give yourself to me now."

I push my cock between her thick thighs that are dripping with her juices and wet my cock, pumping between her flesh to draw as much of her wetness out. I knock her knee sideways with my own to spread her legs wider and slide my fingers into her cunt from behind, soaking them too. "The scent of your arousal is delicious and after you've been thoroughly claimed I'm going to lick up every drop of your essence, from your ass to your cunt and back again."

I finally push one finger into her tight ass, and then a second almost immediately. She gasps and tenses around my fingers, but I don't relent, fucking her with my fingers to open her. She fights against me until August reaches down and begins to stroke her in a way that has her bucking against us both. "That's it, ride my fingers and let the pain mix with pleasure."

She whimpers and I want to eat that sound up. I want to swallow it up. But so does someone else. Joachim leans down, while still holding her arms aloft and kisses her, slipping his tongue into her mouth and back out again, fucking her mouth like I know he wants to take her body.

I match the in and out of my fingers with his rhythm and I think that August does too because soon she's moaning in time with our kisses, touches, and thrusts.

Joachim resumes his position above her and nods at me. Anyone else might take that as his approval or signal that's she's ready, but he needs me to take her as much as I want to. He's going to watch me fuck her because he won't do anything else.

August licks his lips and breaths out the words we all want. "She's close to coming. Her cunt is fluttering around my fingers."

That's what I've been waiting for. Her mind isn't in charge anymore, her body is. I pull my fingers from her ass and grab my cock, then guide my tip to her ass and push in, taking one long deep thrust.

"Vasily, god, Vasily." She stops writhing, but the muscles I'm buried deep within pulse around me.

I grab her hips and pull out only a few inches, and then shove back in hard and fast. I never meant to take her gently, I can't. She's the only one I can be wild and free with. The only one who can handle me when I lose control. And I. Am. Losing control.

I fuck her fast, I fuck her hard, and I fuck her until I can't tell where she ends, and I begin. I'm lost in her and there is nowhere else I'd rather be ever. She makes me feel alive when I thought I never would be again.

I can only hope I'm doing the same for her. Her body responds like I'm making her feel good. But I want more. I want her to come so hard she never forgets this moment, the day I claimed her and became her mate.

"Fuck her, August. Fuck her cunt so that her body and her wolftress know who she belongs too."

He doesn't hesitate and guides his length to her wet pussy, pushing in inch by inch. I can feel him filling her as I fuck her ass, and revel in the moment when he's fully inside. She closes her eyes and lays her head back against my chest, a soft continuous moan wailing out of her mouth and nose and throat.

Joachim is the one who snarls her name this time. "Don't

close your eyes. I want to see the magic burning in you as they fuck and claim you, *boginya.*"

That is more than a want. For all of us. Her magic is our life's blood and only in her do we truly live.

I've lost all sense of myself, I am only feeling, need, lust, desire, and dominance. My cock slides across her sensitive flesh faster than my own heartbeat. Pounding, pounding, pounding. "Please, Vasily. I need you now. Give yourself to me."

I told her she would be begging before I was done with her, but the satisfaction I get is not from her pleas, but in the asking to give myself to her.

I am once again the young novice initiate, trying to earn my place as her lover, her guard, her protector. I'm trying to prove that I am strong, but I'm not, not without her. I am young and untried, and she is the ultimate in beauty, grace, and love.

I am not worthy.

But you are mine and that makes you worthy to me.

With her words in my head, the last bit of myself I'd been holding back, the place inside my heart my wolf worked to keep safe and protected at her death and her absence in my life for the past hundred years, bursts forth. "I am yours, prinsessa. Only yours."

With my words, her body clenches, and every muscle locks as her orgasm takes over. August joins her first, howling out his own climax. He buries his cock deep and his hips jerk as he comes inside of her. He takes her mouth, groaning his pleasure into her. When he's done, he falls back, spread eagle in the grass, dirt, and petals, his cock glistening with their combined releases.

Joachim has his cock in his hand, and he raises his eyes to the sky, mumbling out some kind of apologetic prayer. He steps into August's place and presses his tip to Taryn's lips. "Forgive me, *boginya.*"

He strokes from base to tip and back again and then spills

his seed in her mouth, on her lips and down her chin and neck. The base of his cock is engorged with his wolf's knot, and he'll know no satisfaction from coming when he can't bury that knot deep within her. He lets her arms free and steps away, covering himself, but not taking his eyes from her body as I continue to fuck her.

With one more thrust, my own knot swells and I push into Taryn's ass deeper than ever before. "My Goddess, fuck."

She cries out again, not in pain, but as I bite down on the mark on her neck and instead of blood, I taste her magic pouring from her. Another orgasm rips through her and, with her arms returned to her control, she reaches back and wraps them around my hips, crossing with mine, and holding me tight to her.

I come inside of her so hard that my vision goes black, and I don't see stars, but the bright rays of the moon. I've experienced the bliss of the wolf's knot before, but it's never been like this. My body is vibrating with more need for her than when we started.

Taryn is panting, her chest heaving, and she gives me a soft sigh, leaning her head back. I release her flesh from my bite once again and lick over the new wound to help her heal.

"Mmm. Vasily. That feels good. You filling me is better than I ever imagined." He shoulders sag and her body relaxes with the satisfaction of being well and truly fucked.

My wolf isn't quite satisfied yet and the knot pulses a few more times inside of her, releasing more of my seed into her. Slowly, I lower the two of us to the ground and throw one of my legs over hers, happy to be connected to her in this way.

Happy that she is once again mine.

TARYN

*B*eing taken by all three of my mates at the same time was more than I ever could have dreamed it would be. Yeah, yeah, Joachim didn't technically fuck me. But he definitely lost control and that's more than I could ask of him.

I knew sex with August was amazing but having both him and Vasily inside of me at the same time, that was life changing. Before today, I'd been worried that it was weird that I had more than one mate. Now I'm like, why wouldn't you have multiple mates? One is good, two is great. Three was going to be even better.

When we got back to the *derevnya,* the girls and I were having a talk about how they needed to get themselves, if not another mate, a couple more. Girls, get yourself a whole damn harem.

I quietly giggle to myself. A harem. I have one. Me. A girl who couldn't even get my fiancé to stick with me.

Gasp.

I had an arranged marriage, to a wolf of the...Troika pack. My father wanted me to marry him because it would make a good alliance. We didn't get that far because the son of the Troikas broke it off.

Who the hell are the Troikas?

I can't quite get a grasp on who my father was either. But I get a sense that he was not very kind. Greedy. Elitist. Perhaps the Wolf Tzar was right to kill him and take my pack over from him. There's so much more to that memory and it's just out of my reach. At least I've gotten a glimpse of this life and not another from the past. That's a real first.

I sort of thought that I'd get some new memories, or maybe another burst of power, or an epiphany when I mated with Vasily, like I did with August. I can't ask. Both August and Vasily fell asleep ages ago. Not that I'm complaining. I'm tucked safe and warm between the two of them.

Father Joachim, never even laid down to rest. Once he saw me curled up with these two, he wrapped himself back up and quietly made his way out of the chapel.

I hate that he felt like he had to apologize to me for taking his pleasure in the mating ritual. I'm going to continue to work on him. Someday he'll let go of whatever secrets he's hiding and be himself with me. Just not today.

I yawn and stretch, feeling every muscle ache, but in a good way. I could totally use a hot bath though. I wonder if that's a thing here. Maybe I can magic one up.

I reach my hand out and twirl my fingers around, willing this strange power to do my bidding. The magic comes easier than it did before, and I think that's the gift of this mating. Sweet. Let's take it out for a ride.

I imagine a big round tub, filled with steaming hot water. I want one big enough that all three of us could soak in it together. With another flick of my wrist, something happens, but it's not what I expected or wanted. Instead of a big round tub there's a big round hole in the world. A portal, shit.

I squeeze my eyes tight and clinch my fist. A quick peek out my eyelid and I don't see the portal anymore. Phew. At least I can do one thing. What if the Dark Prince of Wolves had come out of that portal. I could've gotten us all killed.

Don't think you can use your magic to hide from me.

Aw, fuck monkeys. Why did the Dark Prince pick now to pop back into my brain? *You stay out of my head, and away from the people I love. I'm not ready to deal with you yet.*

I get back a slow chuckle. Not the kind that thinks I'm cute, but something much darker and, dare I say, evil. *That's not how this works. You're trouble and I can't allow that. You are a danger to everyone around you, including August and Vasily.*

No, I'm not. My heart sinks down like a rock into my stomach. Oh, who am I kidding. I've known all along that my presence has put August, Vasily, and everyone else around me in harm's way. Vasily almost died the first night I knew him. August has sacrificed himself for me. I don't like the thought of that one bit.

They may be my protectors, but I will do everything in my power to keep them safe too. If only I actually knew how to use my magic for good instead of chaos. That I think I can do with time and practice, just like shifting into a wolf. So, what I need now is to figure out how to stall the Dark Prince, keep him away from the *derevnya* so he can't kill anyone else.

Tell me where you are so I can stop searching the derevnya for you.

I sit bolt upright and both Vasily and August grumble. *Don't you hurt a single hair on any of those people's heads, or bodies, or even their tails.*

I shake my mates to get them to wake up, but they are slow to rouse. I have to take action right now.

Then you'd better hurry and surrender yourself to me.

Is that a threat? Is he implying that he'll hurt the innocent people who have gathered around me? Fuck that. I have to get to the village, and I have to get there now.

I hold out my hand and call up the magic that opened the portal. I don't relish the sickening feeling of traveling through once again, but if I can make the other side open up in the village, we three can get there to defend those people in an instant.

If I screw it up, though... we could end up at the burned-out church, the beach, or who knows where else. I guess if that happens, I just open another one and another and another until I've discovered how it works and it takes me where I want to go. I figure I've got about a thirty-three percent chance of getting it right the first time. Not great odds.

So, I'd better fricking hurry.

I make a dancing fingers motion and push all my intentions out with the magic to make this portal go to the village. A portal opens up just like I hoped it would. Big and black and swirling with magic all around the edges.

That wakes up August and Vasily the rest of the way better than a slap to the face. They're both on their feet and shouting. But their voices are distorted and so are their movements. Weird.

This portal is different than the others. It's magic reaches out and is wrapping itself around me. It's warm, hot even. That's nice, but I don't care what it feels like as long as it gets me where I want it to go.

August and Vasily shift into their wolves and rush toward me but I'm watching everything in slow motion. Except Father Joachim. He's come running back into the chapel. "No, you mustn't open a portal. It leads to Hell."

Oh, shit. That's bad.

Then Father Joachim is caught in the time warp too and all I can see is the warning on his face. He points his hand at the portal, and I turn to see.

The Dark Prince of Wolves steps out of the portal and

zeroes in on me. "Well, well, well, haven't you made it easy for me. How very unlike you."

The moment he touches me, my time speeds back up to normal and I have less than a breath of time to react. He grabs for me, but I dodge him and call up my wolf. This is why Vasily wanted me to learn to shift. With my wolf, I can defend myself against the Dark Prince.

Some of my magic that helps me shift, spills over, and his enormous black wolf shimmers up too. We are each in a state somewhere between human and wolf and it's there that I notice something very peculiar and that I'm not sure I'm ready to see.

As the wolf comes forward, the man is naked, and the reflection of light from the moonflowers overhead shines down on him. His skin in glowing. His eyes are too, but not like the others. His eyes are like eclipses. Complete darkness in the center.

While I'm staring at him, into his eyes, he takes advantage of my lack of action and barrels into me. We go tumbling and roll away. Good thing I did that about a trillion times running around with Vasily. I somersault and spin, so my back is toward the portal, but I'm not as swift as I thought I was.

The Dark Prince is already facing me and stalking closer, his head lowered in that menacing I'm-going-to-eat-your-face way that wild animals have. I back away from him, but the weird, hot magic coming from the portal is nipping at my heels.

I mean... I had planned to jump through this thing before Princy-poo appeared. I could do that now. He came from somewhere. I could just pop though and close the portal, then run and warn everybody. Except that would leave him here with my guys and apparently, they are already mortal enemies.

Okay fine, they're all coming with me then. But how do I do that? They're in some other messed up space-time continuum and it's not like I can ask the Dark Prince to hold up for a second while I gather them up and toss them into my mini black holes.

Aha. That's it. More portals. Geez, I hope this works. I flick my hands around like I'm Spiderman shooting webs, but instead of sticky string I'm filling the place with zings of my magic that opens dozens of portals.

Stop, Taryn. No, you don't understand what you're doing.

Nope, I sure don't. But at least I've done something and he's not attacking anyone I love. In fact, if I don't want him to, I need to make sure I keep a close eye on him, and I'm afraid that means he and I are going to have to go through one of those portals together and just see where we end up.

I use his own move against him and run hard, planning to land hard against him and push him back into the nearest portal. He's not stupid though and sees me coming. He runs toward me too, and just when I think we're going to crash together, he veers to the side and leaps into the air.

Right onto the back of the ugliest ostrich-bat thing I've ever seen. It screeches and flaps its weird wings and spits fire at him. The Dark Prince howls and then snarls at the creature. He slashes at it with his claws and when it ducks and dodges him, he jumps onto its back, ripping the thing's head right off of its body.

There's no death throws or even a wail, the creature just dissolves into an oily black stain on the ground. It's the grossest and most terrifying thing I've ever seen. Holy shit. *Are these the Volkovs?*

Close those portals before you let more of the demon dragon wyrms up from Hell.

But it's too late. These Demons, or dragons, or worms, or whatever they are, are crawling out of every single one of the portals I created. They are flapping and flying awkwardly around the chapel and doing their best to light it on fire. Even in the weird space-time that August, Vasily, and Joachim are in, the monsters are with them too.

Dear God, I've really screwed up.

I can't fix it in wolf form, because I need my hands to close them like I practiced. But I am in panic mode and can only partially shift back. I've got these claws like super long Lizzo nails, and I can't make a fist. Shit.

More monsters are crawling out of the portals and if I don't do something real damn fast, we're all gonna die and then everyone else on the island is gonna die and then this is no longer an island prison for wolves, it's the literal apocalypse end of days.

Okay, what did August teach me about shifting back. Right, imagine him kissing me. I frantically look around the chapel for him and he's mid-air leaping at a demon ostrich, with his fangs aiming straight for its throat. Not exactly kissable at the moment, but I'll take what I can get.

My claws recede and I crush my fingers shut into a tight fist. Half the portals close with that one motion and at least a few of the monsters are cut in half, dissolving into slimy piles of goo. As I close portal after portal, the weird differential in time between me, the Dark Prince, and my mates fades until we're all edging closer together.

I sure could use some back up right now. I get exactly what I wish for. August, Vasily, and Father Joachim each eviscerate the foes they're battling, and one by one, join me and the Dark Prince.

I've yet to close this final portal. "I can't get this one to go away, no matter what I do."

Joachim's voice is the one that answers me back, and I can somehow tell, he's talking to us all. *You are no longer in control of this one. Something from Hell has taken over.*

This is the first one I opened, and the biggest. It bubbles with the black sludge of these demon monsters. I don't know what's about to come out of it, but it's bad. I've got balls of my magic in my hands at the ready, but I definitely don't know what I'm doing.

Vasily steps forward, then August. The four wolves have boxed me in, a guard at each point around me. They work together like a team whose fought many a battle together. I think they have. Even the Dark Prince. We've all faced the bad guys before. Together.

The earth below us rumbles and a screech like the cry of a bird of prey blasts out, just before a black owl, the size of a man bursts out of the portal dragging more of those demon dragon things with it. It flies up and over our heads, circling the canopy that makes up the roof of our sacred chapel of trees. Its wings are covered in wisps of what looks like black smoke, and it drifts down over us.

Oh no. I get that same nauseated feeling as when I was traveling out of the Nothing. This creature is from wherever I was being held. My hands shake as I lift them up and over my head. The blue light of my magic turns to hot flames, and I throw them with all my might at the creepy ass bird.

It dodges one blue ball of fire and throws one of its demons in the path of the other. It flaps its wings and dive bombs the five of us. *Hello, little princess. Rasputin sends his regards.*

VASILY

*T*he God of Chaos, in his deathly owl form, screeches at us and dives, his talons outstretched and reaching for Taryn. I'll be damned if I ever let him close to her again.

I always knew that fucker, Rasputin, had made a deal with the devil to get into Alexandra Feodorovna's bed. He may be a Volkov, but she was the Empress of all Russia, and her husband was a jealous, asshole of a husband. Only the worst of corrupt souls would agree to foster a child for the Volkovs in return for power. The last Tzar of Russia was exactly that corrupt.

I'm glad Taryn doesn't remember much of her life as Anastasia Romanov, short as it was.

But I scent her horror at this threat to us all and hate that Rasputin can still terrorize her even now without even being here. He is a coward and would never come to the Island of the Damned himself. Someday I will have the pleasure of murdering him myself. And this time he will stay dead, deal with the underworld or not.

Taryn, my princess, is so brave, with her fledgling attempts to use her magic to save us, but she isn't ready. She has not yet fully ascended and until she does, we must continue to protect her.

I must protect her. *Shift back into your wolf form, Taryn and run.*

"No, I'm not leaving you to die at the hands of a fucking big bird. Don't ask me to do that." She shoots another blast of her magic and Nergal loses a few feathers. Her aim is improving even if her lethality isn't.

I knew she wouldn't leave us, but I had to at least try. I've played this scenario out in my head, and it goes the same way every time. This isn't the first time we've battled against Hell. The Volkov's unleash their allies on her every time they're afraid she's gaining too much power or memory. Although, they've never sent a god so powerful at us before.

If I ever find out how they gained control over her in the first place, I will burn down the world to destroy the fuckers that did this to her.

The Volkov's must have realized their mistake in putting all four of us together with her. Together, as we originally were chosen as the Wolf Guard of the Moon, we are strongest. Even if I don't trust Grigori with her life, I do believe he'll fight against those that destroyed all that we have. That's enough for right this moment.

I was afraid you'd say that. August, get her out of here. He'll keep her safe. He is her first protector and I have faith in him above all others.

"Don't you dare, August. I'm staying and fighting." She points her finger at a stray demon dragon wyrm trying to crawl out of the portal and zaps it into a pile of stinking oil. "See, I can do this. I'm not weak."

Fuck.

August's concentration on the battle is broken. *Sorry, Vas. Where she goes, I go.*

He stares up at her, glowing in the light of the moonflowers.

Or... wait, the clouds have broken, and the moon is shining through. A crescent moon, rising in the early evening sky. Her power has grown, and she is pushing back the spell that holds us all prisoner on this island once again.

That proves to me even more she must be saved, for the fate of all wolfkind, not just her guard.

I never thought she was anything but powerful, but she won't hear that from me now. She's determined to use her powers to protect us instead of allowing us to protect her as we were chosen to do. If she can't recognize that she is the one that must live, above all else, then I will do what I have to.

I will save her without her consent.

The idea forming in my head makes me physically sick, but my training and the strong constitution of my wolf's healing of this deep, hundred-year-old wound, helps me keep my shit together. If August won't do his duty to save her, I know who will.

Father Joachim has the faith and belief to tear her away from this battle, but in the end, he will give in to her when she demands to come back. He thinks he can keep her at arm's length and put faith in a centuries old vow not to touch her again, but he is so wrong. She has already won his heart, I saw that during the mating. He will hate himself when he gives into her yet again, and she will heal him with her love.

Just as she has done me. I still have some cracks and scars that will never fade, but my wolf and I are at peace with each other once again, because of her. The least I can do to repay her is not let her fucking die.

The one guard who won't give into her demands, her power, or even her love, is the one who let the rest of us down when he was thrown into this prison island with the rest of us. When he decided we could never save her from the unending deaths and rebirths. When he let her die before either he or I could claim her.

Grigori was supposed to take Anastasia away and hide her so that Rasputin couldn't get to her. He failed. She died.

Because of that failure I have hated him, haven't been able to trust him. Until now. He fights beside us once again, even if he won't lead us. He won't fail again. Not this time. There's more at stake than his ego, or our rituals, or even her love.

I open my mind for the first time since that final July day in the wilds of Russia where the Romanov family was executed, and I speak only to him.

You have to take her somewhere safe and don't let her go until she's ready to ascend.

Grigori growls and snarls at me. I know his pain and I return it threefold. *I told you that you couldn't keep her safe. You should have let me hide her before. I should have locked you all up in my dungeon and let you fuck each other's brains out where no demon or minion of the Volkovs could find her.*

The bird swoops down taking shots at each of us over and over. He's trying to divide us so it's easier to get to her. We know better. Grigori may no longer be our alpha, but we still know how to follow his battle plans and we take turns batting the beast away.

But we can't do this long term. We will tire, and a god will not. Then he will pick us off one by one to get at her. I can't even imagine what the consort of the underworld would do with something as bright and precious as her under his control.

Well, you didn't, and I'm telling you to do it now. None of us will stop you. Take her away, kicking and screaming if you have to, and let the rest of us push this evil back to Hell where it came from. We can't do that when we're worried about her safety.

He knows just as well as I do that we've only got a slim chance of defeating Nergal. She will hate him forever if one of us doesn't make it through the battle. Out of us all, he's the one who can live with her hate instead of her love, if it means she is safe.

I will keep her safe. If not happy, safe, until we can get off this fucking island and I can finally seek my revenge on the Volkovs.

That's all I ask. While he's broken his promise to the rest of us, he would never break a promise to her. That's why he was our alpha. Why he truly still is. He will always come for her, and I was selfish to keep them apart.

I quickly communicate the plan to August and Joachim, who both hate the idea but accept it as our only viable possibility for keeping her out of the clutches of Hell and Rasputin.

With one last warning, I set the plan into motion. *Joachim, don't you dare fucking die. She's mated with both August and I, if we die, she can still ascend. You and Grigori must claim her, or we will have died in vain once again. Don't let the cycle start over again. This is our last best chance to end it.*

He is silent too long, and I don't wait for his reply. I give the signal to August and the two of us leap at the owl on his next descent to strike. We each grab a hold of one of the god's legs and climb our way up, tooth and claw, onto the bird's back.

It cries out with the pain we are inflicting on it and jerks, trying to throw us off. I am smashed against the nearest trees but hang on. From up here I watch as Grigori shifts and grabs Taryn.

She fights against him, screaming and kicking just like I knew she would. She shoots arrows of magic at him, but his wolf absorbs each blow, using it to fuel him, as her power always has. We thrive on it. It is what we are made of.

The great owl flaps its wings and tries to throw us off and I dig my claws in deeper. I have no idea if I can kill a god, but I can certainly inflict pain on it. I lose sight of Grigori and Taryn, but that's okay. This asshole can't get to her anymore. She's safe.

Probably pissed as hell. But safe.

August and I put our whole efforts into taking the bird

down. We both rip at its feathers and claw at its skin. This is what happens when you go up against the Wolf Guard. We are warriors that never give up until death.

Joachim guards the exit from the ground and that means our treasure is away. He shifts and pulls out his prayer beads. Fuck, this isn't the time or place. But with his words, the beads glow with the blue light of the moon's magic. All the moon flowers scattered about the chapel and hanging from the trees reflect that light back, and the owl screeches in pain as it hits his eyes and his wounds.

The wing beneath my claws cracks and shadow seeps from his hollow bones. He's losing his ability to fly, and we go careening down, down, down. Instead of hitting the ground, the owl tumbles into the portal and August and I are drawn into Hell with him.

The portal slams shut behind us, and we three crash into a craggy rock wall, shattering stalactites dripping with lava from the cavern ceiling above. Hell fucking sucks.

The owls shifts into a grotesque form of a man, that isn't human enough looking to pass for anything but an abomination of Hell with his horns and hoofed feet. How ever did the Queen of Hell marry this thing? She should have simply kept him as her pet.

He roars and a horde of demon dragons pour forth from the shadows around us. There are more than I can count and their scaley bodies blot out any remaining light until even my wolf's night vision struggles to perceive anything but blurred lines.

The demon dragons attack me and August. I hear his flesh slit under their teeth and nails. Neither of us will last long in this battle.

I swat them away like annoying bugs. The body of my friend and brother of the moon, falls to the ground beside me. August is hurt worse than I am, and Taryn would be mad at me for allowing that. I do my best to protect him, but my wolf has taken over completely and the beast fights against the onslaught without care for anything but destroying every last one of these minions.

Another strikes at my back, then another, and another, until I'm buried beneath the weight of a thousand, and it forces my legs to buckle under me and I'm pushed into the sulphuric ground.

The red rage of the battle shrinks into black as I lose the fight against the demons attacking me. I refuse to die. But the darkness pushes down on me until I have no choice.

Just before the blackness of death overtakes me, I see one brief shining ray of the soft blue magic of the moon and a voice pushes its way into my head, claiming my soul. I will be reborn again in another life to serve her once more.

TARYN

T lay on a cold stone floor, the scent of filth and decay around me. There is a dead body in another cage nearby and I think it might be Peter. He was a liar, a cheat, and a fool, but I don't think he deserved this retched death.

I've lost everything and everyone I care about. My mates are somewhere stuck in actual Hell with monsters so much worse than what I ever imagined were possible, and all because I thought I was stronger and more powerful than I am.

There is an ache inside of me that I push away. My mind and body crave something that I cannot bear to touch. Without my mates, I am back at the beginning, scared and alone, as if I've been thrown back into the Nothing.

I told you that you weren't safe and that I'd come for you.

I don't respond because I can't bear to. Despite everything, he did come for me, and he did make me safe. I want to reach to him for comfort, because I know I would find it there if I simply asked for it.

But because I won't, he's locked me away in a cage, under his lair.

The Dark Prince of Wolves is my captor, and my life is unraveling.

I am undone.

TARYN and her wolves story continues in the next book in the Fate of the Wolf Guard series - Undone.

IF YOU MISSED Taryn's back story, she appears in the Alpha Wolves Want Curves series (in her life back in the real world) - where you can find out exactly who those Troikas are.

Start with Dirty Wolf and enjoy.

UNDONE

FATE OF THE WOLF GUARD - BOOK 3

For every woman who has to learn that she is strong enough from
someone else.
Oh, that's pretty much all of us.
So - learn it from me... You. Are. Strong. Enough.
Save yourself.

Is done an emotion?
  Because I feel that in my soul

                              — GEN X

TARYN

*I*n the beginning, I didn't know who or what I was. I was nothing.

Then I found love and remembered flashes of my life. At first I thought I was an ordinary human, nothing special. How wrong I was.

I thought I was a witch, because magic flowed through me, poured out of me, changed everything. However, like the men that I've claimed, the ones my soul yearns for, who I've fallen in love with, there is a beast inside of me. But it wasn't the wolf I hoped for.

No. What I am is far worse.

I look at the death and destruction around me. The chaos I am responsible for.

I am a monster.

And I've been imprisoned for the crimes that I disguised as courage and love. Maybe this is why I was thrown into the Nothing. Perhaps the people or the pack I belong to back in the real world were only trying to protect themselves from me. If only I'd kept my memories of this life, perhaps I could have controlled the beast, suppressed it somehow and saved those I love.

I'M HUDDLED in the corner of this cold stone and dirt room. It isn't much more than a cave, except for a few wooden support poles, and the bars of four cages that run from ceiling to floor. I don't know how long I've been down here, but it isn't long enough. Not until I rot away like the dead body in the cell across from mine.

The horrible magic of this prison island usually absorbs anyone who is killed here and knowing that even the island is afraid of this dungeon pokes at my fear like beetles trying to eat my brain. I know exactly who killed that poor soul. He was murdered, that I know for sure. No one gets sick, starves, or dies here unless they're killed.

I've seen the beast whose imprisoned me rip the head off a new inmate like it was for funsies. But I'm not better and it's good that he's taken me away from everyone else. That way I can't hurt anyone.

My stomach growls and I hate it for even thinking that I would eat. I don't think it's possible for me to starve to death. The island has kept its other inmates alive for hundreds of years, if Maggie and Will are to be believed. No one gets sick so I think that only deadly injuries can end someone's life here.

Or to be accidentally tossed into Hell.

The tears prick at my eyes, but I refuse to let myself cry. I killed August and Vas, sent them straight to Hell. The actual Hell. I don't get to feel anything but self-hatred for that. I swallow down the tears, but they roil in my stomach. Oh God, I'm going to vomit.

I roll onto my hands and knees and my body takes over. Dry heaves are my punishment now. I gag and my stomach rebels over and over. All that comes up is my own saliva and the thin spittle of yellow bile. It's more than I deserve.

"Feel better?" The voice permeates the stone and dirt around me so deeply that I can't ignore it.

I didn't expect to hear anyone speak to me ever again and his presence wraps around me like a warm blanket. One that I have to refuse, I must brush off.

You can't ignore me, princess. You can try, but I will always be here in your mind. I feel everything you feel.

Even in my current mode of disaster, the magic in me responds to his very presence. Every word he says, out loud or in my mind, lights a fire that as much as I try to mentally tamp out, continues to burn. It's pure, unadulterated arousal, and it's the only thing I can feel outside of the self-hatred and sadness.

I don't want anything to do with it. But it's also the only thing that I have.

I may want to die, but I also know, the Dark Prince of Wolves isn't going to allow that. He is going to be my lifeline whether either of us like it or not.

The mindspeak feels too intimate, but my throat is raw from the heaving. The words come out hoarse and jagged. "No. I don't feel better. I never will. Go away."

I don't want him to leave me, but I can't stand being near him either. He reminds me too much of everything I've lost, or rather what I've destroyed. It's good that he's locked me away where I can't hurt anyone else. I crawl into the corner, wrap the thin blanket around myself and face the wall.

"You need to fucking remember who you are and break the damned curse." There is a dark growl in his voice and I track the sound of him pacing back and forth as if prowling in front of my cage. "If I have to lock you away for a century to make that happen, I will."

Remember who I am. That's what I've been trying to do. I've gotten so many flashes already of past lives, and clues to the life

I'm living now but don't remember. I don't even know who cursed me with this amnesia or why. "I tried that and look what I did."

"That's because August and Vas were fools." The anger in his tone matches the despair in my heart.

Fools for loving me. Yet I can't allow the prince to scorn them or my memories of them. I let some of the power inside of me rise, just enough to give me the energy to stand and spin around, ready to yell and scream and beg him to leave me alone and never speak of my lost loves.

When I turn, the prince is right there, three centimeters in front of me, and the wolf glows red in his eyes. He pushes me against the wall and grabs my wrists, shoving them over my head against the dirty stone. "But I am no fool, princess. I know what you need."

He crushes his mouth down on mine and I don't even try to pull away. Because he isn't wrong. I do need him. I don't want to, but without his touch I felt so empty and alone. The moment he put his lips to mine, the magic inside of me shifts, bubbling up like it did before and filling me with both joy and power.

I struggle to free my hands from his grasp holding me against the wall, not to get away but because I want to tear at his clothes, touch his body and make him mine, just as I did August and Vas. I want to claim him. The need has been growing inside of me, I just didn't understand what it was. I do now.

The connection between us hadn't always been clear, but I've known since the day he attacked me on the beach, that he belonged to me. The mark he left on my throat only confirmed fate has ordained us to be together. But if that's true, why does he hate me even as he kisses me?

Just as he can feel my emotions, his are scored across my heart.

The prince's growl rumbles up low from his chest and if I wasn't already mated to two other wolf shifters I'd probably be scared because that is not a happy sound he's making. I tear my mouth from his and pant. My lower belly clenches and my chest burns with the need to be with him.

He snarls at me and buries his face into the crook of my neck where my skin bares his mark. Zings of pleasure go zipping through me and I want to beg him to scrape his teeth across my throat. I'm lost in a haze of hate and need. I whimper, much to my own disdain, and my hips push against him, searching for contact.

Boy, oh boy do I make contact. He's not just sporting wood, he'd sporting a whole goddess forsaken baseball bat in his pants. Or at least, that's what it feels like. My body isn't the only one losing control. The prince rocks his hips against mine and I can't help it, I wrap one leg around the back of his and make room for him between my thighs.

"You want me to fuck you right here, right now, against this cold stone wall, don't you, princess?" His tone and words are smug, angry, and needy all at the same time.

"Yes. I need—"

He pushes away from me in such a fast maneuver, I bang my head against the wall before I can even finish my sentence.

"What you need is to discover your own power and not rely on ours to help you remember." He says the words like some kind of chastisement, but at the same time his hand drops to the bulge in his pants and he strokes himself through the fabric.

I don't know how to respond. I both want to tell him to fuck off and at the same time want to drop to my knees and claim the right to stroke his cock myself. What the hell is wrong with me? Is this what hate and grief and fate all rolled together feel like?

"I've waited this long to fuck you, I can wait until you

remember who you are and what you can truly do before I claim you."

I'm sure that's supposed to be some kind of threat, but I don't believe him. This draw between us is stronger than he thinks. I don't know how or why I know that, but I have a feeling he and I have been at odds in past lives and still can't resist each other.

"I hate you." The words just come spilling out. I'm not even sure I mean them, but the despair inside of me has to come out or it will eat me alive. If he won't let me love him, I have to hate him. Those are the only base emotions I have left in me.

"Good. It's about time you do." He marches out and leaves me alone in the dark again. I huddle against the wall and rub my hands over my arms. I can see my breath with every exhalation and while I know I won't die of the cold, I can be miserable in it.

"You don't hate him, you know." A creaky voice comes from across the room. "He just wants you to so you find that place inside that fights."

"Peter?" It doesn't sound like him, but there isn't anyone else down her with me. There's still so much I don't know about the supernatural world around me, so perhaps it's his ghost?

"You thought I was dead, didn't you? I wish I was, but this damn prison won't let me rest in fucking peace."

Okay, so not a ghost. I crawl closer to the bars, trying to peer across the dirt room to the cell he's in. "You smell dead."

He replies with a dark laugh. "I'm sure I do. The taint of Hell has that effect."

Hell? "You've been there? Can you take me there? I need to see..." I can't finish my sentence, can't admit out loud what I know to be true. There's some spark inside of me that needs to believe that my men are still alive and surviving in that dark place.

But even that is too selfish. Wouldn't it be worse if they're stuck in Hell? What if they're being tortured by demons or worse? I shake my head hard, trying to erase the intrusive thoughts like my mind is an Etcha-sketch.

They aren't alive. I know better. No one could survive the demons on their own turf.

"You're the one who can open the shadow portals. Why don't you open one now and get us both out of here?" Peter doesn't cough or sound quite so raspy this time.

I back away. I can't do that. I'll never use the strange powers I have like that again. Instead of answering him, I turn my back and forget that he's here. Maybe he isn't, because he doesn't say anything else and the room stays dark and silent. The fetid smell of death wafts over from Peter's cell again and I gag.

I definitely want to punish myself for my part in what happened to August and Vas, but if what Peter and the prince say is true, that's not why I'm here. I'll never forgive myself for what I've done and the pain in my heart will never go away.

I huddle against the wall and close my eyes, but all I see over and over is the demon wyrms, that horrible demon owl, and my men being sucked into Hell.

I shiver and shake, but not from the cold. I'm just so angry. Isn't it better to avenge their loss? Yes, I played a part in that, but so did the ones who threw me and all the others into this prison in the first place. The ones who must pay are the Volkovs.

I may not remember who they are, but I vow right here in this stinking cell, that I will destroy them. Even if that means I have to go to Hell myself.

I may be hurting and broken at the moment, but that place inside where my fight lives, has been awakened. By vengeance.

I may never be able to forgive myself, but I will avenge August, Vasily, and all the people who've been wrongly imprisoned by the Volkovs, if it's the last thing I do.

GRIGORI

*D*amn her to hell and back.

The moment I'm out of the half-dug basement of the old church where I've got Taryn imprisoned, I shift, needing to let my wolf out before my anger takes over. Or my own goddess forsaken lust. I pace back and forth through the ruins and rubble over her head and can still sense her utter despair.

And her arousal.

It's not even her I'm angry with. I'm the damn fool who kissed her. The taste of her skin lingers on my tongue and if I'm not careful I'll drool all over myself. I cannot allow myself to slip under her sensual thrall again. Fucking her won't do either of us any good. It never has.

This time has to be different.

Because I can't take losing her again. I won't. Enough is enough. If I have to deny the both of us the most base instinct we have for each other, I will. Even if she hates me for it. I'm supposed to keep her safe when she's at her weakest. But I think I've kept her weak by saving her from her own powers time and time again.

She's like a little sparrow trying to peck her way out of her shell. By helping her, I'm hating her. Making it so she can never be strong enough to live on her own. Why can't the others understand that?

Perhaps Vas did and that's why he sacrificed both himself and his vendetta against me to save her. I don't deserve his forgiveness, but the princess does.

I catch the scent of Joachim before I see him. He won't find Taryn here. I've made sure no one can smell anything but scorched earth and death here. *Go away. I don't need any lectures or religion today.*

He trots right into my lair as if it is his own. It is a church after all, it should belong more to him than me. He's the one who shared her need to believe in something bigger than herself. All I ever believed in was her.

But look where the fuck that got us.

He sits his ass down and looks around as if this is some normal social call. But there's no such thing when it comes to me. No one but Joachim ever comes here. Not since I razed this church to the ground.

No one even said thanks for finding the Volkovs' secret portal. Now it's guarded and closed to their machinations. I'm fucked if Taryn starts opening portals like she did in the battle with Nergal.

It's been a long damn time since he's been interested in her. I fucking hate fighting gods.

Perhaps you're not the one seeking absolution today, old friend. The bitter scent of her despair permeates the island. Tell me where you've hidden her, and I will tend to her grief.

How fucking right he is. I'm still not letting him anywhere near her. She needs to learn to deal with her pain all on her own. She's no baby chick anymore and I refuse to rescue her from her own self. She will grow as powerful as I know her to be. She must.

August, Vas, and Joachim have forgotten who she is and what she can do. They've made her weak, and I won't allow it any longer.

Fuck off, father. You're not helping. She's safe where she is. This time she does this on her own.

Joachim scratches his ear and looks up at the night sky. He's feigning his disinterest. He wouldn't be here so soon if he wasn't anxious. Or perhaps he needs company in his misery. *She cannot ascend without all four of us. I've searched for them, just as I did you when she sent you into the shadows to Hell. They're not there. They're dead.* Do you still believe there is anything to do?

She's already mated with August and Vas. My throat thickens and for the first time since Taryn died in her last life, my limbs and heart are fucking tired. Even if they were gone, it doesn't change my plans. None of us know what happens if one of us dies in this immortal prison. Perhaps we will be reincarnated, perhaps we'd finally get the rest that none of us have had in five-thousand years.

Vas knew there was a chance they might not make it when he asked me to take Taryn to safety. He could make that sacrifice because he'd already marked and claimed her.

He gave her everything he had, in every life he lived with her. No wonder he thought I was trash.

Even Joachim hadn't predicted Vas and August's sacrifice. No one would willingly leave her side once they were in her good graces again. I may never be. No matter how much I or the others want me to be hers again.

I don't regret not coming to Joachim's well-planned mating ceremony when Taryn first arrived in our prison. He wanted us all to jump through his hoops. I don't take orders from anyone else. I give them. It's when they aren't followed that everything goes to shit.

Which is why I've stopped giving them.

You still think she can save us all?

For thousands of years Joachim has been my confidant. Every alpha needs an advisor, and he's been mine. This is only the second time ever that he's come to me needing guidance. I hear it in his voice if not his words. He is once again questioning his faith.

He didn't listen to me then. I argued till I was hoarse that he shouldn't take a vow to a god he didn't believe in simply so he had an excuse not to mate with her. He swore it was more than that and ignored me. Why would he take my council now?

She won't have to. I will save them.

Joachim doesn't move, except for the slightest wag of his tail. He likes to think he's good at hiding his emotions. I can practically hear the litany of unanswered questions from him, but he's smart enough to answer them all himself without even asking.

Yes, August and Vas are alive.

Yes, I've seen them through the Volkov's shadow portal.

No, I haven't told her she didn't kill them when she opened a portal of her own and they were sucked into the mouth of Hell.

Let her suffer, feel her grief, and come back stronger because of her heartache. I can handle her anger and hatred for not telling her, if it means she breaks the curse on her once and for all.

When? I will go with you.

A third predator joins us and he is one I can't ignore. *As will I.*

William, the lion King of Scots, prowls into my domain so rarely. He wasn't involved in our battle with Nergal, so I don't know how he knows of Vas and August's fate. He and his strange mate always seem to know more than they should.

I answer them both at the same time. *The next time the Volkov portal opens, and no you will not. Someone has to guard it from this side.*

There aren't many I trust to slay the monsters from Hell, but the King in his impressive lion form can and will get the job done. We can't keep the portal from opening if a god like Nergal wills it so, but we can make sure nothing gets through to terrorize the inmates of Fire Island.

Last time I was distracted from my duty here, two demon wyrms emerged and it took me far too long to hunt them down. Taryn still had no idea denizens of the underworld had been hunting her in the forest. Perhaps I should have made her face them and forced her to reawaken her powers on her own. I won't make that mistake again.

Will prowls around the church ruins until he finds a place to sit and begins cleaning his paws as if the stench here makes him feel dirty. *I will accept those terms. My luscious bride didn't want me going to Hell anyway. But don't fuck up the rescue effort, lad. There are a few too many women in our lives who will make us wish we were in Hell if you don't bring those boys back.*

One alpha to another, Will knows better than most what's at stake here. He's been around so much longer than anyone else, I wouldn't be surprised if he knew who and what Taryn is. Even if he doesn't, his mate is special enough, that he understands what it means to be in love with a powerful woman that the rest of the world wants to destroy.

Fuck. I am not in love with Taryn. Not this time. I can't afford to be.

This reincarnated life of hers has to be different, and I'm the only one who seems to understand that. We've been doing the same thing for thousands of years, over and over. We find where she'd been hidden away, work to protect her, keep her safe, help her discover her true self and the power within, and then she is taken from us and we have to start from scratch in her next life.

No more. The Volkovs have made too many mistakes that I will take advantage of, and if I have to drag the rest of the Wolf

Guard kicking and screaming into my plan, fine. I may have forsaken my position as their alpha, but that doesn't mean I don't still know their strengths and weaknesses or how to control them.

If a trip to Hell and back doesn't change their minds, my prison for them will.

What would you have me do with Taryn while you're off saving the world? Joachim's tone is a bit more snide than I'm used to hearing from him. He's always been the peacemaker and doesn't pick fights. He's more cunning, but no less of a warrior.

You'll stay away from her. She doesn't need to be coddled. He had his chance and once again denied himself and Taryn that comfort. Too late now.

I wait for his rebuttal, but none comes. Good. I don't want to argue with him. No doubt this isn't the end of it. Joachim has machinations of his own that I've never understood. He'll search for her, but I'm ready for him. He won't like the plans I have.

In the end, when Taryn ascends to her rightful place once again, they'll thank me. *Go away, you won't find her here. Tend to your sheep in wolves' clothing. They're the flock that needs a man of the cloth and the platitudes of a messenger of God.*

I full well know that he'll look for her. In fact, I'm counting on it. With the bait laid out for him and my trap ready to spring, I'm done with talk and still have this angry energy to burn off. I hadn't planned on going through the portal so soon, but what better way to work through the feelings I don't want to acknowledge than by destroying minions of hell?

Joachim doesn't budge and simply sits there staring at me. I can't give him what he wants, because he wants me to be something better than I am. That's what he's always wanted for all of us. But with each life, he gets more and more desperate.

Perhaps that's why he twisted the way he interacted with her. He no longer fulfilled his duty to her by being her mate.

How is what I do now any different? I no longer serve her as the alpha of the Wolf Guard. I cannot be her lover as much as I want her.

Huh. For the first time since Joachim took his stupid vows and decided to forsake her bed, I understand his decision. Yet, he condemns mine even as he tries to find forgiveness for me.

Well, he was going to have plenty of time to ponder his mistakes, and mine, once he is imprisoned and can no longer manipulate Taryn's life... or mine.

I'm going to make sure there are no traces of Taryn's portals. Be gone when I return. I turn my back on him and trot off into the forest, toward the chapel in the woods, not wanting anymore talk. Will has never cared about manners, so it's not as if my abrupt end to the conversation will offend him. He may not know the details, but he inherently knows what I have to do will be both hard and the right thing.

I hear the two of them moving around my lair. Joachim didn't even wait for me to get very far away before he defied my orders not to search for Taryn. He won't find her this time. But he'll be back.

When I get back from this foray into Hell, I suspect he'll be waiting in a cell alongside Taryn. A strange pang spreads across my chest. I have no right to be hurt that Joachim is trying to rescue Taryn from me. In fact, I planned on him doing just that.

He, August, and Vas are the ones who suffered because of me. At any time I could have used my alpha voice to command them to my will. I may have abdicated my position, but in truth, they are still my pack, and I, their alpha. Taryn ensured long ago that the four of us would always be bound both to her and each other.

Not even my anger can break that bond.

About ten minutes after leaving Joachim and Will in my lair, I sense a new presence on the island. It doesn't have a scent, and

I don't even know which direction to go to stalk this being. But I know that it isn't wolf, isn't human, isn't good.

Something evil has come to Fire Island, and it's my responsibility to destroy it.

Until Taryn ascends and then her light will destroy all the darkness and evil once again. Just like it did for our people five-thousand years ago.

TARYN

*I*f I'm going to avenge the death of my mates, the first thing I have to do is get the hell out of this stinking dungeon. Who has a dungeon, anyway. It's not like I'm a Disney princess locked away in a tower by an awful beast. Well, the Dark Prince of Wolves is pretty beastly.

I doubt true love's kiss can save him.

Doesn't mean I don't want to kiss him.

Ack. What is wrong with me. He's a complete douchepotato and I should want nothing to do with him. So why in the world does he make my girly bits go all tingly even thinking about him?

I don't want to admit that I already know.

He's mine. Just the same as August, Vasily, and Joachim are. I can't have Father Joachim either, and I've lost August and Vas to the depths of Hell.

Fine. It's fine. I'll be fricking fine.

I will figure out what to do about the tornadoes of emotion I'm having about all my wolves later. I can't think about that now. I'll think about it tomorrow. For today, or tonight, I can't tell what time of day it is in all this darkness, I will simply focus on finding a way out of this prison within a prison.

"Hey Peter, any chance you know of an escape route?"

He doesn't answer. What a creep. Ooh, or maybe he's really dead this time? He didn't sound great when I was talking to him earlier. That's just got to be another thing I can't think about right now. Get out. That's all I can do. I'll send help back for Peter if I can escape and get back to the *derevnya.*

There are real bars on two sides of my cell and the others are dirt and stone walls as if this place is simply a big hole dug into the ground. I shake the bars, but they don't budge. I drop to my knees and scrape at the dirt beneath me. If I can find the bottom, I could dig underneath. Like a dog, or a wolf.

This whole shifting thing is still so new to me and I sometimes forget. I take a moment to clear my mind and pull up the emotions that Vas taught me. I think of him and his unwavering love and devotion to me, I think of August and the way his arms and body felt wrapped around mine. There is the warmth and passion of their love for me and mine for them. Those are supposed to be the ones I use to shift back to my human form, but I know what's coming next.

The tear in my heart pains me just as if the stupid thing has been torn from my chest again. The wolftresses rises up just as she did when Vas taught me how to embrace this other form. Sparkling blue light, my magic, rushes over me and for a moment this underground prison is illuminated.

If I weren't in the middle of shifting, I'd throw up. There are bones, human bones scattered everywhere in three other cells. How many people have died down here?

I can't think about that now. I am not god-damn dying down here. I've got shit to do.

In wolf form my senses are overwhelmed with the stench of this place. It's more than death. If I had to guess, this is what brimstone smells like. I push away the thoughts that the Dark Prince of Wolves got his darkness from Hell. He protected and saved me from the demons, even if I didn't want him too. I watched him destroy them, ripping them apart until they turned to oily stains in the beautiful natural chapel.

If he was in league with them, I don't think he would have killed as many as he did. But what do I know?

I ignore the worries and set to digging. One by one my claws break off on the earth here that is frozen hard like cement. It's impenetrable permafrost. After fifteen minutes my paws are bloody and I've hardly made any progress. There's nothing more than a slight depression in the dirt. I shift back, avoiding looking around when my magic lights up the room again.

This digging out idea isn't going to work. Okay, maybe digging up?

I crawl up onto the makeshift wooden cot and scratch as high up as I can reach. My fingers are bloody in my human form too from my nails being torn off and I'll I do is leaves smears of dark red on the stone. If it's even possible, the dirt here is even harder than on the floor. This plan to quickly dig hole in the ground or the wall to escape isn't going to work. The dirt has been compacted and the bars are solid immovable objects. Without someone else coming to my rescue, I'm not getting out of here.

Unless I open another portal.

A shiver that has nothing to do with the cold ripples through me. I can't. I won't ever use that kind of magic again.

But if I can open a portal into hell, couldn't I use my magic to open some stupid jail cell bars? I wish there was someone around who could teach me more about where my magic comes from and how to use it. Where's a Hogwarts when you need one. Ooh, another thing I've just remembered. I used to like to read. A lot. That was my escape.

If I'm stuck on this stupid prison island for the rest of an eternal life, and I hope I'm not, I'm going to start writing books. Romances between women who aren't perfect, in their minds or bodies but who are kinda badass anyway, like me, and some super schmexy wolf shifters. Hmm. Maybe I'll start doing that if we all get out of this supernatural prison anyway.

At least that will give me something to think about other than stewing and being sad or mad, or smad, like before while I'm stuck here in the dark. Wait, no, I don't want to think that way. I will get out of here. Then I'll kick the Dark Prince of Wolves delicious butt, and go rescue my mates. Just putting that out into the universe.

After several deep breaths, I close my eyes and search inside of myself for the magic inside of me. This time, it's easier to find that then it is was to find the wolf. The blue light flickers in my mind and I imagine it working it's way down my arms and bursting from my fingertips.

When I peek one eye open, there is indeed, tiny sparkles of blue shimmering from my fingertips. It's not as strong as when I was in the fight against that owl demon thing and trying to open portal. This is more like I've stuck my fingers in a pot of blue glitter. But it's going to have to do, because that's all I've got in me at the moment.

I wiggle my fingers and waved my hand back and forth over the bars and imagined them splitting open wide enough for me to walk though. The bars creaked and groaned and I mentally pushed harder. Is there a wider space between the two metal rods in front of me, or am I imagining it?

"That's not going to work," Peter's voice croaks out from the other side of the room.

Poof. He's broken my concentration and into my self-doubt. The magic fades away and I drop down onto my knees. That push sucked out every last drop of energy I had and now I have a headache. When we were out in the moonlight before, I could feel the drain, but the night air seemed to refill me. Here in the cold, damp darkness, it's like I can't breathe.

"Don't be a dick, Peter." I need people around me who believe in me, not haters. He doesn't respond so maybe he's learned his lesson. Or he's dead. He really smells dead.

I'm not giving up yet, but I don't think I can keep trying to escape until I rest, and hopefully get some food and water. Will the Dark Prince even give me those basic necessities? I can't I even starve to death or die of dehydration on this horrible immortal prison island, but I can feel the effects of it on my body.

I both want the Dark Prince to come back and the thought of seeing him makes me shiver. I want to wrap myself up in him, and never want to see him again, all at the same time.

I bow my head and do my best to conserve my energy. I don't know how long I'll have to wait, but I can do nothing else. A hundred scenarios run through my mind of what will happen when the Dark Prince returns. If he ever does. I can try to seduce him, or beg, or cry, or fight.

I don't think any of them will work. What I need is help. Then as if I manifested what I wanted, I hear a scratching above my head and am immediately on my feet. "Hello? Is anyone there? Help me, help."

That was probably dumb. I'm sure it's just my captor again, but if it isn't, I'm not missing the opportunity to be rescued. I may be powerful and working my way into being the badass everyone else seems to think I am, but there's no shame in getting help, especially when it's dire freaking straights.

"Please, anyone. I'm down here." I pound against the wall, which doesn't do much, so I run over to the metal bars. Running my fingers back and forth across them also doesn't make much sound and I needed a racket. There's nothing in my cell to help. What I need is a tin cup to bang against the bars like they do in the old movies.

I search the cell quickly and there's nothing in here that will work. The Dark Prince must have cleared it out especially for me. But the cell next to mine has those bones. Oh God - sorry father - I have to get one, pick it up, and bang it against the metal, or I have no chance of being heard.

I swallow hard and turn to the set of bars separating my cell from the next. There's a skull, but thankfully it's all the way on the other side and I couldn't reach it even if I wanted to. The only one that is within reach is a handful of small bones that seem as if they're pointing right at me. This was someone's hand. Someone big, because the whole thing is twice the size of mine, even with my skin and muscle still intact.

But still, even the largest bone will barely be big enough to work like I want. I quickly grab two of the biggest of the bunch, trying not to think about who this might have been, and drag them back and forth across the metal bars like a macabre xylophone. "Can anybody hear me? I'm down here. Help me, please."

I paused for a moment to see if I could hear the scratching or any other movement above again. Everything was deadly silent. Crapballs.

But then a sliver of light shot into the darkness from the stairway. "Taryn, quiet. I am here for you."

Oh my God - sorry Father - I'm saved. It's Father Joachim, in the flesh. When the Dark Prince ripped me from the battle with the evil owl demon and those horrible oily wyrms I didn't know if he'd survived. I'm so happy to see him, that I could pee my pants. Except I'm not wearing any.

I shout whisper to him, "Hurry, I don't know if there are keys or what. It's so dark down here and you do not want to see what it looks like in the light."

Father Joachim doesn't hurry. He squints his eyes and looks around as if there are a hundred booby traps. I'm pretty sure I have the only two boobs in this place. I wave him over and he creeps forward, sniffing the air. "Taryn, are you alright?"

"Yes, mostly. I'm more mentally hurt than physically." I look down at my hands, but the wounds from digging are all healed up. "That's Peter you're smelling."

"No, there is something worse down here than a rotting corpse."

"You gotta get me out of here so we can open another portal to hell, and..." I don't have the guts to ask him if he knows what Vas and August's fates are. When we get back to the derevnya, and I can safely curl up in his arms, then he can tell me the truths of what I've done.

He still isn't moving faster than an exhausted sloth. I've never seen him so cautious before. His wolf is shining in his eyes and the sliver of light from the stairwell allows me to see that he's fingering the prayer beads at his waist. That one singular ray of light is heaven sent.

"Come on, Father. Before the Dark Prince comes back."

Once again, as if I conjured him, the Prince's shadow blots out the light. I know it's his because I can feel his presence from my skin to my soul. "Too late."

Father Joachim spins to face our nemesis, but the trapdoor at the top of the stairs slams shut enveloping us all again in utter darkness. All I can see now is Father Joachim's glowing blue eyes. "Hide, Taryn, now."

His words barely make it out of his mouth before he drops his robes and shifts into his wolf. But before his paws even hit the dirt, he's thrown across the room. I scream because I don't know what else to do.

Crap. Duh. I shift into my wolf form too, and now with my wolf's vision I can once again make out shapes. But where I expect to see the Dark Prince and Father Joachim fighting, there is nothing. Like... Nothing. The next cell over where the father was thrown is filled with the black fog that I was held captive in before the island. The fog that stole all my memories.

I snarl and bring up the magic inside of me. I don't have much left, but what I do have explodes out of me in so many rays of light. It pushes the Nothing back, as if it's a sentient being retreating in pain. Good. Fuck off you disgusting bit of evil.

It finally dissipates enough that I can see Father Joachim's wolf lying prone in the next cell over. I hurry over and snick my snout through the bars between us. *Can you hear me, Father?*

I don't even know if he and I can mindspeak like I can with the others. Father Joachim has never marked me, although we've done some stuff that only mates would do with each other, so I'm hoping.

He doesn't respond, not even a twitch. But I don't know if it's because he can't hear me or because he's hurt that bad. He's not dead. He can't be dead, I would know. I. Would. Know.

I shift back because there's nothing I can do as a wolf if he can't hear me and maybe I can reach my arm through and try to at least touch him so he knows I'm here. Even stretching as far as I can, I can only barely get a hand into the tips of his scruff.

But I can see feel the up and down movement of his breathing and that makes me feel loads better. Finally after a few moments he shifts and moves closer to me. He's still not awake, but he must have sensed my presence. I stroke the back of his neck until I come across something strange, stuck in his fur.

Carefully I untangle it, hoping it's not like a blood clot or something. I haven't felt any other bleeding, but maybe I missed something. When I finally get the thing out, I pull something that's hard like a stick, but covered in something soft. When I get it close enough to my face to see what it is, I'm holding a black feather.

Just like the evil owl.

Gulp. The Dark Prince of Wolves saved me from the battle

with that demon. This must just be a leftover feather from when Father Joachim was fighting too.

The Dark Prince couldn't be in league with Hell. Not if he was one of my mates. Damn it. I was going to have to save him too, wasn't I?

GRIGORI

*F*ather forgive me for what I've done.

That's what I should be thinking. But I'm not. The feelings running through my blood as I lock the hidden trapdoor to my secret dungeon tight is not remorse. Hmm. This is more like a good old-fashioned gloat.

It took a good amount of work and planning to set a trap for one of the Wolf Guard. Only in the wake of Taryn's destruction would he have been vulnerable enough to get caught. But I used bait he could never resist.

Joachim can resist anything but temptation. And temptation's name is Taryn.

He'll spend his time comforting her guilt because it means he can avoid thinking about his own. The two of them together tucked away safe in my dungeon gives me the breathing room I need to attempt to rescue August and Vas.

I fucking hate Hell, and I don't want to go. But I will. For her.

I shake my head to clear away the thoughts of her in the dark, awaiting her fate. Will she remember the last time she was trapped in a damp dark basement? I would spare her those memories if I could. They haunt me every time I see her.

A hundred plus years imprisoned on this island isn't enough to forget the last time she died. In my arms, by my own hands.

Father Joachim thinks he has guilt. Over what I don't know. But he doesn't know what it means to kill your beloved. He could never do what I had to that day. I can never forgive myself or the Volkovs for letting the Bolsheviks run roughshod over the last Wolf Tzar to rule over Russia. Even if Nikolai Alexandrovich Romanov was the worst kind of idiot, and his wife a cheating whore, their children didn't deserve to die that way.

I should have fucking known Rasputin would get his revenge.

There was no way I was going to allow my sweet Anastasia to be... no. I couldn't even think about what they would have done to her if I hadn't taken her life first.

Enough. It's been too long since I allowed those memories to crawl into my brain like flesh-eating scarabs. I made the choices I did, and it didn't matter if no one ever forgave me. Including myself. That wasn't what mattered now.

I may not let him know that I agreed with him, but Joachim was right. Taryn couldn't ascend and take her rightful place unless all four of us were here to guard her. Without August and Vas, we were incomplete and she would never rise again.

I cover the trapdoor so no one else can find it, use the mix of herbs I'd meticulously gathered to block anyone else from finding their scent, and prepare myself for a trip to Hell. The shadow portal at the alter sometimes opens on its own, but I couldn't wait for that.

Only gods, goddesses, and those with a gift from either could open a portal. I was none of the above so I shouldn't be able to do it. I never had before being imprisoned here. In fact, I never had until a little more than a quarter century ago.

When Taryn had been reincarnated into this new life.

Everything was different this time. All four of us knew it. I was just the only one who had the guts to defy our duty and do what had to be done with this last chance.

I pushed away the dark stain on my soul and pulled upon her power. The light from her magic, bubbled up inside of me and I opened my hand. The darkness of the shadow pooled like a cauldron being stirred, opening wider and wider, until the fires of Hell flickered through, lighting up the burned out shell of the church.

Sometimes when other portals were open, I could see through them like an eyeglass telescope. I suspected this was how Father Joachim predicted Taryn's arrival, and not some mystical precognition or message from God.

At least this time, there were no demon dragon wyrms or the God of Chaos to fight off. Which must mean they were busy. If anyone could survive a trip to Hell, it was August and Vas. But the sooner I got the two of them out of there, the better.

Then I was going to throw their dumb asses into my dungeon too.

I take several deep breaths of the cool Siberian night air, shift into my more powerful wolf form, then dive into the portal. The heat hits me right in the face. No amount of panting is going to cool me down. I never thought I'd appreciate eternal winter, but fuck. I'm wishing for snow right now.

The first thing I do is reach out through our pack connection. *August, Vas, tell me where you are.*

No response. I don't even feel the touch of their minds. Yet somehow I also know they aren't dead. They're here, but something is blocking us from communicating. I know only a little about the Queen of the Underworld and her powers, but her consort, Nergal doesn't have the ability to do this.

One more item on my to do list while I'm in Hell. Find out

why the rulers of the underworld are interested in Taryn, and why they're working with the Volkovs. Even for Rasputin, this was a dangerous game.

The maze of tunnels carved out of the sharp and craggily rock is endless. I open my senses as wide as I can, searching for any sign of my fellow guardsmen. Their scents are nowhere near, but I catch a faint whiff of something other than demons and brimstone ahead. That's the only clue I have, so that's where I'll start.

I give one last glance at the portal, hold up my paw and let the magic flow to close it. I can't risk leaving it open for any wyrm to come upon. Not if I'm not there to protect the island. My tether back is Taryn. As long as she lives, I will always have a way to get home.

Because she has always been and will always be my home. No matter what century, what continent, what life, she is mine.

It's no use trying to hide in the shadows when the demons can appear out of even the smallest sliver of it. I stalk down the tunnel where the different scent is the strongest, keeping ultra alert for signs of August and Vas, or danger.

What I find is neither.

Dragging a sword as tall as she is, and a belt full of daggers, the little girl we met the last time I was thrown into Hell, trots down the corridor as if this is nothing more than a school hallway. I still don't understand what the fuck a human girl is doing in Hell. She shouldn't have been able to survive even a moment, much less be walking around like this is her personal playground.

She spots me and hauls her sword up in front of her, and points the tip right at me. "No, puppy. Bad. Go home. Go home, right now."

I don't move an inch. I have no idea what kind of a creature she is. She definitely human, but more. What I do catch is the distinct scent of wolves. She isn't one, but she's been near them.

The little girl sighs, rolls her eyes at me, and drops the tip of the sword into the dirt. I almost laugh because she's so very clearly irritated that I am causing her some kind of inconvenience by not doing as I'm told. If I had robes and could shift so that I wasn't a large naked male, I'd do so and ask her who she is and what she's doing down here. Since that isn't happening, I can't waste anymore time. She may be the key to finding August and Vas.

When I rescue them from these depths, we can bring her back to Fire Island with us. She'd eternally be the same age, but being six-ish years old for a lifetime has to be better than growing up in Hell.

Slowly and carefully I approach her, with my head slung low, so she knows I'm not a threat. I'm twice as big as she is, but she seems completely unafraid. Her scent is strange, like nothing else I've smelled either. It's almost like a dragon. But there is no such thing as female dragons. I don't smell the telltale bitterness of fear or aggression from her. She won't attack me. Not that I think she could do much damage with a sword she can barely lift.

She watches me with narrowed eyes, but when I put my snout into her hand to show her I mean her no harm. She sighs again like she's put out. "Dumb puppy. Come on."

With a tug of the fur at the scruff of my neck, she leads me deeper into the depths of the tunnels. It's clear she knows exactly where she's going and I have to pay a lot of attention to make sure I can get back. The thing keeping me by her side is that faint scent of wolf on her.

I can't tell if it's August or Vas. There are simply too many other scents surrounding her and I can't pick out any one in particular. Who or what is this child?

She holds her fingers up to her lips to signal that I should be silent. It's not like I'm going to run around howling or anything, but I nod my understanding anyway. Together we creep up to a crossroads of tunnels and I can hear a horde of demon dragon wyrms nearby.

"Bad demons," she whispers and points around the corner. The way she says it makes me think that there are good demons too. Uh. I didn't realize there was any other kind.

She darts across the opening to a different tunnel and waves to me to follow. I can't help but glance to where the dumb demons are gathered. Even that short glimpse turns my stomach. The Black Dragon of Hell is fucking some other kind of demon I've never seen before.

That is something a little girl shouldn't see. I hurry across the gap and give her a little shove forward. She takes several steps, then turns and smacks me on the nose. "Don't touch. Ouch."

She curls in on herself and puts a hand on one of her daggers. I take a step back and sit, trying again to make myself less threatening. She's injured somehow, but doesn't want me to see her pain.

My heart pounds in my chest like a battle axe cutting open my chest. This child reminds me so much of Taryn with her fierce bravery. If I didn't know Taryn was in my dungeon and not awaiting reincarnation, I'd think this is where she went between each life, that this was her.

A moment later, she pulls the dagger from the belt at her waist and holds it out in front of her. "Jett."

She says this name as if she was swearing. There is no fear in her. Again, more like frustration. I move to get in front of her, the need to protect her just as strong as with Taryn. Whoever this girl is, she's important to the world.

Another horde of demon wyrms trample down the tunnel towards us. I growl and prepare to rip these demons apart, but just before they are within striking distance, the largest of the demons stops. It hisses at me but doesn't move any closer. I recognize it as the same one she protected us from before.

The little girl crawls underneath me and pops up between my legs. "Puppies not yours. Go away." She sticks out her tongue at the demon wyrm and points her dagger at its face.

The demon hisses again and the way they react to each other reminds me of the Romanov siblings. Always bickering, but they cared for each other. I don't see how a demon and a girl of unknown species could be related. Then the demon spoke. It actually said real words and pointed at me. "Fallyn have two. Jett want one."

Hell was getting stranger and stranger by the minute. The girl, Fallyn, has two puppies. That had to be August and Vas. Thank the Goddess.

Fallyn stomped her foot. "No. Puppies leave."

"Jett leave Hell," the beast shouts. He directs his next words at me. "Wolf take Jett to portal or wolf die."

TARYN

*I*t doesn't occur to me until what felt like hours later, that my magic could probably help Father Joachim heal. Duh. I already knew that the shifters heal faster when they were in their animal forms. I still didn't really think of myself as one of them, I realize.

My own shift was different. Their skin split and their bones cracked when they went from one form to another. My magic just sort of made me into a wolf. I wonder if I can shift into other animals too. Or for that matter, other forms all together. Like can I become foggy like the Nothing? That was something I would try after Father Joachim was awake.

I rest my hand on his back, right between his shoulder bones and close my eyes. Wait. Why was I always doing that? It's not as if I need total darkness to call the magic up or something. In fact, everything worked better when there was light. Specifically moonlight.

Whatever I am, human, wolf, witch, something else, I think the wolves Goddess of the Moon had maybe bestowed this magic on me. I'd felt something stir inside of me when Alida was telling the story of how she'd given their people the ability to defend themselves.

I wish I'd had more time to hear more and ask questions. But I absolutely didn't regret getting busy with Vas and August instead. But if my powers also came from her, why didn't she just make me a wolf shifter too? What makes me so special?

I promise myself, sitting here in the dark, that I will find out who this Goddess is and why she chose me to have this magic. I suspect she also has a hand in matching me up with my wolves. There's so much more to the feelings I have for them, even the Dark Prince, than simply attraction. Even love doesn't feel like a strong enough word.

It's that feeling that I draw upon to pull the magic up now and try to heal Father Joachim. I watch very closely as my hand begins to glow. I bring up the memories of him comforting me with his soft wisdom when we first met and I was still so lost as to who, where, and why I was here.

He doesn't move and nothing changes. I need to do more. The instant attraction to him is a pretty damn strong emotion, so I let that bubble up next. The light in the room increases, and not just my fingers are glowing now, but my whole arm.

Vas taught me that the most instinctual base emotions are what I should use to control the shift, and I guess it's the same with this magic too. What's more instinctual than sex?

I reach out to Father Joachim with my mind, even though I don't think he can hear me. I push the memories of how much I wanted him when I mated with August. The way he touched himself because he couldn't help it turned me on so much.

He stirs, just the slightest movement in his legs, as if he's really only a big dog having a dream. It's working so I pull up the next memory. This time he's pressing his cock to my lips, letting his orgasm overwhelm him and me. I felt so happy and guilty at the same time that I wanted him to let me taste him, but knowing he thought it was wrong.

What I wouldn't give to see him lose all control.

Our entire side of the room is glowing with my magic and something is definitely happening to Father Joachim. He's breathing is better and he doesn't seem to be in as much pain as before, but he's still unconscious. I need to give him more, but I'm fresh out of memories.

Well, here goes nothing. In my mind's eye I imagine what I really want to do with Father Joachim. I want him bared to me, not just his body but his soul. No more secrets, no lies. He'll bite my neck and mark me, and he won't feel guilt, but the same pleasure that I do. Then with August, Vasily, and even the Dark Prince as our witnesses, I want him to claim me.

As I think about this scenario, I can literally feel the magic doing what I want. Father Joachim's internal bleeding slows, then stops, and the injuries knit themselves back together. His broken bones mend, and I sense the moment he becomes conscious again.

Out of the corner of my eye I see his prayer beads, nestled in the pile of robes he dropped when he shifted to fight the Nothing. They're glowing with the same blue light of my magic. I always assumed Father was an ordained priest of the Russian Orthodox church. But what if his religion is that of this Goddess of the Moon? That makes a heck of a lot more sense.

He does talk of God, but also of the Goddess. He's the one I understand the least about. So far I have no past memories of him, but there is a very distinct sense that his vows to Christianity are comforting to me, but that a religion that stems from the mythology of wolf-shifters and the moon is also right for both of us.

"Father Joachim, can you hear me? Are you all right now?" I gave him one last push of magic and he shifts from wolf to man. At least I know how to do that one thing right.

His back is to me and he slowly rolls over to face me. He has that same kind of dazed look as when I made him shift from wolf to man the other time. When I remove my hand and let the magic recede back inside of me, he gets more alert pretty fast.

"Taryn? I'm the one that should be asking if you're alright. I'm supposed to protect you, not the other way around." He sits up and scrubs his hand over his face and looks around. "Grigori always did like a secret dungeon to punish those that would harm you."

In just those two or three sentences, Father Joachim has revealed more about who and what he and the Dark Prince are to me than the entire rest of the time I've been with them on this island. Maybe I should use more magic on him to make him spill all his secrets.

I get a yucky indigestion rumble in my stomach from even the thought of using my power to manipulate him. Vas said I had to discover who and what I am for myself, that they couldn't tell me. I want to trust in my wolves, that they know best. They certainly all remember more than I do.

Father Joachim grabs his robes and his prayer beads. The beads, he wraps around his wrist securing them with a quick loop and a twist. He shoves the robes through the bars to me. "Put these on, *boginya*. You shouldn't be subjected to such cold."

I'd rather he and I snuggled for warmth, but I suppose the bars would make that hard. Besides, if I put on his robes, Father Joachim can't hide himself from me. Gah. I know I shouldn't be thinking about anything but escape, but the attraction I have to him just takes over my brain sometimes.

Besides the fact that I've just spent the last few minutes imagining all the deliciously dirty things we have done and could be doing together. I'm so going to hell.

Why do I have sex on the brain when I should just be working on getting out of here and avenging August and Vas? I'm blaming the Dark Prince and that red hot kiss. Okay, time to get my mind out of the freaking gutter...dungeon...whatever, and get back to the plan.

I slip into the robes, and the scent of Father Joachim send all the tingles to all the places I want him to touch me. Later, body. Geez, get a grip. "Father, can you get out of your cell? I'm locked in tight."

He looks around, and examines the bars. "Does the demon who pushed me into the cell appear often? Is it guarding you?"

"The Nothing? I didn't realize it was a demon." That would mean, what? The Nothing had eaten me and I'd been living inside of it, then it puked me onto the island. Horrifying. "The only other time I've seen it was before I came here."

"The Nothing is a good name for the shadow. But it is merely the element the demons use to travel. There was also a demon here, that came from that cell over there. That's what I fought against."

"The only other thing down here is Peter, and he's mostly dead." I pointed in the direction of Peter's putrid smell.

"*Demon, ty govorish' cherez Pyotr Fyodorovicha?*"

Uh, that's interesting. I don't understand how or why, but I know that Father Joachim is speaking Russian and that he asked if the demon was speaking through Peter. When I first landed on the island Peter had spoken several other languages to me and I hadn't understood them at all. This had to be a side effect of the Goddess's magic, but what a strange one.

Or was it because more of my past life memories were manifesting and I'd lived so many of them in Russia that the language was latent in my mind?

Something moves in Peter's cell. I squint to see, but it was still so dark. I call up my wolf trying to focus on only shifting my eyes to use the better vision. Slowly the shapes in the room became more clear and a very raggedy looking Peter, his head lolling to the side and his limbs at weird angles was standing behind the bars. Eek.

"Why do you think I'm possessed by a demon, priest?"

I grab Father Joachim's hand through the bars. Whatever that is on the other side of the room, it is not a person. If the creepy crawlies of disgust feels like bugs crawling through sludge dripping down your insides, then I am infested with both heebies and jeebies, because eww. The sight and sound of the demon coming out of Peter is beyond disturbing.

"Because Peter is clearly dead, but his body has not been taken by the island and his soul has not been claimed by the Goddess, as is her right with all her people." Joachim's tone was calm and even as if he is having a conversation with any Joe Schmoe.

"Your Goddess has forsaken her people. Or have you not noticed?" Peterdemon's arm flings around as if he is trying to indicate the dire circumstances we're in, but instead he just looks like a marionette doll that the puppeteer doesn't have much practice using.

"Your mind tricks won't work on me." Father Joachim waves the demon's threat away.

I cover a snort because I almost said - These are not the droids you're looking for - out loud. It is so weird how my memories come back to me in these little blips. It never seems to be the important ones, always just tiny slices of my life. But I do know now I had a bit of a crush on young Obi Wan Kenobi. Which explains a lot.

Father Joachim gives my hand a little squeeze and continues to chastise Peterdemon. "I am not your average priest. My connection to the Goddess is stronger than you can imagine. Now, tell me your name so I can banish you and be done with your insolence."

The Father's confidence and bravado with this creepy beast is delicious. It makes me want to jump his bones even more. It also gives me a bit of bravery. I bet if my magic repelled the

Nothing, the shadow, that this demon hid in, I can help banish the actual demon too.

"Yeah. I want you gone, Darth Creepo. Go back to where you came from." I point at Peterdemon and give a little wiggle of my fingers. Father Joachim grabs my hand, covering it with his fist so fast, I didn't even get one sparkle of magic out.

I give him a what-the-literal-hell, but don't say anything because his eyes are wide and he's giving me the same look back. "Don't let him see what you can do, *sladkaya boginya.* It is my duty to protect you from Hell's beasts."

"But I want to help. I can do it."

"You can. Why do you think he did not attack you already? But I have failed you for so long, allow me to do my duty."

Peterdemon shakes the bars and the shadow bubbles up around his feet. "You can not hide her from me any longer, priest. She will be forever vulnerable in the darkness without her guards. I have three and your soul is already tainted by my realm. Give her to me."

I rip my hand from Father Joachim's hold, rush the bars of my cage and shoot a beam of magic at this pile of poo. My light grabs him up just as it did my wolves at the beach. But this time through the connection, I can feel the chaos and darkness that embodies this beast of Hell. "Are you saying you have August, Vasily, and the Dark Prince imprisoned in Hell?"

Peterdemon flails and squeaks. Father Joachim joins me at the door to our cells and clears his throat. "I guess we're doing this your way. Fine. The demon speaks through Peter and you're crushing his windpipe. He cannot answer."

"Oh. Does it hurt the demon when I do it?"

"I think not."

"Too bad." I concentrate and lesson my magical hold. "Now, talk you shitstick."

His voice comes out raspy and broken, but darker and more menacing than before. Whatever remnant of Peter may have remained, it's gone now and only the beast from Hell remains. "Choke me harder, mommy."

I'm sure that is supposed to shock me, but I've got no fucks left to give with this guy. "My pleasure."

I narrow my eyes and clench my fingers around the magic as if it's actually the demon's throat. Peterdemon gurgles and scratches at his throat as if he can pull my fingers away. He can't. Ha. He doesn't like this and I do think it hurts him. I relent a little and ask again, "Do you have my Wolf Guard imprisoned in Hell?"

"No," he says and cough laugh.

Father Joachim crosses his arms. "He's deflecting. Ask him in a different way."

I think Father Joachim has done this kind of thing before. Have I done it with him? "Do you know where August, Vasily, and the Dark Prince are?"

"Yes. They're in my domain. You can't touch them in Hell, or you'll face my wrath."

Father gives his wrist a shake. "Hell is not yours though, is it. It's Ereshkigal's. Does she know the chaos you're wreaking on the mortal plane, Nergal."

Nergal? This super evil demon from Hell's name is Nergal? Worst villain name ever. He apparently doesn't like it either because he screams and writhes around like a rodent caught on a fishing line.

"Quickly, sweet light, while you've still got him in your hold, demand he bring them back from Hell to you. Your power over him will compel him to do as you say."

It will? Badass. "I want my Guard back, Nergally Wergally. Bring me the Dark Prince, Aug—"

Before I could get out August and Vasily's names, Peterdemon's body goes slack and all the shadow bubbling around the dungeon fades away like fog in the early morning sun. I pull my magic back and drop the body of the thing that used to be a man to the floor.

The light in the room dims back to the near complete darkness. I like this new hold on the powers inside of me. The first lesson I learned when I got to this island was one of love. But the second one was that I am powerful. I forgot that.

I won't again.

GRIGORI

*I*f not for the little girl, I would have probably just ripped this talking demon dragon to shreds. I'd take my chances with the rest of his brethren. But I couldn't do that if it would put her in danger.

I'm not shifting out of my powerful wolf to my more vulnerable human form just to have a chat. I have shit to do and none of it involves parlaying with minions from Hell. I could run the other way and hope to catch August and Vas's scent, or I could stay and fight.

I didn't like either option. What I need is more info from the little girl on where my fellow guards are, not a fight.

Fuck. I was going to have to shift.

I growl and snap at the demon wyrm and it backs off a bit. As the magic of the shift rolls through me, I stay in a position low to the ground, squatting, to be able to protect my stomach and groin areas. Not to mention, I'm not walking around naked in front of a child.

The moment I'm in my human form, the girl claps and smiles at me. "Good job, puppy. My turn."

A different kind of magic than what I'm used to seeing rolls across the little girl and before my eyes, she goes from six to something like twenty. Her hair looks like it's made of flames, and the once heavy sword looks much more deadly hanging from her belt along with a dozen or so daggers.

The demon wyrm doesn't seem bothered by the fact that she's become and adult in the blink of an eye, leaving me to believe that this is not the first time she's done this. A disguise she uses, perhaps? "Do you know where the other wolves sucked down into Hell are, Fallyn?"

The demon wyrm moves closer. "I know. You show portal. I show wolves."

Fallyn smacks the demon on the nose just as she did me. "My turn, I said."

The demon wyrm pouts, like actually scowls and looks hurt but doesn't do anything more than sit back and wait for Fallyn to have her turn. She looks at me again and says, "Izzy said I should help your moon, because her children are going to be important later. Do you know the babies?"

What? "I don't have children, and who is Izzy?"

She rolled her eyes at me like I was stupid, but then turns and clearly hears something the rest of us can't. "He's coming. Hurry. I will help you, you help Jett, Jett will find the unicorn, she will help the dragons, and then I can help the mermaid's children, and they can help the sacrifice and the savior, and..."

I understand the individual words coming out of her mouth, but not when they were strung together in some kind of fairy story. Whatever kind of creature this Fallyn is, she's been in Hell too long, and I want to make sure she gets out of here with me. "Yes, I will help Jett."

Was I lying? A little bit. If Jett the demon dragon wanted to get out of Hell, as long as he didn't come to terrorize the island, fine. I wasn't sure how to help him. It's not as if he could borrow magic from the Goddess to open a shadow portal. But I would certainly show him how I did it and fulfill my end of the bargain.

"Where are the other wolves?"

The ceiling of rock above us rattled and small stones shook loose falling down on us. Fallyn and Jett looked at each other with worry in their eyes. Fallyn wrinkled her nose. "Uh-oh. You run, I go hide with the puppies. Come back later."

"No, I need to take the wolves back with me now. We don't need to run and hide, we can fight." If no one else had ever defended this woman besides herself, I would. No way I was letting another special woman die on my watch.

I shift back into my wolf form and push my senses out to pinpoint the threat. The ground around us shakes even more and a shadow portal opens above our heads not more than a few feet away. Many of the demon wyrms who'd had Jett's back when he was ready to attack me, bolt away in fear.

The portal warps and gyrates like no other I'd ever seen. Out of the darkness, the God of Chaos, half man-half owl, like a winged demon of death, drops to the dirt. This is no power move by Nergal. He isn't attacking, he's been attacked.

If he's been back to Fire Island again, while I was down here and couldn't defend Taryn, there's no telling what kind of havoc he's wrought. Father Joachim seems to have done his job though, because Nergal is looking like shit. What I don't understand is his interest in Taryn. He hasn't bothered with her or our people in thousands of years. Not since his attacks so long ago that prompted the Goddess to give us our shifting abilities in the first place. Why now?

I'll just have to kick his ass and find out.

To his credit, Jett moves next to me, pushing Fallyn behind us both. But she is the one who strikes first. One of her daggers flies through the air over my head, striking not Nergal, but the unstable rocks above him where the misshapen portal had been. A landslide of stone falls down on him, blocking my path back to where I need to go to open the portal back to the church.

"Now we run and hide." Fallyn grabs me by the scruff of the neck and slaps a hand against the wall. Trails of sparkling fire magic drop from the ceiling and reveal a dozen small caves that were previously hidden. I've lived long enough to see the rise of elemental magic and realize, the girl is some kind of a fire witch. Although, she's using magic in a way I've never seen or heard of.

She drags me toward one of the caves and as we pass through her curtain of magic, I feel a zip like lightning in the air. I can see out, but the way the demon wyrms are looking around, they can't see in. Inside is more weapons in various states of disrepair and the distinct scent of August and Vas. But they aren't here.

Outside Nergal has broken out of the pile of rock and is advancing on Jett and his fellows that did not flee. I won't have them sacrificing themselves while I stand here in relative safety, but I also can't let that beast get anywhere near Fallyn. I sniff around the cave loudly doing my best to show her that I want to know where the other wolves are.

She's very clever and shakes her head and holds her finger to her lips. "Not here. Sleeping, shhh."

The sounds outside the cave are muted, but I think she's trying to tell me they can still hear us. Likely as much as we can hear them. We're safe for the moment, but won't be for much longer.

Nergal is advancing and he swipes at one of the demon wyrms. It goes flying and smacks against the nearest wall. Jett goes berserk and runs forward on the attack. Right behind him, from the darkness, two huge wolves bound into the fray.

August and Vasily.

They're looking a little worse for their time in Hell, singed fur, dirty muzzles, unhealed cuts and scrapes. But their healthy enough to fight, and the pins and needles of worry I've felt for them dissipates. Taryn's the one who has been worried about them, not me. She needs them. I don't need anyone.

I lower my head and growl as August and Vas coordinate their attack on Nergal. They won't be able to defeat or kill the God, but we can incapacitate him and keep him from attacking long enough to escape.

"No, puppy. Shh." Fallyn holds her daggers at the ready, but she doesn't want Nergal to see her. I don't blame her. She's safe here in her cave, but I can't stay while other fight for us. Gently I place my head against her shoulder and back her up to the farthest wall of the cave, then stare at her unmoving, willing her to understand that she mustn't move.

She nods and while I doubt she'll hear or understand, I tell her what I wish I'd said to Taryn so many times over the years. *You're strong,* oomnyashka. *You don't need anyone to save you or protect you.*

My sweet fierce Taryn. It was my duty to protect her, but she always had the power to do it herself. Even before the Goddess made her the Queen of Wolves and touched her with the magical power of the moon.

I shake off the memories. Nothing better to distract myself than a good old fashioned brawl between good and evil. That same zip of fire magic passes through me when I go through Fallyn's hidden barrier. I've got the element of surprise and I'm taking full advantage of it.

With one big leap, I rebound off the wall and over the heads of most of the demons. The momentum from my push off the wall propels me straight into Nergal's chest. He falls backward, because he'd been bracing himself for a head on attack by August, Vas, and the demon dragons. Surprise, asshole.

Well, well, look who finally showed up to the fight. August blasts forward, rushing past me to land on one of the demon's wings, and Vas is right behind to pin the other one to the ground.

The scent of irritation, anger, and disappointment waft off Vasily so strongly that I don't have to guess what he's thinking right now. *If you're here, who is protecting the princess?*

Your sacrifice was not for nothing. She is safe. Joachim is with her. He doesn't need to know that they are both imprisoned, only that they are together and Taryn is out of harms way. Soon the two of them will be too and I can finally rest.

I follow Vas and August's defense strategy and charge forward to land directly on Nergal's chest, pinning him to the ground. Since he is a God and I am an alpha, he can hear me though mindspeak. *What is your interest in Taryn?*

It's not like I expected him to answer. It seemed like he had beef with August and Vas and I'd bet they'd been tracking him while down here, and not the other way around. I'd expect no less from elite warriors I'd trained. Even if Nergal did nothing but squawk, I'd bet the two of them had some intel on Hell's plans.

This asshole thrashes around like a bird caught in a trap, and it surprises me that he hasn't yet thrown us off. Perhaps when we battled him in our realm we weakened him, because there was no way this was his full strength. He wasn't mentally in the game either.

My end game is supposed to be to get August and Vas out of Hell, and rescue Tar...uh Fallyn. Fucking around with the God of Chaos wasn't getting that done. I swipe a claw across one of his wings and he thrashes about, throwing August and Vas.

Get to the tunnel where the portal back to the church is. I'll be right behind you to open it.

Both of them hesitate, but then take off running. The demon wyrms are closing in, and I think they'd like to take advantage of the weakened position Nergal is in. I'll happily let them chomp on him.

I jump away and they move in. None of us are fast enough. The demon beast snatches one of the wyrms and rips its throat out with his teeth, drinking down the beasts blood. Jett makes an unholy war cry and the room explodes into battle. Demon wyrms are attacking and being attacked if Nergal was dazed from where ever he crashed in from, he's got his wits back now.

And he's pissed.

At me.

I'd intended to grab Fallyn and slip away during the fight, but if I even attempted to get close to her, I'd be exposing her. I'll be back for her, I swear it. I turn and run down the tunnel after August and Vas. They have to be my first priority.

I owe a debt to Fallyn and Jett that I must find a way to repay, but not now. I don't get more than a few leaps into the darkness, when I hear Nergal screech and in an instant he's flying over my head. His great claws dig into my fur and the muscles on my back, snatching me up into the air. He slams me into the wall and lands in front of me, talons extended, going for my throat.

I dodge, but he catches me on the chest instead, ripping me open all the way to the bone. Fuck that hurts. This wound is deep enough that even my wolf was going to have a hard time healing this wound. I slide down the wall and all I can do now is pray.

My hubris has screwed us all. Because while I marked Taryn, I did not claim her, we did not mate, and without that bond, she cannot ascend as the Queen of the Wolves. I pray hard to the Goddess who gave me the responsibility to keep my Queen safe to spare me this one last time. If I die, here in Hell, I pray that she brings me back to life and shows me the way to find Taryn once again.

I pray.

But there is no answer.

Only Hell.

Nergal grabs me again and lifts me up by the scruff of my

neck. "Your Goddess sent me for you. But she didn't say I had to send you back alive. Death is so much more fun."

The last of my life's blood trickles down through my fur and the world around me is fading to black. I barely understand the words the God of Chaos hisses. The Goddess wants me. That's all I get.

Nergal plucks a feather from his arm and slaps it against my chest. "Give her this for me."

A shadow portal opens above me and I can see through all of space and time. My queen is waiting for me, and I want nothing more than to go to her. I'm not even bothered when Nergal squeezes my throat, choking the last of my breath from me.

In my very last moment of consciousness, I see a dagger, alight with the flames of fire magic fly through the air and strike Nergal's feathered head right in the temple. His feathers burst into flames and he screams out, dropping me into the portal and clawing at the dagger and flames.

I fall into the darkness of the shadow, into nothing, and I die.

TARYN

*S*omething has changed and I don't like it. Everything feels wrong, like a piece of me has fallen off and gone missing. I gasp at the wrenching in my chest and clasp Father Joachim's hand harder. "Do you feel it too?"

He nods gravely. I think he knows what's happening but before I can ask him, a portal opens up right where that demon vanished into the dirt and a body so bloody and torn he's unrecognizable crashes into the room. Oh no. Oh no no no no no.

It's the Dark Prince of Wolves. And I think he's dead.

Did I do this? When I told that vile demon to bring him back to me, I set a dangerous being on him. Now he's suffered the consequences of having me in his life just like August and Vasily did. I scooch away from Father Joachim. If I'm not careful, he'll be next and I need him to not be. He's my last life line, the only thing keeping me sane.

I can't lose the Dark Prince, August, and Vasily. I can't.

I can't breathe.

I can't think.

Little spots are swirling through my vision. One second I'm a badass demon shit-talker and the next I'm a pile of cortisol.

"You're going to be okay, Taryn. Breathe." Father Joachim's calm voice filters in to my full on panic attack.

"N-no. I won't. It's too much, Father. I'm not strong enough to handle all the death and despair of this island, this prison. I want to go home." I've never said that out loud before. I don't even know where home is, but I know I had one. Anything is better than the constant threats and killing.

Words pop into my head that I don't want to hear right now. *You're strong. You don't need anyone to save you or protect you.*

Tears form, blotting out the little vision I have in this darkness. They pool, but don't fall. Why is that the one thing I needed to hear? It pools in my heart and I blink, letting the tears fall just so I can wipe them from my face. From the moment I was thrown out of the Nothing and onto this island, I've let everyone else take care of me.

I wanted their protection.

But did I need it?

I've made a lot of mistakes in the short amount of time I've been here. I'm sure I made mistakes before this, in my life outside the prison that I've only started to remember. It's probably what got me thrown in here in the first place.

But these words, telling me that I am enough, they mean everything to me.

I take a shaky breath and push the sentiment deep into my heart. I'm sure I'll screw up again, but it's even worse if I fall apart and lose all hope. Nope. No. No way.

There is always hope. I'm done with these rollercoaster emotions. Either I've got the grit, determination and hope inside of me to survive or I don't.

And I know that I do. It's scary to even think about letting it all out, becoming who I'm meant to be, but I have to, because continuing to react to everything that happens to me feels to much like I'm a victim and that's never what I want for myself. I'm better than that, God dammit.

Okay, so what do I do now? I'm done freaking out, and I need to deal with this situation. Which is a dead mate out of reach, two more somewhere in Hell, and another one mentally out of reach on the other side of these bars. Yes, I was now 100% sure that all four were absolutely mine. They belong to me, and my heart to them.

It's time I did something about that instead of idly waiting for them to save me and make me stronger. I blow out a long breath and turn to Father Joachim. He's not going to like my plan, but I must convince him it's the only way.

I consider a million different ways to ask for what I need, but in the end, I just blurt it out. "You need to bite me, give me your mate mark."

Father Joachim jerks back like I'd slapped him. "Taryn, I can't. I vowed that--"

I hold up a hand to stop that line of discussion. "You don't have to have sex with me. I know you don't want to, and I swear I won't push you beyond this. But I know that we belong to each other just as I do with August and Vasily. The same as with the Dark Prince. I can't let him just die, and I can't let you deny what we both want and need any longer."

Father Joachim bows his head and I think that he's praying, probably for the strength to resist temptation. I want to respect his beliefs, but I want a real life more, and I want it with him, with all of my wolves. That means I'll do whatever I can to save the prince.

I know I have power in me and that it can heal, but I also know there's a lot more potential than the little bit I've discovered in myself. Every time I bond with one of my mates, I get more glimpses of my past lives, and more access to power.

I've been marked by three. Something inside of me knows that completing that circle will open up this power inside of me. If I can heal, maybe I can also bring someone back from the dead.

The voice that told me I am strong was his voice. There is still a spark of life in him, I can feel it. We can't wait a whole lot longer though. "Please, Father Joachim."

He slowly raises his face and looks me in the eye. There isn't pain, or reticence, or even anger there. There's fear. He's afraid, and I didn't think that was possible. He's always the calm and confident one with all the answers. I've seen him fight, literally tooth and claw, and he's so centered that I didn't even think fear was in his emotional wheel house.

But he's scared, and I think it's of me. Well, shit. Add that to the list of things I need to figure out and resolve.

He fingers the prayer beads that are his ever present companion. They glow with the same light as my magic again and I realize for they were a gift from the Goddess. They are his comfort. "I am yours, Taryn. I have been and always will be. I want only to do what is best for you. If you need me to break these vows for you... I will do my best to live with the consequences."

My heart fills with overwhelming joy and breaks at the same time. I don't want his love, his mind, body, and soul out of obligation. But right now, in this moment, for today, I will take this as a step forward. Not a win, but the move in the right direction.

"I don't know what to say, except thank you." That doesn't come out sounding the way it did in my head. This isn't some cold transaction, and I don't like the clammy swirl in my chest. "I'm sorry."

"No, *boginya*. I am the one who should apologize to you. I hope someday I will get the chance to do that. Until then, we will make the best of what we have to do. Come, let me fulfill your simple request."

This is anything but simple. I didn't want this intimate act to feel like a transaction and now it's all awkward and weird. I can't let that stop me. Whenever I figure out what in the world is going on in Father Joachim's head, I'll get him to reveal the secrets that are keeping us apart. Because it has to be more than a vow to a religion.

Until then, I'm going to try to make this as good for him as I know it will be for me. This isn't my first marking rodeo. I've imagined what it would be like to be held in his arms, for him to kiss me with all the passion burning inside of him, and to mark me. More than that, I want him to take me, just as August and Vasily have.

I'm imagining what that would be like right now, and Father Joachim groans. Is he scenting my arousal, my desire for him, or can he hear my thoughts like the others? I can feel the connection between us bringing the magic up inside of me already.

I'd love to take our time, to seduce him, entice him, make him forget all about these other vows. But I can feel the spark of life in the Dark Prince sputtering, reaching out for the bit of magic too. I want them both, but can't have them both at the same time. Not while one doesn't want me and the other one is dying.

I have to take what I need from Father Joachim and help the prince. Then I'm digging into him hard to find out what's keeping us apart. With that resolve in my mind, I move to the bars between the two of us with my arms open.

The fear is still banked in his eyes, but I can see that he's trying. He understands what's at stake here.

"Will you kiss me first? I understand if that's too much, but I'd like it." And I think he would too.

"*Boginya*, I want very little more than that, but I think it's best if we do this quickly. I can sense the power in you reaching out, ready to heal Grigori, just as you did me. If he can be saved, only you can do it."

See? Awkward. But fine. I'll deal with that later. "Okay. Bite me."

Did I say that with a little too much snark? Yes. Did I still mean it? Also yes. I really, really wanted him to bite me and bite me hard. In fact I was really giddy inside. Like my magic is turning into butterflies on crack in my lower belly.

Both of us press our bodies against the bars between us. Never did I imagine I'd ever be trying to get busy in an actual jail. What is this the Old West? Ooh, just the anticipation of having Father Joachim's lips on my skin, his teeth digging into my flesh is bringing up memories.

I'm so close to breaking through the mental barriers that the Nothing placed in my mind, that I can almost reach out and touch them. What I do in reality is reach out and touch Father Joachim. I cup his cheek and slowly caress my way down his throat. He swallows and his breathing goes shallow and raspy like he's trying not to let me see him sweat.

"Kiss me. Let me have just a little of what you don't want me to have." I lick my lips, imagining his on mine.

Why is it so deliciously sensual to be with him? I already know he's mine, and I assume we've been together, like in all the ways two souls can be intertwined. I know I'm asking for something he doesn't want to give. Except he does, I could never even ask if I thought he truly didn't want me.

"I do want it, I simply can't." He leans into my touch. "You are more tempting to me than you could ever know."

He runs his lips softly across my cheek, from nose to temple, in a kiss so light it sends shivers across my skin.

I guess I'm asking for something he isn't supposed to give, and that rebellion, against everything in this life, and possibly all my past lives, is thrilling. No more will I cower and take what's been thrown at me. Yet I also cannot force myself on this kind, gentle warrior.

Again, I tell him that I'm sorry. Not with words, but with my heart. He whispers my heart's sentiments back to me. "I wish I could give you more. I'm sorry."

He buries his face in the crook of my neck, and scrapes his teeth across the skin there. Magic and lust rush up through every cell in my body and I reach through the bars and clasp his head, holding him to me. As he sinks his teeth into me, all the need for him that I've tried to hold back explodes through me.

I go from zero to orgasm in less than a moment and cry out with the nirvana of it all. The magic inside of me flows out in crashing waves, filling the room with light and warmth. The bars between us melt away, and I slip the robes off my shoulders and arms so I can be that much closer to him.

It isn't only magic and lust that crashes into me. I'm flooded with memories and power. I see flashes of our past lives together, and how he has always been the wise council for not only the rest of the Wolf Guard, but for me as well. We've always shared the love of knowing there is something greater in the universe than we.

In more lives than not, we have both turned to religion, even though it doesn't quite hold the everything we need to believe in. No wonder he's made vows to a God that can't be broken. He's done that for me.

Before either of us are done reveling in each other, I pull away. I've taken more than I should from him. "Forgive me, Father."

I have sinned.

Against him.

But I would do it again, and I'm not sorry.

Father Joachim steps back, bows his head, and covers his groin with his hands, in a way that's less hiding his erection from me, and more genuflecting. I'll let him be for now because I've gotten all that he promised he could give me.

The room around us is still bathed in my magic's blue sparkling light. The jail cell bars between all three of us are nothing more than stalactites and stalagmites of melted metal. I touch his cheek one last time and step around the debris left in the wake of my newfound power.

The magic is growing inside of me this time, not fading away. The more Joachim's mark on my skin takes on it's final form, the stronger I feel. There will be no more hiding in the shadows and darkness. This light is mine and it's never going out.

I cross to the broken body of Grigori, my Dark Prince, and reach for the spark of life in him. When I press my hand against his chest, hot, blue light surrounds him and the great tear in his skin and bones knits back together. He gasps and his back bows, the life in him reawakening. For one shining moment, he opens his eyes and looks at me, not with the anger and disdain of before, but with the love in his broken heart.

I can heal his wounds, but it will take more than magic to heal his heart.

JOACHIM

*W*hat have I done? Oh Goddess, what have I done?

I shake my bowed head and swallow back the gut-wrenching spasms, the bile rising up my throat, the mournful howl of my wolf inside my head.

I vowed not to touch her.

Why can I not resist the temptation of her flesh, even with the guilt of man's religion bearing down on me. It worked four-hundred years ago when she was Sophia Alekseyevna, my sweet and fierce Sophia, and I swore not to mark and claim her in this life. I knew then everything had to change.

We couldn't keep living these lives over and over, with no progress to breaking the curse on her. The curse I created. I did my penance, and it paid off, even though I didn't get to see it. I heard all about Ekataryn, the greatest ruler of both the Russia and the Wolves. August, Vasily, and Grigori had almost gotten her to the peak of ascension in that lifetime.

She was once again the Queen of Wolves, though called the Tsarina as befitted the time. She lived a long and mostly peaceful life for once in a thousand years. All because I wasn't there. When August told me the stories of his time at her side I was both relieved and disappointed I couldn't see her come into her power.

But she hadn't truly regained her magic.

Not like she had just now.

I was in awe of her. In five thousand years, a hundreds of lives lived and relived, I hadn't seen such magic and power manifest in her. She was truly Goddess touched. I had forgotten.

I watch as she heals Grigori's wounds, brings him back from death, as if she's doing nothing more than plucking a summer flower for herself. As if marking her, tasting her for the first time in hundreds of years wasn't enough, my body responds even more to this display of her true self.

My cock is so hard that it's painful. My wolf pushes me to finish my bond with her, to claim her as she wants me to, our bodies joined. The wolf's knot pulses at the base of my member, begging to be touched, stroked, buried in her sweet body.

I've already broken my vow not to touch her. I could not refuse her need to be marked. But I must deny us both that final connection between her and I.

She's not ready. Nor am I.

I know it's a lie the moment I think it.

Best not to even let those old wounds into my mind now that we are linked. I push all thoughts of the past away and concentrate on the here and now. With one final mental chastisement of myself for the way my hands shake with wanting to touch her beautifully naked and plush body, I pick up the discarded robes on the dirt floor and bring them over.

Grigori is alive. He breaths, his heart beats, but he is unconscious and in this state, even his wolf can't push through to shift and finish healing him. He's been touched by Hell and I can only pray that August and Vas are better off.

I lay the robes over her shoulders and then get down on the

floor with her. She's trying to lift Grigori so she can lay his head on her breast, and it's interesting to me how she can use her strength to stave off death, but doesn't realize she can do anything else with her gifts.

"Let me help you, my lady." I'm careful with my words, and I feel stiff and clunky next to her charm.

She smiles and I'm dumbstruck by grace. She's had to beg me to help her save a life and I am ashamed. Of so much.

Together we lift Grigori, and she pushes one hand into his hair to hold his head to her, and puts her other arm around his shoulder. I want nothing more than to surround them both and hold them as if I'm pressing two broken pieces of my heart together. She is my queen, he is my alpha.

He may deny it, but if not for him, none of us would be in her service. He chose us so that she could share her gifts from the Goddess. I give in one more time and fold them both into my arms.

"Thank you, Father." The words are quiet and solemn and for once I don't have a reply.

For just this moment, I will revel in her light and pretend I haven't destroyed her.

We sit together for a long time, and yet her light does not fade. She is glowing from within now, just as if she is the moon herself and only the passing of the month could dim her light. But there is no time passing in this prison, and I could be content to stay and hold her for an eternity.

In this peace I could hide from the reality of what is waiting for me when she learns the truth. No amount of prayer or even self-flagellation will save me from her punishment when she comes into her full powers. In trying to save her and keep her safe, I have failed not only her, but all of our people.

I can't forgive myself, why would she?

She knows that I'm stewing deep in thought. I can feel her mind pressing against mine. She's gentle, like the caress of moonlight on night blooming flowers. I keep my mind closed to her, but she is like an open book, wanting to know if I'm okay.

I never will be, but she doesn't need that burden. Instead I distract her with questions I don't want the answers to. "What did you remember, *boginya*?"

She's quiet for a long minute, thinking, letting memories flash through her mind. "Us."

I nod, pressing her to say more. "I understand now why you're drawn to religion. You're longing for the oldest of days."

I can hardly breathe. Does she remember all the way back to our first life together, when I found my calling in serving her?

"But what I don't understand is that so long ago, you were mine. You shared my bed and my heart. You want to recapture that as much as I do. Religion shouldn't be the thing that keeps us apart, but that which brings us together." Her voice is like the sweet whispers of a lover in the dark, but her words stab me. Her fingers caress the prayer beads wrapped around my wrist in a reverence no one else could understand.

It's time I got up and put some space between us, but I can't. I haven't held her in so long, and now that I have her body pressed to mine, I can't let go. "Any attempt to explain won't make sense. Just know that what I do is always in your best interest."

Her silence is recriminating enough for my non-answer. She strokes Grigori's hair and I feel her mind and magic at work again. "That's a load of crap, Father."

Well, fuck.

The power she's regained is not only in her magical abilities, but in her soul too. I have spent many a long night roaming the woods of our prison island simply to avoid thinking about how much I love her. She fights so hard in each reincarnation, against all odds. When she finally finds that inner strength, that's when I lost my heart to her each and every time.

Except once.

I glance over and see the mark I've made on her skin still swirling with the mating magic. Just as the other three have, this bite will form into an intricate design like a tattoo on her skin, that represents me and my role in her life. Even thinking about marking her reawakens the wolf inside and my instinctual need to claim her. No matter how much I will my body to still, my cock grows again and my pulse quickens.

All because of her sass and the way she's no longer afraid to call me out.

"It is. But we have bigger worries at the moment. Once Grigori is awake, we must find out if he was able to pull August and Vasily from Hell. I worry for all of our souls if he hasn't."

She allows me change of subject, but I know we aren't done. Someday soon I will have to own up to all my...crap.

Taryn presses her lips to Grigori's brow. "I don't think he's getting any better. I don't know what else to do for him. I wish you would just teach me about my magic and how to use it. I miss them, and I want them back. I need for us all to be together." Her voice is gentle, but her frustration buzzes in my mind.

"As Vasily explained, we have tried that before, and with catastrophic consequences. You must discover the gifts of the Goddess yourself, just as you did today."

Her mind goes to work again and I both dread and revel in her train of thought. "When I figured out that you should mark me."

"Yes."

"But you won't claim me as August and Vasily did." It's not a question.

"No." Not yet. I withdraw but she grabs my arm and holds me to where I can't move without outright rejecting her touch.

"But you'll do... other stuff with me. Like you did when I mated August and Vasily."

I want to say no, but I can't. I indulged in the sins of the flesh during both of her matings. She couldn't know, but I'd done the same off on my own in the woods when I should have been praying for absolution. I dream of touching my cock to her lips, of seeing her come with such ecstasy that I can hardly breath.

I can't say any of that so I say nothing at all. But she sees me. Down to my very soul.

Taryn nods and strokes Grigori's hair some more and I'm fucking jealous of his broken unconscious state. She nods in understanding of everything I am.

"You all say I have to figure this out on my own. Well, here's what I've deduced. The Dark Prince isn't getting any better now that my fancy fit of magic is over. I also understand that there is power in the connection and bond I have with each of you. Am I wrong?"

My chest constricts but I push out the answer. "You're not."

"There is power and magic in sex, isn't there? Not just fucking, but sharing our bodies because it's an expression of our deep, abiding love."

A whisper in both of our minds answers before I can. *Yes.*

No. If I could quiet Grigori's mind, I would. I don't want him giving her any ideas. But it's too late. Her clever mind is already sending me images of what she wants and what she thinks will happen.

"I need him to get better, Father. We both do. I know I said I wouldn't ask for more, but if it can help me access more magic and heal him so that we can save August and Vasily from Hell, we have to, don't we? There are lots of ways to have sex that doesn't involve--"

"I know, *boginya*. I know exactly how you like to be touched, and what will make you whimper with need. I can deny myself, but I can deny you very little." I have tried.

"I... I don't want you to think that this is enough. Someday when you're ready, I want you to fulfill the claim and make me your mate under the moon and stars. If you can't do that, then I will try to find another way to learn more magic."

I take her hand and kiss her palm. "All I am is yours. It is my failing, not yours that keeps us apart. I swear to you when the day comes when you no longer allow me this vow of chastity, I will be yours. It's always been in your power to break me and put me back together again."

I hear the echo in her mind of my words. *I don't want to break you.*

But she must and how well I know it. Until she does, I will be whatever she needs me to be. Man, wolf, protector, almost lover. Because she knows her own power and it's almost time for her to ascend and reign again.

I move behind her and shift the robes so they cover Grigori's body, exposing hers to me. The ripeness of her hips, the dimples of her behind, and the soft rolls of flesh on her arms, back, and belly are so sensual that I reconsider for a moment what it would mean if I did claim her right here, right now. My wolf pushes to the surface, my fangs drop once again, and my cock pulses as if I'm already inside of her.

The wolf part of me wants to bury the knot deep inside of her, locking us together, until I'm sure she's mine once again. "Lay back against me, with his head cradled, and spread your legs for me."

She repositions herself, being careful not to jostle Grigori too much, until she is tucked against me with her ass against my cock and her knees spread. I'm reminded of the times when the two of us shared her body to bring her pleasure, his mouth on her pussy and my cock in her cunt, until she cried out with pleasure and her magic filled us all to repletion.

I'll never know days such as those again, so I will savor what I can have with her here and now. I will memorize every soft curve, every plump handful of belly, breast, and pussy. It's been so many hundreds of years since I've touched her, but my hands remember every little touch that turns her on.

I skim my knuckles across my mark on her throat and my heart tremors to match the shivers of her skin. She leans into me and my cock presses against the seam of her ass. I cannot indulge in the lusciousness of that feeling or I won't be able to focus on what she needs.

Light as the petals of a flower, I trace the curve of her breast, and then tease her nipple until I grows hard as if reaching for my touch. The prayer beads rattle as they too caress her skin. She lets out the softest sigh and the blue sparkle of the magic of the moon dances across her skin, trailing my every touch.

I want to take my time with her, but I feel the push of Grigori's mind, wanting me to hurry. He knows what it means that I'm willing to do this for him. It's not only for him.

I can feel the urgency of the news he brings from Hell, but he isn't actually strong enough to just tell me or Taryn. He needs me. It's been a long time since I felt that. I kid myself that he wants me around for my counsel, but we both know that it is I who wants to be near him and who needs his advice.

"You are so very beautiful, *boginya*. I am a lucky man who gets to see, touch, and bring you pleasure." I get the feeling from the way the soft pink of a blush crosses her cheeks and chest that she hasn't been told that often enough in her most recent life.

I will tell her as often as I can until she tosses me aside.

TARYN

I'm reveling in Father Joachim's touch. I feel guilty and dirty, and I've only felt this wanted two other times in my life, when August and Vasily took me as their mate and claimed me in our special chapel of trees in the forest. While Joachim isn't properly claiming me and we aren't in that same place, we are in a church of sorts, and that feels right.

I didn't know until I used my magic to heal the prince where we are. This dungeon in the ground could be anywhere. But as the power inside of me swells with each of Joachim's caresses, our minds connected and, I see so much more than I imagine either of them want me to.

I lean into Father Joachim's touch, to where he is teasing my breast. I love it and want so much more from him at the same time. "Please, Father."

Even those two simple words feel dirty when I say them like that, and he responds with a push of pure need into my mind.

I don't wait for him to hesitate and I grab his wrist, clasping his precious prayer beads, and drag them it across my belly and down between my legs. I'd have some guilt for pushing him, but I can full well feel the hard length of his cock pressing against my butt. Vasily had taken me there and it fulfilled every forbidden desire I had, until now.

I want Father Joachim to claim me in that same way. In fact, I want each one of my wolves to give me their bodies in every way possible. I want them alone, I want them in pairs, I want all four touching, tasting, teasing, and making me come, at the same time.

To make that happen, I have to save them all first. I would heal the prince, I would rescue August and Vasily, and I would draw Father Joachim out of his self imposed prison of punishment, and I would love them all until there was nothing left of their hurts and heart aches.

Another shot of power sizzles low in my belly and the marks on my neck burn, not with pain, but with passion. "Touch me, Joachim. I need you."

I need you to love me. I don't say those words, but there are no secrets between us in this moment. Not secrets of mine anyway.

"You're so wet. I wish I was inside of you right now." The words rasp out like an ardent prayer.

Is he saying that just to amp up the lust and thus the magic or does he really want to break his vow right here, right now? "Then do it. Take me and make me your mate."

He groans and drops his mouth first to my head, giving me a kiss to the crown of my hair, then my temple, drags his lips and teeth down my neck and scrapes right over my mark. He bites into that same place again and as he sinks two of his fingers inside of me, the beads light up, glowing as if in approval of what we're doing.

"Oh, oh God - sorry Father." The words escape. Any filter I had left is gone.

He crooks his fingers inside of me, pressing his knuckles against the sweetest spot that I shake with the thrill of it. "Never apologize for taking your pleasure from me."

He rocks his palm against my pussy, the beads tickling the patch of hair on my mons, until I spread my legs even wider and his hand slides over my clit. The light in the room bounces around as if I am shooting off fireworks or lightening. The prince moans against my chest and his eyelashes flutter over my skin.

The magic is working, just as I knew it must. He is waking up. "More, Father, more."

I ask for what I want, what the prince needs, and what Joachim needs to give. His cock thrusts against me and his fingers mirror the movement. With each jerk of his hips, he sends me higher and higher. I can almost imagine his cock and not his fingers are buried inside of me.

"Let go, boginya. Give everything you have to Grigori. He needs you." His own words of the same sentiment echo in his mind. *I need you.*

But the prince doesn't need me to give him more. He awakens with a howl, his eyes alight with the sparkling blue magic of the moon. Before I can even breathe out gratitude that he is healed and returned to us, he twists in my arms and takes my nipple into his mouth. He suckles as if he is drinking in the magic from this joining and it pushes me higher, closer to climax than I've ever been, without going over the edge. I feel as though I could touch the moon and stars, floating among the heavens, the Gods and Goddess jealous of my rapture.

I throw my head back, reveling in the feeling of having two of my mates here with me, sharing my body, pushing us all into such perfect bliss.

The Dark Prince grabs me by the waist and crawls between my legs. "Do you like having his fingers in your cunt, pretty princess? Are those damned prayer beads rolling across your hard clit?"

His words are a low growl and he stares down to where

357

Father Joachim is pleasuring me. "It's been far too long since he gave into these sins of the flesh."

"Yes, and yes." I pant the words both as an answer and a cry because I am so close to coming I can do nothing more. The way he looks at what Father Joachim is doing to me, makes me want even more of this delicious drug called sex magic.

The prince licks his lips and then looks up at Father Joachim. Some quiet but meaningful communication passes between them and I want to know what, but not enough to ask anyone to stop touching me. This is just supposed to be a way to help me access the magic inside of me, but just because I'd healed the prince, doesn't mean I want Father Joachim to stop.

It doesn't take but a moment for me to learn what they have in store for me. The prince presses two of his fingers into his mouth, wetting them, then he puts his hand between my legs too and pushes inside of me alongside Father Joachim. "Have you truly found the power inside of you? Do you remember who and what you are?"

How am I supposed to remember or think of anything when two of the hottest men on the planet are double-teaming to make me come? When one's fingers withdraw, the other pushes in and my body is going crazy for it.

They aren't even taking their own pleasure. Both their cocks are hard and pressing against me, but neither are doing anything to make themselves come.

There is definitely access to this sex magic in what they were doing to me, but I can feel the potential for so much more. If we could just join our bodies as one, then I know, I know with all of my heart and soul, I would remember everything.

I reach up and wrap one arm around the prince's neck, drawing him down and into a kiss. He bites my lip on one side and then the other. "No, no, princess. You don't get anything more from me unless you can tell me you're ready to break your damned curse and take back the power stolen from you."

Father Joachim wraps his other arms around my waist and holds me tight against his body. I think he too is lost in the magic. Neither of them stop thrusting their fingers inside of me, and yet, the tension won't break, I can't yet come.

"I. Am. Powerful." It's so hard to get the words out because I can hardly breathe. "I. Am...."

"What Taryn, what are you?" The wolf in him is so close to the surface I can see it in his eyes.

I want so badly to give him the answer he wants, but I don't know. I've found the place where the magic in me lives. With a little practice, I even think I can wield it without going out of control and hurting anyone. But while I have more memories than an hour ago, there are still so many holes in my Swiss cheese of a brain and I can sense the Nothing, the shadow blocking out the most important part of me.

So I say the only thing I know to be true. "I am yours."

Darkness flashes across his face, as if a cloud has passed over the moon. He withdraws his fingers and sits back on his heels, pulling his body so far away from me, I can feel the cold between us. "You're not mine until you know who and what you are. You're so fucking close I can taste it on you."

I want to cry out that I could know everything if only they would take this sex magic to the next, much more important level. I don't get that chance.

The Dark Prince stands, and throws the robes across my body. He sneers and then growls at Father Joachim. "Finish her."

There's an edge to his voice I've never heard before, and Father Joachim reacts to it too. His hips jerk against me, thrusting his cock between my legs, but only to slide between my thighs and not inside of me. He lowers his lips to my ear and whispers. "Come for me, *moy malenkiy agnets.*"

My little lamb.

The moment he calls me that, I know he is firmly back in the arms of his God. Even though he's thrusting his cock between my slick thighs, everything has changed. To late for me to pull away, I give in to what my body has been waiting for and let the orgasm pour over me. Wave after wave of terrible pleasure courses through me and the only joy I take is the splash of Father Joachim's seed on my thighs and his tight grunt as he too comes.

I close my eyes and lean into him and say a prayer of my own, letting the words wash over both of them. *You are mine, I am yours.*

When the final tremors of my orgasm subsides, I listen to the harsh rapid breaths behind me. My senses are wide open now, as if I am in my wolf form, even though I am not. Everything in the room is clearer to me. I can see each individual speck of dirt, feel the tiniest of rocks digging into my knees. The smell, not only the death and evil that invaded this space, but the foul mood of the Dark Prince, and the guilt of Father Joachim are potent in the air. As is the new chill that wasn't there before.

I can taste the magic we performed by joining and exalting in joining our bodies and minds together, and that's what I grasp onto. I let that satisfaction swirl around and around, and when I open my eyes, the prince is staring down at me with a scowl, but also surprise.

Ha. So there, princey poo. I have learned something about myself. I wasn't lying when I said I am powerful. He's the one who got me to believe it.

Father Joachim kisses my temple and pulls the robes up and over me. I love how he's doing is best to take care of me, even under the scrutiny of the prince. While I know he has retreated back to the place in his mind where he isn't allowed to have feelings for me, we made strides toward each other. I'll take the win.

I turn into his embrace and give him the lightest of kisses to his throat. He hisses, but tries to hide it. I know what I'm doing in choosing this particular spot. That's the place he'll carry my mark someday. I'm simply saving it for later.

Then I lift his arm and kiss the beads wrapped around his wrist. I can taste myself on them, and his eyes go wide at my blatant attention to his sacred symbol of prayer and worship. The way he rolled those beads across my clit when he was thrusting his fingers inside of me is a much better use, in my opinion. "Your God may have hold on your conscience, but your heart and soul is mine. Our love will be your religion, when you are ready."

He turns his face away, and I let him. This has been a lot for him today. While he recovers, I will move my attention to my Dark Prince of Wolves. He's pretending to examine the damage I wrought on one half of his carefully constructed prison. But the conflict in his heart is as clear as if I am reading a book.

I pad across the dirt to him and slug him in the arm.

He doesn't even flinch and I know I haven't hurt him. That wasn't the point anyway.

He picks up a melted piece of metal that used to be the latch of the cell door. "What, pray tell, dear princess, was that for?"

"I think you know. Don't do that to me again." I wish he would look at me, but if he wants to push my buttons some more, then fine. I can play his game. I have his number now, he just doesn't know it.

He tosses the lock to the ground like so many other pieces of detritus. "I won't have to if you'll break the curse."

I'm down for some you're-an-asshole- banter. "I would if you and the good Father would do what I want."

He half laughs half scoffs. "It doesn't work that way."

You know what, I'm done with this I'm a man-wolf, I know better than you, little princess bullshit. The prince has intimidated the hell out of me since the first day. But I just saved his god-damned - sorry Father - life. If that doesn't put us on equal ground, nothing does. "It works however I want it to."

AIDY AWARD

That gets his attention and he finally turns his head and looks at me. "Does it now?"

"Yes." We stare at each other for a good long minute and something new passes through his eyes. It's either relief or respect. I'll take either or. "Now tell me what happened to you and what news of August and Vasily."

Uh-oh. The eyebrow raise of disdain again. There goes my R-E-S-P-E-C-T. "None of that it matters."

I need to add some more creative swearing to my vocabulary to deal with the prince, because oh my God - sorry Father - isn't going to cut it. "Of course it matters, you boob. I need as much information as I can get if I'm going to rescue them from Hell."

"You?" He folds his arms and the other eyebrow goes up.

I fold mine, mirroring him. "Yes, you couldn't, so I will."

That ought to get his goat, or wolf as the case may be. I think I see him smile, but I won't tell him that.

He waves me toward the steps in an invitation to leave. "Then let me know when we leave for Hell. But I suggest you practice using your magic without someone else's hands between your legs. You're going to need every advantage you can get if you're going to take on the God of Chaos and risk angering the Goddess of Hell.

GRIGORI

She thinks she's going to take on Hell all by herself. Ha. She's either got more hubris than I do, which will get her ass burned to a crisp, or she's finally found her fierce fighting spirit.

Warrior, fighter, protector. Those are supposed to my job. Mine and the rest of the Guard. She's the one we fight for. But if she's this close to remembering who she truly is, the Queen of the Wolves, Goddess touched, wolf cursed, then she's going to need everything she can to prepare for the battle ahead.

Especially if we're going back to Hell. I don't like that Nergal has a hard on for my princess. What has him interested in the affairs of wolves? Is this just a five thousand year old vendetta for the goddesses gift when our people pushed him and his demons back into Hell? It feels like somethings more, something new.

"Can we please get out of your red room of pain and get working on our plan to rescue August and Vasily?" Taryn motions to the stairs.

"Red? If anything you've turned my dungeon blue." Her light is everywhere now. I have to guard myself from basking in her radiant glow. I can't imagine even standing next to the Goddess herself could feel anymore resplendent.

"I read it in a book in some lifetime. I used to like to read, you know."

Oh, I know. I spent hours reading poetry and philosophy to her when she was Katherine the Great. The first and last time I saw her even close to reclaiming her throne. Until now.

"I don't have any books and you don't have time to read." I've already made too many mistakes from our past with her. Poetry isn't going to win us the upcoming battle.

She rolls her eyes at me and looks to Joachim for solidarity. He's withdrawn into himself completely. I'm surprised he hasn't shifted into his wolf form to avoid talking to either of us all together. Although, he's marked her now and she's in his head.

He moves to the stairs without looking at either of us, and I get the feeling he'd bolt if he could.

"Come, we have work to do." I push the trapdoor open, busting the lock that should prevent anyone from getting out from this side.

"I already came, I think it's your turn." Taryn sashays her way up the stairs as if she owns the place.

If I'd known all it took was some orgasms to bring out the sass in her, maybe I wouldn't have needed my dungeon. No, no. I will not fuck her, I will not put my face between her legs, or better yet, make her sit on my face while I fuck her with my tongue until she's shaking and weak. I will not fuck that sweet and sassy mouth of hers, and I will not claim her under the light of the full moon.

Not until I know he is safe.

She needs to grow in her powers if we're going to take on Hell.

I don't want her anywhere near Nergal and his forces of Hell, but I have a feeling there won't be any choice. I've seen this determination in her before. She'll burn down the world to reclaim her rightful place and protect her people.

This world needs to burn, especially this prison island. I just thought we would be fighting the Volkovs to win our freedom, not the forces of hell. Perhaps they are one in the same. The portals they use to transport their prisoners here and to keep us contained are of the shadow. That means someone made a deal with a demon because no mortal wolf can control that element without help from a God or Goddess.

I'd like to blame that dickface, Rasputin, but even he isn't as old as this prison the Volkovs have been using for centuries. No someone either long ago or much older made this Hell on Earth. If Taryn is to ascend, I need to find out who and why to make sure her life and power is never taken from her again.

Joachim and I follow her up the stairs of my destroyed little dungeon. In the cloudy spring light, I see Joachim flinch at being back in the shell of the church. For a brief moment when I first awakened, I thought finally he was ready to discard the mantle of protection he wears in the form of religion. I was sure she'd won him over. But he has retreated to that place again.

I root out some worn and tattered robes so that he can cover himself. His body got the gratification I've denied myself, yet both of us are still hard. I don't think my cock will ever rest until I've buried myself in Taryn's body and claimed her for my own.

My body and soul ache for her, my wolf is chomping and snarling at me for denying that pleasure. I will not do it until she is ready. Only when she is strong enough to save herself, will I bow at her feet, and ask her to be mine. That has to be the difference this time.

I can't protect her, as much as I'm driven to.

"Okay, who wants to practice some magic so we can go to Hell and rescue my lovers." Taryn claps her hands and rubs them together. "That is not a sentence I ever thought would come out of my mouth."

She flicks her fingers and shots of sparkling magic surge through the rubble of my lair. Moon flowers spring up turning the fearsome ruins into a nature reclaimed sanctuary. How, after everything that has happened to her, is she filled with such light?

Joachim takes the robes, slips them on and moves his prayer beads from his wrist back to his waist. He busies himself with his task and doesn't look at me, but his voice rings clear in my mind. *Because she knows her darkness is safe with you, Guard of the House of the New Moon, Dark Prince of Wolves.*

A new bond has forged between the two of us. Something we haven't shared since our last shared life with her. Since the last time we shared her body. I don't want him in my head, unguarded, listening to my thoughts. *I cannot protect her from the darkness any longer, priest.*

I want to poke and push him away. His failings only remind me of my own.

It is not the darkness of others, the world, or even Hell she needs protecting from, but her own. The rest of us get to see her light and bathe in her love. You are the only one strong enough to bear the shadow in her soul.

My hands and fingers go dumb. The rustling of the wind in the trees goes quiet against the ringing in my ears. My wolf surges up as if I'm in danger and the shift pushes at my skin.

In a thousand lifetimes, no one has ever said as much to me. I was chosen to protect her at her weakest, when there is no light from the moon, because I was the strongest warrior. I became her Dark Prince. But what if all this time, it wasn't my job to keep her safe from the darkness, but to help her embrace it?

Isn't that what I've been pushing her to do, locking her in

my dungeon in the dark, and forcing her to face her demons all on her own.

I look over at her, glowing for us all to see. Even in the burned rubble of this once beautiful but tainted church, others will be drawn to her light. How can they help it?

Am I the reason her powers have been hobbled in life after life? My chest is caving in, my heart stutters and has forgotten how to beat the blood through my veins. This is why I've been so angry for so long.

No. That fault lies with... that doesn't matter.

There's more he needs to say, because it does matter. I will tackle that later. Much, much later. Once I remember how to breathe, live, and do my duty to her once again. *Why have you never said anything before?*

We both know there are some lessons that must be learned, not taught. I only speak now because you've realized already what you have to do. You've been doing it since she arrived in our keep once again. I'm the one who didn't understand that until today.

It took me taking her life and being thrown into supernatural prison to break my own soul open to see my mistakes. All this time on the island, I thought I was rebelling against our fate as her Wolf Guard, but my true nature was just trying to get through, just as hers has been.

I don't know how to... her strength is in her light, her magic comes from the Goddess gift of the moonlight.

Without darkness, there is no light. She needs you just as much as the three of us combined. That's why you're our alpha.

An honor I tried to give up.

She's never embraced the dark side of her nature. I've always protected her from that.

Not always. Do you remember when she was Olga of Kyiv?

A life from long ago that lives among the other regrets in my heart. I died, killed by her enemies, leaving her vulnerable.

She burned down half of old Russia to avenge your death. Her vengeance was glorious, but frightening. Left unchecked, her darkness flowed like rivers of blood.

I shouldn't be able to, because she's always been such pure light to me, but I absolutely can imagine her wreaking a horrible wrath on the Derevlyanins. I found I liked the idea.

I didn't know.

I didn't know. She avenged my death, she brought me back to life, and I couldn't even deign to do my own duty for her.

You do now. Do better than I have. Go, claim her, and help her ascend to her rightful place.

She cannot ascend until all four of us have taken our places by her side. I am chastising myself as much as I am Joachim. If I would have done as he asked when she first arrived, shown up for her mating ceremony with August, and joined them, we could have... no, we all have lessons to learn in this life with her.

I pray, which we all know I don't do, but I'll make the exception now. I pray that Joachim is close to learning his as well. As his alpha I should have been helping him just as much as her. I vow to be better.

She makes me a better man, wolf and guardian. As is her right. I've forgotten that. But I won't again.

I move quietly to the part of the sanctuary she's in considering how to tell her that I understand my duty now without revealing too much. A line of her moonflowers pop up along the path ahead of me.

I want to bow at her feet, kiss the very ground she walks on and genuflect before her. That is not what she needs from me. If I am to help her embrace her darkness, assist her in using that to defeat the forces of Hell to rescue our brethren, then guide her back into her light, she doesn't need submission from me.

I too must embrace the shadow in my soul. That's what has brought me this far, and I can't be afraid of hurting her now.

Because she is strong, she can save herself. I'm only here to be by her side as she does.

She's using the soft side of her magic and not only are the flowers blooming, but the trees are growing back out of the scorched ground filling in where the wooden and brick walls used to be. It was never church buildings that she loved, just places of worship.

Left over, I'm sure, from when we worshipped her.

I drag her against the nearest tree she's pulled into being, and clasp her tight in my arms. Her eyes sparkle with surprise and lust. For me.

I've made love to her, fucked her, claimed her as my mate in more lives than I can count. I've always wanted it to perfect for her. I've always been gentle, putting her pleasure first. I understand now, that was wrong. She needs me as harsh and punishing as her lover, as in her guard.

Taryn wraps one leg around the back of mine and smiles up at me with her saucy, knowing grin. "What's this, my Dark Prince? Couldn't get enough of me?"

Her. Dark. Prince.

I growl and shove my hips against hers, ripping the robes she's wearing open to her round goddess's body is exposed to me. "Never."

Her eyes goes dark and she licks her lips. The scent of her arousal overwhelms me and my wolf pushes to the surface, wanting to claim her in response. Hot damn. My sweet princess wants me to be rough with her. What the fuck have I been doing for the last five-thousand years?

The shoddy mark I placed on her neck sings out to me to bite her again. I wrap my hand around her throat, caressing the symbol of my wolf in the darkened moon with my thumb. She lets out a sensual sigh and her eyes flutter shut.

"Mark me, claim me, make me yours."

I'm not sure if Taryn is saying these words to me, or my ancient queen.

Dusk is upon us and the ever present clouds in sky part. Rays from the moon shine down on us both and she glows as only a true mate does. This is not her goddess given gift of moonlight on her skin, it's the manifestation of our fate sparkling, tempting me to her, something no one could resist.

"You are mine, my queen. I won't fail you again." I lower my mouth to her skin and scrape my teeth across the ragged mark.

Her fingers lace into my hair, just as they did when she was healing me, but this time she isn't gentle either. She grips my scalp, scraping her nails from the crown down, holding me to her. "More, my prince, more."

Saliva drips from my fangs, my mouth literally watering for the taste of her. I shoot my hand up from where I've had it around her throat to her hair and wrap her locks around my fist. I tug hard, forcing her to expose her most vulnerable soft flesh to me. I could rip out her artery with one bite, and yet she trusts me.

Before I bite down, I slide my hand around her thick thigh and hoist her up so she has to wrap her legs around my waist. My cock slides through her already wet folds, my tip caressing her clit. My wolf is begging to bury every hard inch of my dick so deep into her cunt that already the knot at my base is pulsing. I thrust against her, not into her to tease us both. "I'm going to mark you, claim you, and then I'm going to fuck you so hard you black out from screaming my name."

She sucks in a hissed breath, then does the opposite of what I told her she would. She whispers my name. For the first time since I took the innocent life she lived as Anastasia Romanov, she says my name. "Grigori."

I am lost. I bite down, sinking my fangs into her skin, tasting her blood, and arousal, and magic. She shatters in my arms, her body going tight with the first orgasm. It's not enough for either of us.

She says my name again, whimpering her need for me. "Grigori."

I lick the wound reopened and push the healing power of my wolf to close the bite. My cock throbs and grows harder watching the tattoo symbol swirl and connect with the others on her skin. I wish the rest of her guard was here with us now to witness this claim. *Joachim, come, perform the ancient ceremony and witness my claiming.*

He is beside us before I even finish the thought, but I don't wait for the ritualistic words. I grip her thigh tight, knowing there will be a bruise there tomorrow, and slide my hand around her throat once again. She bites her lip and stares deep into my eyes, her magic swirling between us, and I thrust my cock all the way to the hilt in one rough push of my hips.

The beautiful blue glow of her light, goes from bright like lightening to dark like the shadow on fire. I withdraw and shove in again, harder, until I'm filling her body, working my knot into her tight cunt. I fuck her hard and she moans with each ever-deeper thrust.

Never once does her gaze leave mine. Her pupils are blown, and taking over the whites of her eyes. Her cunt pulses around me and her body shakes, on the verge of another climax. Then she lifts her arm, palm to the sky, and the world goes dark as the moon shining down eclipses and we are baptized in her utter darkness.

TARYN

*G*rigori, my Dark Prince has finally come to me. He's marked me, and is claiming me. I'm sure in all of my lives, I've never experienced sex like this. He's fierce, rough, and it's exactly what I need. What I didn't even know I needed.

His dark desires wash over me, through me and bring up the shadows buried deep in my soul. They balance out my light and I am finally able to push away the Nothing left in my mind. Magic and shadow, light and dark swirl around us.

I remember.

I remember everything.

I remember too much.

All my lives, all the loss, all the love, good and bad, heaven and hell are whooshing through my mind and it's threatening to drown me. I don't even know what I'm doing when I raise my hand to the sky. I just know I need to release the rising tide of magic bubbling up from centuries and centuries of lessons learned.

More power than any mortal being can possess flows through me, and I am filled with hope and rage. If I can't control the flow of magic, I don't know what's going to happen, but it won't be good. I need something to ground me and it can't be just anything.

I need my Wolf Guard.

Grigori, my Dark Prince of Wolves is with me, inside of me, connecting his soul with my own. He is my chosen one, the strongest of them all, the one who guides all the others. He is fearsome and yet broken. I've put too heavy a burden on him and he doesn't think he's strong enough.

I can hear his thoughts, and he truly believes in his heart, that he has failed me. They all do. Because they couldn't protect me from the evil in our world, the chaos around us, they think they are not worthy.

What they don't understand is it is I who is supposed to be protecting them.

Without thought, I reach out and touch Grigori's soul. The wolf inside of him howls and his body explodes into pure pleasure. His cock sinks deep into me and the wolf's knot locks into place as he spills his seed into my channel. We are one and while this is meant to be his claim on me, I am the one who asserts my dominion over his soul.

He is mine.

They all are. Every person on this island... oh save the Unicorn and the Lion, are mine. But two are special to me. I reach out to Joachim's soul and pull him to me. He's saying the words I taught him so long ago, to bind us all together.

"We gather together in this, our sacred circle to honor the Goddess of the Moon who bestowed upon us the very nature of our wolves and gave us the light by which to find out way to our true fated mates."

He is using the old ritualistic words, if not the old language. None of us have spoken them in thousands of years. "If your fated mate be here, declare your claim on them and let your pack know that they are yours and that you belong to them."

He takes Grigori's hand from around my throat and places it over my heart. My prince is still breathing hard and it takes him a minute to shake of the euphoria of our mating. But in a moment, he nods and says the words I need to hear from him. "Taryn, I Grigori, Dark Prince of Wolves, Guard to you of the House of the New Moon, claim you as my mate. You are mine and I am yours for all time."

His words and his claim, pull me down from the heights of overwhelm and help me focus on him and this moment. Father Joachim takes my hand and places it on Grigori's chest. The words flow from me easily. Grigori, my guardian of the new moon and my darkness, I claim you as my mate. I am yours and your are mine for all time."

His chest shudders under my palm as old heart wounds knit back together. He swallows and takes a long, deep breath as if he hasn't had one in a long time. His cock surges inside of me, and the wolf's knot gluing us together throbs. He leans forward and brushes a soft kiss across my lips.

"Don't forget who you are to me, Dark Prince." I nip at the corner of my mouth with my teeth and he smiles like I've never seen him do before. There's dark promises in that grin. He squeezes my hip and shoves his other hand into my hair, gripping it tight in his fist once again. His mouth crashes down on mine and we are a mess of lips, teeth, tongues, all rolled into one fierce kiss.

Through the haze of this sensuality, I hear Father Joachim speak again. "Friends, join us in the sacred circle to witness the claiming and renew your own bonds."

Both Grigori and I look up, for the first time breaking eye contact with each other, and we are surrounded by everyone from the *derevnya*, including the new packs that joined us, and Maggie and Will.

Will gives us a salute, and Maggie says, "The eclipse darkened the island so that only your light could be seen. We thought we ought follow that beacon, and here we are, witness to your mating."

She winks and steps back, into the arms of her mate, the King of Scotland, and protector of the Tuatha Dé Danann. Strange. I know who these two beings are, but not why they are here. They do not belong to me, yet they are integral to my life. Maybe I don't remember everything yet.

Grigori throws back his head and howls his pride, his happiness, and his desire for me into the far reaches of the night. Joachim joins his howl and the rest of the pack joins in, echoing through the night.

The howls resound through the sanctuary that makes up another new sacred circle of the moon, and each and every wolf lifts their voices up.

But two voices are missing.

I touch Grigori's face and he nods in understanding. His wolf is satisfied that we are once again connected soul deep and the knot recedes. He slips from me and lowers my feet to the ground. I slip out of the robe and hand it to him. I don't need it anymore.

With an easy swish of my fingers, I dress of moonflowers, knitted together with vines, covers me from head to toe. The magic I fought is now at my disposal and my powers are almost limitless.

Grigori dons the robes and then as one, he and Joachim kneel before me. Grigori says in a loud, clear voice, "All hail, Taryn, Queen of the Wolves."

A hush rolls across the gathered crowd and in a wave, everyone kneels and bows their heads to me. I allow them this moment of exaltation, but it's neither necessary or wanted. I may have lived a thousand lives, but not since that first life, when they were given the ability to shift, have I fulfilled my duty to them as Queen.

They've had to fight and scrabble for every scrap of dignity and respect, and not this proud lot of them have been imprisoned by false rulers. The days of the Volkovs are numbered.

"Stand and greet me as friend. I may have the gift of moon magic, but I am still the same woman you welcomed into your fold and helped to survive in this harsh prison."

The women I have come to think of as my girl gang are the first to break the spell and approach me. I open my arms to them and hope they aren't intimidated by who they think I am now. I may remember al my past lives, how to use my powers, and who I am, but that doesn't mean I don't need friends.

I look into each of their eyes, Alida, Killisi, Bridget, Jeanette, and even Maggie. I return to them the calm and confidence they lent to me when I first arrived in the *derevnya*. Maggie smiles and gives the other girls a shove forward until I'm wrapped up in a big group hug.

"We didn't know you were the Queen of Wolves, my lady. Sorry." Alida shrugs and blushes just a little.

"Well, to be fair. I didn't know either." That gets a good chuckle all around and I'm happy to be back in their fold. "I'll need more help, ladies. Are you up for bringing out the claws for me again?"

Bridget scoffs like I've asked something daft. "Of course. Anything for you."

"Good. Because you're going to need those fighting skills I've come to count on. My magic is powerful, but it has limits, especially when it comes to the evil forces of Hell. I can either fight, or I can protect everyone. I can't do both at the same time."

Killisi gave an eyebrow waggle and her wolf surged up, glowing in her eyes. "We can fight for you. It's fun kicking the asses of the baddies that have terrorized us for so long."

Grigori and Joachim joined us. I would be even more powerful with my fervent priest's claim on me too, but he's got a dark mark on his soul, that I will have to heal before he can accept my love again. That will be easier for me to tackle with the rest of my Wolf Guard at my side.

Grigori, with his mantle of alpha firmly back in place, put his hand on my lower back. "What are you planning, my Queen."

"Would everyone please stop calling me that? This is the twenty-first century, and not ancient Sumer. Just call me Taryn."

Maggie chuckled. "It's hard when they find out who and what you are, isn't it, love?"

"I mean, how do you all think I feel? A hot minute ago I was an amnesiac Hogwarts drop out?"

"Now, now, sweet queen, you don't look like a hog or have warts."

"Oh God - sorry Father - I forget how long you've been out of the real world. That is step two on my agenda. But first, we mount the rescue party to save August and Vasily from Hell. Raise your hand if you're tired of this cold Siberian winter and want a trip somewhere really, really hot."

Everyone around me put their arms in the air, but Grigori scowled at them all and they put them back down. "No one is going to Hell."

"I thought we were done with the whole you have to protect me from everything bit. That's my job now and we are getting August and Vasily back." I glowered at him and he sent me an image of me over his knee getting a spanking back into my mind.

Ooh. Fun. For later.

Joachim rolled his eyes at the two of us. Pretty sure he got that image thrust into his mind too. Sorry not sorry. He shakes his head and says, "If you truly have your powers back, you can open a portal to Hell and summon them back."

"Oh. Sweet." I know I just said I remembered everything, but that's a lot of memories to sort through in a short amount of time, so I'm giving myself some grace on not knowing all the things stored in the giant filing cabinets in the castle in my mind.

"Right. Let's do this." I raise my hands into the air, but before I let the magic flow, I pause just a moment. "Maybe you all should shift and get ready for battle anyway, because we've already had a run in with the dickhead of Chaos and some demons. They could also pop up while I'm getting August and Vasily."

In a flurry of popping bones and flying fur, a hundred wolves, ready to take on the forces of Hell, stand before me. It's good to be Queen.

"Ready, everyone?" I hold my hands up in the air again and call on the magic of the moon so bright in the sky.

My question is met by a chorus of howls. I'll take that as a yes. I give a little swirly, swirly, flick and swish and a shadow portal open before us all.

I feel August and Vasily's souls immediately and push my light through the portal to search them out and pull them back to me on this strange piece of the mortal realm. There's some interesting magic in Hell that doesn't belong there.

I touch the minds wielding the elemental magic of the Goddess Inanna. I think I'll bring these two back with me too. Near the little fire witch, I find my wolves. My soul connects once again with theirs and fills in the holes left in my heart from their absence.

But my light has been noticed by the evil chaos. Damn. Before I can bring August and Vasily back, the great owl with his oily stained wings, and chaos in his heart burst up and out of the portal.

Grigori and Joachim jump in front of me. I must trust them to fight while I protect even though my instinct is to keep them safe. Ten wolves attack, and half are thrown free from Nergal's wings. He isn't fighting claw and beak like he did before. It's almost as if he's tethered by someone or something else.

A stream of demon wyrms pour out of the portal after him and right behind them are my lovers, my life, August and Vasily.

They attack the demons from behind while my army of wolves slaughter them from the front. It doesn't take long before the forest around us is covered in their oily stains of death. Gross. The only threat left is one large demon wyrm who has taken on the shape of a black dragon. He's being protected by August and Vasily. Grigori rushes over and stands with them.

My queen. This beast is different from the others. He wants only to escape Hell's grip on him and his brethren. Grigori shows me his interactions with this demon dragon while in Hell and August and Vasily back him up.

Fine. I have no beef with Dragons. "He can stay, but I have to close the portal. There's something darker coming."

I stare deep into the portal, and can see a dark spell tethering Nergal, the God of Chaos once used against me and my people to terrorize me into using my powers. But Nergal is just flying around, up above our heads, and isn't attacking anyone. Something tells me he's a few french fries short of a happy meal today.

Someone else is controlling him. The only being I can think of that has that kind of power is Ereshkigal, the Goddess of the Underworld, and his wife. I don't really want her popping out of hell to our little island. That would make this prison camp into a death camp. No, thank you.

I also see in the shadow, the face of a young woman. The fire witch. A dragon's daughter. I offer my light to her, but she shakes her head. She is not one of my people, so I can't force her to come along. She turns away from the portal and disappears.

Then it's time to shove Nergaly Wergaly back into Hell and close this sucker up before whatever is on the other side of his leash comes through.

I close my hands, willing the portal to close. It doesn't.

"Come on, come on. I'm all juiced up on love, so do as you're told shadow." I close my hands into fists, trying again to close the entry and exit to Hell.

No go.

And now I see why.

I'm not the only one holding it open.

A tall bearded figure, in black robes, with the stench of evil on him steps through the portal.

"Hello, Taryn. I wondered where my incompetent minions stashed you."

Rasputin?

He reaches his hand out of his robes and closes his fist the same as I did, but instead of closing the portal, his black magic grabs me by the neck and crushes my throat. Nergal swoops down and his claws did into my shoulders and he lifts me into the air and toward the shadow portal.

Oh, fuck no.

I'm not going down without a fight.

JOACHIM

I feel the very moment my Queen remembers the first life we all lived together. I was a lost and lonely soul back then, looking for any way to survive.

Grigori was my first savior, recruiting me to the priesthood of the Goddess of the Moon. I was in awe and wonder at the splendor of her temple. I learned to pray, I learned to fight to defend and protect her, and I learned to love.

I went from initiate to priest, without once ever seeing the Goddess herself.

I didn't need to, just the meaning she gave my life when I worshipped her, was enough. I could have lived a peaceful life and died happily bowing at the steps of her temple.

But then the demons attacked and Chaos reigned. Those I called friends and family were killed before my very eyes. We were terrorized because we loved our sweet Goddess.

Then she bestowed upon our people the ability to defend ourselves against the vile evil attacking us. Our bones broke and reshaped, our skin split and covered our fragile bodies with fur, and our nails became killing claws. We howled to the Moon in thanks and praise for her gift.

Forever more the people of the Moon didn't have to be afraid. But because she gave so much of herself to keep us all from harm, she floated down from the heavens, and become a mortal.

The Queen of the Wolves.

Grigori, as her Dark Prince, chose me, along with August and Vasily to be her Wolf Guard. We would live life along with her, and protect her from the harshness of the world.

She loved us, each and everyone, and we became her mates.

But as time passed, I grew scared. Our Queen was so vulnerable, even with the remnants of her magic to protect her. I decided to do something about it.

I have regretted everyday of my existence since then.

I have waited in fear for the day she would discover what I have done to curse her, and condemn me.

I deserve her punishment, even as I seek her love.

Today is the day she will know what I have done and forsake me.

She is powerful.

She is a Goddess once more.

NEED MORE of Taryn and her adventures with her Wolf Guard? Read the finale book in the series - Undefeated

UNDEFEATED

FATE OF THE WOLF GUARD - BOOK 4

For all the women who give everything of themselves and ask nothing in return.
Quit it.
Don't sacrifice everything because you fear losing love if you don't.
Ask.
Those that love you will be happy to return that love to you, and those that don't... fuck 'em.

Her enemy is loneliness or isolation.

— GAIL CARRIGER

TARYN

J am not going down without a fight.

I have been a sister, a daughter, a priestess, a tsarina, a queen, and now I am a fucking goddess and a true mate to four sexy, amazing, delicious guards. No one, not even the god of chaos is going to take that away from me.

This giant demon owl form Nergal has taken may have me in its talons flying around like an unhinged chicken who caught the magic worm, aka me, but I refuse to freak out.

Why? Because my mates are here, all four of them, back together again, and that above all else gives me strength. I've learned that when I use my magic in a knee jerk reaction kind of way, I don't always like the consequences.

I'm going to breathe through the pain and figure out how to escape without killing anyone this time. Although, it would sure as shit help if I had a clue how to control my powers, or even what they all were. Somehow I don't think the ability to heal or turn into a werewolf is going to help me escape Nergal's powerful talons.

I let out a growl anyway and kick and jerk around, half hoping he'll drop me. I bring up one of my blue balls of magic, but don't know where to aim it. I don't really want to go crashing to the ground, but maybe I can get that new black dragon dude we've pulled onto Team Taryn to catch me. He looks pretty damn grumpy for someone who's just escaped Hell, so maybe not. "Let me go, you foul fowl, or I'll pluck your feathers out one by one."

Nergal squawks or screeches or whatever it is he does, and is unperturbed by my threats. Fine. I toss my magic up into the air, directly in his path, hoping it defeathers him as is my intention. Instead of doing a thing to hurt him, hundreds of moon flowers sprout along the branches of the trees.

Great. That's useful.

Dammit. I just spent an eternity in a dungeon forced to use my own wit and magic. Come on, powerful inner strength, let's get this show on the road. What else can I try? Opening a portal comes to mind, but those have all just led to Hell and what got me into this crapload of trouble in the first place. We just finished eviscerating all his demon wyrm buddies, I don't want to let more out into the world.

I also have the uncanny ability to make people shift into their human forms, but they're always naked, and I have no desire to be anywhere Nergal's peen. Blech. Which means, I'm loath to use my other magic powers. The kind that pours out of my eyes, ears, fingers, toes, nose... and vagina.

See? Yeah. No. My vagina and Nergal do not go together. Ever.

Nergal may have me in his grasp but I'll figure out how to get away, in another couple of seconds. I take another deep breath and remember where my abilities come from. Even the thought of August, Vas, and Grigori marking me and making me theirs gets me all tingly with magic and more than a little lust.

Even though I haven't yet mated with Joachim, I know he's mine too. He cares deeply for me, but has forbidden himself from fulfilling the bond between us. After this, I'm not going to let him keep anything between us. I am not fricking dying again to be reincarnated without my mates. Nope. Nuh-uh. Nyet.

The power rises inside of me like moonlight shining through the clouds. What I see in the darkness around us gives me a lump of dread in my throat. A gray shimmer of magic emanates all around me and Nergal. It is like a fine layer of dust and I can feel it gripping both of us.

And it's coming from Rasputin.

Yeah. That Rasputin. The one who controlled the last Tzar of Russia because he was in love with the Tsarina. My memories of him are strange and spotty, but there's one thing I know for sure. He's a dickmunch if I ever knew one. Worse than Peter, even. Makes me wonder if dumb old Petey was in league with the Volkovs. He probably was.

How and why this band of wolves came into power and decided they got to rule my people is what I don't understand. I remember almost everything about who I am and my hundreds of past lives now, but not how and where the Volkovs came from.

Rasputin is not a god. He is one of my people. I gave him the gift of shifting into a wolf, as I did all who descended from those who worshiped me in the beginning times. That piece of my own soul, my magic, doesn't give him or his buddies this kind of power.

"Bring her to me, Nergal so we can be done with this." Rasputin raises his arms, and if I squint just right, I think I can see a tether of magic pulling on Nergal. That's some weird bullshit right there.

Grigori gives me a mental push. *Princess, shift, use the abilities you've mastered to free yourself.*

My wolves are surrounding Rasputin, but they aren't attacking. All eyes are on me. Is this my everyday life here on this island hellhole? Fight, recover, only to fight again? I don't accept that. My one goal since the day I popped out on the beach with no memory of who or what I am, was to escape this prison. I am taking each and every man, woman, wolf... and lion, and whatever Maggie is, with me too.

The Volkovs, our jailers, don't get to decide who is good and who isn't. Rasputin wouldn't know a moral compass if it bit him on the schlong.

Instead of using my powers, since I don't feel fully in control of them, I'm going to try an age-old tactic. "Hey Nergally Wergally. I always knew Ereshkigal had you under her thumb, but now you're letting the mealy-mouthed Rasputin hold your leash too?"

Negral makes a weird growly screechy sound that sounds more like a dying pigeon and Rasputin throws death glares at me.

Men like these two, who have to puff themselves up and try to control others, are the ones with the most sensitive egos. My time as Russian royalty taught me that. I ruled all of Russia as Katherine the Great, started a revolution as Princess Sophia Alekseyevna, and burned down the world around the men who thought they could control me as Olga of Kiev. I can certainly take down one minor god and a defunct monk.

Nergal screeches like the underworld bird-thing that he is and it definitely sounds like an avian version of 'fuck you'. That's exactly what I want to hear. But strange that he didn't try to mind-speak. I'm pretty sure gods and goddesses can do that whenever we want.

"Yeah, that's right, ya big schmoe. He's got you by the short and, uh, featheries, doesn't he? You and I could take him on, don't let him control you." The more I talk, the better I can see that Nergal isn't himself. Rasputin's control over him is a dangerous element in this battle for all of us. When he breaks free of the leash holding him, someone is going to die.

That needs to be Rasputin, not me or my family and friends.

Nergal takes my bait and swoops down, dive bombing the ground. I scream out of pure instinct and surprisingly that's what gets him to drop me. I would have screamed my head off from the get-go if I'd known he was startled by that.

I'm just about to release a stream of magic to cushion my fall when another set of talons snags me out of mid-air. What the shit?

Jett is on our side, Boginya. Don't fight him. August's calm but commanding voice takes me from a level eleventy-hundred on the what-the-hell scale to the usual. Except he's flying me away from the fight. He's got me cupped in his claw so I could jump out if I wanted to, but if August says he's working with us, I'll believe him.

I grab a hold of his leg and point toward the battle. "Wait, where are you going? We can't leave my wolves."

It's not like they can't defend themselves, but I don't want even another minute of separation from them. I just got August and Vas back. We didn't even have time to say hello, I love you, I missed you, I'm so glad you're not dead and can't wait to get back in your pants.

The dragon swoops in a wide arc, turning us back around, but keeping us at a distance. At least I can see what's going on. Nergal is literally pecking at Rasputin as if he is no more than the giant bird he appears to be.

Whatever magical tether Rasputin has on him, has a hold of his true powers. The guy is a god of the underworld for goodness sake.

Rasputin is asking for a smiting. Ooh. That sounds fun. I should try doing that. I rub my hands together to juice my powers up and shoot a stream of light right at Rasputin. I was hoping more for a bolt of lightning, but whatever. Maybe next time.

The beam of light shoots toward him, but right before it gets there, it splits in four and gives each of my wolves a shot of my magic. Shit. The last time I did something like that, they all turned human, and drooly, half-conscious ones at that.

This time, only Father Joachim shifts back into his human form. He looks up at me from the ground, once again butt naked except for his prayer beads, with a quizzical look on his face. If I wasn't being flown through the air by a fricking dragon, I'd shrug, because damned if I know why that happened. "Sorry, my bad, Father."

I shoot another quick burst of magic at him and he shifts back once again. At least I know how to do one thing right. Right-ish.

My magical fuck-up has given Rasputin time to get his poop in a group. He shoves Nergal away and drops his own robes. Blurgh. I've never seen anyone, much less a wolf-shifter, so wrinkly and bone thin. But his wolf form pops out as his skin and bones break and reform just like anyone else, and his wolf is big and intimidating. Uh-oh.

"Dragon dude, put me down, I need to help them." Dragon dude does not put me down. He flies up a little higher. Dammit. From this angle I can see everything happening in one glance.

Rasputin lowers his head in a stance that looks like he's ready to attack, but is slowly backing away. Ooh, without Nergal as his weapon, he's frightened of my wolf guard. Good to know. Vas lunges, but too late. Nergal scoops up Rasputin just like he did me, and tosses him right into the trees. Well, well, well. Isn't that interesting?

Vas and August stalk in the direction Rasputin careened, but Grigori stops them. He shifts and the others follow suit. If they're having a confab, I want in on it. I tug on the big dragon leg as if I can steer him back to the battle ground. "Take me back down now, please. I'll give you a dragon treat if you will."

The dragon makes a sound that I'm pretty sure is a snort-laugh. Rude. August waves up to us, and sure, fine, that's when the dragon dude decides to take me back down. He's got some kind of loyalty to August, so I guess I'll forgive him.

When we land, I run straight into August's arms and pull Vas into our group hug. If they're happy to stand around in their more vulnerable, and not to mention naked, human forms, they must not be worried about Rasputin anymore. I'm happy to take advantage of the moment.

"I'm so, so, so, so sorry I accidentally sent you both to Hell. I swear I was trying to help. I thought I'd killed you." The tears are bubbling up and dribbling over my eyelashes totally uncontrolled. August responds by peppering kisses and licks across the mark he gave me, sending shivers up and down my spine.

Vas tucks himself against me and wraps one arm around my waist so tight, I think he'll never let me go. Which is fine by me. He shoves the other hand into my hair and cups the back of my head, tilting my face up to him. His eyes are burning with the wolf inside of him. I see no hurt there, only lust and relief. He brushes his lips softly across mine, but leaves me with a nip to my bottom lip that promises more.

Grigori clears his throat. "We can all have a naked reunion later. Let's get Taryn back to the *derevenya* while Nergal and Rasputin are having their spat and figure out what the fuck we do next."

I know what we need to do. "We need to get everyone off this island, and for that we need me to be at full power."

August smiles down at me. "You remember now who and what you are, don't you?"

"There's a few holes still in my Swiss cheese of a brain, but I think if you all fill in some of the missing details, I can use my powers to finally break the spell or curse or whatever is holding us all here. Isn't that right, Father Joachim?" I spring that last bit on him. He's still keeping both his true self and secrets from me. I haven't wanted to force his hand up until now.

That's a little bit of a lie. I've pushed him into doing what he claimed he wasn't ready for multiple times. That needs to end now. He's mine, and I am his, and there's a freedom in that which we've all been waiting for. All eyes turn to him.

He fingers the prayer beads and nods his head. "Yes, *Boginya*. It's time I repented for my sins against you. Against you all."

JOACHIM

On the retreat to the *derevnya*, I let Grigori, August, and Vasily keep watch over Taryn and her dragon ride. I need a few moments to compose myself. Few times in my life have I known real fear. That base emotion was trained out of me once I submitted myself to be a priest to the Goddess of the Moon.

I learned to fight for her, pray to her, live and die for her. None of it would I give up for even a moment. It's everything that came after that I regret.

My actions, my hubris, is what fucked us all. And she's about to find out.

I have known since the very first death and rebirth that the only way to break this curse is for all five of us to be together again. For centuries, I've wondered how the Volkovs have ensured that no more than three of us were with her in any given life. Now I see I wasn't the only one who made a deal with the devil.

Seeing Rasputin use her power to tether the consort of the underworld has shaken me and my faith to the very core.

I can no longer keep my transgressions against her and my

fellow Guards a secret. But by admitting everything to her now, I could also be putting her ascendance into jeopardy. Why would she ever want to take me as her mate, when I'm the cause of all of our problems for the past five-thousand years?

I am so fucked.

I have to tell her, tell the rest of them, but it's a secret I've kept for so long, that it's buried deep in my soul. The truth will either set us free or destroy us. Damned if I do, damned if I don't.

If she forgives me it will be a miracle. If August, Vasily, and Grigori do, well, that's more than I can ever hope for. I haven't forgiven myself. Why would they?

If they would have all followed my plan to mate with her at once, when August claimed her, maybe it wouldn't have come to this. Once again, I thought I knew best, and once again the universe showed me just how wrong I was. One would think I'd learn my damned lesson and stop making the same mistakes.

Only in her light, can I be healed.

Grigori gives me a mental poke, and I realize the dragon flies faster than I expect and I've fallen too far behind. None of us know how long Nergal and Rasputin will take to battle over who controls whom. The faster I act, the better.

My wolf pushes at me in ways I haven't allowed it to in centuries. I used to be able to rely on the rituals of the one-God faith I adopted to control myself and my urges. But not anymore. Prayer only goes so far. Especially when it's to the wrong God. She is the only one I've ever truly worshiped.

Mark.

Claim.

Mate.

The ever present lust I feel for her rises up, spurring me to hurry to her side. I likely have precious little time left with her before she casts me out, so I quicken my pace to be there when the black dragon lands in the center of the *derevnya*.

Will, in his great lion form, with Maggie by his side as always, waits for us. He paces like the predator that he is and it's not hard to sense his unease at a beast from Hell entering his domain. Many of the other wolves shift into their animal forms, ready to defend and attack if need be, but they hold off because of Taryn.

I shift and hold up my hands to calm those waiting. "Please, be calm. The dragon is our ally, and we'll need all we can get this day."

My own life may be on the verge of utter destruction, but I will still do all that I can to minister to the forgotten and down-trodden of this island. Too many have been cast in here spuri-ously by the Volkovs and Taryn's presence has given them the only hope they've known.

The dragon lands and carefully opens its talons, allowing Taryn to crawl out. She smiles and waves to Maggie, and that in and of itself, calms everyone around us much more than my placating words. A moment later, August, Vas, and Grigori come up on either side of her and they shift too.

"Can someone get these hunka-hunks some robes? We've got a lot to talk about and nobody needs to be distracted by their, uh... butts."

August grins at her in a way that's so easy I want to groan for wanting the same with her. *Sweet princess, I would happily do each and every one of those things to you right here and now if we weren't fresh out of Hell with a war on our hands.*

Taryn's mental images of all five of us naked and worshiping her body are projected right into our heads. She never was any good at hiding her feelings, or her wanton lusts. She hides a blush by handing over robes that some of her newfound friends provide.

I've squandered too many lives denying myself the pleasure of making her blush and an ache pounds deep in my belly. The sooner I tell her everything, the less I have to live with these pangs of guilt manifesting as actual pain. Either she will forgive me or she won't. Either I'll continue to be her Wolf Guard, or she'll cast me out. Either I will be allowed to be her mate once again, or... more than likely not.

There can be no in between. She loves me despite my transgressions, or we all suffer for my hubris.

Grigori gives me a sideways glance and even without saying anything, he knows something is amiss. "We need to gather as many fighters together as we can. Rasputin and Nergal are here and they're after Taryn."

A gasp goes through the gathering. Rasputin is the one who sentenced most of them to this prison and many fear him and his powers. Powers he never should have had in the first place.

"Who is Nergal?" A younger wolftress steps forward and asks what many are wondering. The stories of our Gods and Goddesses are centuries old, and mostly forgotten, in the absence of no one to worship them like in the ancient days.

I doubt anyone but the five of us, and perhaps Will and Maggie, know much about any of the ancient gods and goddesses. They barely know the tales of the Goddess of the Moon and it's become only folklore. They are in for an awakening. Assuming we all survive the day.

Even I am loath to speak about Nergal in an open forum this way. Taryn is the one who finally says something. "He's an asshat is who he is. If you see a big, ugly owl flying around here, I guess, hide. He's bad news."

"But is he a Volkov, or one of their minions, or something else?"

It's useless to keep them in the dark, seeing as they will be fighting him soon. I step forward, next to Taryn, wanting to be near her. "Nergal is the God of Chaos, and the consort to Ereshkigal, Goddess of the Underworld."

"That sounds bad. Why is he here? Can he hurt us, kill us? Is he working for the Volkovs?" The crowd gathers closer and peppers Taryn and I with questions. They're frightened and she is the closest thing they have to a safe place.

Grigori growls, letting his wolf rise up and it doesn't take long for everyone to back off. They don't yet trust him. Only Taryn's presence makes it okay. They trust her implicitly without even knowing why.

Taryn puts her hand on his shoulder and soothes his savage beast for all to see. His quick glance her way shines with the deep abiding love he has for her. "It's okay, my prince. They're just scared."

"They have nothing to be scared of. We have kept you and your people safe from the machinations of the gods for centuries. We will not fail them now." He scoffs as if they should all know who and what we are. They don't even yet know she is their Queen, their Goddess.

"Okay, so let's make sure they feel protected. Do your thing. Alpha it up." She looks out over her people and gives them a smile. "I know this is asking a lot, but I need you to do exactly as my Guards ask of you. We need some time to come up with a plan to free us all from this dumb island. We can't do that if we're worried you aren't safe."

Her skin sparkles and shimmers with the blue light of her power as she speaks. She was always at her most powerful when she was taking care of her people.

"You've got this, my queen." Grigori takes a step back, but Taryn grabs his hand.

"I know I do, but if I've learned anything recently, it's that I don't want to do anything alone, ever again. Help me. Each of you, help me make them safe from Nergal and Rasputin."

I doubt she even realizes, but moon flowers are sprouting up out of the ground around her and the clouds above us are parting, exposing the blue sky for the first time. In an instant, the cold frost of Siberian spring melts, and warmth like we haven't known on the island invades us all.

It doesn't take long for people to realize the pure awesomeness of who she is. In a fast moving wave, starting with those directly in front of us, her people drop to their knees, and bow their heads before her.

"Wait, no. That's not what I want. Please don't bow to me. Get up, and let's work together." Taryn squats down and lifts her friend Alida by the arm, then Bridget, and Killisi. "You're my friends, not... worshippers. You've saved me so many times already. I need you, all of you, if we're going to finally get off this island."

Alida was the first to move and accept Taryn's proffered request. It didn't take the other girls long to follow suit. Once they did, the rest of the crowd joined, although most were still in awe. I understood. The first time I got a glimpse of her power, I'd prostrated myself before her too.

It was time I did so again. "Ladies, as her trusted friends, can you organize the people and packs? Most need to go into hiding, with a few to keep watch."

"We'll take care of everything." Alida gave a dip of her chin to me, and a shy smile to Taryn. Before she turned away, she asked, "Do you truly believe you can end our imprisonment?"

Taryn took a deep breath and the light around her brightened even more. "I'm going to do everything in my power."

Maggie waved the wolftresses off and wrapped arms with Taryn. "It's so good to see the real you, love. Now come inside, we'll make a cuppa, and you all can get to work on your plans."

Taryn tipped her head to the side and looked Maggie deep in the eyes, then her eyebrows went up and she let out a small laugh. "It's good to see the real you, too."

The two went into Maggie's cabin and the rest of us looked back and forth among each other. Will broke the silence. "Yes, your Goddess knows what my Maggie is. None of the rest of you lot need to, so shut your open traps before the flies get in. We've got battle plans to make. This should be fun."

We filed in and while it was cramped, there was room for me to stand before what would be my tribunal. I didn't know how to begin.

Grigori helped me along the way by asking the question everyone wanted to know. "How has Nergal found her now, after all these years? He stopped hunting for her upon her first rebirth."

August nodded. "I thought since she didn't go to the underworld she was somehow safe. Is it because Vas and I were in Hell? Did he find her through us?"

A flash of guilt passed through Vas's eyes, and above all, I couldn't take that. Vasily had dealt with his own worries that he'd let her down for the last hundred years, he didn't need this on his conscience. Not when I could save him the heartache.

It was time. I wasn't strong enough, but I had to be.

"I alone know the answer to that question." As I expected, all eyes turned to me. The three men that meant the world to me, the ones I fought and loved beside, waiting on my explanation. The guilt bubbled up inside of me and I tasted the bitterness of my betrayal in the back of my throat.

Grigori motioned for me to continue.

I couldn't.

I must.

"August is correct that when Taryn died in that first life, and was reincarnated, that she and her powers were then hidden from Nergal."

"That's what we all wanted. To keep her safe." Vas said.

Taryn scrunched up her eyes and it didn't take her long to fill in the memory. "He was trying to capture me, wasn't he?"

"He would have done the unspeakable to you if he'd succeeded. Our powers were nothing compared to his, and we were desperate to keep you safe."

"I was weak, from giving up a part of myself to my people so they had the ability to defend themselves. His demons were the ones who persecuted us, killing everyone. I knew he was an asshat."

Grigori's lips thinned as he looked at me. "We've always guessed, but how do you know? And if her powers have been hidden all this time, how has he found her now?"

"Because I'm the one who gave her powers away, and took her life."

TARYN

ather Joachim, my priest, since the beginning of time, my most trusted advisor, the man that I want as my mate, and my guard, gave away my powers?

And killed me?

I can't...

No, no, no, no. This can't be true, and yet, somewhere in the darkest depths of my incomplete memories, I remember.

I was in my temple, bathing in the moonlight, trying to rebuild my energy and my power knowing Nergal was coming for me. Joachim came to me, he held me, kissed me, brought me pleasure as we relished each other's bodies...

And then there is nothing.

Wait. Not nothing. A searing pain, and then nothing.

"You..." My voice comes out barely loud enough to hear. "What did you do?"

Grigori, Vas, and August are all standing there staring at Joachim like he's a ghost, or a demon himself. Grigori is the first to recover and he jumps forward and pins Joachim against the nearest wall. He growls and his wolf rises up, his claws extend and his fangs drop as he partially shifts. "Yes, Joachim, what did you do?"

Joachim gives me a look that makes me ache inside with emotions that are both mine and not my own. I should interfere, stop Grigori from hurting him. I just... don't. It's not that I want to see him in pain, but my arms and legs have gone numb. But this pain projecting from him, it's made my mouth, vocal chords, and lungs stop functioning. I'm broken.

Everyone else is frozen, or not willing to get between the two of them.

Father Joachim doesn't fight against Grigori's death grip on him either, and I think that more than anything is what stops the Dark Prince from tearing his head off.

Vas gets himself back together after this bomb and is the only one to act in the way that I should. He puts a hand on Grigori's wrist, the one around Father Joachim's throat. "We will hear what he has to say. There is more to his story than that simple confession."

Grigori growls and his words are barely intelligible. "How do you know? Were you in on this conspiracy? Am I the only one who doesn't know what the fuck is going on here?"

I can literally feel Grigori's anger, like little spears poking me from the inside out. Yet I still can't move. I flash August a look trying to ask him to help with my eyes alone. Not only does my voice not work, even my mental voice that allows me to share my thoughts and feelings with my mates is broken too.

August apparently doesn't need me to say anything, and I am ridiculously grateful that he understood. With nothing more than a nod, he steps up to the other side and puts his hand across Vas's and folds over Grigori's grip. Slowly, he pulls the fingers off, and Grigori lets him, but with a snarl. "Let him speak, Grigori. Taryn wishes it."

Grigori glares at me, but takes a step back. Father Joachim doesn't even move a centimeter from the wall, even though he's free. His back is still ramrod straight and his eyes are a storm. The wolf is right there, but he's not allowing it out.

"No one else was involved in my mistake that has betrayed you all. It is mine alone to bear."

Grigori growls and turns away. Father Joachim takes two harsh breaths. This discordance is literally paining him and that in turn hurts me. I don't like the idea that we're not all on the same side. I want to fix it, and I can't. I can't.

Joachim reaches out for me, and I shrink away. "Please, *boginya,* understand I didn't do any of this to harm you. Everything I did was to keep you safe from Nergal. You were weakened and we were not yet strong enough to protect you."

August asked the question that I couldn't seem to get out of my throat, even though I was desperate to know. "What exactly is it that you did?"

I thought I knew everything about each of my guards now that I had most of my memories back. But now I realize that there are some distinct blank spaces when it comes to the Father. I thought that was only because we hadn't yet claimed each other and become true mates.

In fact, we hadn't bonded that way in several lifetimes. Is this secret he's been holding onto a blade between us? It hurts like a dagger to my heart, and it isn't something I can forgive easily.

Father Joachim avoids looking at me, bowing his head. He clicks the prayer beads at his waist and they take on an eerie glow, a blue light similar to my own magic. His voice is almost a whisper, but I can hear him as if his mouth is right next to my ear. "I made a deal with Rasputin."

Grigori jumps and slams Joachim against the wall again. August and Vas grab him by the shoulders to restrain him, and all of their wolves are so near the surface it would be only a moment before they all shift and tear each other apart. For me.

But none of this feels as though I am their queen and they are my guards, consorts, lovers. This is hell. Worse.

I raise my hand and they are all still. I still can't seem to find my voice again, and I don't think I will. Not until Father Joachim tells me everything. Then I can breathe again.

He opens his mouth and then closes it. His memories are thousands of years old and he's lived almost as many lives as I have in all that time. Somehow though, I don't think these events have faded from his mind. He takes a shallow breath and then brings his eyes up to mine.

"I used our access to you, and the way you opened yourself to give us the gift of your magic, to siphon off that which attracted Nergal to you. But it wasn't enough. Even with all but the tiniest drops of magic, you still glowed like the moon in the night sky. You were a beacon for Nergal's dark and chaotic soul."

He held his prayer beads aloft. "So, I went to the last place I thought Hell would go to look for you."

How clever my priest is.

Grigori snarled. "You fucker, you took her power to the priests of Ereshkigal herself?"

Grigori made the same intuitive leap as me. Nergal may be a god, but he is forever beholden to his queen, the Goddess of the Underworld. Joachim hid my power in plain sight.

"Nergal would never suspect the acolytes of Ereshkigal as the hiding place of the object of his desire. Even if he did, he wouldn't dare torment them." For the first time since the beginning of his sordid tale, Joachim's wolf shines in his eyes. His inner strength doesn't waver, even under the onslaught of his guilt at having caused us all so much pain. "And I was right. She's been hidden from him for five thousand years. Until now."

"I remember." Funny how something that happened five thousand years ago could be both fuzzy in my mind and also as clear as if it happened yesterday. "You came to me in the temple at Ur. I was tired and weak, and you laid with me, tried to give me strength through your love. But there's nothing after that."

It was as if I fell asleep, but when I reawakened, everything was different. I was an infant, newly born and the world was bright and confusing. My life as I knew over, and a mortal life started anew.

Grigori fills in the next part. "We all died that night, though none of us should have. You bound us to your immortality so that we could be by your side as eternal companions, lovers, and protectors of you and your light."

Vas shakes his head and takes a step back. The hurt wolf I met on the shore on my first night flashes through his eyes and I think if I weren't standing here folded in on myself and needing him by my side, he might retreat to his beast once again. "We've all wondered life after life what curse befell us, and all along it was you, Joachim?"

Joachim ignores everyone else and stares only at me. "Your death sealed the spell. Rasputin swore that when we all reawakened, you would be safe from Nergal. He may have become a greedy despot who used your power for his own gain, but in that he did not lie."

The first time I saw any of my guards again, Grigori and Joachim only, I'd been a poor, but happy little peasant girl, no cares, no enemies, no demons of the underworld chasing me, trying to devour me and my powers.

No magic, no people worshiping me, no one to be a goddess for.

"You murdered her. You took her magic, you took her from us and her people." Grigori's anger rises up again, and this time, I find the strength inside of me to quell the rage.

I open that part of me that's been asleep for far too long. I connect to August, Vasily, and Grigori, feeling the love and connection between us. They are all the keepers of my magic, of my power, not Rasputin. Moonlight fills the room and settles first onto Grigori's shoulders, soaking in until his muscles unbunch and his mind calms.

He bows his head, shakes it, his disappointment, hurt, and sadness palpable. He comes to my side, takes my hand and kisses it, finally understanding that at least in this fight, I don't need his protection, only his support.

Vas comes to my side, then August joins, flanking my back. They are my strength, because of their love for me, and mine for them. We are a team, more even, because when we are all as one, we are an unbreakable force.

We cannot all be together as we are meant to be without Joachim, and right now, there is too much hurt flowing between us all for that to happen.

However, Joachim is wrong in one aspect of his story. Rasputin had lied to him.

His death spell may have hidden me from Nergal, but he hadn't taken my power. He simply used what I'd already gifted him as one of my people, along with the gifts he must have received from Ereshkigal when he became one of her priests.

I understand how that would appear to be an overabundance of my magic. He'd used it to his advantage, not allowing all four of my guards to be reincarnated into any of my own lives, thus keeping a part of my memories eternally bound.

While Joachim didn't believe in the strength of the five of us united, I did.

I too am hurt and angry at the way Joachim decided to act without talking to the rest of us, that he thought he knew what was best for us all. To me, that was his greater sin, the rest could be forgiven. He'd done it all to protect me and keep me safe.

But he hadn't thought I, his Goddess, his Queen, was strong enough to do that for myself. Nor that my chosen ones, the guardians of me, my heart, my power, my soul, were smart enough, strong enough to keep me safe.

Joachim looks between the four of us and drops to his knees in front of me. "Please, *boginya*, forgive me. I have committed too many sins to expect your favor ever again, but I can't help but ask for it."

I breathe in, I breathe out. The power inside of me swells and my body reacts to his nearness. He is mine, and he always will be, but… I don't know how to be with him. He's sorry he hurt me, hurt us, and yet he doesn't entirely believe what he did was wrong.

I reach down and cup his chin, tilting his head up. He defers his eyes down so low, it's as if they are closed. "Look at me, Guard of the Divided moon."

His gaze snaps up to mine.

"I can forgive everything you did in trying to protect me." I end my first sentence on a cool note. They are all waiting for some kind of verdict from me.

His face falls because he sees that my forgiveness isn't complete, as much as he's hoped it would be. I am not his false god who forgives those who confess their sins.

"Because you did all of that out of love for me. What hurts me is that you alone decided how to best keep me safe. Without one another we are nothing. How can I trust you with my heart, my body, and the safe-keeping of the Divided moon if you don't trust in me?"

"My goddess, I swear on my very soul, that I will not—"

"Words are not enough, Joachim." I'm not having it. I've spent plenty of time among men with excuses of why they thought they knew better. That more than anything else is what disappoints me. That's not who I thought he was. "You've spent five thousand years demonstrating to all of us that you didn't believe we were worthy of your trust. You could have told me and Grigori what happened in the very first life and hundreds of times since, yet, only now when we would have found out anyway, did you finally admit what you've done."

He jerks his chin, trying to break eye contact with me, but I don't allow it. He blinks, but if he is trying to hold back his emotions, it doesn't work. They pool and then drip from the side of his eyes.

"I'm sorry, my goddess. So sorry. I have failed you more than I ever realized. I'm so sorry."

My spine, my heart, my very soul, tingles with pins and needles. I absolutely hate this discord between us all. I want nothing more than to wrap him in my arms and tell him everything will be fine. But right now, I'm not sure anything will ever be okay between us again. I can't fix this with simple love and forgiveness. "I know."

The whooshing of great bird wings sounds outside, and the respite we had ends with a new battle to be fought.

I squeeze my hands into fists. "This isn't over, but we must fight off the forces of Hell and greed once again. I don't want anyone else hurt by our fight, so it's time we get everyone off this damn island. Once my people are safe from Nergal and Rasputin, then we will figure out our fates."

GRIGORI

a shadow passes over the windows and we hear Nergal's screech. The bastard has horrible timing and if I could I'd rip his feathers out one by one and roast him on a spit over an open fire. But Gods are hard to kill.

I touch Taryn's mind with my own, and do what I can in that brief moment to make sure she knows she is still loved. She's closed herself off and I can only sense her hurt and her need to escape. One I can't do anything about, but I will make sure she can get off this island. I'll kill Rasputin and send Nergal back to Hell if I have to take him there myself.

Except my sweet princess has taught me that I'm not alone in my duty. We have friends among the people here who are on our side. Without Joachim, we're going to need all the help we can get.

"Will, you and Mags defend the barn, we may need it for triage." Will nods, allowing me to take the lead, even though this *derevnya* is his domain and has been for a very long time. Maggie takes his hand and I hate that such a solid, loving couple has to see the lowest point in our relationship. We'll never have what they do. Not now.

"August, Vas, get out there and don't let those pack alphas fuck up the plan. The last thing we need is more chaos." I really didn't even need to tell the two of them what to do. They react instantly, both giving Taryn a brief kiss before shifting and bounding out the door. I need that extra minute to think. Never before have I worried that I couldn't completely trust one of our own.

Joachim has been a complete fuckwad for the last five thousand years and I can't believe I didn't know or even have a clue. Taryn's hurt seeps through our connection and digs deep into the armor I have around my own anger. I don't want her feeling any of that. She doesn't need to contend with my emotions too.

I've never been one to coddle her, but it is my duty to keep her out of danger, and it'snot fucking safe right now.

Without him, she won't be able to fully regain her powers and ascend to her rightful place as Queen and Goddess. If that wasn't the case, I'd already have his throat torn out and be feasting on his betraying heart. Out of anyone in this forsaken existence, he's the last person I would have expected this from.

All those years I trusted him with the darkest parts of my soul and he couldn't do the same.

When this is over, regardless of the outcome, I will rip his fucking head off and feed it to the wyrms. Unfortunately for us all, we still need him. Especially right now when Nergal is once again attacking.

No way I'm sending Joachim into battle with the Volkov he'd made a goddess-damned deal with. He turns toward the door as if he's leaving. My wolf rises up, wanting to shift and make him supplicate himself to me, make him show me his throat. I don't suppress the warning growl that rumbles up from my chest.

Joachim freezes, bows his head, and slowly turns back. "I will defend and protect her, Grigori, whether you want me to or not. I will not allow more harm to come to her on my watch."

We both know that I can use my alpha voice and demand his obedience. That won't fix a damn thing. He isn't worthy of being in my presence, much less my pack. I won't deign to use the power of the alpha within me on him.

I'd rather let my wolf eat his fucking face. It's clawing to get out, and the only reason I can keep in the rage my beast wants to unleash is the utter despair in Taryn's eyes. I can taste her bitter sorrow in the back of my throat. "It isn't your watch any longer. Stand down."

Instead of doing as he should, Joachim stands up straighter, his own wolf glowing in his eyes. "I will not let Rasputin or Nergal touch her, not now, not ever again."

"You should have thought of that when you were making your deal with devils." I expect my words to hurt him, but he doesn't even flinch. He's gone numb to my anger and that pisses me off even more. "I'd kill you here and now if I didn't know the consequences. Defend your own life so that she may decide your fate. I am done with you."

I've bared everything to Joachim time and time again, as a leader in need of counsel, and as a man who needed a friend. Turns out I got nothing in return but platitudes.

I don't wait for his response or even Taryn's. I've got shit to take care of. We need more time to figure out how to enact Taryn's wishes to save the souls on this island and I need her safe.

Nergal and Rasputin are incoming and we don't have the time we need. Joachim picked a fine time to destroy our world. I didn't think it could get any worse than it's been for the past hundred or so years without her in it. But he's done it, he's eviscerated the last remaining bit of faith I have.

How the fuck will she accept him as her fourth mate and guardian? I don't want him anywhere near her... or me. Yet without him, she can't realize her full self and ascend to her goddess state and powers. The only way off this island is a portal, and without her full powers, that's not happening. Unless we'd all rather live out the end of our lives in Hell. Fuck.

Fuck.

Fucking.

Fucker.

I slam the door shut and breathe in the cool spring air. Taryn's magic is at work all around me and I breathe it in, needing her strength more than ever. I've walked into a battle in progress, but the fight and adrenaline is muted. I must shake this utter betrayal off or I'll make a stupid mistake. We've got a war to win against Hell.

Nergal swoops high in the sky above us, in some kind of waiting game. Rasputin must have regained his control. But where is he? Gathering more allies from Hell or perhaps bringing in more slaves made loyal to the Volkovs?

Taryn yanks the door open behind me, and when I spin to shove her back inside, the wind is blowing through her hair, the light is shining down on her, or maybe the light is coming from her. I can't tell because even without her full powers, she is the embodiment of the Goddess of the Moon, and I'm awed by her.

"I can't afford to lose anyone else. That includes you." She pokes me in the chest. "Don't go off doing anything dumb, my Dark Prince."

"I'm not the one who did something stupid, my queen." I try to look behind her, to glare at Joachim, but she moves to block the doorway.

"That's debatable. I think I could make an argument for quite a few things you've done that weren't so smart." She folds her arms and a warm wind whips around me. Stars above, I fucking love her so damned much.

She's not wrong. I spent the last hundred years tearing the world around me down because I couldn't have her. That's the reminder I need that through her, all things are possible. Even when I don't see how we can possibly go on to defeat our enemies, both the ones we face on the field of battle and the ones within ourselves.

I grab her and pull her into my arms, needing her more than anything else. She lets out a startled gasp and I swallow the sound as I take her mouth, crushing our lips together. She doesn't melt in my arms, no, not my queen. Taryn kisses me back with all the fervor of our first kiss, but with so much more love behind it.

I want to live in this moment forever, forget about everyone else, and revel in her, her body, her love. But the battle is oncoming, and we break our kiss short. She touches my cheek and looks so deep into my eyes, I'm sure she's looking directly into my dark soul. "This is what I need, more than protection. I don't know how to do what I must without all of you by my side and in my heart."

In that plea, and that's what it is, a request from her heart to mine, there is the vision of the future she needs. I must be strong enough to help her grasp it. "It is exactly what we all need. Even fucking Joachim."

I don't know that I can ever forgive him. But maybe she can.

Her eyes flick back and forth over mine and I see the gears in her mind working. "I... I don't know how to be with him."

"You'll figure it out." I leave part of what she needs to hear unsaid. I can't simply tell her she still has to mate with him, claim him and be claimed by him, so that she can ascend.

Shouts come from the far end of the *derevnya* and we both look, even though I know full well the battle is beginning without me. I release her, though she doesn't entirely let me go.

"I will save them, Grigori. But I'm going to need your help, and August's, and Vas's, because I know what I have to do and I don't know if I can."

417

I didn't know either. I could never again trust Joachim with anything, how could she trust him with a claim and her body? I couldn't placate her this time, although my sentiment that she could figure it out for herself was sincere. She didn't and shouldn't have to. That is why she had us in the first place. We are a team, a unit, four hearts beating as one. Five was better.

"You don't have to save everyone right this moment. Let's get rid of the imminent threat and then we can all drag Joachim over the coals and we'll decide what you want to do with him after that."

She gave a small grimace and a shake of her head. There was so much more to this than my oversimplified solution, and we both knew it. Emotions and empathy aren't my strong suit and I was shit at doing this kind of caring for her.

Joachim was the one we all turned to for this.

I am strategy, action, and utter belief in my goddess. "Come, let's throw some chaos back at Nergal and see how he likes it."

We leave Joachim behind in the cabin and dash over to where August and Vas are forming our first line of defense. They've got the dragon warrior who'd joined forces with them in Hell and he's shifted to his human form. I'm wary of any beast of Hell, but they've got a bond with him and he did help keep Taryn out of harm's way. He may be useful to us in this ongoing fight.

Taryn looks around at the wolves gathered to protect her and the *derevnya*. "I don't like this. I don't want anyone hurt. I'm supposed to be protecting them, not the other way around."

"They won't have to fight. You're going to open a bunch of portals to Hell, let's see if we can throw Nergal off guard and back to Hell." Then we'll deal with Rasputin wolf to wolf.

"No, but the demon wyrms will come again." Taryn looks at her hands, already glowing with her powers. She is stronger than I've ever seen her. I can't even imagine how much more she would be if not for Joachim's stupidity. If all four of us had fulfilled our duties to her, she might not even need us to protect her from Nergal any longer. She certainly could take out Rasputin like a bug under her shoe.

The dragon warrior glares at me. "My brethren recognize the goddess's gift of my freedom as our one true hope of breaking Ereshkigal's curse on us. We've got centuries of experience in deflecting Nergal's commands."

Taryn eyes the dragon warrior. "I think I need to have a chat with Ereshkigal."

I imagine a conversation between the Goddess of the Moon and the Goddess of the Underworld would be... illuminating. "Let's work on getting rid of her consort first. We've seen Nergal's attack patterns twice now, and I suspect they're being directed by Rasputin. We lay a trap with your portals, sending Nergal back to Hell, and capture Rasputin so we can break our own curse."

The dragon warrior points toward the nearest treeline. "You don't have time for plans or traps, your enemy is at the gates."

We all turn to see what he's indicating. Yep. There's Rasputin coming out of the treeline, with Nergal flying figure eights in the sky overhead. Behind them the animal eyes of dozens of wolves blink in the brush and trees like lightning bugs.

Rasputin has brought reinforcements. I should have killed him already and not given him the chance to call up an army to hide behind. He'll be harder to get to now and that makes Taryn more vulnerable. But I must trust that she is the powerful warrior woman I love.

"Ready, my queen? Looks like we've got a shit load of Volkovs to send to Hell."

She narrows her eyes and I see her own wolf rising up, ready to defend her pack with the ferocity of a wolftress who's been wronged. "No, but let's do this anyway."

Taryn touches August, me, and Vas, shooting a warm bolt of

her magic inside of us, giving us a layer of protection. We three form a phalanx in front of her and with her at our backs, we step forward and onto the field of battle.

If it is for the last time, I will haunt Joachim in this life and the next and the next.

JOACHIM

I drop to my knees and bow my head. I've spent an eternity like this in prayer, to my goddess or someone else's god trying so hard to will my trespasses away. I know the sins I've committed. August, Vasily, and Grigori's disappointment in me isn't unexpected. Their condemnation is not any worse than my own.

But somewhere buried deep in my heart was the stupid hope that my goddess would forgive me. She shouldn't. I didn't even expect her to.

I am still crushed.

The prayer beads click and clack as they run through my fingers. I'm not speaking the incantations nor even thinking them to myself. The motions themselves soothe me and the moment I realize that, I stop. I deserve a good flagellation, self-inflicted or even better a lashing from my Goddess. Something, anything other than this devastating withdrawal of her love.

As if in a vision from God, I know what to do. I can't let Rasputin have a hold on Taryn's magic for another moment longer. I either must kill him or be killed. But reclaiming the magic I gave to him will destroy every single thing about our world, and I'm not ready to lose her forever.

I get to my feet and throw off my robes. For far too long I've suppressed my wolf because when I do, the base feelings I can't control are also buried. Today I can let all my rage run wild. I can face the sacrifices I know I must make but am still unsure of.

My bones break and reform, claws burst out from beneath my fingernails, my skin splits and the fur pushes out, my fangs push my other teeth aside and burst through my gums, and I let the wildness overtake me.

I will end Rasputin. The island will claim his body, and may his soul be a snack for Ereshkigal.

I scratch at the door, ready to break it down, but Maggie opens it and gives me a disapproving look I don't have the capacity to interpret right now. Am I repeating the same mistake again?

Taryn hates me not for my mistake in giving her power over to the Volkovs, but for making the decision to do so on my own. I can't and won't ask her or Grigori's permission. Not for this. Because they'll say no.

I must repent.

The battle has already begun. Taryn's put up a shield around her heart that sends a chill up and down my spine. Her love for me is there, but it's as if it's covered in the same frigid snow that has covered the ground on this forsaken island for so long. Until she came and warmed all of us up with her love.

My mistakes can't be the reason she gets hurt in this battle or gets stuck here for the rest of eternity. I have known since I first felt her magic come through my prayer beads months ago, that this was our one and only chance to all be together once again.

I fucking tried to get the rest of them to come to the first mating ceremony and we all could have joined with our

Goddess once again. Then she wouldn't have found out about what I'd done and we'd all be safe and wrapped up in her warm love and body once again.

But no. They had to have their little pouts and... I'm being the ultimate asshole once again, deflecting my pain onto the brethren I trust in above all else. What the fuck is wrong with me? When did I become worse than a man like Rasputin, self serving, and narcissistic?

I will repent, I will sacrifice everything I am, and I will not disappoint Taryn or the rest of her Wolf Guard again.

I run toward the battle already in progress. The wolves of the *derevnya* have joined the phalanx that August, Vas, and Grigori have formed in front of Taryn. I'm sure it's driving Grigori mad that she's putting herself in the center of the fight, but maybe he's finally learned to trust that she knows herself and her abilities.

Taryn is opening portals that still look like they lead only to Hell. But our new ally, the black dragon, Jett, is flicking in and out of them, using his own power over shadow, and that must be why no new demon wyrms are joining the fray. It's just the Volkovs against the prisoners.

Rasputin sends a small pack straight for Taryn and her guards and it kills me not to rush to their assistance. Vas quickly dispatches the first two, and August rips the head off another. We were all trained to fight by Grigori and there's no one better to keep her safe.

Except maybe Taryn herself. I stumble when I look up to see Nergal, wings tucked in, dive bombing my *boginya* herself. Before I can even react, she's shot her magic into the sky and opened a handful of portals, creating an obstacle course that even the God of Chaos can't navigate safely.

Although, he should be able to. His connection with Rasputin has weakened him and Grigori is smart to take advantage of that mistake.

With all this activity, no one notices me moving to the front line. Good. I don't need any grief from Grigori for doing my sworn duty. I will protect my Goddess whether any of them want me to or not. This gives me the leeway to hunt for Rasputin.

Since I'm clearly not needed there, I continue to push my way forward through the gathered ranks. I itch to stop and give platitudes and prayers to those in line for battle, but I am no longer a spiritual advisor for her people. That is no longer my path.

I will destroy the prayer beads he possesses that hold that portion of Taryn's power. She may never forgive me, never claim me or allow me to claim her, but hopefully the magic Rasputin possesses will be enough to boost hers to the point where she can free her people.

That is a cause I can be worthy of. I will save her so that she may save others.

"What exactly do you think you're doing, Father?" Taryn's voice pops into my head and I stumble for a second time. She may not trust or love me any longer, but our connection hasn't been severed and that gives me hope.

By the time I regain my footing I've formulated my response. *"My duty, boygina."*

I finally make it to the front line and I'm happy to release the guilt and anger pulsing through me on those who would serve the despotic Volkovs. Two wolves come at me, and I swipe at one with my claws and snap at the other. I am twice as big as they are and better trained. With only a bit of effort, their blood pools at my feet and the island absorbs their bodies. *"May the Goddess bless you with the ability to choose the right side in your next life."*

August and Vas leave a trail of blood and destruction in their wake too. Yet somehow the Volkovs keep coming. How many souls has Rasputin corrupted in the years I've been imprisoned? Without her guards to find her and help her rise to power in wolf society, Taryn must not have been able to influence the wolf tzars. We haven't had enough new prisoners to the island with news of the outside world to understand the current political situation.

And Rasputin has definitely taken advantage of our absence. Even if I die this day in my mission to get those cursed prayer beads from him, it will not be in vain if Taryn can rule once again over our people. Because there is no way she will allow this piece of trash to control the lives of those she holds most dear.

I tear through another swath of Volkovs and like the progress I'm making toward Rasputin's position. His forces and attention are torn between holding back the Wolf Guard and me. The closer I get, the more I can see he's also struggling to control Nergal. His own goddess doesn't favor him quite enough to give him total control over her consort. That is a strategic mistake on his part.

One of desperation.

He knows his reign is coming to an end.

I'll be the one to end it.

"Stand down, Guard of the House of the Divided Moon." Grigori's demands are easy to ignore as long as he doesn't use his alpha voice on me. I've been neglecting what he wants for thousands of years, mostly because he trusted me, and didn't know to command me to bare my transgressions for all to see.

"Only she can take away the responsibility I bear in service to her, Alpha." I'm not even sure if he did use his all powerful alpha voice on me it would negate that calling.

Vas growls into my head. *"You're a distraction and that's going to get someone killed."*

Even as he says it, he smashes two Volkovs into the trees so hard I can hear the wood and their bones break from way the hell over here. I'm so close to Rasputin, I can see the wolf shining in his eyes. He hasn't shifted and is vulnerable. This is my chance. *"Then stop talking to me and treat me like any other wolf out here fighting for our Goddess."*

I feel Taryn's frustrated sigh at my rebuttal all the way to my broken heart. *"But you're not any other wolf. You're mine and I'm tired of fighting."*

That halts all four of us in our tracks. Something has changed in her tone and her demeanor. Is she giving up? That's not what I want. *"Boginya?"*

She doesn't answer and from my position, I see the blue glow of her magic is spreading out around her and absorbing all those around her like a shield. Rasputin finally shifts and the beads around his neck glow with the same light of her power.

It's not a shield, but a beacon, one where she is at the center. Nergal screeches right above my head and dives, his talons outstretched. Grigori, August, and Vas spin to face her in a panic and move to cover her, but they aren't going to be fast enough.

Everyone is racing toward her and time around us slows until only my Goddess is at normal speed. She walks through the wolves frozen in battle, toward me. The air around me shimmers, and I blink through a fog that's covered my eyes. Have I been killed in the fight by some rogue Volkov? I must be dead and she's coming to claim my soul after all.

Except August falls in line behind her, he too stalks toward me. I know he hasn't been killed, I would have seen it happen. Then Vas joins, and finally Grigori. The glow of her magic surrounds them too, and we are all under her spell.

They surround me and Taryn cups my jaw. In that brief moment I am not a wolf, I am not a man. I am both and I am neither. I am only what she wants me to be. I lean into her touch and, for the first time in as long as I can remember, I give myself permission to revel in her physical affection.

The heat of her touch intensifies as if she was summer itself.

"Don't you see the magic in all of us together? This only works when I have all of my guards, and they have me."

I close my eyes and wish away the last five thousand years where I lived the very embodiment of sin against her. *"I know."*

"Then why do you continue to hold yourself apart?" She pulls me to her chest and strokes my hair as she would if we'd just made love and weren't ready to let go of each other. But these are not sweet nothings she's whispering to me, but condemnations of my entire existence.

"You don't want me anymore." A shiver takes over my entire body and I almost cry out from the chill of it. I try to pull away, but Taryn doesn't let me go.

"What I want is for you to give yourself over to me as you once did so long ago. When did you stop trusting in me, in us?"

"I..." I'm about to say I haven't, but isn't that what's got me into this mess in the first place? I didn't trust her to know whether we four guards were enough to keep her safe in those early days when she was so weak. I didn't trust Grigori, August, and Vas to be smart enough, strategic enough, to even consult with my plan.

I still didn't trust them. No, no, that couldn't be right. I trusted all of them with my very life. There was something deeper inside that kept me from sharing what I knew to be the right thing to do. I was afraid.

Of what, I don't know. Probably because I've been fobbing those fears off on my spirituality and religion. It was a convenient and easy place to hide it away.

She trusted me to be her spiritual advisor in life after life, when really she was mine. I wanted to feel all of that again. To do that I have to let all four of them back into my life.

All of it.

The moment I make that decision, the world snaps back to the frenzied fray of the battle. I'm still near Rasputin, and Taryn and the rest of the Guard are in the heat of their part of the fight.

The only clue I have that anything happened is the fact that Nergal is still dive bombing toward her, and she's looking directly at me.

If I hurry I can use the outcropping of rock ahead of me to catapult into the air and stop Nergal's attack. He can't be allowed to touch her. But if I do, I move away from Rasputin and the prayer beads holding her captive.

I don't know the right path.

I don't know.

Now is the time to let go of my fears and trust my beloved and my brethren with not only my life, but with their own.

TARYN

*W*hoa. I had no idea I could do any of that. I'm not even sure I know what I just did. I was in Joachim's mind... or his consciousness... or his soul. Whatever or wherever I was, we were so intimately connected that I can still feel every single one of his emotions.

It's similar to how August, Vasily, and Grigori felt to me when we mated. But that settled into a softer but constant connection. Somehow this new link I have with Joachim feels like it's always been there. It even makes my connections with the other guards feel older too.

I wish I could make it happen again, but I'm not even sure what I did in the first place. I sensed what he was doing even though he's still trying to keep it from us. I won't let him sacrifice himself. He can't die on me now.

Am I mad at him, sure. Can I see the two of us getting naked and intimate with each other? I've been fantasizing about that even when I thought it was completely inappropriate. I'll never give up that need I have for him. I just need some time to work through these feelings.

But in that moment, I was simply desperate for him to be

with us, no longer separate. I don't feel whole without him. None of us do. Just because we're hurt doesn't mean we don't still love him.

There's a shift in his mind now, and we can all feel it. He's letting us in. Thank God. Oops. Uh, I mean, thank Goddess? I'm gonna need some new vernacular when this is all over. Let's go with thank the Universe for right now.

"Boginya, we must get to Rasputin." He wasn't only projecting his thoughts to me, but to August, Vasily, and Grigori too. What he is saying isn't a demand. My heart melts a little because despite his open and fresh emotional wounds, he is trying to reconnect.

"No shit. What do you think we're trying to do." Grigori snaps and the tension between them pings like an off key set of bagpipes. While I'm working on forgiving Father Joachim, Grigori isn't quite there yet. I get it, I do. The wounds are fresh, and Grigori isn't made for forgiveness. It's going to take him a long time.

I simply want us to have that time, and Joachim going off and getting himself killed isn't the way.

Guilt pervades our connection and while I don't like it, Joachim needs to work through it. His mistakes aren't just something any of us can just brush off. *"I'm trying to learn from my past mistakes and not simply act on what I think is the right thing to do."*

That's what I like to hear and I want to run over and snuggle him right in the face and see his tail wag. Which is slightly ridiculous because he's a six foot tall werewolf and not a puppy. I'm just so tickled that he listened and is trying to work on his shit.

Any other day and we'd be making our way to the church in the forest so we could claim each other. Maybe I'm being too forgiving, but while I was hurt, I still believe in the power of us all being together. I'll be mad for a while, but just because I'm pissed doesn't mean we aren't going to save the world.

Or at least this island and all my people who've been trapped here. *"You're right, August. That's not the real problem. I can get to Rasputin, but what we really need are those prayer beads. Only that can break this curse. But I don't know that I can survive."*

Well, God dammit. Sorry Father.

Break the curse so that this half existence we've been living finally ends, but not be able to be the Goddess I truly am or save the last of my beloved guards so that I can once again ascend? To me there is no question. I will not lose Joachim.

As I'm trying to prove to them all, it's not only my choice. But I do get a say. If I say it now, it may sway the others. "This isn't exactly a great time for a meeting. Can this be an email?"

"If an email is a death spell, then yes, this should be an email."

Oops. Sometimes I forget that my guards have been imprisoned without the modern technologies of man for a hundred or more years. It's gonna be fun to reintroduce them to my world. Because we are getting out of here. I will reclaim my power and then Rasputin and Nergal are going down. Literally. Hell has their name on it.

Nergal swoops down again, but I've got his attack pattern down pat now. Or rather, I've got Rasputin's because I'm more sure with every passing moment Nergal is going to break free of the Volkov's compulsion over him, and then we're all in a lot more trouble. Rasputin is predictable. The God of Chaos, not so much. I throw up another series of portals and he can't get to us. I wish he'd just miss and go popping off back to Hell. I'm so telling on him to Ereshkigal.

How in the world did she ever let Rasputin have such free rein on her powers? Now that I know what he is, I can smell her on him. The Queen of the Underworld has a certain scent of death about her. No wonder I've been repulsed by the Volkovs. Not that worshiping a goddess is bad. They can venerate who they want. This is something wrong. They are my people and I'm not a fan of sharing.

If they left me of their own free will, fine. But that scent of death on them is unnatural. Missing pieces of my current life snap into place. I'm letting the Volkov minions off too easily. These wolves are who the Troikas were fighting against. The one-bloods.

They chose to leave me.

Because I wasn't there for them? My people have lived in fear, and that's the opposite of why I gave them the gift of shifting into powerful beasts. I see everything in my past through a dual lens now. That of the wolftress who's lived a thousand lives and seen the evolution of life without the guidance of a goddess, and that goddess herself, imprisoned, unable to help her own people.

I understand better and remember more about how they've been the ones to manipulate my lives. I remember Rasputin being around me as a young child more often than not. He influenced my parents, my life, and the lives of my guards to make sure I couldn't remember who or what I truly was. I doubt if Ereshkigal even understands what kind of liberties he's taken with her powers here on the Earthly realm.

He is the epitome of the modern day one-bloods. Greed and power, to the point of corruption over all else. Why did he choose to worship the Queen of the Underworld instead of the Goddess of the Moon?

My sweet August is the first of the protectors to let down his guard. *"Of course you should attack Rasputin. That's not really a question, is it? Try again, dickhead."*

Okay, maybe August isn't ready to let Joachim back in either.

Several more wolves attack us, but at this point, I'm not sure why Rasputin keeps sending them our way. None have even gotten close to me. A few have torn some bits off my guards though. It's as if they aren't even trying to get to me.

Gasp. Shit. Whooo boy. They aren't. Dammit. Why didn't I see it earlier? Rasputin wants my guards dead because without all four of them, I can't get back my full powers. He won't hurt me if he can help it, but he'll sure as shit hurt my men.

"You're right, August. That's not the real problem. I can get to Rasputin, but what we really need are those prayer beads. Only that can break this curse. But I don't know that I can survive."

Well, God dammit. Sorry Father. Joachim wants to redeem himself. I don't like his whole sacrificial vibe, and no way we're losing him when we're so damn close to being one heart, one soul once again. *"No, Father, wait. It's better if we all attack together."*

I don't know how but Nergal reacts to what I'm saying and changes his tactics. He swoops up into a wide loop, avoiding all my portals to Hell and aims his talons right for Father Joachim. Rasputin cackles in the back of my mind and I brush my hair and skin as if I can wipe him away like a bug.

"Get out of my head you dickmunch eye of a potato." I bring up a bolt of blue magic and pull my arm back to give it my all and throw it directly at Rasputin or Nergal, or both. Argh, can I make this two birds and one stone?

I hurl what I've got and Grigori jumps directly in front of my missle of magic. Shit. Shit. Shit. I make a fist to try and pull the spell I've thrown in anger. It still glances off Grigori's haunches and I close my eyes and scream.

I can't look. What if I sent his lower half to Hell, or turned his butt human and nothing else. Oh no... human bits are so much more vulnerable. If I've killed him by exposing him from the waist down, I'll die and then die again.

Grigori makes an ooph sound and I can't take it. I have to see what I've done. I expect his ass to be on fire at the least, but it's not. He's been propelled by my magic like a freaking firecracker. He barrels through a whole swath of bad guy wolves and runs right into Rasputin.

They tumble claws over ass, and that's the exact moment Nergal breaks whatever bond Rasputin has over him. He dives directly toward me and I shoot out a hundred portals, but just as I predicted, there's nothing stopping him this time. His razor sharp talons are about a foot in front of my face and I drop to the ground and roll away.

August's body slams into the owl's body and Vasily sinks his teeth into a wing. Nergal squawks, but tosses them both aside. Without Rasputin hindering him, he's much more powerful. Grigori and Joachim come rushing toward us, but with one big flap of his wings, Nergal blows Grigori halfway across the town and he goes crashing into the barn.

Rasputin pulls out the prayer beads that we have to get to break the curse and crushes them in his hand. They glow with a blue-black hue and Joachim falls as if he's been shot, skidding across the ground, hitting Rasputin and knocking him down.

Aw, hell no. Nobody hurts my wolves. I jump up and explode with power. My magical blue light pours out from everywhere and I am going to fuck this guy up with my magic god-damned vagina if I have to.

Sorry Father.

I am all fired up and quite literally using my rage as rocket fuel. I fly up into the air, just a foot or so feeling like SuperGirl or Wonder Woman. I shoot a bolt of blue magic at the approaching asshat birdman. Nergal screeches, but flounders and my shot misses him. Crap.

Rasputin is back on his feet and is chanting some kind of incantation. His eyes are rolled back in his head and Father Joachim lays at his feet unmoving. That fucking bastard. Rasputin, not Joachim. Although, if my sweet priest has died before we can be mated, I'm going to kill him.

Maybe it's time one of us grabbed those cursed beads off Rasputin.

Joachim can't be dead. I can still feel his soul reaching out for mine, and the island hasn't taken his body. He is injured though and his wolf needs time to heal him. I search for anyone that can run interference. Grigori is rushing back through the *derevnya* with Will right on his heels, but they're so far away. August is fighting his way through a gauntlet of Volkovs, but more keep coming. I hear Vas's howl and see him scrambling through his own battles to get back here.

It's got to be up to me

We should have just let Joachim attack Rasputin when he wanted to. It was a good plan. There's always risk involved when it comes to fighting evil. I don't know that he was really going to sacrifice himself just to break the spell.

Now he's hurt and none of us are close enough to save him.

"Joachim, don't you dare die on me. Get up and fight. For me, fight for me." Even if he can't move, I will fight for him. If he dies without knowing how much I love him, I will never recover.

With every bit of my power I can muster, I speed toward Rasputin, feeling more magic building up inside of me. I don't know what's in those beads he's got, but they are mine, dammit. They're. Mine.

Grigori, Will, August, Vasily, and I are all rushing toward Rasputin, and converging with us is that flying rat eater Nergal. I won't use my magic willy nilly, I've learned the consequences too many times. So that just means I have to get to Joachim faster.

I'm a breath away from him when he opens his eyes and relief pours through me like a hot toddy. But like the drink, it burns a moment later when his eyes go wide. I know Nergal is right behind me. I won't take the effort to look because it will take away from the power I'm using to hurry to get to Joachim.

Rasputin cackles and his eyes go white like a fucking

zombie. Nergal screeches and sinks his talons into my back, piercing me all the way through my shoulders and chest. Blue light shoots out of my wounds and into my four wolves.

Joachim receives the full force of it first and his eyes, claws, and fangs glow with my magic as if he's a radioactive werewolf. He pounces on Rasputin, crushing him into the dirt, sending the prayer beads flying. He uses Rasputin's spine as a springboard to jump into the air and crashes into Nergal, sending all three of us crashing to the ground.

Just as we hit the Earth below us, I catch the prayer beads and clutch them to my chest. When I smash into the ground, it knocks the air clean out of me and I'm dazed, my ears ringing, and I taste the blood bubbling up my throat.

I roll and cry out with pain. Not because of my own injuries, but because lying next to me is Father Joachim, the severed talon of the God of Chaos through his chest. No light is in his eyes, no soul left in his body.

He's dead, and the island is taking his body right before my eyes.

JOACHIM

*G*od dammit. Yeah. This is bad enough that I very willfully will take the Lord's name in vain. He's not my lord anyway. I don't have a lord, but a lady, and I've lost her.

How?

I'm dead.

How the fuck am I dead? Again.

Wherever I am is not the underworld. Am I in some kind of purgatory? Has the Christian God I adopted laid me on his altar to be weighed and measured? He'd most certainly send me to Hell for my sins against him and my own Goddess.

Taryn.

My beautiful *boginya*.

My mind is fuzzy but I'm sure I saw those fucking prayer beads in her hand. The curse is broken. She will be free. Only in that knowledge can I find any respite.

I deserve to die for all the ways I've wronged her. Even in the end she loved me, and what did I do for her but fuck up her life?

So many regrets circle me like vultures waiting for my body

to rot in my grief. This death is so unlike the thousands of others. I know this time, I won't be reincarnated. There is no second, third, four-thousandth chance with her.

"Phew. This one sti-inks. Are you sure we're supposed to be here?"

At least I know she is strong. She's almost regained all her powers and with the curse broken, perhaps she will still be able to find a way to lead her people off the island.

"Yes, my love. I'm sure. Just keep your voice down. We don't need Ereshkigal or anyone else getting wind that we're interfering with one of my mother's people."

I would so like to be able to have seen her ascend...

"Aha. I knew it. We aren't allowed here. I shall be as stealthy as a super secret sneaky spy."

Who or what keeps invading my melancholy memories of my final life. "Do you mind? I am trying to wallow in my grief and remember those I've left behind."

"Oooh, he's feisty." The deep rumbling male voice is getting closer, and I wonder if this is one of Ereshkigal's annunaki come to drag me off to her domain. Somehow I assumed they'd be a bit more reverential to the dead. This demon or whatever it is has a distinct flippancy that I don't like. *"A spicy, salty douchepotato. Shall I knock him around a bit? Show him who's boss?"*

"Kur." The female voice sounds as irritated with her partner as I am. Perhaps she is the true annunaki and this other one is... her pet. *"We need him to do our bidding, so perhaps a more gentle approach is called for."*

Their bidding? Shit. Is this my penance for a life of sin? I'm to become a demon and wreak havoc on the unsuspecting? That would be my hell, indeed.

I have no sense of my body or I would get up and have a look around. I doubt there is any avoiding the fate of my afterlife, but then again, August and Vas survived what must have seemed like an eternity in Hell. Not that there will be any escape for me.

Since I don't seem to have an actual body, I instinctively reach for my wolf and am surprised to find the spirit of my beast ready and prepared to act. The wolf is ruffled by these strange visitors, but isn't afraid. More like irritated by their presence. I reach out with my senses and scent... a dragon?

What. The. Fuck?

No, I must be wrong. Perhaps it's a demon dragon like Jett. Even with the darkness in his soul, he wasn't evil. But as I expand my senses to understand who and what is here with me, I feel only a mix of emotions including grief, but also hopefulness.

A bright white presence appears before me and I'm overwhelmed by her beauty. A soft, plump woman with dark olivey skin and a radiance so like that of my own Goddess appears before me. Robes of white decorated with prismatic rainbows sparkle all around her and if I could, I would bow and genuflect before her.

Because I know exactly who this is.

"Inanna, Goddess of Love. I would bow before you if I could. I am overwhelmed by your favor." Perhaps I wasn't destined for Hell after all. She was the goddess associated with heaven back when I was little more than a young man in what was now an ancient civilization.

"Ooh, we've got ourselves a smarty-smart pants over here. Don't forget the part about being the Goddess of Beauty, Sex, Fertility, War, Justice, Political Power, and Prostitutes too." The male voice hovers around us like an irritating fly. Fucking dragons. *"Oh, and my very luscious mate, thank you very much."*

"Yes, of course, my lady of many domains." But she was not my goddess. Not the one I chose to worship, not the one I'd betrayed. "But why do you seek me out? I am—"

"Yes, I know who you are, En of Ningal, Guardian of the House of Divided Moon. That is why I am here. I need you to give my mother something that will... well, that's all very complicated. But

when you wake up, please give this to Taryn. She'll know what to do with it."

Wake up? I'm not asleep, I'm dead.

The dragon finally appears before me and shifts into a human form. He slaps me on the shoulder, which I wasn't aware I even had until he touched me. He leans in to say something to me, as if to share a secret. *"And get your shit together, wolf. Goddesses don't like to be kept waiting. Especially not for their orgasms."*

"What?" I got no answer. What I did get is a sensation like a thousand knives stabbing me from the inside, while from the outside I'm being snuggled by a hundred and one fluffy kittens. The discordant sensations push my mind and body into overdrive. Utter and complete sadness tears me apart, while the most intense joy puts me back together again, but not as I was before. I am young and untried, I am thousands of years old and tired, so tired.

I am earth, I am wind, water flows through me, over me baptizing me anew. Fire and brimstone burn me back up again.

Death consumes me, and then...

I gasp and sit bolt upright. My ears are ringing, my vision is fuzzy and it hurts to blink. My lungs burn, but I find the strength to croak out just one singular word. "Taryn."

A soft cool hand touches my forehead and gently pushes me back down to a prone position. I don't have the strength to resist but I do say her name again. "Taryn."

"I'm right here, *dusha moya.*" I blink, but still can't focus to see her. "Quiet now, you've been through hell and it's going to take a minute to recover.

"I wasn't in Hell. I don't know where I was." I try to recall what just happened to me, but like a dream, the memory is fading faster than I can grab onto it. Something about a white light, a mother, and some kind of rainbows? None of it makes a lick of sense.

Taryn's face starts to come into focus, and as my vision clears I see Maggie and Will beside her. Another couple of blinks and Grigori, August, and Vas come into view too. Grigori is glaring at me, August is swiping his tongue across his fangs like he's going to eat me, and Vas is smacking his fist against his open palm.

I may have just been resurrected, but I think I'm about to get my ass kicked. Until Taryn holds up her hand and the three of them sag. "I can feel the anger rolling off the three of you. Knock it off. You can kill him again later after we've mated."

Mated? Uh. I think I'm feeling better already. In fact, I feel some blood pumping through my veins and most of it is going down below my belt. I open my mouth and close it again, not knowing what to say. I'm not worthy of my Goddess or her forgiveness.

"You don't think you're going to put me off again, do you, Joachim? Your vows to the Christian God can't possibly be as sacred as your one to me, can it?"

Fuck. "I never should have hidden behind the chastity of priesthood. I... I needed something to believe in when I thought I'd failed you."

"You're a dumbshit," Grigori calls from behind Taryn.

Yes. I am. A douchepotato even. I don't exactly know what that is, but I assume it's much worse and I'm deserving of it.

Taryn runs the back of her fingers over my cheek and across my jaw. "They're not wrong, but that doesn't mean I didn't die a whole lot when you did."

Oh goddess. I did die. I wasn't entirely sure, because, how does one recover from death if not by reincarnation. When she has her full powers, even my Goddess can't bring people back from the dead. "But how? What happened?"

I sit up, despite Taryn's hand on my shoulder. We're in Will and Maggie's barn and there are a few other wolves laid out on makeshift beds suffering from battle wounds. None are in any desperate condition and our wolves' supernatural healing abilities will take care of them. A day ago I would set aside my own injuries and help tend to them. I no longer feel qualified to help anyone.

I am not the same man, or even the same wolf as I was even an hour ago. I have been reborn and can't make the same mistakes of my past with this second chance.

Taryn slides her hand into mine and for the first time, I notice her tear stained face. She swallows and shakes her head, then looks to Grigori. He steps forward and caresses her hair, giving her comfort. My own hands tingle with wanting to do the same, but it is because of me that she needs soothing in the first place.

Grigori takes a deep breath and he's either about to berate me or—

"You don't even know what you gave Rasputin when you made that cursed deal, do you?"

Okay, a tongue-lashing it is. Even I know dying for my sins isn't enough penance. But Taryn gives my hand a squeeze and for the first time, I don't feel as though I need to be punished anymore. "I do. My mistake was not in hiding her magic from Nergal, but in not trusting the rest of you. I will use the rest of my existence working to repair the harm I've done to our relationship, but I won't apologize again for giving Rasputin a piece of Taryn's magic. It saved her, and it saved us until she could be strong enough to defend herself once again."

A tear drips down Taryn's cheek and I swipe at it with my thumb. "No more tears, *boginya*. We'll get through this together."

She nods but a few more tears escape. "Yeah, we will, now that we have you back for real."

I don't understand what that means. I look to Grigori and he glares at me. That's going to be a long road to regain his trust. I'm willing to walk it. For all of them. "You didn't give Rasputin her magic. You gave him the ability to reincarnate us when and where he liked, to track her and all of us in each of those lives, and manipulate us all."

"But he hid her and us from Nergal. How could he do that without her magic?" I put almost everything I had into those prayer beads, keeping only my connection to her in my own.

"You're the dumbest smart guy I've ever known. Rasputin was and is a priest of the cult of Ereshkigal. They deal in life and death, not magic. They deal in souls."

Taryn lifts her hand from mine and I see my prayer beads wrapped around her wrist. But not just mine. The ones I gave to Rasputin as well. The two strands were intertwined becoming whole once again. I knew she'd be able to break the curse when she got them back. So what was I missing?

She unwinds the beads and dangles them between us. They're glowing with her pure moonlight as if her very essence is inside. "The prayer beads you were so careful to cherish held that bit of magic I shared with you when we claimed each other and mated that first time. That can't ever be taken away. Ever."

Oh holy Goddess. I have no words. Her love is so all encompassing and I'm basking in it, undeserved or not. I belong to her and always will. Always.

"What you gave Rasputin was the bond not only between you and me, but with August, Vas, and Grigori. What you gave him was your soul." As she says these heaven and earth-shattering words, Taryn shoves the beads directly into my chest and I'm literally filled with a sense of awe, wonder, love, and finally, finally, peace.

Everyone is staring at me, and I don't care about anything but the beautiful goddess who has saved me. I reach out and slide my hands into her hair. For so long I've denied myself anything that was good and right because I felt so unworthy.

No more.

I look her directly in the eyes and it takes me a moment to find the words, I'm so lost in her. "I am yours, if you'll have me."

For the first time since I reawoke, she smiles and gives me a slow nod. There are new tears in her eyes, but these ones aren't sad. I kiss one, tasting the tang of her joy, then another, and another. With my brethren as my witnesses, I press my lips to hers and kiss her. Kiss her like there's no tomorrow and let the magic of loving her break free from my hardened heart. "I, Joachim, Guard of the House of the Divided Moon, claim you, Taryn, my Goddess, as my own."

TARYN

*J*oachim is finally mine.

I mean, he always was, but now he understands. Hallelujah.

Too bad it took him dying to figure it out. I despise Rasputin with all of my being, but if he hadn't been keeping Joachim's soul in those damn prayer beads, I would have lost him forever. Holding his soul in my hands was the most spiritual experience of my existence. I will forever be awed by everything he's sacrificed for me.

I would not have been able to call him back from dead without the deep connection the five of us have. Even through their anger at him, August, Vasily, and Grigori joined hearts and minds with me and only together were we able to give him renewed life. It's brought us all even closer together and I know the rest of the guard are anxious for Joachim and I to finally mate so we can all feel whole again.

With his soul restored, I have before me the real Joachim. The one I fell in love with so many moons ago. I find myself strangely nervous now. It's not because Nergal is still on the loose, nor the fact that I'm about to be able to fully ascend into my true goddess state.

I know what will happen afterwards. I've got a plan. But Joachim has denied us both the connection of claiming and mating for several lifetimes. This one is special, and I want it to be just right, and I'm afraid that can't happen. I always did enjoy the ritualistic part of worship and religion. Especially when they worshiped me.

The cults of the Sumerian gods and goddesses are all long gone, and I don't really care. Tonight I only want to be worshiped by one man. Well... maybe a few more. I need to claim and be claimed by Joachim. He and I will mate. But this will also be the first opportunity to be with all my guards, all my lovers, at once for the first time in five thousand years.

I didn't realize how alone I've felt without them all by my side and in my heart until right now.

A rattling and shouts come from the far side of the barn. "It will never work, you stupid beasts. Nergal will destroy her and then there won't be anything stopping me from ruling the wolves the way they should be."

All eyes turn to the weak and now frail man Rasputin has become. He turned out to be incredibly hard to kill. Without Joachim's soul connecting him to the five of us, all he has fueling him now is Ereshkigal's gifts and bitter rage.

Vasily takes a few steps over and punches him in the face. "Shut the fuck up."

I'd snicker if it wasn't so sad. Once upon a time, this man was one of my people. He gave that all up for greed and power, for control. It's disgusting and I've had enough. I stand and have to push both August and Grigori out of my way to get to where we have Rasputin chained up in the corner.

"Why did you forsake me for Ereshkigal, Rasputin?" His answer doesn't matter, I merely want him to have to think about what he's done before he feels the consequences of his choices.

He snarls at me as if he's feral. I know better. He's scared. I wait in silence and he can't stand it. "You chose your favorites and the rest of us were left with nothing but your curse."

Vasily cracks Rasputin in the face again. "The Goddess gave us a gift that you've manipulated and squandered, you fool."

"There's no power in being hunted by humankind and having to hide from the world when we should be masters over them all." There's no wolf in his eyes where there should be, and that's sad. He's suppressed that part of his nature with his hate and shame. "Being a slathering beast, a monster who cares only about finding and fucking a mate is no gift."

"Watch your mouth." Vas punches Rasputin so hard this time, I hear his jaw crack. His wolf will be able to heal it quickly.

Joachim joins us, moving tenderly, as his own wounds are still healing. He should shift and let his own wolf finish healing him. I hate to see him suffering. I hate to see any of my people in pain. "You've never understood the gift for what it is. You wanted power, when what she offered us was so much more."

"There was no offer. I never wanted this." Rasputin jerks against the restraints. "One day I was a man and the next an abomination."

Huh. I only offered that piece of myself, my magic and the ability to shift, to those who worshiped at my altar. He absolutely was one of my people, so how did it all go so wrong with him?

"I ask you again, Rasputin. Why did you forsake me?" I thought my memories were completely restored, but I have no clue why Rasputin hates me or being a wolf shifter so much. This is one of the last mysteries left by the holes in my formerly Swiss cheese brain. Or perhaps is something I was never privy to in the first place.

"You're the one who rejected me, you fickle goddess." Rasputin spits at me, but Joachim moves so the spittle strikes him instead of me.

"She didn't, I did." Grigori doesn't move from his spot, but that tenor of power resonates throughout the whole room. "You were not worthy of her then, and you aren't now."

"I would have been a better choice than this fool who literally gave up his soul and then killed her by his own hand." Rasputin jerks his chin at Joachim. "Did you really think that would keep her safe?"

That is apparently all August can take of Rasputin, because he's the one who punches him this time. "You didn't get chosen to be one of her guards so you made a deal with demons? Tell me again who the fool is."

"Dumuzid offered me a hell of a lot more if I worshiped Ereshkigal than any of you ever did. Look at the last five centuries. Who has been at the core of our society, manipulating all the pieces just so. Me. While you all just scrambled about trying to get your dicks sucked."

Dumuzid? The same Dumuzid who betrayed my daughter Inanna?

Wait. Holy shit.

It is well past time I get all my damned memory back and reassume my throne in the heavens because I am tired of memories just popping up like burnt fucking Pop-Tarts. I have two daughters and a son. I had a husband who was also a god. Where the fuck is he?

I want like five billion years of back child support.

Although, I guess I've been a bit of an absentee mother. I'll have to work on that later. Right now I'm going to set a few things straight.

Both Vasily and August are winding up again to beat Rasputin, and while he deserves to be a pile of pulp, I'm going to do them one better. "Gentleman, allow me."

They step aside and I press my fingers to Rasputin's forehead. I see all of his memories. All. Of. Them. He deserves much worse than what I'm going to do to him and I've got some new to-dos on my list for once we get back to the real world. "I rescind my gift to you and denounce you as one of my people. Never more shall you bask in the light of my glory. Let the darkness in your soul be no solace to you until Ereshkigal reclaims your life and you serve her in the Underworld for eternity."

The spirit of a wolf, battered and sad, rises up from the place where I'm touching Rasputin's head and howls with an eerie mournful bay. I release the poor spirit and its light shimmers and fades away.

Rasputin collapses, his body withering before our eyes. He has only whatever offerings he received from Dumuzid or Ereshkigal left to sustain him. He won't perish here and now, but it won't be long before the Anunnaki come to claim his soul. Good riddance.

But with this severance, I can also see the tether that Rasputin has held over Nergal slip away. I listen for his tell-tale screech, but none sounds. I doubt we have very long before he attacks once again, but of course he'll wait until the most chaotic time to launch against me.

Which probably means right when I'm mating with Joachim.

Fuck him. I'm not waiting another minute to claim my mate. Not one more minute.

I spin around and find exactly who I'm looking for standing there waiting for me. "Maggie, Will, I hate to ask more favors of you, but do you think you could hold off any attack from Nergal for just a bit? I have something I need to do."

Maggie grins with a sparkle in her eyes. "I think ya mean you have someone to do. We've got this lass, go get on with yourselves."

Will gives me a wink. "We've got quite a vested interest in you reclaiming your throne, my lady. What do you think we've been doing waiting around her for all these years?"

He shoos us away toward their little cabin before I even have time to ask what that means. I've always known there was something special about the two of them and I'm going to find out what it is. Later.

I take Joachim's hand and then look each of my other guards in the eye, one by one. "I know all is not forgiven, but I'm asking you to set that aside and both witness my mating, and then join with me as I ascend to my rightful place among the gods."

August grins and leans in to give me a quick but hot and tongue tangling kiss. Whew. Not that I needed any help getting all hot and bothered, but that got my engine revving. He gives Joachim a partially playful slap to the cheek and goes to hold the door to the cabin open for us.

Vas gives me a nip on the lips instead of a kiss and then scrapes his teeth across his mark on my throat. I love the tingles that sends through my whole body, that pools right between my legs. The little pinch he gives my butt as he walks past helps too. He only gives Joachim a nod, but it's his approval none-theless.

It takes Grigori a little bit longer to decide he's down. I don't get a kiss from him, but he pushes his hand into my hair and grips it tight, forcing me to look up at him. The alpha wolf is in his eyes and it's both protective and wants his dominance too. "If he doesn't make you come a thousand times to make up for denying you the pleasure you've deserved from him, I'll cut off his dick and use it myself."

I smile up at him through my lashes. "I know you will."

"Good. As long as we're straight on that." He releases his grip on me, slides his hand down across my throat and holds his palm over his mark. My skin burns for him and he hisses, the alpha's base instinct in him turning from protectiveness to desire.

Oh, this is going to be fun.

Joachim squeezes my hand. "No pressure then."

I can feel his own nerves that match mine, radiating around us. It's silly because this feels more like our first time together, even though we've claimed each other and mated hundreds of times before. I stand up on my tippy toes and press my body against his. I'd forgotten how delicious it is to have his hard muscles against my soft curves.

I brush my lips across his in a teasing not-quite-kiss. "You have nothing to worry about. The moment you touch me with no reservations, I'll come apart. I've wanted you for far too long, and I don't think I have to tell you how many dirty fantasies I've had about your cock and every bit of my body."

Joachim swallows hard and makes a choking sound. But I also feel exactly how hard he's getting beneath his robes. I can't wait to strip them off and know that this time, he isn't going to hide himself or his desires from me.

"Take me, Joachim. Claim me, mate me, make me yours."

JOACHIM

*F*uck. What if I've forgotten how to pleasure her? It's been too many lifetimes since we mated and while my cock has never been harder, I'm not sure what to do with it. I can fuck her, sure. But that's for my pleasure and not hers.

I have lifetimes of orgasms to make up for.

What I do know is that part of the wolf mating ritual has always been about a certain amount of dominance and submission. I asked her once long ago before I'd taken my vows of celibacy for the first time, why she wanted that, and her answer was simple.

In the rest of her daily life, she had to be strong and take responsibility for everyone and everything. She was the strongest, most powerful woman, always finding her way into a leadership role in our world in every single life. In this one aspect, when she was with her men that she knew she could trust above all else, that was the one place she could let go of it all.

She didn't have to be the strong one, she could give up her control. And that turned her the fuck on.

I hadn't felt worthy of her trust back then, and the very next life was the first where I chose not to mate with her. I thought Grigori was going to kill me for that decision. He almost did.

Now for the first time in far too long, I could give her what she wanted once again. Starting immediately.

"As you wish, *boginya*." I wrap my hands around her waist and do the one thing that I know gets her going every time. I pick her up like the princess that she is. I love the weight of her in my arms and if she'd let me, I'd carry her around the rest of my life.

She giggles and puts her hands around the back of my neck to pull me down for a proper kiss. At first she keeps her lips closed, and I know what she wants.

"Don't think you can be disobedient now. I'll have you on your knees praying for a kiss and your orgasms if you even try." I bite her bottom lip and push my way into her mouth with my tongue. She moans so sweetly that I could fucking come right then and there.

I want nothing more than to take her on the altar we've made for her in the blooming trees in the woods. That is what would make this moment perfect. If we could claim each other in the ways of worshiping her in ancient times, I could want for nothing more. But the sooner I get her to a bed the better, not only because of the imminent threat of Nergal, but for my own selfish need to be inside of her at last.

When we finally step outside of the barn, the island has changed so much I don't even recognize it. Gone is the ice and snow, and a warm summer evening has bloomed in its place. The constant cover of clouds is gone and the stars twinkle more brightly than I've seen in any of my lifetimes.

The only thing missing is the glow of the full moon.

That's only because I'm holding the moon herself in my arms.

I hurry the twenty steps to the cabin where the others are waiting. Vas ushers us inside, and both Taryn and I gasp at the sight before us. I don't know when and I don't know how, but the interior of the cabin has been transformed. It is no longer a well-lived-in room that functions as living, dining, and kitchen, but now so closely resembles the temple of Ningal at Uruk, I forget how to walk, talk, or even breathe.

The walls are draped in vines of moon flowers that glow with her blue light, that is all directed at a table, nay an altar, in the center of the room. Nothing more, nothing less. Simply a place to worship. To worship her.

Grigori is the first to step up to the altar and drops his robes. August and Vasily follow suit.

I step up to the altar, set Taryn on her feet beside me, and look to my alpha, waiting for his cue.

For the first time since I admitted my wrong doings, the anger is gone from his eyes. "Ready, Guard of the House of the Divided Moon?"

"I am." As like never before.

He nods to Taryn and begins the ritual. "We gather together in this, our sacred circle to honor the Goddess of the Moon who bestowed upon us the very nature of our wolves and gave us the light by which to find our way to our true fated mates."

He is using the old ceremonial words, if not the old language, that I have spoken three times before. Once for each of them. "If your fated mate be here, declare your claim on them and let your pack know that they are yours and that you belong to them."

Magic as old as time sparkles through me. Taryn presses her hand over my heart just as she did with August, Vasily, and Grigori. She speaks first and I'm grateful because I'm too over-whelmed to say a thing. "I claim you, Guard of the House of the Divided Moon, as my mate. You are mine and I am yours for all time."

Grigori takes my hand and places it over Taryn's heart, but he does not pull away. August puts his hand on top, and then

Vas completes the union. I repeat back the words, claiming her for myself, for all of us. "I claim you, Goddess of the Moon, as my mate. You are mine, you belong to us all, and I am yours, as are they, for all time."

My wolf delights at finally getting to claim her and I'm so close to shifting, feeling so free. I throw my head back and howl my pride, my happiness, and my desire for her into the far reaches of the night. August joins his howl and then Vasily's voice joins us and echoes through the night. Grigori lifts his face to the sky and he too blesses this union with his bay to the moonless night.

The howls resound through the unexpected sanctuary and even though we aren't in our new sacred circle of the moon, I feel her blessings. But they grow even more when each and every wolf on the island lifts their voices up and sings the song she gave to us to worship her and the gifts she's bestowed upon our people.

I realize then that we are in a sacred circle. The whole of this island that's always been damned is our sacred circle and a little more of Rasputin's curse, and Nergal's pursuit of innocence is broken.

I'm the first to stop howling because there's something very important I need to do. I drop my mouth to Taryn's throat and whisper against her lush skin. "I love you, my queen, my goddess, my Taryn."

I scrape my teeth across the spot that's been calling to me for an eternity, and relish the deep, sensual moan that comes out of her mouth. "You want me to mark you, right here, right now, don't you?"

"Yes, Joachim. Please."

"Even though you asked so nicely, you'll just have to wait. Because when I mark you, my cock is going to be buried deep in your wet cunt, because I want to feel the first orgasm I give you."

She wobbles in my arms and I hold her tight to keep her upright. "Then don't make me wait any longer. Claim me, take me."

I would love nothing more than to drag this out, fulfilling every one of her desires, but I won't with Nergal's presence weighing over us. Once she'd defeated him, and I know she will, then I'll fulfill every dirty desire she has. With a gentle, but direct shove, I push her back into Grigori's waiting arms.

He can't help it, and wraps his hand around her throat, lifting her chin. Her focus is on him, and it's the opportunity I need. I shift just a few claws and use them to rip open the robes she's wearing, exposing her plump breasts to me. She gasps, but I don't give her even a second before I yank the shreds off her body, revealing every pillowy curve of her body to us. "On your knees, *boginya*."

Grigori gives me a quick side-eye, but I know what I'm doing. I know what she wants from me.

She drops to her knees, the robes padding the hard table beneath her. I push my hand into her hair and tilt her head back so she's looking up at me. I'm the only one still dressed and we both feel the power in this exchange. "Open my robes, Taryn. Take out my cock and see just how ready I am for you."

She licks her lips and reaches her hands into the folds of fabric. As she splits them open, August and Vas each grab a shoulder and drop the coverings to my elbows, making way for her to touch me.

Taryn wraps her hand around the base of my cock and leans forward, her lips parted, and I think I'm about to die. I've dreamed of fucking her mouth. I want to come down her throat, I want to come on her body. I want the evidence of my claim everywhere.

But even more, I want to come inside of her as I mark her, claim her, take her body and give her mine. I wrap her fist with my own and hold her mouth mere centimeters from the tip of my cock. She whimpers and I almost give in.

We both need just a little something to satisfy this craving that we won't get to fulfill today. Slowly, I pump our two hands up and down my shaft watching her eyes follow the movements. It only takes a few strokes before the first drops of precum pool at my slit. "Lick it up, Taryn. But nothing more. I want to feel your tongue on me, see you taste what is yours, but don't take more than I'm allowing you to have."

"Yes, Father."

Oh, holy fuck. Why did she have to go and call me that? I still both of our hands and grit my teeth as I watch her little pink tongue dart out and lap at the bead growing on my cock. The wolf inside of me snarls and growls inside, pushing me to thrust forward and shove my cock into her mouth and all the way to the back of her throat.

I let one of those snarls out as she pulls my seed into her mouth and sucks her own bottom lip in with it. "You want more, don't you, my little lamb?"

She nods and her tongue pokes out again, just as I thought she'd do. "Ah, ah, ah, naughty girl. I didn't give you permission for more than that taste, so now you'll have to face my punishment."

Her eyes go dark with desire, and how I want to play these games with her for hours, taking her to the edge of her desires, and keeping her there until we're both praying for relief. This is all we'll get for this first time. I silently promise her so much more. "August, Vasily, hold her down for me, and Grigori, give her a good spanking to warm her ass up for me."

I turn my back, dying to see the looks on all their faces, but playing my role by turning my back and finally dropping my robes as if readying myself to fuck her. But this is so much more than a ritual fucking. I'm openly giving her my heart, my body, and finally, my soul.

I listen only as I hear Grigori's hand land on her backside and the little whimpers and moans she lets out with each one. If I were a better man, I'd let each of them fuck her now, but I'm not. This time, she is mine. I've watched, I've needed, and I've let each of them have their own marking and claiming of her. It's my turn.

I wait for one more slap and then turn back around to see her deliciously reddened ass up in the air for me and her face pressed to the hard table below. Perfect.

"That's a good girl. Now you'll get what you want." I get down on my knees behind her and grab onto her heavenly hips. Good goddess, she was so soft and lush everywhere from her big, round ass just waiting for me to fuck, to her thick thighs I wanted to bury my cock between. The dimples in her flesh, the stretch marks where her skin couldn't contain her exquisite curves were all like the best aphrodisiac.

How had I ever denied myself, or her?

I push her knees open further with my own and press my hand to her back so that she has to arch her back, opening her pussy to me. My senses are overwhelmed with her scent and my wolf is drooling for wanting a taste.

I almost gave in, until she begged. "Please, Father. I need to feel you inside of me."

That was the end of my control. I thrust my cock into her wet cunt until I was buried, and then I fucked her in long, hard strokes, setting up a rhythm.. "Ask, and it shall be given to you. Seek, and ye shall find. Knock, and it shall be opened unto you."

With only a few thrusts, my wolf is satisfied with her submission and is ready to mark her with my seed. But first I would give her the mark for all the world to see that she belonged to me. I push the others aside and pull her upright. My cock is buried so deep inside of her that we both groan as this new angle tightens her inner walls around me.

"Are you going to be a good girl and come for me, *boginya?*" I reach around and slide two fingers between her slippery wet pussy lips and tease her swollen clit.

She bucks against my hand and she's panting with need. "Yes, Father. Yes. I want to come for you."

I'm going to fuck the hell out of that dirty mouth of hers someday. "That's my girl."

The long, hard thrusts from before are gone, and I now I'm fucking her fast and deep. My wolf's knot is rising up and it's bigger than it's ever been before. I'm pushing hard to get it inside of her and we're both on the edge, but I won't let either of us spill over into that blissful climax until her cunt has taken the whole of my knot. We'll be locked together, vulnerable, and bound in spirit and body.

"Come on, good girl, you can take it, come on, let me in, that's it." I thrust hard and her body finally opens for me. I grunt out my words, too overcome to even find my real voice. "Good girl. Fuck, Goddess, you feel so fucking good."

Her pussy quivers around me, her clit pulses between my fingers and with the last bit of control that I have, I press my mouth to her throat and sink my fangs into her delicious flesh.

Taryn explodes into her orgasm, taking me with, and I spill my seed deep into her cunt, into her womb, and cry out my final prayer claiming her as my mate, my one true love.

TARYN

*W*ith my mating with Joachim, I am finally free. I see the past, I see the present, I see the future. Our orgasm spread to my other guards who've been stroking their cocks while being witnesses to my final mating. They all spill their seeds and their knots of the wolf swell at the base. While only Joachim's is buried in my body now, satisfying the beast I gifted him with, I will take the others into me soon too.

I chose these four men so long ago to protect me when I was weak and vulnerable, and in return I offered them my devotion, my body, and my love.

They protected me, but they gave me so much more than that. They gave me purpose and a family.

For the first time since I died in Joachim's arms five thousand years ago, my full power floods into me, and the final tears in my memory heal. I know exactly who and what I am, and no one will ever take that away from me again.

Not even the God of Chaos.

He's been waiting until I was in this most vulnerable moment to attack, but that was his greatest mistake. He wanted the essence of what makes me a woman, the purity of the feminine that lives inside of me. What he's never understood is that is exactly what makes me strong.

He's nursing his wounds from my wrath when he killed Joachim, hiding in the shadows. It won't be long before he's ready to attack again, and I want only to lay here a bit longer and snuggle with my mates. But I have real responsibilities to my people now. I will protect them. I will save them. I will sacrifice everything to defeat Nergal if I have to.

In a minute.

There's a knock at the door and someone calls out to us, interrupting my thoughts on how to get rid of Nergal for good. But I'm glad because I also want to focus on freeing my people from the Island of the Damned.

"Ah, ahem. Sorry to intrude, but there's some people here wanting to see ya, and that pesky owl to take care of." The lilt in Maggie's voice, even trying very hard to be discreet, is unmistakable. I always thought her accent was Scottish, as is her mate's, but I recognize it now for what it is.

She's a queen in her own right, and she's exactly the right person to help me end the curse on this island. No cage can imprison her, not even this one. It's a wonder she hasn't busted out already.

I snuggle into Joachim's embrace for just one more moment, and reach out to touch each of my mates. I wouldn't leave them behind, nor would Maggie leave hers. My heart gives a small ping of pain knowing the beautiful sacrifices that our lovers are willing to give for us.

With a deep breath to resolve myself to crawling out of this bubble of love and getting back to work, I magic us all up some clothes. It's easy peasy magic and moonlight squeezy to use my powers now. It wasn't the holes in my memory that needed to be filled, but the ones in my heart.

"Ready to face our new world, my loves?" Once I get everyone out of this prison and take care of Nergal, everyone has a big culture shock coming their way. Not a single one of them has a clue how much the outside world has changed. I mean, the internet alone is going to make their brains explode. I just hope I'm there to see it.

They each give me an affirmative, and I pop us outside where not only are Maggie and Will waiting for us, but so are hundreds of my people. Maggie dips her head in reverence and I give her the same respect. I can't believe I didn't figure out who or what she was before. Her unique beauty and abilities are so obvious now.

Will takes a knee, and I think I liked it better when he didn't know exactly who I was. Inanna always was an excellent matchmaker, and I'm happy to see she's rewarded him with a love match of his own. It does make me wonder if she placed him in my path on purpose. It's not like her to give up someone as powerful as her lion, unless she had a very specific reason for doing so.

If she did, I'm appreciative. He's been the perfect protector of my people while they were trapped here, and I will have to find a way to reward his service.

The rest of the people gathered follow suit. I allow them the moment of veneration, but this isn't ancient times, and I don't want to be worshiped. Except in the bedroom by my mates.

"Thank you, but please rise. I may have changed a bit, but I am still your friend, and don't expect anything more from you than that."

There are rumbles through the crowd, but eventually most of them get up and don't seem to know what to do with themselves. The wolftresses I've come to think of as my girl gang approach us first.

Brave and bold Alida is the first to say something to me. "My lady, it's an honor to be in your presence."

This is the first time in the last five thousand years that anyone besides my mates knows who I truly am. So, I don't have any precedent for how to tell them I don't want to be treated any differently. "You don't have to call me that. I'm still Taryn, I just have a little more power and magic at my disposal now."

"Uh, you're a bit more than that." She snort-scoffs, then covers her mouth and looks as though she's committed a grievous crime. "You gave of yourself so we could be who we are, and I'm... how did you say it... right, I'm kinda freaked out by that."

"Yeah," Bridget continues. She bows her head and holds a low curtsy. "You're a goddess. Our Goddess."

I'm overwhelmed by their adoration and look to my mates for help. August steps in. "She is, but you've always known there was something special about her, haven't you?"

The girls all nod, and look a bit wide-eyed at me.

He pats Alida on the arm. "And yet you befriended her just as you would any other wolftress. Just because she's our goddess, doesn't mean she doesn't still want your friendship."

"Really?" Alida says what's written across all their faces, but while there is surprise written there, I can also see and sense a release of their initial fear.

"Really, really." I'm going to need them to continue to be the girl gang if we're going to defeat Nergal. I may be very powerful now but so is he, especially unhindered by the yolk of Rasputin. We will be evenly matched. The mates, my friends, and this community is what I hope will give me the advantage.

Am I being the goddess they deserve if I put them in danger again? I'm not sure I can do that and respect myself. But do I have a choice?

I take one of Alida's hands in mine, and encourage the others standing near us to join in too, until we're forming a circle. "We've got some more fighting ahead, both to defeat Nergal, but also to get off this island and start new lives. I'm counting on you to be the wolftresses who keep our community safe and glued together the best we can in the coming days, and hopefully, years."

With my words, I imbue each of these already powerful women with just a little more magic. I want them to have everything they've been denied in this imprisoned life. Maggie joins us and I insert her into the circle as well. She's not one of my people, so I can't give her my magic, but she doesn't really need it. It's just nice to have even more girl power on our team.

The wolftresses relax as they accept the magic and their beautiful beasts rise to the surface, howling in a chorus for only our ears. Every bit of power and magic I've given to them and all of my people returns to me, three-fold. My mates join in and soon everyone is raising their voices to the sky.

I can feel the pride and courage in them all, and that gives me the strength to finally destroy the barriers of this prison. The portals set up to keep us contained here pop, one by one, and as the light of the real world shines through, I feel Nergal slink deeper into hiding.

He's utilizing the permanent portal in the old burned down church and I'm almost ready to bring the fight to him. Just as soon as I'm sure everyone I love is free. Now I know exactly where the final battle will take place.

As the final gray veil of the Volkovs' curse burns away, the lushness of the island's true form emerges. It's green and sunny, with rolling mounds, and not of this Earth. We are not in Kansas anymore, Toto.

Maggie lets out a huge sigh of relief and her true form shimmers like an iridescent rainbow come to life. Her lion steps up beside her, his huge beast form unleashed as well, and protects her with his mere presence. The voices of all those around me slowly fade as the spell breaks and I have to giggle as they gawk at our hosts.

I guess if I had never seen a unicorn before either, I would also have my jaw hanging open.

"Maggie, if I knew we would emerge in *Sìthean*, when the veil dropped, I would have done this another way. I didn't mean to expose you." The Sidhe were very protective of a Queen like Maggie. They didn't like it when too many knew her true form. Too many unicorns were hunted for their magical blood that could heal any wound or curse.

"Auch, it's fine, lass. The people of the derevnya *are my family just as much as the Sithe."* Maggie's voice in my head is like a tinkling of bells.

"Sorry, but I don't entirely understand," August says.

"The Volkovs stole a chunk of Tir Na Nog, one of the seven fae realms, because of this perfect fairy circle smack dab in the middle of this Siberian lake. My people had used the island as a retreat for years." Maggie indicates the circle of houses of the *derevnya*. What were once cozy cabins in a circle, are now clumps of brightly colored mushrooms. The other buildings have become fairy mounds of green grass, and yet it's all still recognizable as the village where everyone lived for so long.

"Will and I were visiting this sanctuary when Rasputin discovered the magic here, took it, and turned it into the monstrosity of a prison for himself. We've been trapped in this damned place ever since. Then you lot started showing up, and we figured we'd best try to take care of ya if we could."

Joachim tilts his head and I see the gears working. "But legends say unicorns can't be trapped."

Will lowers his chin onto Maggie's mane. *"Legends also say there hasn't been a dragon in the isles since St. George, yet there is one here now, isn't there?"*

We all turn to look at the black dragon we've befriended and brought along with us. He's looking a bit bewildered at his current surroundings. There's no shadow in Sidhe, and I'm sure that's making him pretty damn uncomfortable, but it confirms what I thought.

This is the perfect place to battle Nergal. And that is the

exact reason I must not. His chaos and evil would taint this precious land and perhaps even spill over into the other six realms. I won't have it.

I'll have to open a new portal and get back to the part of our island prison that isn't in Sidhe. I already have a connection with Grigori's lair in the remnants of the church. It will be easy to get back there and root Nergal out.

Fae folk poke their heads out from the hills, the flora, and approach us. They greet my people and offer food and drink. One woman comes over and bows to Maggie. "My lady, we are gratified to have you and your mate return to us. We'd all but lost hope of ever seeing the great aon-adharcach again. It is dark times here in Tir Na Nog. I am so sorry to report, your daughter has gone missing."

Maggie and Will exchange looks as if this isn't actually news to them. She addresses the woman who is clearly a leader in this realm and who feels horrible about having to deliver this sad news. *"Absolve yourself of any guilt, Cait. Her destiny has called her, and in that we cannot interfere."*

Weirdly, she looks over at me and then to the black dragon and while I might be a goddess, I can't read the mind of a unicorn. I don't have a clue what's going on, but I'm pretty sure Maggie and I are going to have some tea together later.

Cait bows her head again to Maggie and looks relieved. "How can we serve you now, my lady?"

"I'm afraid more darkness is coming. Gather those who are willing to fight at our sides and evacuate those that cannot."

"No, Maggie, your people do not have to fight this battle, it is mine alone." She and Will have given enough of themselves.

My mates are instantly around me. Grigori growls in warning and Joachim shakes his head. "Never alone, *boginya.*"

Alida steps up and repeats Grigori's sentiment. "Never alone."

Maggie whinnies, and says the same. *"Never alone."*

Well, crapballs. My heart and soul fills with the warmth of family and friendship that even as a Goddess worshiped by thousands, I'd never truly known until now.

I'd finally resolved to go back to the portal to Hell and fight Nergal on my own and now that plan was shot to shit. All because people loved me and I loved them.

Goddess dammit.

Not sorry, Father.

TARYN

*W*ith all this ooey, gooey, mushy, gushy, lovely feelings brought on by the love of friends and family, I got a whole new idea. Long ago, I had a family too and I'm about to call on them.

Nergal wasn't going to get the final battle he wanted. I'd promised to tell on him to Ereshkigal, and that's exactly what I was going to do.

But I had a sneaking suspicion that her sister was involved in these shenanigans too. They were constantly bickering even back in ancient times. That's what I got for having daughters.

Yep. Along with the ascension back to my full goddess magic and powers, I also got the motherload of my memories.

Honestly, I hadn't wanted anything to do with either of them even back then. Selfish of me to leave them to their own devices? Yes. But it wasn't like they were some helpless humans. They were goddesses in their own rights. It was my fault, however, for not teaching them how to wield their responsibilities better.

Perhaps we all had to go through the trials of life to learn our lessons. Mine just happened to be a couple thousand lives.

It's not like either of them ever reached out to me during those years when I'd been trying to figure out who I was, so I didn't feel too badly about being an absentee mother.

Besides, it was my own daughter's consort who'd been hunting me all along. She was going to be responsible for setting him straight. Not me.

"I know what to do, but it means bringing three fairly dangerous gods into our midst. I can't guarantee nothing will go wrong, so, I guess, everyone just be prepared to stand your ground. Or better yet, hide behind me."

August, Vas, Grigori, and Joachim surround me, one at each of the four points, and take up a warrior's stance. A day ago, even an hour ago, I might have been surprised that they put themselves between me and the potential danger.

I could use my magic to protect some of the wolves and fae who insisted on being here with us, but not while summoning my family. This little trick was going to use all my power. And since that was the case, I wanted a quick top up.

I turned to Joachim, standing behind me in the position of the divided moon. I pulled him down to me and brushed my lips softly across his. He responded with a needy groan and deepened the kiss until we were both breathless. The mark on my neck lit with the reflection of his love. "You have my heart, now and always."

I slipped from his arms and put myself directly in front of Grigori, my Dark Prince of Wolves. He wrapped me up in his embrace and slashed his mouth across mine. He nibbled and bit at my lips, until I wobbled in his grip. His unique dark glow of the new moon pulsed through his mark on my skin and I was the one moaning with pleasure.

"Come here, Princessa." Grigori carefully passed me to Vasily. I pressed my body to his and we stared into each other's eyes until we were both lost in a sensual haze. He tucked my hair behind an ear and kissed his way from the nape of my neck, where his mark of the quarter moon already burned from within, to my mouth. Our tongues danced and tarried, filling me with passion, joy, and promises of so much more to come.

Vas sent me in a perfect spin, right over to August. My sweet, lovely protector, my rising moon. It all started with him, and I wouldn't have it any other way. He smiles down at me and I fall in love all over again. The kiss he gives me starts soft and turns deep and sensual so easily that I don't want to come up for air. As the final mark on my skin, from being claimed by all my mates ignites, that last bit of magic snaps into place and August lets me go, knowing I'm ready.

I stand in the middle of the four of them, and let the magic flow out of me like the beams of the moon. My moonflowers sprout up in a rapid line all up and down the wolves and fae, family and friends, at my back, and their fragrance fills the air. The sunny day turns to night and I am the only light.

"Nergal, God of Chaos, I summon you to me." I put a good amount of fuck-around-and-find-out into my call, because I'm feeling a little spicy and am looking forward to this confrontation.

A portal between Sidhe and Siberia opens and Nergal screeches like a petulant child. Yeah, that's right you ass of a jackass, come and get me.

He flaps his wings, lifting up into the air and swoops around in his chaotic pattern to begin his attack. "Not this time, birds for brains. It's time for you to go straight back to Hell."

I let more of the magic flow through me and bring the Goddess of the Underworld, my daughter, Ereshkigal. In that same thought, I summon her sister Inanna, the Goddess of Love and War to witness and answer for her part in all of this too.

With one last push of power, Ereshkigal walks through the portal, bringing a swath of shadow with her. August, Vas, Grigori, and Joachim tighten the circle around me, not trusting my daughter. Which is fair. She is the Goddess of Death after all. "It's okay, guys. I got this."

Nergal swoops down, and much too late notices his Queen by my side. She frowns up at him and snaps her fingers. With only that small motion he shifts into a human form, and falls to his knee, his head bowed at her side.

"What are you doing here, husband? Why do you attack my mother?"

Nergal says nothing, but hisses. Ereshkigal looks to me for his answer. "Your dickface of a husband has been making my lives quite hellish. Would you be so kind as to lock his ass up in Hell, please and thank you."

Ereshkigal shoots a death glare at Nergal and he shrinks under her wrath. I'm having a bit of a proud mama moment until she turns that cranky face on me. "I'm a bit busy at the moment, mother. Why don't you take care of him yourself if you've finally gotten your powers back. It's about damn time."

Sigh. What is she thirteen? I can't help but roll my eyes at her. "Because he is your responsibility, child. You can choose to take care of this as I've asked, or you can reap my consequences. I brought you into this world, I can take you out."

That's the most mom thing I've ever said. But it is true. I don't know who'd take over the running of the underworld, but I'm sure I could find someone.

Ereshkigal pouts and folds her arms. She's looking much more the crone than I've ever seen her and for a minute, I almost feel sorry for her. Which is my mistake.

"I'll do as you ask, but I want something in return."

Oh, here we go. "Tell me what you want, and we'll see."

"Stay out of my business with Inanna."

In a poof of rainbows, Inanna appears before us all with a very colorful dragon at her side. I look around to see where our friend the black dragon has gotten to so I can ask if he knows this one and if he's trustworthy. But Jett is nowhere to be found.

He must have skedaddled when Ereshkigal showed up. I should have warned him. He wouldn't want to get coerced back to Hell. Hopefully, he finds what he needs out in the wide world. Perhaps he'll run into Maggie's daughter and return her to Sidhe.

"Inanna, you're late. Who is this?" My wolves growl at the dragon. They don't seem to like him much.

"Mother, nice to see you with your powers back. This is my mate Kur, the First Dragon." The dragon beside her winks at me and waggles his eyebrows. I am both charmed and irritated at the same time. Which is of course exactly the kind of mate Inanna would choose for herself.

"Mother, she murdered my first husband." Ereshkigal doesn't even wait for or say, *hello, how are you*, before she starts bickering with her younger sister.

Sigh.

Inanna isn't any better. "I did not touch Gugalanna. Enkidu and Gilgamesh slayed him."

Shadow bubbles up around Ereshkigal's feet as it often does when she is upset. "Because you sent them to kill your little pet when he brushed you off."

"Well, I said I was sorry, sentenced Enkidu to death to prove it, and I came to the funeral." Inanna's elements go a bit haywire and snowflakes blow around our heads like wasps. "You hung me from a meat hook and stole my first born son."

Her mate wraps his tail around her and her elements calm. Hmm. Interesting. Maybe he is a better mate than I took him for. They have at least one child together and I take a moment to open my mind to this mate of hers. Ah, they have many children together, and they are grieving the loss of one of them. Among the feelings he lets me access is a great deal of love for my Inanna. Not unlike that which my mates and I feel for each other.

That I can work with.

Nergal on the other hand remained on his knees and didn't do a thing to support Ereshkigal. Not that she needed him to defend her, but we all wanted to know our mate had our back. She continues on her defensive as if he isn't even there.

Ereshkigal has her nails out now and points them at Inanna. "As a replacement for you in Hell when you snuck out. Nobody leaves the Underworld little sister. He's mine now."

I snap my fingers and dampen both of their powers temporarily as a reminder that I am still here and I am the mother. "Daughters, enough. First of all, get with the times and get more modern names. No one even speaks Sumerian anymore. Grow up."

Geez, they're such old fuddy-duddies. I may be their mother, but I feel about five thousand years younger in spirit than they are. Both of my daughters could use a stint on Earth living as a human. I just may have to arrange that.

"Secondly, you've brought more than enough suffering on those that would worship us and I will not stand for more of your bickering. Don't make me send you to your rooms." Granted that wouldn't exactly hurt them since Ereshkigal's realm was the entire underworld and Inanna's was the heavens. Ugh. How did I end up with two such selfish children?

I'm blaming their father. Which is a story for another time. I wound up with my guards for a reason.

Inanna was, and is, impetuous and a bit greedy, but I like this mate she's found for herself. He's changed her, even if she's reverted to her selfishness in this moment. He will be good for her while she learns the lesson of what it means to sacrifice for the good of her children.

I will watch that with interest.

But my poor Ereshkigal hasn't yet learned what real love is.

She's hardened her heart. I suppose having one bull-headed husband and then utter chaos as a second consort hasn't helped. If Inanna wasn't so stroppy I'd have her help me find the right mate for her sister.

The two looked at each other and then at me. In unison they apologize. "Sorry, Mother."

"Good. You two need to learn to solve these problems on your own. I'm not getting involved." Inanna opened her mouth to protest, but I shut it up with one look. "Nor are my people. Don't you dare involve the wolves in your little feud anymore. Do you see what kind of grief it's caused me? Five thousand years is enough to make me want to end both of you. Do you hear me?"

"Yes, Mother."

Hmm... somehow I didn't believe it.

"Good. Now Ereshkigal, I've said I won't get involved, so send your consort back to Hell, and I expect you to keep him there. If I see him on the mortal plane again, or if he even thinks about harassing me or my people, I will call your grandfather."

She rolls her eyes at me and I almost expect her to stick out her tongue. I don't care how irritated she is, as long as she keeps her stupid boy toy under control and far away from me.

"And Inanna." I don't know what I am to do with her.

"Uh-oh, Mother. Gotta run." She cupped her hand to her ear as if she had mortal hearing. "Kur needs to use the little dragon's room. Nice to see you again, bye."

She pops back through her portal, Ereshkigal stomps her foot, glares at me, and then does the same. If the two of them hadn't grown up in five thousand years, they weren't going to now just because I wanted them to. Fine, as long as they left me and my people alone, I didn't care.

Maggie sidles up next to me. "Well, kids are fun, aren't they?"

"If you say so." I certainly wasn't having any more.

"That dragon certainly was a handsome fellow. If I didn't have a sexy lion waiting for me, I'd take a bite out of his scales." She giggles and I can't help but laugh at her. "So what will you do now? You and your people?"

Oh, shit. It's my job to take care of them now. I gently touch their minds and see that most just want to go home if they can.

They can't. So many have been imprisoned here for hundreds of years and their homes as they knew them don't exist anymore. "For those of you who want to start a new life, I know of three very good and righteous alphas who will take anyone who is true of heart into their packs."

I open a portal to my last home in Crescent Bay. Niko Troika is in for a surprise, but I expect the Wolf Tzar to be able to handle any kind of situation for his people. Even one this extraordinary. As soon as I take care of some other business, I'll make my way back to America to help these refugees get settled as best as I can.

Many of the prisoners of the Volkovs look a bit shocked, but I push a little bit of calm and confidence into their minds and most make their way to, and then through, the portal. We'll follow behind soon and I'll need to talk to Niko right away to make sure we find a place for everyone.

I imagine he'll be a bit shell shocked when I show up.

Alida, who I have a lot of affection for, has clearly been made spokes-wolftress for the band of stranglers. "Is it okay if some of us stay here? Without the endless winter, this isn't such a bad place."

"Well, that's not entirely up to me as this is not our realm, is it, Maggie?" I turn back to the Queen of Tir Na Nog and smile.

"Auch." Maggie returns my smile and snuggles up close to her mate. "I'd be happy for any of your people to take refuge in my land."

"We can stay if we want? Even though this isn't our realm?"

Alida's eyes danced and I could practically see the possibilities blooming in her mind.

"Of course. We've been family for a long time, lass. I'd be sad if you did leave."

With that settled, I turn to my own mates. "Up for one more adventure with me, my loves?"

I get such dazzling, self-assured, promising smiles from all four of them that my heart skips a beat. This life is going to be our best one yet.

TARYN

*J*oachim slips his hand into mine and I find a slip of paper folded there. "I just remembered I was supposed to give you this from Inanna. She said you'd know what to do with it."

I look at the missive and then let it disintegrate into the rainbow dragon scales it was actually made of. "Looks like we've got a little trip to Hell to make later. I knew she couldn't leave well enough alone."

August, Vas, and Grigori all make a face at me for that plan and I can't blame them. "Don't worry, I'll just pop down to run this errand and be right back."

Grigori raises an eyebrow at me. "I'll give you five minutes."

It shows just how much he's grown that he truly trusts me to do this all on my own. Although, I have no doubt he'll wear a path in the grass pacing until I get back. Adorable.

"And what will you do if I'm back late?" Two can play his game. It's one I rather enjoy.

Joachim answers for him. "A spanking for every minute you're late."

I'll be sure to be at least five or ten late then.

I open my powers and find who I'm looking for. The girl is feeling small, lost, and alone, and I decide to take her a present. Because I cannot save her from her fate and she's got a hard destiny. She will change the world, and I promise both her and myself to do what I can to make her life a little brighter while she undergoes the trials ahead of her.

I pluck a star down from the sky and put it on a dangling cord. It looks a bit like the Christmas ornaments I hung on the trees in my happier childhoods. But I also slice her a sliver of the moon and fashion her a sharp dagger. A girl should have the tools to defend herself when she needs to.

I did promise I wouldn't interfere, but my girls are bit manipulative, and I can play that game too. With a blink, I'm just outside one of the small caves she's claimed for herself. But not in today's underworld. I've jumped back in time several hundred years to not long after she was captured.

She's already drawn upon the magic of her ancestors, witch and wolf, making her a little bit mine. She may be the daughter of a dragon, but she's got a long line of supernatural power in her blood, witch, and wolf. It's the only reason she'll survive under such harsh conditions.

She sees me through the spell she's cast to keep Ereshkigal out, and studies me for a long time before she drops the shield and lets me in. "Who are you?"

"I'm Ningal."

"Oh, you're grandmother."

I suppose I am. "I've come to bring you some presents."

"Yes, give them to me, they're mine." She sits on a bit of the stone carved out from the wall and holds out her hands.

Her lack of manners doesn't bother me. It's not like her own mother has been allowed to raise her beyond her first few years, and that makes me so sad that I want to simply whisk her away. But if I did, she wouldn't be able to build up the strength she's going to need to save her world.

I hand her the dagger first. "This dagger is very sharp and will never go dull. Can you use it wisely?"

"Of course I can." There's a very distinct *duh* in her voice and I forget for a moment she's much older inside than her few human years.

"Good. This one is to bring some light into your life when you need it." I dangle the star and this time she takes the gift with much more reverence.

The star and the dagger have the magic inside that will allow her to save the world someday. She'll help bring the dragons and the wolves together in their darkest hour.

"I want more. Please." Her face flushes, and I'm not sure she's ever used that word before. She feels the power of the magic and its draw. She won't understand why she can hear more, see more, and be more than everyone else around her.

"I'll bring you more, but you have to promise never to tell anyone that I was here. I'm cheating a bit by visiting you."

She nods. "I promise."

"I've got one more gift for you." My time away is more than up, and while I don't want to leave her, I know that Grigori and the others will be worried if I don't hurry along.

She holds out her hand again, but I shake my head. "This one isn't a thing, but something else. It's a gift to say thank you for helping my wolves when they need your help someday soon. Okay?"

She narrows her eyes at me and I touch my finger to her forehead. With one brilliant burst of my moon's light, I push one more bit of my magic into her soul.

It won't make any sense to her for a while, but once she is ready to leave Hell, Inanna and Ninshubar will help her use it to find her own mate. It's the least we'll all owe her for the sacrifices she'll have to make.

Her eyes flutter, and she sighs, her body relaxes, and I help her to lay on her makeshift bed.

"Good night, Fallyn, sleep tight. I'll see you again soon, little lady bug." I establish her protective wards so that no one can disturb her rest and then shift back to the current day, pop back up to Sidhe and my mates.

August wraps me in his arms and holds me close. He doesn't say anything, and it's exactly the support that I need from him. When I'm ready, I extract myself and look toward the portal.

"Ready, boys?" We have a new life waiting. One that I can't wait to get started.

"Yes, but for what? I'm not sure what to do with myself now that we're not fighting to protect you," August says, but I could tell by the waggle of his eyebrows he knew exactly what he wanted to do.

Vas joined in. "Yes. I can think of a few things."

Grigori snorted but the dancing wolf in his eyes said he was game for some, umm, games. Joachim rubs his hands together and I think he's already counting those spankings.

The five of us wave to Maggie, Will, and the wolves staying behind in Sidhe. We make two or three real quick stops directed by Grigori to pick up some things he says we'll need for our new life, and then finally step out of my portal to Troika lands. We pop up on the beach, along with the rest of my people. They've huddled together in small groups and while I get the feeling of some nervousness, they too are excited for this new life.

"Come on, everyone. I've got a favor or two to call in." We make our way up the beach to what used to be an old, yellow, dilapidated inn. It's had quite a bit of work done since I last saw it, as have the cabins surrounding it. I hope Heli and Kosta are ready to have a full house.

I signal to the group to wait on the porch and walk up the restored front steps and into the double doors of the new Bay Inn. I look around at the light and breezy ocean-themed decor of the lobby. It's both homey and vacationy at the same time.

There's an old friend working behind the counter, but she's tapping away on the computer and hasn't spotted me yet. "Is there any room at the inn?"

Heli spins around, searching for the voice, finally finds me, and her eyes go from normal surprised to holy shit surprised. "Taryn? Oh my God, is it you? Where have you been?"

"Hi Heli. It's a long, long story." A really, really long story.

"Something has changed about you." She looks over my shoulder and her eyes go even wider. "Uh, I think I can see what."

"Heli, meet August, Vasily, Joachim, and Grigori, my mates."

"Lucky girl." She winks at me. "Nice to meet you all."

Time to get down to business. "It seems I'm homeless, now that Niko and Zara have taken over the Crescent pack."

Heli makes an uh-oh face, but I smile so she understands I'm not upset. "Oh, uh, I'm sure Niko would love to talk to you about that."

"Yes, I will want to chat with them, but when you call them," which I'm sure she will immediately if not sooner, "please assure them, I'm not here to challenge him. I'm very content with all that I have. I do have some people who'll need his help."

It's really interesting to see how the wolftress in her is reacting to my presence. Somehow her newly transformed beast knows who I am, but hasn't let the human woman part of her in on the secret yet. My original gift had transformed all my people, and for a while, they kept to our own kind. But it didn't take long for one of my wolves to fall in love with a human.

Humans are so interesting and unique that when my gift is transferred to them, it doesn't always result in the ability to shift. I wonder if there is a common denominator to the ones that do, and the ones that develop other supernatural abilities.

I'd be paying a lot more attention when I meet other new mates of my wolves in the future.

"So, for real though. I really am homeless and was wondering if you had a room, or rooms, available for us."

"Of course." She taps on her computer for a second and says, "I think I have just the thing. We just finished refurbing the old Presidential suite. But I hate that name, so I'm calling it the Goddess suite. How long would you like to stay?"

"Umm, indefinitely. I'll need a home base while I figure out where I belong in the world now." I'd love to be somewhere nearish to the area I grew up in, but I don't think I'd actually be comfortable back in my not-father's old territory. It's better off with Niko and Zara.

"Okay," she tapped the keyboard a few more times. "I'll just charge that to Niko, since you know, he took over your pack, and umm, you know, he's the Wolf Tzar now and all. I think he can afford it."

"Well, I'm going to need more than just that suite." I wave to the guys and they bring in the first wave of other guests I'm hoping she can accommodate. "I've got some friends who don't have anywhere to call home either."

Heli takes a quick peek out the window, then down at her computer. "Uh, yeah. Good thing we haven't opened yet. Anyone up for some beach camping?"

She was so cute and kind. "Thanks, yes. We'll take anything and everything you've got. And if you're up for a bit of trade, I've got some old family heirlooms I could give you to cover the first few days or so."

I pulled out a ring made of emeralds and diamonds that Grigori had given to me when I'd been Katherine the Great. I may have turned an entire room of the Winter Palace into a jewelry box, but he had hidden away even more precious items that he'd intended to bolster my wealth and position in future reincarnations. I'd only had one more life in Russia after that, and I'd only lived to seventeen and in an extremely privileged life. I hadn't needed the fortune he'd amassed.

It was going to come in handy now if I was to live among the humans and my people. I pressed the ring into Heli's hand and she shivered. "Holy shit, Taryn, is this real?"

"Yep. That should cover any expenses we might incur. Although, these guys eat like they haven't been fed in hundreds of years, so let me know if you need anything more." I wasn't going to be wanting for money anytime soon, and now neither were Heli and Kosta.

Heli tapped away on her computer, handed out keys, and called back to her kitchen for Kosta. When he came up to the desk, he looked around at all the people, then at Heli, then at me. I gave a little wave, and he dropped to one knee and bowed his head.

Heli laughed. "It's just Taryn, sweetheart. Well, and a whole bunch of her friends. Oh, and her four mates."

Kosta didn't lift his head, but spoke out the side of his mouth at his mate. "That might be Taryn, *zaika*, but she is also the Goddess of the Moon."

Heli tilted her head one way, then the other, and I give her a little wave. "That's cool as shit. I think we'd better call up Gal, Zara, and Selena and invite them over for some tea. Or, uh, maybe something stronger."

"Yes, let's do that. But maybe tomorrow?" It had been so long since I'd lived as a goddess and not a mortal, that I actually wasn't entirely sure what to do about my old friends and connections. But I could think about that tomorrow. For now, I knew I wanted to spend a lot of time rekindling a lot of old fantasies.

Oh. I had a great idea. I leaned over the counter to whisper to Heli and she snort giggled when I asked about their in-room entertainment.

"Like I think you'll need it." She handed over the keys to the suite and pointed us up the grand staircase. In true guard fashion, August picked me up, threw me over his shoulder and sprinted up the stairs three at a time. He didn't set me down, despite my protests and squeals, until we were at the door to the suite.

"Come on boys. You've been locked up for all of the modern era and I'd like to introduce you to running hot water, a luxurious hotel room, room service hamburgers and fries, and maybe pay-per-view porn."

Joachim lifted me up into his arms again and kissed my brand new mark of his wolf. "I don't know what any of that means, but where you go, we go. So let's go pay to view porn.

And we did. For an entire day.

In the light of the full moon that evening, I snuggled deep into the arms of two of my lovers, fingers intertwined with others. I am powerful, I am a Goddess and I am worshiped.

While others may pray to me and give me thanks for the gifts I've given them, I too am thankful. I close my eyes, and send my gratitude out into the universe. It hasn't been an easy journey, but I wouldn't have it any other way, because it's made me who I am.

I love myself, I love my mates, and I love my fate.

My fate with my wolf guards is my very own happy ever after.

WANT MORE WOLVES? Pop over and see how Taryn is having fun doing a little matchmaking with the wolf-shifters of Rogue while definitely interfering in the war between Inanna and Ereshkigal.

Grab the next book in the series - Filthy Wolf

W̶ONDERING what's going on between Inanna and Ereshkigal? Or how about Maggie and Will's daughter? Just where did Jett the black dragon disappear off to? And what is going to happen to Fallyn?

You're gonna want to read Dragons Love Curves!

Start with Chase Me.

Get it now, or turn the page for an excerpt from chapter one.

EXCERPT FROM CHASE ME

CHAPTER 1: ALWAYS THE WEDDING PLANNER, NEVER THE BRIDE

*A*gh. Ciara's feet ached, her back was stiff and the headache she'd staved off with some ibuprofen four hours ago was rapidly creeping back behind her left eyeball. Nothing like the sweet pains of victory.

One more commission like this and she could afford to take that beach vacation she'd been promising Wesley for the past three years.

"Oh Sarah, there you are." The bride's mother, who was reason number one, two, three, and forty-three for said headache, waved her over. Mother-of-the-Bridezilla paid the bills, so Ciara pasted on her most helpful smile and greeted the table.

"Hello everyone. Having a nice time?"

Headache mom turned to the couple sitting next to her. "Bill, Thi, this is Sarah, the wedding planner. You simply must book her for your Linh's wedding. She is the best—always available for her clients. I called her last week at two in the morning when I simply knew that Bethany needed to have three more wedding cakes at the reception. Sarah never says no."

Oh, great. That's what she wanted to be known for. Being the slut of the wedding planner world.

"Well, I like to hear that. We want our baby to have everything she wants for her wedding. No expense spared. Do you have a card, Sarah?"

"It's Ciara actually, and yes, of course." She handed Bill, who she could already tell was wrapped around his daughter's little finger, a card. Bill handed the card to his wife. "Let me write your time and date on the back for you."

She pulled a pen out of her kit. Always prepared, true to her Girl Scout roots. She scribbled on the back of the card.

"Ciara Mosley-Willingham. Do you own Willingham Weddings, dear?"

Sigh. Not yet. Not ever if her mother had anything to do with it. "That honor goes to my mother, Wilhelmina."

"Ah, I see. Well, nepotism has its benefits." The table all chuckled at Bill's little joke.

Benefits schmenefits. If only they knew.

"I've got an appointment that just opened up for two weeks from Monday. Will that work to bring Linh in for a consultation?"

"Two weeks?"

She nodded. "I'm afraid the next available is in August."

The couple glanced at each other. They were not used to waiting patiently. Most of her clients weren't.

"That's almost three months from now."

Headache mother raised a glass of champagne. "You wanted the best. Better get her while you can."

Thi raised an eyebrow, trying to intimidate Ciara. Not

gonna happen. Ciara gave the mother her award-winning account-getting smile.

Thi gave in. "We'll be there."

Bali with Wesley, here she comes. If she could ever get him to ask her out in the first place, and in another three years when her schedule cleared up. Not that her mother would ever allow her to take a vacation, but at least now she had a plan to get that date with the hunk of the office.

Ciara made her rounds, vying for a chance to run into Wes with the good news. News that should be celebrated, with a night on the town, a nice dinner, some satin sheets.

She checked in with the catering staff and found out he was in the kitchen. Wes, in a perfect three-piece suit with the purple pocket square and matching vest, just about took her breath away. How any man this good looking would be interested in her blew her mind.

By interested, she meant he flirted with her constantly at the office but hadn't ever asked her out. Ciara had made it perfectly clear she was willing and available.

He hinted, she smiled and nodded, and then nothing.

A girl could only wait so long for the man of her day dreams to make a move.

"Hey babe." He kissed her on the cheeks while holding his cell phone to his ear. "We've got a champagne shortage crisis on our hands."

No need to stress. Cool, calm, and collected. Always. "No problem. I'll bring in the secret back-up case I keep in my car."

Wes hung up his phone and winked at the disheveled waiter with the empty tray. "Told you Ciara would swing some of her magic."

He was such a sweet talker. She hoped he was a dirty talker too. Whoa, wait. Down girl. She had to get a date with him first. "I'll go grab it, but the bouquet toss is in a few minutes. Go chat up all the single girls and talk them into standing up to catch the bouquet."

One wink or an eyebrow waggle from him and they'd all be smashing each other in the face to catch those flowers whether they wanted to or not.

"I'll go get the champagne, you go catch the bouquet." Wes shook his head and shivered.

Lots of bouquets were in her future, but not for catching. Always the wedding planner, never the bride. Yet.

Here goes nothing, or something, or gah, just ask him.

"Hey, I just landed the Barton wedding. We should celebrate."

Wes grinned. "You are going to make us all zillionaires. I cannot even keep up."

Okay, this was going well. Ask him. "So, you'll go out with me to celebrate?"

"You bet."

He didn't hesitate even a little. She should have asked him months and months... and months ago.

"Are you free on Wednesday?" They had weddings on the weekends, but she hoped she didn't sound lame for suggesting a weeknight.

"Nope. But, I could do Thursday. Dinner, drinks, and I know the greatest place to go clubbing."

Dinner, drinks, and dancing. Perfect.

She wanted to jump up and down and clap her hands.

Not appropriate.

Be cool.

Ciara drew upon her inner cucumber-ness. "Sounds great."

Enough said. Right? Yeah, that was fine. She didn't want to look overly enthusiastic. She'd save that for the in-bed portion of their evening.

Geez, she needed to get her mind out of the gutter. She'd

gone from dinner and dancing to handcuffs and blindfolds in seconds. Oh, please let him be at least a little kinky.

"Ciara?"

"Yeah?" She blinked, still caught up in her fantasy sex life with Wesley.

"You feeling alright? You look a little flushed."

She'd be fine and dandy if she could get the real Wesley into her fantasy life. "Yep. Great. Go grab that champagne and get it on ice."

"You're the best, you know that, right?" Wes grabbed her in a bear hug and danced her around. He jerked back and rubbed at his chest. "Ouch, your necklace bit me."

"Oh, geez. Sorry." Ciara put her hand over the colorful pendant she'd gotten a few days ago. She didn't feel anything sharp.

"Pretty but painful, doll." Wes examined the charm, staring a scant inch above Ciara's boobs. "It would go with everything. Where'd you get it?"

Damn. She'd kind of hoped Wesley had sent it. Not likely, but she was ever hopeful. Must be from her mother, who rarely gave gifts. Weird.

"Oh my god, Ciara, there you are. I'm getting a divorce, or is it an annulment? Whatever. George is such an ass. I want out of this marriage right now." The bride ran into the kitchen and faux collapsed into Ciara's arms.

She glanced at Wes, who shook his head and smirked. He mouthed the words good luck and backed away from them.

This woman wasn't the first newlywed to freak out at the reception and she wouldn't be the last. Ciara had a long track-record of calming them down and helping them focus on what was important, their happily ever afters. Wesley called her the bride whisperer.

Ciara put a hand on the bride's arm and sent all the happy

calming positive thoughts she could muster. They took a deep breath together.

"You can do this. Everything is going to be fine."

The bride nodded, looking a little dazed and repeated Ciara's words. "Everything is going to be fine."

A few hours later, the bride and groom had more than made up. The bouquet was tossed, the champagne chilled and toasted, the candles blown out, all topped off by the perfect sunset.

At two in the morning, Wes escorted the last of the drunken groomsmen to the limos they'd arranged to drive the non-sober home and Ciara collapsed into the nearest chair.

If she took her shoes off now, they were never ever going back on, but she'd limp home barefoot rather than take one more second in her not-so-high heels.

A lonely uneaten piece of wedding cake had been calling to her ever since she saw the fit groomsman walk away from it several hours ago. After that marathon wedding and reception, she needed a good sugar fix.

"Stop right there, thief." The deep rumble of a male voice halted the fork midway to her mouth. Sounded like he was back for his dessert. Oh God. How embarrassing.

"I'm just doing a bit of quality control. Have to make sure the cake is up to Willingham Weddings standards."

Please don't let him mention the fact that the wedding was over. Ciara turned to give the groomsman her best don't mind me I'm just the chubby, dateless, wedding planner stealing a piece of leftover cake smile. The man-slash-movie-star-slash-romance novel cover model standing three feet behind her had his arms crossed and a mad as hell glare on.

He wore a tight black t-shirt, dark jeans and a beautiful bright green crystal on a cord around his neck, so he wasn't the groomsman, or any other guest of the Ketcher-Fast wedding. She'd remember all that fantasy material.

He glanced down at the glowing charm at his throat and

stilled. He faltered for a second and had to grab on to a chair to keep his balance.

Great. Another drunk guest and all the limos were gone. No way was she driving him home herself. Hmm. Well, maybe. He was awfully sexy and all those daydreams she'd had about Wes all night suddenly starred this magnetic stranger.

Until he growled at her. "I don't give a damn about the cake, unless that is where you've hidden my goods."

"Your goods?" The only goods Ciara could comprehend at the moment were six, or maybe eight, of the most beautifully defined abdominal muscles in the whole Four Corners.

He crossed the scant yard between them in two strides, hauled her up out of the chair, and got so far into her personal space bubble she could smell his cinnamony breath. A zing whipped through her from every place he touched and strangely, she really wanted to stand up on her tippy toes and press her lips to his, taste that spice, lick up every essence of that erotic flavor.

She might have too if he'd held her for a second longer. But, after searching her eyes, he released her and began pacing, prowling around her, his eyes roving her from head to toe.

He might have the body of a god and she the body of a cupcake, but she would not be intimidated by wandering eyes. "First of all, you have to tell me what brand of toothpaste you use, and second, back up out of my business, buster."

"Do not try to beguile me with your talk of hygiene products, your hair of gold, and your body made for sin. Where have you hidden my Wyr relic, witch?" He stopped circling and stared straight at her butt.

Body made for sin? Was he kidding? Body made of sins, maybe. Namely the sins of Swiss meringue buttercream, chocolate ganache, and too many I Love Lucy reruns. "Stop staring at my tuchis. Whatever you're looking for ain't in there."

She wiggled her backside to emphasize her point. That

made her intruder damn irritated, probably that her rear wasn't dropping any evidence of wrong doing based on the growl rumbling from his chest and his eyes glued to her ass.

"Stop enticing me with your curves, thief. You cannot distract me from what is mine."

Ciara cleared her throat, gently at first, but when that failed to bring his eyes up to hers, she about gave herself a sore throat trying to get his attention.

"Are you ill? I won't have you dying before you tell me where the statue is hidden."

What an asshat. A cute one, but a real douche canoe nonetheless. "I think maybe we've gotten off on the wrong foot here." Ciara extended her hand to him. "I'm Ciara Mosley-Willingham." Her hand hung there for a full count of ten. "And you are?"

He recoiled from her hand. "Wondering what kind of spell you're trying to work on me. Whatever it is, I assure you a Wyvern is immune."

"I was trying to be nice, but I've had a very long and tiring day, so my patience is wearing thin. I don't have your thingy, and I don't know what a why Vern is. I thought for a minute I might help you try to find it, but I'm done now." Ciara turned and began looking for her torturous heels. It would be much more fun to stomp off if there was some clack.

"As am I. If you won't return what you have taken from me I will be forced to bring you before the AllWyr council."

"What the hell?"

He grabbed her hand and pulled her through the ballroom toward a terrace. Good thing she'd already kicked off her shoes or she'd have been tripping all over her feet at the rate he was dragging her away.

"Hey, stop right this instant or I'll bring out the self-defense moves."

"Save your defense for the council. You'll need it."

This dude was seriously a wackadoo. Where was the pepper spray when she needed it? Oh, that's right, still in the bag from the store her mother had insisted they buy in bulk from.

"Let me go."

"Return my relic."

"I'm gonna make you a relic."

"Save your spells, witch."

"Your face is a witch."

The scary man released her and grabbed at his face. When he didn't find anything wrong with it, he narrowed his eyes and glared at her. "Good try, witch. You'll pay for that."

Ciara pivoted and bolted weaving her way between the tables. One second she was zigging and zagging, the next she was airborne.

Great talons gripped her shoulders and a deep whoosh-whoosh-whoosh sounded above her.

She wriggled and screamed, frantically trying to see what was happening above her. Her feet crashed into empty glasses and caught a centerpiece of giant lilies dead-on as she was dragged through the air above the tables.

Before she could even take another breath to scream again, they swooped out of the French doors, over the balcony and into the night sky.

Ciara lost her effing mind as the ground beneath her sunk down into tiny squares of land. She couldn't look any longer, or she'd throw up. So instead she glanced up, not fathoming that she'd see flying above her the giant wings, flapping gracefully through the sky, of a dragon.

———

JOIN in Ciara's adventures with her Dragon Warrior Jakob in Chase Me

ACKNOWLEDGMENTS

Great big thanks to my Mushrooms - JL Madore, Claudia Burgoa, Dylann Crush, M. Guida, and Bri Blackwood. I appreciate all your help and patience as I burn hard.

I'm so grateful for my Amazeballs Writers - Danielle Hart, Stephanie Harrell, Davina Storm, and Cara Bryant who are always willing to get on and do writing sprints with me. I appreciate it more than you could know, and am infinitely proud of your successes in publishing.

My Amazeballs Facebook group is so much of the reason I keep writing and I look forward to logging onto the FaceSpace every day and seeing what kind of fun and games we've got going on!

I had some help making this book the best it could be right out of the gate.

Big thanks to my borrowed BETA Readers:

- Dianah Stedman
- Fiona Hennessy-Collard
- Carin Diepstraten - Boersma

Extra super duper hugs to the Just in Time Proofreaders:

- Elaine H
- Fiona Hennessy-Collard
- Dorothy-Helen L. Billmeier
- Julie Coxon
- Jeanette Merrick

- Lara
- Lahudyne

Big thanks to my proofreader, Chrisandra. She probably hates commas as much as I do now. All the remaining errors are all my fault. I'm sure I screwed it up somewhere.

I'm ever grateful to Elli Zafiris and Becca Syme for telling me I'm worth fighting for when I'm sure I've effed up my book and my career. You two are my energy pennies.

I am so very grateful to have readers who will join my on my crazy book adventures where there will ALWAYS be curvy girls getting happy ever afters!

Without all of you, I wouldn't be able to feed my cats (or live the dream of a creative life!)

Special thanks to everyone who went through the weird cover fiasco with me and supported my use of a real, plus-size, ba-donka donka curvy girl on the individual book covers of the Fate of the Wolf Guard series.

It was a risk to put a woman on the cover who wasn't a drawing, and wasn't what society thinks of as the ideal body. It's a risk I was willing to take for all the curvy girls out there who've been told or thought they weren't deserving of love because of your size, shape, or what the scale says.

Yes. You. Are.

Thank you so much to all my Patreon Book Dragons!

An enormous thanks to my Official Biggest Fans Ever. You're the best book dragons a curvy girl author could ask for~

Thank you so much for all your undying devotion for me

and the characters I write. You keep me writing (almost) every day.

Hugs and Kisses and Signed Books and Swag for you from me! I am so incredibly grateful for each of you and am awed by your support.

- Helena E.
- Alida H.
- Daphine G.
- Bridget M.
- Stephanie F.
- Danielle T.
- Marea H.
- Marilyn C.
- Mari G.
- Cherie S.
- Jessica W.
- Katherine M.
- Kelli W.

Shout out to my Official VIP Fans!
Extra Hugs and to you ~

- Jeanette M.
- Kerrie M.
- Michele C.
- Corinne A.
- Deborah S.
- Frania G.
- Jennifer B.
- Hannah P.
- Janice M.
- Nicole W.
- Sandra B.

- Sherrie W.
- DebbieJoy G.
- Heather R.
- Janice W.
- Robin O.

ALSO BY AIDY AWARD

Dragons Love Curves

Chase Me

Tease Me

Unmask Me

Bite Me

Cage Me

Baby Me

Defy Me

Surprise Me

Dirty Dragon

Crave Me

Dragon Love Letters - Curvy Connection Exclusive

Slay Me

Play Me

Merry Me

The Black Dragon Brotherhood

Tamed

Tangled

Twisted

Fated For Curves

A Touch of Fate

A Tangled Fate

A Twist of Fate

Alpha Wolves Want Curves

Dirty Wolf

Naughty Wolf

Kinky Wolf

Hungry Wolf

Flirty Wolf - Curvy Connection Exclusive

Grumpy Wolves

Filthy Wolf

The Fate of the Wolf Guard

Unclaimed

Untamed

Undone

Undefeated

Claimed by the Seven Realms

Protected

Stolen

Crowned

By Aidy Award and Piper Fox

Big Wolf on Campus

Cocky Jock Wolf

Bad Boy Wolf

Heart Throb Wolf

Hot Shot Wolf

Contemporary Romance by Aidy Award

The Curvy Love Series

Curvy Diversion

Curvy Temptation

Curvy Persuasion

The Curvy Seduction Saga

Rebound

Rebellion

Reignite

Rejoice

Revel

ABOUT THE AUTHOR

Aidy Award is a curvy girl who kind of has a thing for stormtroopers. She's also the author of the popular Curvy Love series and the hot new Dragons Love Curves series.

She writes curvy girl erotic romance, about real love, and dirty fun, with happy ever afters because every woman deserves great sex and even better romance, no matter her size, shape, or what the scale says.

Read the delicious tales of hot heroes and curvy heroines come to life under the covers and between the pages of Aidy's books. Then let her know because she really does want to hear from her readers.

Connect with Aidy on her website. www.AidyAward.com get her Curvy Connection, and join her Facebook Group - Aidy's Amazeballs.